Beverley Harper was born in New South [Wales]. At the age of twenty-six she went 'walkies'. In the course of her travels, Beverley took one look at Africa and fell in love. She stayed for nearly twenty years, living at various times in Durban, Cape Town, Johannesburg, Botswana, the Ivory Coast and Malawi. She also spent time in India, London and Scotland, before returning to Australia in 1988 with the spoils of her wanderings – one husband and three sons. Despite an almost pathological hatred of flying, Beverley returns to Africa once a year for research purposes. When she's not travelling, she lives, with husband Robert, on the Northern Tablelands of New South Wales. *People of Heaven* is her fourth novel.

Also by Beverley Harper

Storms Over Africa
Edge of the Rain
Echo of an Angry God
The Forgotten Sea
Jackal's Dance

PEOPLE
of
HEAVEN

BEVERLEY HARPER

PAN
Pan Macmillan Australia

This book is for my family —
Robert, Piers, Miles and Adam
for their continuing support and love
and above all
for being who they are.

First published 1999 in Macmillan by Pan Macmillan Australia Pty Limited
This Pan edition published 2000 by Pan Macmillan Pty Ltd
St Martins Tower, 31 Market Street, Sydney

Reprinted 2000 (four times), 2002, 2003

National Library of Australia
cataloguing-in-publication data:

Harper, Beverley.
People of heaven.

ISBN 0 330 36197 X.

I. Title.

A823.3

Typeset in 11.5/13pt Bembo by Post Pre-press Group, Brisbane
Printed in Australia by McPherson's Printing Group

I am indebted to Anne and Jim Boyd;
Ann and Bob Cochrane;
and Beryl and Basil 'Mac' McMenamin;
all of Swaziland for three incredible days and
nights at Nkankanka Lodge overlooking the
Mlawula Stream in Mbuluzi Game Reserve.
The stories of old Zululand will stay with
me forever.

Also to Gloria Goold and Robin Jones,
many thanks and much love
for reasons too numerous to mention.

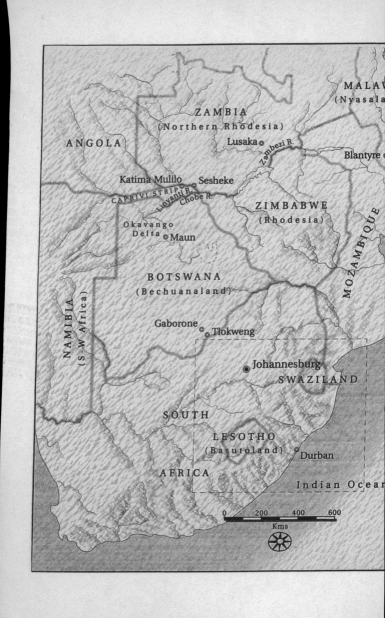

AFRICA

South
Africa

Zeerust
Groot Marico
Rustenberg
Pretoria
Johannesburg
Soweto
Sharpville
Breyten
Heilbron

Transvaal

0   100   200
Kms

SWAZILAND

Balelesberg
Range

Zululand

Drakensberg
Mts.

Ulundi
Empangeni
Umfolozi
Kwa Mbonambi
Amatikulu

LESOTHO
(Basutoland)
Mpendle
Underberg
Sani Pass
Tugela R.
Umkomaas R.
Pietermaritzburg
Kwa-Mashu
Durban

Drakensberg
Mts.

Indian Ocean

PROLOGUE

She was running hard, as fast as she could. Panic flooded her body. Flecks of froth gathered at her mouth. She had almost reached the end of her endurance. It was dark, virtually impossible to see. She had to get away – hide somewhere – it was the only way.

The pain was awful. Rolling waves of it through her body. Still she ran, seeking sanctuary, fleeing the danger, concentrating on only one thing. To reach a safe place.

Stumbling over a low bush, she nearly fell. Air whistled through tortured lungs as she sucked it in. Her heart thudded painfully. Limbs trembling with exertion, she pushed on. Here was not safe. They would find her. She needed something deeper, darker, more inaccessible.

Finally, she could go no further and sank down, exhausted. The pain had intensified until it was the only thing left – banishing even her terror. Somewhere off in the distance, hyena chittered and giggled their hideous night noises. They would come for her, following the blood smell. She needed to regain strength.

She lay gasping for air. A shard of agony ripped through her. Summoning the very last of her reserves, she staggered up and headed for dense bush nearby. It would have to do. Ignoring sharp thorns and pushing through to the centre of the thicket, she lay down again, thoroughly spent. There, she trembled with pain and fear, listening for any warning that danger approached. A hunting leopard gave a sawing cough nearby but she knew it would not harm her. The hyena were further away. At last she had no option, giving herself up to the insistent rolling waves of agony as her time grew near.

The urge to push was irresistible and she obeyed her natural instincts, even though she had no experience – for this was her first baby. For nearly an hour, she bore down with the pain and strained. Everything else – her earlier panic and fear – went away as she laboured alone in the thicket in the blackness that was the African night.

At last she felt something slippery between her thighs. It was coming. She gave one last mighty push and the baby slithered out onto the ground, mewling feebly. The new mother could not rest. Staggering to her feet, she knew she had to get away, take the baby and flee from the blood and sticky mess of afterbirth before hyena found them.

Tired as she was, her only instinct was to protect her new baby. Lowering her head, she nudged it gently, licking away the cocoon of mucus from the birth sac covering its face. The small creature found wobbly legs and the mother nudged it again.

Nose to nose, making soft noises, she coaxed her baby away from the scene of its birth, stepping backwards and waiting until it followed, before taking another step. In this manner, mother and child made a distance of several hundred metres before stopping for a well-deserved rest.

The infant found teat. Wearily, the mother allowed it to suckle. At last, just as dawn lightened the sky to the east, the baby settled down to sleep and the mother – solitary, bad-tempered, aggressive creature that she was – allowed herself the luxury of love. She hated all other things. In three years or so, she would also hate this one but, for now, licking gently, she nuzzled and bonded with her baby.

She was unaware of something very important. The rest of the world were too. After all, the birth of a black rhinoceros deep in the wilds of Zululand would probably mean nothing, even go unnoticed by all but a few.

But this tiny creature symbolised hope.

Hope for a species so endangered that only a handful remained outside captivity.

Hope that this baby might be allowed to live and breed before the species disappeared forever.

Hope that man, in his insane quest for the so-called aphrodisiac powers of powdered rhinoceros horn, might not find and kill this one.

Hope that someone, at some time out there in the world of men, might come to their senses before it was too late.

She was just a dumb, plodding animal and her continued existence was beyond her control. The terror from which she had fled had been no more than an instinct to hide from the night creatures of the African bush. If given the power of reason, the black rhinoceros mother would have known that she had far more to fear from the two-legged day creatures.

PART ONE

1945–1952

ONE

J oe King shifted on the hard leather seat as the train lurched crazily from side to side. He'd had two choices, take the milk train from Durban to Empangeni or hitchhike. He'd opted for the train but was beginning to wish he hadn't. He scowled through the window which rattled and shook and stared out unseeingly at the dark land beyond. He was bone weary. His thin body, wrapped in an oversized greatcoat, was perpetually cold. An ache, deep and raw, burned in the upper part of his right arm where the bullet had cracked bone. The quacks had said he was lucky to have the use of it. Bugger them! What good was an arm that only half worked?

He could see his reflection in the window, thrown back at him in the soft light of the carriage. Joe rubbed his good hand wearily over his face, feeling the stubble of three days' growth. What was Claire going to think of him now?

Claire! He could barely remember her face. He thought that was strange. He had loved her so much – she had been his life. He pulled his wallet from the deep greatcoat pocket and took out a faded and creased sepia brown photograph. It had been a long time since Joe had looked at it. There. There was Claire. Standing on the verandah of her parents' home, head back laughing, fine strong legs slightly apart, a breeze ruffling her long blonde hair, pressing the thin cotton of her dress against a firm, slim body.

Joe stared at the photograph of his wife. They had married young, she was just twenty, Joe nearly twenty-two. Joe's father had divided his vast estate between his four sons and Joe, the youngest, had nearly 2500 acres to administer. He needed a wife, he was in love with Claire, he had his own land. What more could a man ask for?

For eighteen months they had been happy. Claire was a wife to make a man proud. She ran the household and took care of the farm's bookwork. She organised the gardeners and kept a firm but fair grip on the house servants, leaving Joe free to run the farm. At night, while never initiating intimacy between them, she willingly submitted to Joe's advances, never developing the convenient headache which some of his friends complained afflicted their wives regularly. If Claire said she had a headache, then Claire *had* a headache.

When she told him she was pregnant, Joe believed his life was complete. He enjoyed the sight of his young wife growing heavy with his child. He revelled in the ribald teasing of his friends. He had visions of teaching a son to play cricket and rugby.

Claire blossomed but the realities of parenthood

soon had Joe longing for the peace and privacy he'd enjoyed before his son was born. Too late, Joe realised that by rushing headlong into marriage and a family he had become stuck in an inescapable rut. He hadn't taken time out to live. Claire was his first love but, as responsibility weighed heavily on him, he began to question that too.

Then came the war. Like all the other eager and fit young men, Joe listened to the rumblings intently. And while the young wives sensibly worried and feared for their menfolk, their husbands fidgeted and grew excited at the prospect, spurred on by inevitable dreams of glory and heroism. Joe and Claire were no exception.

'God!' Joe thought, as he sat in the rocking carriage. 'If only we'd known.' Men maimed or killed, others left tormented by memories. Was this what the women had feared? He sighed and put the snapshot back in his wallet. Out of sight, out of mind. That's how it worked. Not entirely though, there were some things he found easy to remember.

He could recall every line of her body, the feel of her under his hands, the smell of her hair and the softness of her in that private place between her legs. Sometimes during the past three years, in despair, if he closed his eyes he could almost imagine she was under him, that his hot thrusting was not onto his hand against the flea-infested straw mattress. Sometimes it had helped. Mostly, though, it had increased his agony and frustration to the point where he would weep hot tears of hopelessness and despair.

Especially when he became too sick and dispirited to get those urges any more. Or, more correctly, to do anything about them when he did.

Joe blinked and the past went away. He was left staring into the darkness that hid the land of his birth. The hot, steamy sugarcane belt of Zululand was just out there. He wanted to open the window and breathe it in but he was too cold. 'Welcome home,' he mocked his reflection. 'Welcome back to all those things you went to war to save.' Joe sneered at himself. 'Bullshit!' he thought. He'd gone to war for excitement. He'd gone because the reality of his life hit him squarely between the eyes and frightened the shit out of him. Twenty-six, married, a father, and a farm around his neck. Joe had gone to war to experience life before it passed him by. If the war hadn't come along, he'd have lived his life out in plodding monotony. But the war *had* come along and Joe seized the opportunity, telling himself it was for king and country. It was for king all right. Joe King.

October 1939 – Joe had been among the first to sign up. Too impatient to wait for South Africa, Joe had used his parents' country of birth and his own British passport to join the Royal Air Force. He could still see Claire, in tears, holding their son's hand as the ship cast off, turning slowly towards Durban Bluff and its deepwater channel to the Indian Ocean. Michael was only three years old. The sight had left Joe unmoved.

Watching Claire grow smaller as the ship pulled away came as something of a relief. He still loved her but she represented everything about his life that tied him down.

'What will it be like now?' Joe wondered. 'It's been five years. I've changed. Will she have changed? Will I love her? Can I do this? Do I want to?'

He wondered if his son would be as demanding. Michael would be nearly eight. 'Christ! I have an eight-year-old son I don't know and a wife I can barely remember. We're strangers.'

He had been twenty-six and he was never going to die.

Joe had been flying his own aeroplane for several years, a fact which the Royal Air Force put to good use. They threw him at the Germans time and time again. Desperate dogfights over the English Channel, raids over Berlin, moonless nights flying parachute drops over France.

Joe was having the time of his life. The beer, once he got used to it, was good. The men, living as they did with death riding their shoulders, were a wild and reckless crowd. The women, who did it for England and who were turned on by the possibility that this fuck could be his last, were plentiful. Joe forgot Claire, forgot his son, forgot his farm, even forgot his country. He was having fun, lived with gut-churning exhilaration and bowel-liquefying fear, with bravado a constant companion and with dark and terrifying nightmares. Not that he'd admit them. He was Joe King, he was tough and he was going to live forever.

Until he was shot down over France and nearly burned to death in the cockpit of his plane. Only the actions of two brave peasant farmers got him out alive but not before both legs were badly burned. His relief at being saved had been short-lived. Before he could be carried from the wreck, he had been captured. His uniform saved his life, the Frenchmen had not been so lucky – shot as they stood with hands in the air.

Joe shook his head but the past stayed with him. It was there in his reflection, in the thin face and haunted eyes, in the tight mouth and hunched shoulders. 'Bastards!' Joe hated the Germans. Not for their arrogance and cruelty. Not because they had become the enemy. But because they'd taken a young man and turned him into an old one. His once jet-black hair was flecked with grey. His once strong body was wasted and aching.

For as long as he lived, Joe would never forget his capture and three years of hell. His first impression of the camp would remain with him forever. It had been winter. The ground was churned up and frozen solid. Three separate fences of barbed wire ran around the perimeter. Inside, the forty-acre camp was segmented with more barbed wire, with trenches running parallel.

Wooden huts, or converted barns, housed the prisoners. Each building accommodated around 200 men. They slept on planks of wood covered with a thin layer of straw. They were jammed in like sardines with no thought for comfort or privacy. No blankets were provided, no lights and no heating. The prisoners huddled together, human contact their one source of warmth.

Camp food was so terrible that the men quickly lost condition. Bread and coffee in the morning, thin soup at midday made with chickpeas, lentils or vermicelli, and the same soup in the evening.

The fittest, usually those newly arrived, were put to work building roads in the area. Once their undernourished condition took its toll, they were given lighter tasks – cleaning huts, emptying latrines, burying the dead and various other jobs necessary to keep the camp running. Despite his burns, Joe was expected to carry out the heavier road-building work. His legs eventually healed, leaving them badly scarred. And they ached, oh God how they ached, in the cold of winter. But at least he was alive.

The dead were buried naked. No new clothes were ever issued and the men had to find replacements where they could. Joe quickly swallowed his disgust at wearing dead men's shoes as his second winter in the camp bit deep and the cold split his feet raw open.

Worst of all were the rollcalls. Four times a day, in all weather, the men assembled for anything up to an hour. They were expected to stand completely still, any fidgeting being punished by a swift and ruthless blow from a rifle butt.

Despite the rigid routine of rollcall, security was surprisingly lax. Joe quickly realised that his best chance of escaping was from the road-building gangs who worked outside the camp. The Germans were undermanned. Road gangs usually numbered around 400 men and they were never controlled by more than eight guards. When one of the prisoners announced he was going, the others tried to create a diversion. The Germans were fairly relaxed about it. Many tried to escape. As far as Joe knew, only one had succeeded. The trouble was the arid terrain. There was simply nowhere to hide.

Joe had seen one man, desperate to get away, break into a run when the guard told him to stop. He was shot in the back. The Germans left him there, a gruesome reminder to others. Those caught trying to escape were punished by two weeks' isolation, on a diet of bread and water. If conditions in the camp were unbearable, the cramped outdoor lock-up was worse. At least in the company of others, Joe knew he was not alone. However, the prospect of solitary confinement never prevented him from trying to get away. And he'd tried, God how he'd tried. One time he remained at large for two weeks. On that occasion he'd been plain lucky. The snow was falling so heavily it was thirty minutes before his absence was discovered. They tracked him down though. The French peasant farmer who had hidden him had been shot. Poor bastard!

Towards the end of summer last year, rumours began to circulate around the camp. There were always rumours but these, coupled with the behaviour of the guards who seemed more keyed up than usual, alerted the prisoners that something big was happening. 'Have you heard?' one man said to Joe. 'Paris has fallen. The Germans are on the run.'

'How do you know?'

'I heard two guards discussing it.'

By then Joe was too weak to care very much but when, the next morning, everyone in camp was rounded up and told they were being moved to another prison he saw this as one last chance to get away. They left the camp an hour later. They walked two abreast, the strong helping the weak. Joe waited until the guards were busy elsewhere then simply walked off the road. The command to stop was immediate but he ignored it. He was desperate to get away. Death was preferable to the half-life at camp. That's when he'd been shot in the arm. His right arm exploded in numbing pain before the impact registered.

He truly thought they would kill him. He stood his ground, holding on to his shattered arm, expecting another bullet. Instead, he was roughly bundled back into line and the march continued. They marched for two days. No-one had the slightest idea where they were going. More rumours. 'Austria. Germany.' Speculation laced with suspicion and dread. The Germans kept up a cracking pace, not giving the men any chance to rest. Then, after two days, they reached another camp. This one was better fortified and had more guards. The ordeal of getting there was over but their captors, perhaps out of bitterness or anger over the direction the war had taken, turned against them and made no effort to accommodate the newcomers. They had to find their own places to sleep in the already overcrowded buildings. They had to fight, like ravenous dogs, for every morsel of food.

Joe received no medical attention for his arm. The bastard Germans left the bullet there, hoping he would die of gangrene. But he didn't die, much as he would have liked to.

The war ended and the Germans went away. Rumours had been circulating for several days that it was only a matter of hours. The prisoners went to sleep one night in their miserable huts and woke to find their captors gone. They left behind the sick and dying. Joe was among them. The camp gates were open, he was free to go, but he didn't have the strength.

The following day, as the retching, pale-faced Americans picked their way through the bloated, flyblown bodies of dead prisoners, they found Joe. Fever and dysentery had him hovering on the very edge of life. They moved him to a hospital in Paris. A French doctor dug the bullet out and told him that if it had been left for just one more day the gangrene poisoning would have been irreversible. Joe could have told the doctor that. Instead, he asked how long it would be before he could use his arm.

'You'll never get full use back,' the doctor said. 'You're lucky to have any mobility at all.'

Joe had shut his eyes, telling the doctor to 'sod off'.

Nurses set to work on his body, clearing up the scabies and hair lice, curing the debilitating dysentery which had him bent double with pain and constantly soiling himself, cleaning out the ulcers which ate away at his flesh, washing away the grime and stench of three years in a prisoner-of-war camp. They catered for his every need and, with the good food and medication, his wasted body began to respond. The doctors said how delighted they were with his progress but their eyes could not hide the pity, or sometimes disgust, at what his body had become.

When he was well enough, he was sent to a rehabilitation hospital in London. There, among amputees, paraplegics, burn victims and others, psychiatrists tried to heal Joe's psyche. They asked questions and wrote down the answers. They placed broken puzzles in front of him and told him to put them back together again. They showed him ink blobs and asked him what he saw in them. They drugged him or hypnotised him and then probed his subconscious – sessions which invariably left Joe weak with emotion and fear.

When they had no more questions or puzzles, they left him to the mercy of the generals. Joe had made a dozen attempts to escape. The generals wanted details. 'Why, for Christ's sake?' Joe railed, not willing to relive the memories. 'What good can it possibly do now? All I did was walk off.' But the generals persisted and wrote down his answers. Joe knew they were just keeping busy, reluctant to let go of their status and return to the mundane existence they led before war put authority at their disposal.

At last he was free of them. Joe assumed that

someone would have let Claire know he was alive. But because he moved from one hospital to another, her letters, if she'd written any, did not reach him. Joe didn't care. Filled with a sense of loss for the three years stolen from his life, he went looking for the women he had known before he'd been shot down.

The madness which had affected everyone had, just as quickly, disappeared. The willing women had married their wartime sweethearts or returned to their husbands. Joe found it amusing that many a returning hero must have asked where on earth their loving and faithful little wife had learned such things. He wondered if Claire had remained faithful and found that whether she had or hadn't didn't really bother him.

Joe did manage to meet up with one of the women he had known before. He wined and dined her and took her to bed. That was when he discovered that he couldn't get it up. The woman was understanding, patient and very skilled. But Joe still couldn't get it up.

Five months after the war ended, and released from active duty with the rank of Flight Lieutenant, Joe thought it was time to go home. The doctors, psychiatrists and generals had finished with him, the fun of the war days was over. Although the beer still tasted good, whisky was better.

So here he was. Joe King. A good deal thinner, a whole lot older, a hell of a lot wiser with a liking for whisky he hadn't known before. 'Ladies and gentlemen,' he thought sardonically, 'I bring you Joe King – pilot, escapee, emotionally wrecked and riding the fucking milk train.'

He was thirty-one years old and going home to a wife and son he did not know. Going home to a farm he'd forgotten how to work. The young man who had left, the one who was planning to make a difference to the war, was returning covered in nothing more than the lingering stink of three years in prison camp and the scars of unsuccessful escape attempts.

Joe shifted his position on the hard seat. He was sitting on the bones of his arse, quite literally, and it hurt. He rummaged in the large pocket of his greatcoat and brought out a flask of whisky, unscrewing the lid and tipping it back. He hardly tasted it. It was the sting and the hot feeling in his belly he was after. 'Should have shaved,' he thought.

South Africa did not notice his return. The tickertape, the celebrations, the hero-worshipping were finished. Not that it bothered him. What did he have to boast about? Still, it would have been nice to see it. Instead of that, he'd disembarked in Durban, hoisted his kit bag and walked down Point Road towards the station. The milk train left Durban for Zululand around two in the morning. No-one knew he was coming. Good! That was how he liked it. 'Still,' he thought again, rubbing his hand over his chin, 'I should have shaved.'

It crossed Joe's mind that he should have let

Claire know he was coming. And his brothers. How had they fared? Had they all survived? Joe knew, from a letter Claire sent early in the war, that his father had died. He had read the news with total disinterest. Old man King might have divided his farm equally between his sons and he would have left each with a sizeable inheritance, but he had been a domineering and cruel father. Joe hated the old bastard.

One of his brothers, Colin, had lost both legs in a landmine explosion within a month of going into action. 'How would that be?' he wondered dispassionately. 'To go marching gloriously off to war one minute and be dragged back on stumps the next?'

It was as black as pitch outside. Joe lit a cigarette and closed his eyes. He wondered what Claire looked like now. Without the photograph to jog his memory, he couldn't remember her face. He remembered other things – her tinkling laugh, her long, strong legs, her breasts. He remembered she had large grey eyes and blonde hair. She hated people who drank too much, he could recall that. 'Hard luck,' he thought callously. 'She'll have to get used to it.' Then his thoughts mellowed. She had the softest lips he had ever known. Why couldn't he put it all together to make a whole picture? What was it going to be like, to be with one woman again? Joe thought long and hard about that. He tried to remember how she looked, all spread out under him, wide open for him to take. But although he found he could recall that part of his wife quite clearly, nothing stirred between his legs. Down there, he was dead. The doctors said it would come back.

He thought about UBejane, his farm. When Kingsway, the original estate, had been split four ways Colin had retained the name for his share. One of the other brothers named his estate Kingsmead while the other opted for Kingston. Joe, much to his father's ire, broke with the name King by calling his farm UBejane Estate, the Zulu word for the black rhinoceros which once roamed freely in Zululand. He thought the name appropriate in more ways than one since *uBejane,* translated into English, means 'the vicious one', which summed up his father rather well.

Now, Joe was wondering how run-down the farm would be. Five years was a long time for any business to be without a leader. Would the farm even be solvent? A woman couldn't run a sugar plantation. Claire would have done her best but it wasn't work for a woman. She'd never have controlled the bloody Pondos for starters. *Dirty buggers.* Joe wondered if the farm still employed them, those savages from Pondoland down south, who would shit where they stood and seldom bothered to wash. A lady shouldn't have to come into contact with them. And the Indians. They'd rob a man blind as soon as he turned his back. 'Christ!' Joe thought tiredly, as the day-to-day problems of sugarcane farming came back to him. 'I don't want this any more.'

Mechanical breakdowns, rains that didn't come

or, if they did, came usually at the wrong time. Fluctuating prices, arguments between the native cutters and their *indunas* that made squabbling children look like adults, the black fungus disease smut, which affected young plant cane. And that was just on the sugar side. A large portion of the estate ran cattle, with all their attendant problems: innumerable diseases, stillbirths, fences that needed repair, fodder crops to be sown, not enough rain, too much rain. The cattle were probably breeding at will and not, as Joe had them before he left, over a two-month period. He would need at least a year to put that right. And the cane? He tried to remember. 'Let's see, it's October. The mills close in December. So it's all happening now. If we miss this season we can't cut again until April.'

With a start, Joe realised how different his life would be from now on. He'd run wild for those first two years in England. Then he'd been treated like a wild thing for the next three. Claire was a lady. He'd have to treat her like one. He hadn't treated a woman like anything but a whore for five years. Claire liked all the little niceties. Opening doors for her, pulling out her chair, asking if she'd slept well or had a good day. Sex with Claire was a case of get on, get in and get off. He had been innocent and inexperienced before he left. It wasn't going to be good enough now. He wondered, with some amusement, what Claire's reaction would be.

And Michael, his son. Joe had never had much contact with children. Who did he look like? Claire had written of course, recording all the

22

milestones, trying to involve Joe in their son's progress. It hadn't been terribly relevant all those miles away. In fact, after a while he stopped reading her letters. Now he was coming face to face with his family. *His* family. His wife and the child they had created between them. His seed in her warm, moist pussy. Only he couldn't call it a pussy. It was 'down there', or 'down below'. That was how Claire referred to herself.

Did he want this? Did he want to go home and try to pretend that nothing had changed? Because he had changed. He had changed and changed again. From idealism to recklessness. And from recklessness to hopelessness. Could he now dredge back idealism? Was it possible to go from cynic to optimist? Joe opened his eyes and sneered at his reflection. The boy had gone. There was no trace of him. 'Dear God,' he thought, softening a little. 'Poor Claire.'

Sighing, Joe rose, steadied himself with his good arm, and let himself out of the compartment. The toilet was at the end of the carriage and he needed to pee. Lurching at the erratic rocking, Joe made his way slowly down the passageway. All but one other compartment were empty. The black man who sat three compartments from Joe took no notice as Joe went past. In fact, he appeared to be in a trance.

Joe had frowned in annoyance when the African had boarded the train. Not that the African shouldn't have been on the train – apartheid was being bandied about even before the war started but, as far as Joe was aware, laws to prevent Africans from travelling in the same carriage as whites had not been brought in yet. However, very few of them did it. They appeared to be content to travel third class, with their own kind. At least this one was a Zulu and not a stinking Pondo. He wore the uniform of a sergeant in the Natal Mounted Rifles. Joe hadn't known that Africans had joined up. Oh sure, something called the NMC, the Native Military Corps, had been established. *Military Corps! What a bloody joke. Fancy name for training the kaffirs as stretcher bearers.* Joe also noticed the medal ribbons on the Zulu's chest. That rankled. It rubbed in the fact that while Joe had sat on his backside in a filthy prisoner-of-war camp for most of the war, this cheeky kaffir was out getting decorated.

Joe wondered what he'd done to get them.

Wilson Mpande was not in a trance. His eyes were open and he stared, unseeing, dead ahead. The vision was being played inside his head where no-one else could see. Wilson was watching the last few years of his life, trying to make sense of them. It was a trick his father had taught him many years before. 'Concentrate on something close to you. It is the way to find peace when anger clouds your judgment,' his father had said. And Wilson Mpande was very, very angry.

Nothing had changed. In fact, it had grown worse. 'I think you mean third class,' the clerk said when Wilson asked for a first-class ticket.

'No.'

The white railway employee had gaped at him, taking in the uniform and ribbons. 'What they give you those for, man? Polishing boots?'

Wilson swallowed an angry retort, remembering he was back in the land of racial prejudice. 'Bravery,' he said briefly.

The clerk shrugged insultingly and pushed a ticket under the grille. 'Must have been a very savage boot,' he commented, sniggering. He stared at Wilson for a moment. 'A Zulu who thinks he's a white man,' he mused finally. 'When the sons of Blood River still live among you.'

It had been a calculated insult and it hit home. It took a very brave man to speak like that of the 3000 warriors who, at King Dingane's bidding, lost their lives without killing a single white man at the battle known as Blood River. A very brave man, or one who spoke from behind the safety of a mesh grille. Wilson made no comment, however, and climbed aboard the train. A porter, a Xhosa from down south by the look of him, stopped Wilson. 'Wrong carriage,' he said.

The porter's eyebrows rose when Wilson showed him his ticket. 'May I pass?' he asked calmly.

The porter stepped aside, but he had not finished with Wilson. He followed him down the corridor and into the compartment. 'Why are you doing this? It will bring trouble.'

'If I can pay for it there is no reason why I cannot sit here.'

'Why do you wear that uniform, man? Where did you steal it? You are trying to draw attention to yourself. It will bring trouble I tell you.'

'The uniform is mine.' Wilson sat down.

The porter hovered at the doorway. 'You fought with the white men!' His expression showed that he found the concept disgusting.

Wilson had had enough. Who was this Xhosa dog to question a Zulu? With an effort, he controlled his reaction. 'A Zulu gives no mercy and expects none in return,' he said stiffly. 'But I would not expect a Xhosa to understand such things. We have fought the white man in the past, we have won and we have lost. We may fight them again one day. It is what is in our hearts that matters. That is the Zulu way.' He looked the porter up and down. 'You are not a Zulu. Do not comment on things about which you know nothing.'

The porter smiled but it was not a friendly gesture. 'Hau, arrogant Zulu! You pride yourself on your warrior skills and you boast that a Zulu quickly flares up and just as quickly forgives. Tell that to the white man. You might have fought for him but if whites are on the train you will be asked to leave the carriage. You may be a *Zulu* . . .' he sneered the word, 'but do not think you are good enough to share their carriages.'

Wilson knew the porter spoke the truth but he would not give in. 'It is not against the law.'

'No,' the Xhosa agreed, 'but it soon will be.' With that prediction hanging between them, the porter left the carriage.

Wilson shook his head. Injustice heaped on top of injustice. 'Will it ever end?' he wondered bitterly. It seemed to him that the Zulus had nothing left to give. Then he shook his head again. 'The whites took our land but they will never take our dignity.'

A Zulu did not hold a grudge against an old enemy and so, when the call to arms rang out, many Zulus offered to fight on the side of the British. That they had fought each other a century earlier was irrelevant. But what the Africans had not been told was that the white South Africans had no intention of actually arming their black units. The Zulus had been signed up for the sole purpose of looking after the needs of their fellow countrymen. For this service, they were rewarded with the gift of a bicycle and a greatcoat or blanket.

Wilson was one of only a handful of Zulus who had been accepted for active duty. He was sent to North Africa with the First South African Division. There, together with the Ninth Australian, the Fifty-first Hungarian, the Second New Zealand and the Fourth Indian Divisions, the South Africans were part of 30 Corps which played such a decisive role in what became known as the battle of Alamein. Alongside 10 and 13 Corps and various extra formations, 30 Corps were involved in Field-Marshal Montgomery's successful plotting and execution of a break in Rommel's lines. Wilson had been in the thick of the fierce fighting which took place between October 23 and November 4, 1942.

Wilson still remembered the stirring words spoken by the Army Commander. Words worthy of any Zulu chief to his warriors before battle:

'When I assumed command of the Eighth Army I said that the mandate was to destroy Rommel and his army, and that it would be done as soon as we were ready.

We are ready now.

The battle which is now about to begin will be one of the decisive battles of history. It will be the turning point of the war. The eyes of the whole world will be on us, watching anxiously which way the battle will swing.

We can give them their answer at once. It will swing our way.'

And the rousing punchline.

'And let no man surrender so long as he is unwounded and can fight.'

It was rhetoric Wilson understood and responded to with the fiery blood of his ancestors singing in his veins. Now he was home, decorated, a hero, a man who had risked his own life for that of a white man, and he was being told he was not good enough to sit in the same carriage. What really rankled was that this attitude was held by a black man as well.

Walking to his compartment Wilson had noticed that the only other occupant of the carriage was a white man dressed in the uniform of a British airman. Had a rough time of it too from the look of him. As he passed the compartment where the white man slumped, Wilson had been ready for confrontation but none was forthcoming. The white man had frowned at him, then looked away.

As the train pulled out of the station, Wilson forgot the white man. He forgot the ticket clerk's words and those of the porter. His anger was directed at none of them. It was an anger with himself and his own people. He realised now that he had been used, coldly and dispassionately. He had been nothing more than a means to an end. That he had endured five years of separation from his wife, Nandi, who had been pregnant with their second child when he left to fight; that he had been wounded in North Africa and then, a few months later, nearly killed in an attempt to rescue a white captain pinned down by heavy fire; that he'd received word that his second child had been stillborn; none of this mattered to those who had ordered him to join up. 'In the coming years,' they had told him, 'we will need men like you. Men who know how the white man thinks.'

And so Wilson had joined up fighting side by side with white South Africans. He was good enough to die for his country, just not good enough to eat, sleep and relax with his country-men. As soon as the novelty of his presence wore off, even those who claimed to be liberal thinkers generally left him to his own company. Which didn't help him much since he was there to learn how the white man thought – some harebrained scheme of the African National Congress.

Did he now understand the white mind? He did not. No more than a white person could ever know how a black man thought. It was a game of guile they played with each other. Thrust and parry. Thrust a thought and parry back another. Neither of them a complete answer. Just enough truth to keep the deceit alive. A game of semantics. A game threaded with mistrust. A game that had its roots in past treachery and greed that had forced such a wedge between blacks and whites that Wilson doubted it could ever be removed.

He'd come closest to an understanding when he got drunk with the captain he had saved. 'What you did was incredibly brave,' the captain acknowledged.

'Zulus are brave,' Wilson replied matter-of-factly. 'They can't help themselves.'

The captain had smiled. 'Thank God,' he said quietly. Then added seriously, 'I would not have done that for you.'

'I know,' Wilson said.

Their eyes locked and, at that moment, both men knew they had breached the normal barrier of truth. Both of them retreated instantly to safer ground – ground that was both familiar and comfortable.

Wilson expected that the fight against oppression in South Africa would have made progress while so many of the country's white men had been off fighting for king and country and many more, who were considered to hold sympathies with Germany, had been incarcerated in camps. But the struggle had, in fact, gone backwards. And that was what made him angry. It filled him with a frustration that was crushing in its intensity, weighing him down with a sense of helpless futility.

He had been back in South Africa for three months but, in all that time, he had not been allowed to travel north to see Nandi and his son. As a member of the African National Congress, as a man the ANC considered to be potentially powerful within their cause, the uncertainty of the times meant that Wilson was required to be on hand. They refused his numerous requests to go home, even for a couple of days. Jan Smuts, they told him, was about to be ousted. In his place, lined up and anxious to put into practice their fervent Afrikaner racial purity beliefs, was a plethora of Nationalists determined to raise a defeated people from the ashes of shame.

Wilson knew a little of the Afrikaners' grievances. He knew they harboured a fierce resentment of Britain's attempt to colonise South Africa. He also knew they feared being overwhelmed by an African majority which they believed to be inferior in the eyes of God. Slowly and quietly, the Afrikaner culture had gathered momentum. Inspired by Hitler's National Socialism, the idea of racial purity seemed like an ideal method of dealing with the majority of the population.

Like so many radical changes, the movement which started slowly began to escalate until it gained a life of its own and became unstoppable. The speed with which Afrikaner nationalism took control caught the ANC on the hop. They had been lulled by the fact that Jan Smuts, and his United Party, had at least been willing to listen to the African point of view.

Wilson had quickly realised that the ANC had become impotent. The original ideals of putting tribalism and racism to one side for the good of all people had broken down into a mishmash of petty tribal hatred, ineffectual leadership and a lack of any clear policy or direction. Dispirited and disgusted, Wilson resigned from the ANC.

With a conscious effort, Wilson controlled his anger. He was going home. Home to Nandi, home to Dyson, the son he had not seen in five years, a son who was a baby of two when he left. His face softened. *My son!* There would be more, many more. And girls too. A man needed daughters to help care for the men of the family and bring a bride price of many cattle. He was going home in uniform because he was proud of his medal. And why shouldn't he be? He had acquitted himself well and he was returning, like the warriors of old, in triumph.

How would Dyson look? Like Wilson, not tall but powerfully built, with skin the colour of polished mahogany, a high bridged nose and strong cheekbones giving his face a hawk-like arrogance? Or would he take after his mother – short, a vision of burnished gold, skin that felt like the soft feathers of a bird and smelled of winds which blew in from the sea? Would his son have Nandi's small nose and wide mouth?

Thinking about Nandi, Wilson was uncomfortably aware that he had an erection. It had been such a long time since he had lain with a woman.

Nandi. The sweet one. Her name, when he

learned it, told Wilson she was high born. The Nandi after whom she had been called had been the mother of Shaka, first king of the Zulus and the man responsible for uniting all the clans into one great nation. Wilson himself carried the royal name of Mpande, third king of the Zulus and a half-brother to Shaka. When he learned her name, Wilson had spent some time worrying that he and Nandi would be forbidden to marry. But, though her family had ancient royal connections, they were of a different clan and too removed from Wilson's to cause problems.

He remembered when he first saw her, how he knew instantly that she was the one for him. Her short hair and the simple beaded headband she wore told him she was unmarried and did not belong to his own clan. If she noticed Wilson, she gave no indication. She was in the company of others, collecting water from the river and Wilson, who was visiting her village to pay his respects to an uncle, returned to his own home immediately and enlisted the aid of his sisters.

'Her name is Nandi,' they reported back. 'She is not interested. She calls you a dog.'

Wilson had been encouraged. Nandi would not have insulted him, not even have given her name if she were not interested. 'Go and speak with her again.'

Nandi played hard to get for three agonising months. Wilson had to move slowly and with infinite care through the human minefield that were her sisters and peer group. Before he could concentrate on

Nandi, he had to convince these others that he would make a good husband. He spent a great deal of time with them, chatting, laughing, entertaining them, with Nandi always present but never taking part. Then, one day his sisters told him, 'We have spoken with Nandi's sisters. They say she might be interested.'

A meeting between Nandi and Wilson was arranged. Her entire peer group were with her as usual. Wilson arrived alone, wearing an otter skin headband, and a new leather belt with strips of hide hanging down the front and back. This meeting was different from any that had gone before. This time, her relations directed a series of explicit questions at him. Would he beat his wife? Only if she were lazy or disobedient. Would he lie with his wife often and would she be his number one wife? He would lie with her as often as she would allow and she would be his favourite. Would he prepare for her a fine thatched home of which she could be proud? He would prepare for her the finest home he could. On and on the questions came. Nandi sat facing away from him, apparently oblivious of his answers. But she was listening avidly. Wilson could tell from the tense way she held her shoulders.

At last, the group fell silent. The moment had arrived when Wilson would know his fate. She made him wait. Wilson could still recall the feelings of dread and excitement which churned together in his stomach. The tension within the small group was electric as they all waited for Nandi's response.

She stirred, rose slowly and stood, with her back to him, for a long moment before turning to face him. Wilson's heart had beaten wildly when he saw the betrothal beads in her hands. When she placed them over his head he tried to look deeply into her eyes. But Nandi, with fetching modesty, would not meet his gaze.

Wilson returned home and raised the white flag outside his home to let everyone know that he would soon be taking a wife. Feeling worldly and important, he visited Nandi's home the next day to begin the courting process. Her brothers were waiting for him, as he knew they would be, and they thrashed him soundly and chased him away. For three more weeks, each time he visited Nandi she would refuse to see him, refuse to go with him to his home and her brothers would chase him away. After that first visit Wilson never let them catch him again. Love lent adrenalin to his legs and he would go whooping and leaping back to his own village, strong and fast, keeping well out of the way of their sticks.

It was all part of the game, Wilson knew that. He could not rush the process but waited impatiently for the day when, with the assistance of his brothers, they abducted Nandi and bore her away to be locked in his mother's hut. Nandi wailed and screamed and moaned until Wilson's mother went to his father and told him, 'Our son has done a bad thing. You must go to Nandi's home and put this thing right.'

Wilson's father had bemoaned his son's rashness

for abducting Nandi and complained that, since he had done this bad thing, he would have to pay one extra cow to her family as part of the bride price. There followed more delay while his father calculated the *lobola*, a delicate balancing act that had to take into account the importance of Nandi's family, the status of Wilson's, while at the same time satisfying both sides that a good deal had been struck. Offering too little would be an insult, too much may lead Nandi's family into thinking there was something wrong with Wilson.

While Wilson's father was procrastinating, Nandi's family sent a contingent of young men to release her and return her home. Wilson's brothers were waiting for them and, although outnumbered, put up a good fight with their sticks. Again, caution was required. Dignity had to be maintained on both sides which required great skill and discipline. Some minor injuries would be tolerated but a split skull could cause a major rift between the two families. Likewise, if one side felt the other to be holding back.

While Wilson chomped with impatience, negotiations over the bride price and attempts to make peace between Wilson's brothers and Nandi's were taken over by both their parents. Then, at last, came the wonderful day when everyone agreed that a marriage between Wilson and Nandi was a good thing, when she came willingly to his kraal bearing her clay pots and sleeping blankets, followed by her sisters and peer group. At the wedding feast, Nandi's pots were ceremoniously broken to cut the links with her own family.

The wedding ceremony lasted three days. Nandi spent most of the time sitting in Wilson's hut, her face covered by a special beaded fringe as a mark of respect for Wilson and the male members of his family. The guests drank beer, ate all manner of specially prepared food, played music and danced.

On the third night, after everybody had departed, Wilson joined Nandi in his hut. She fought him like a wildcat. Disgruntled and dissatisfied, Wilson complained to his father the next morning. 'Now I see her closely, she has the scars of cuts on her chest. She must have had an illness. We have been robbed by her parents. You must go and claim one cow back.'

Negotiations over Nandi and the bride price went on for several more weeks. In all that time, she refused to lie with him. Outwardly, Wilson became bad-tempered with frustration. His own peer group teased him unmercifully. Wilson was, in truth, having a wonderful time. He was very proud of his young bride. As much as he wanted to lie with her, he would have been shocked if she had behaved in any other way. Every night he would go to her sleeping mat. Every night he would leave it again, ranting and raving that he and his family had been cheated.

In the end, Nandi's family returned one cow. It was the signal from them to their daughter that she should allow her husband to bed her. When she came to him that night, shivering and trembling with both fear and need, and when at last he found sweet relief, he held her close and told her how much he loved her. They did not kiss; the mouth was for eating – to lick someone else's was a dirty habit. But he held her and whispered how proud he was of her and he mounted her again and took her gently and with great care so she would know he would always look after her well.

Wilson came out of his reverie with a grunt. Soon he would be able to hold her again.

The white man went past his compartment towards the toilet. He was painfully thin and walked along the passage with the gait of a man who had recently known great pain. He held his body hunched forward, one arm pressed tightly to his side, as though it hurt to move it. Wilson thought he must have been injured in battle.

'Mind if I join you?' Joe King surprised himself as much as he did Wilson with his question. Joe had intended to return to his seat but, at the last moment, the thought of being alone with his memories was too much. That, and the fact that his whisky was finished. This black man was better than nothing. Besides, the decorations intrigued him.

'Aren't you going to ask me to leave this carriage?'

Joe took the question seriously. 'I don't think so.'

Wilson removed his feet from the seat opposite and Joe sat down. He looked across at the Zulu who stared straight back. Suddenly, Joe was glad to be home. This black man who met his gaze with all the proud dignity of Zulu tradition made Joe realise just how much he had missed his country. Africa was alive with difference. This man was a part of it. Despite the uniform, his eyes shone out of a hawk-like face with . . . with . . . Joe struggled to think of the right word . . . with Zulu. That was it. Pure Zulu. There wasn't another race like them in the world. 'I take it you were in the Western Desert. Did you see much action?'

'More than I would have liked.'

The man's English was excellent. 'What made you join up?'

It was a good question. Not many blacks had. Wilson had been asked many times and had devised an answer to satisfy the curiosity of the white man by talking about his belief that blacks and whites should pull together and if that included going to war, so be it. Now he was sick of the lie. 'To see as many white men die as possible.'

To Wilson's surprise, Joe King threw back his head and roared with laughter. It was a strangely hollow sound. 'A kaffir with a sense of humour,' he said loudly. 'That's good.'

Wilson winced inside at the word 'kaffir' as he caught a whiff of whisky turned sour in the man's stomach. All he said, however, was, 'Where are you going?'

'Empangeni. You?'

Wilson nodded. 'Same.'

'You live there?'

'No. I am two days' walk towards the mountains from there.'

Joe whistled. 'Long way to go, man.'

Wilson looked at him. 'You are South African?' he asked, surprised.

Joe indicated his uniform. 'I joined the RAF so I could fly.'

'You could have flown with the South Africans.'

Joe nodded. 'I know. But not like I could fly with the British.'

Wilson shrugged. Aeroplanes were a mystery to him and he'd prefer it if they stayed that way. He was intensely suspicious of them.

'What are the ribbons for?' Joe asked suddenly, unable to curb his curiosity any longer.

There was something like aggression in the white man's voice. Wilson ignored it. 'I saved a captain's life.'

'A white man?'

Wilson pulled a wry face. 'It was war. He was fighting on my side. If there's one thing Zulus understand, it's the rules of war. I suppose you think it doesn't make sense.'

'Not a lot.' Joe regarded the African carefully. He was typically Zulu, yet his manner was not. Yes, the Zulus understood the rules of war and they held a brave enemy in great respect. One only had to look at the respect accorded to the British soldiers at Rorke's Drift. It was said by the Zulus that many had to be stabbed twice, like a lion needs to be stabbed twice, before they would die. This impressed the Zulus. Fighting was in their blood but that still didn't explain why this man volunteered. He seemed to be a strange mixture of traditional and modern Zulu. 'Trust a bloody

Zulu,' Joe thought grudgingly. It both irked and impressed him that in the face of what must be a bewildering transition process, this man accepted his Zulu fighting heritage with the same equanimity as he regarded defending his country. The two, in Joe's mind, were poles apart.

Wilson wondered what the white man was thinking. He looked at the window and watched his reflection. The man's face was thin and sour, disappointment etched in the lines around his mouth. There was an air of sad resignation about him. Turning back he said, 'My name is Wilson Mpande.'

'Joe King.' The white man hesitated, then awkwardly put out his left hand. 'Sorry. Bit of a problem with the other one.'

Wilson grasped his hand, then let it go. 'Joe King. Are you joking?'

Joe smothered the rush of irritation. All his life he had lived with that pun and it annoyed him. He was surprised, however, that the African's English was good enough to make the connection. 'Very funny,' he said sardonically.

The African thought it was. He grinned slightly, then asked, 'You were injured?'

'Trying to escape.'

'You were captured?'

A flush spread up Joe's neck. 'So what?' he asked belligerently.

Wilson shook his head. 'Nothing. I just asked. You weren't the only one.'

'Twelve times?' Joe asked bitterly.

Wilson smiled. 'A man who tries to escape twelve times need have no shame in him.'

'I am not ashamed,' Joe said angrily. Wilson's eyes went blank. A neat trick to which Joe was not blind. He knew it was to hide inner feelings. 'Shot down a few Germans though.' Inwardly Joe cringed. The statement had sounded boastful, almost as though he were trying to justify something. Anger stirred against the Zulu. The man had him on the back foot and it irked him.

Wilson's eyes were still blank as he asked, 'What do you do in Zululand?'

Joe took the proffered olive branch. 'Sugar and cattle,' he answered shortly.

Wilson raised his eyebrows. 'Together?'

Joe knew what he meant. It was an unusual combination. 'Sugar mainly. I keep the cattle on higher ground.'

Wilson nodded. Sugar was an alien world about which he knew little. Cattle, on the other hand, were almost a religion to him. 'You are a fortunate man.'

'So I keep telling myself. And what about you?'

'I am a Zulu. I live the old way.'

Joe thought he heard defensiveness in the African's voice. 'Nothing wrong with that.'

'I did not say there was.'

Joe shrugged. It was no skin off his nose.

Wilson allowed emotion back into his eyes. 'It is a way of life that is dying. The white man takes our best land and lets us keep what is left.' He stared impassively at Joe. 'Of course, this is generously granted only because the white man has found no use for it. You have your cattle. They grow fat and healthy on the rich grasses you take from us.'

Joe was taken aback by the outburst. He had never really considered that the annexation of Zulu lands was wrong. It had never occurred to him that the Zulus might actually resent it. After all, this was what colonial powers did best. They took land from a bunch of uneducated savages and turned it into neatly divided, profitable farmland which fed a nation and boosted the national economy. What was wrong with that? The Zulus could never have done it. All they were concerned with was owning a few head of cattle, they never thought further than that.

Okay, he was aware that cattle were important to a Zulu. They were a symbol of a man's wealth, measured as such from the humblest of men right up to the king himself. The cattle kraal was considered a sacred place where only the men were allowed to enter. But Jesus, South Africa was developing fast. If the white man could adapt to change then the bloody Zulus would have to as well. Joe thought it time to teach this arrogant kaffir a lesson. 'You'll have to make do with much less if Daniel Malan wins the next election. If you think you're hard done by now, wait and see what happens then.'

His words struck at the core of Wilson's anger. 'The Afrikaners are a minority group. You English speakers will not let their man lead the government.'

If Joe was surprised by the Zulu's grasp of South African politics, he did not let it show. Instead, he said in a hard voice, 'You are wrong, my friend. It is true there are more English speakers in South Africa but many of them cannot vote. They cling to their British passports. The Afrikaners may well have the numbers. And there's something else too. It may be the English who control much of the business in this country but if Nationalist Party policies work for them, they'll vote for Malan.'

Wilson knew he spoke the truth. The knowledge rankled. 'And you? You who farm my lands and wear an English uniform? How will you vote, if indeed you can?'

The unexpectedly frank exchange surprised Joe. 'I keep my British passport,' he said angrily, 'for without it I am a man without a country.'

'You have a country. You have taken it from me. The least you could do is show some faith in it.'

Joe rose stiffly, losing balance and staggering a little as the train rocked – or perhaps it was the whisky. 'I have faith in only one thing, black man. I did not take your country. You lost it.' He moved off up the passageway, back to his compartment, before he could see the blank stare of suppressed rage in Wilson Mpande's eyes.

Wilson had also been surprised by the turn the conversation had taken. In the dark, rocking carriage the gloves had come off. Here, at last, was the undiluted truth. Did it help him to understand how the white man thought? He concluded, sadly, that it did not.

TWO

Michael King waited until the scotch cart gathered speed, dust kicked up by the hooves of the mules, before bending and removing his shoes and socks. He stuffed them into the canvas satchel, liberally covering its contents with soil. Eyes screwed up to cut the glare from the sandy white road, Michael carefully checked the ground for footprints. Moving with the stealth of a leopard, he sneaked up to the curved stone wall to the right of the gate and, standing on tiptoe, peered over it. Satisfied, he moved to the left wall and repeated the exercise. With a grunt of serious relief, he flung the satchel over his shoulder, passed through the imposing arch on which was emblazoned the name 'UBejane Estate' and started up the burning hot track towards the house. It was a two-kilometre walk.

UBejane was the only home Michael had ever known. He knew it had once been part of a much larger estate owned by his grandfather, that crusty and sharp-tongued patriarch, the memory of whom still filled Michael with awe. When the old man died four years ago Michael had felt relief that he would never again be subjected to the cruel barbs which his grandfather fired at random to anybody and everybody within earshot. On more than one occasion Michael had seen his mother reduced to tears by a calculated criticism or by stinging sarcasm. With three out of four of the old man's sons away at war, and a fourth, the eldest, trying to come to terms with the loss of both legs, the old man's funeral was organised by the women of the family. Not one of them had liked their father-in-law sufficiently to even pretend they were sorry he had gone. Claire King had given Michael the choice of whether or not to attend the funeral. Even at four, Michael wanted to see the old man buried and forever out of reach.

Now he was nearly eight and with memories of his grandfather fading, Michael, if he thought about the old man at all, would concede that he owed his grandfather if not love, then at least gratitude. With the war over, countries were struggling to get back on their feet. At school, Michael was taught about food shortages. It didn't mean much to him. The vegetable gardens, orchards, henhouse, pig styes and fields were overflowing with an abundance of food which fed not only Michael and his mother but the entire population on UBejane, with enough left over to help those less fortunate in the nearby town of Empangeni. Money was tight, Michael understood that, but his belly was full, he had a roof over his head and he knew he was one of the fortunate.

Walking up the road, Michael's world turned

green. The tall sugar cane on either side closed around him, muting all sounds and forming a mini-climate. The silence was unusual. Normally the smallest breeze would have the dead lower leaves rustling, like small scurrying creatures. The absence of any movement in the air was an eerie sensation. He stepped off the road and up to the plants, searching for a succulent young shoot. When he found one, he snapped it off and, walking up the road, he sucked the sweet juice from it with pleasure. Soon, his chin and hands were sticky with it. His eyes darted from left to right. Today he had to be careful. An attack from the cane fields was long overdue.

Michael sniffed. Summer was coming, he could smell it. Storm clouds were building out towards the sea but, so far, had not delivered any rain. The air was heavy with anticipation. Michael focused his attention on the three-metre strip of grass bordering either side of the track. It was long enough to hide in. He scanned ahead as he walked, looking for telltale signs. There were no workers in these fields, everybody was up at the northern end sowing new plant cane. The fields where Michael walked were nearly ready for burning. He hoped he could see it. Usually, depending on weather conditions, they put the fire in very early in the morning, when he was still asleep. Sometimes, though, they fired the cane at night and, if it wasn't too late, he was allowed to watch.

The road was dead straight, cut at intervals by crossroads dividing the cane into blocks. It was dry now but there was a strangely sweet smell coming from the cane field. Occasionally, when the road and fields were wet, or the grassy verges were newly cut, the combination of scents was almost overpowering. It was more noticeable since his mother put in the irrigation.

When Claire first talked of watering the cane, Michael had thought she was mad. All the farms in the area relied on the rains and no-one irrigated their fields. She went ahead anyway, and it worked. Tonnages increased and seasonal variations reduced. Once ground moisture could be controlled, Claire went a step further and they were now deliberately burning off the dry trash before cutting mill-ready cane. It was dirty work and the Africans hated it, wearing hessian sacks over their clothes to protect them. Claire persisted. The cane was cleaner with little or no loss of sucrose. At first, other farmers derided Claire King and continued to remove the trash with cane knives in the old manner. But, once they saw her tonnages compared to their own, one by one they followed suit. Michael had overheard one neighbour saying, 'There's no doubting it, she's right. She's got a good head on her, that woman.'

He reached the first crossroad and turned right. Raj Singh, the tall Sikh farm manager, was pedalling towards him. Michael breathed a sigh of relief. The feeling of imminent attack had been strong today. Seeing Raj coming down the road was comforting. He looked ridiculous perched on the bicycle, turban slightly askew, his white pants and tunic top billowing, and the ends of a broad red sash flying behind him. Hopping one foot on the ground as a brake, he wobbled to a stop beside Michael, his thin brown face with its severely hooked nose wide open with genuine pleasure at the sight of the young boy he loved like his own son.

'Good afternoon, Master Michael.'

'Good afternoon, Mr Singh.' Michael adored Raj but he was always careful to observe the proper formalities with him. He had received more than one clip around the ear for not doing so. Not that it hurt physically, the reminders were delivered so they barely skimmed him. But Raj's approval was important to Michael and the Sikh's displeasure was something he strove to avoid.

Raj held a special position on the farm, not only because he was the manager. With Joe away at war, Raj had taken it upon himself to attend to Michael's farming education, taking him along whenever possible on his daily routine, explaining what he was doing and why, teaching Michael the finer points of sugarcane farming, about which he knew a great deal. While he was doing that, he threw in a few masculine pearls of wisdom for good measure.

'Never,' he said emphatically to Michael once, 'let a woman think she is clever.'

'Why not?'

Raj had favoured Michael with a pitying look. 'Because she isn't.'

'Some women are clever,' Michael had objected.

'Katie Fisher comes top of the class in maths *and* English.'

'Pah!' Raj waved his hand in dismissal. 'That means she has a good memory.'

Michael rather wished his memory was as good and said so.

Raj had treated him to a skimming cuff and told him, 'Can she run a farm? No. Can she fight in a war? No. All she can do is have babies.'

Michael thought his mother ran UBejane rather well but, wisely, did not mention it. Instead he asked, 'Why can't men have babies?' He had been glad Raj mentioned babies. He'd watched the cattle, the farm dogs and that horrible old rooster, and his young mind had put two and two together. Even while he was rejecting the idea as disgusting, the subject fascinated him – there was definitely something taboo about it – and he longed to find out more. This had been his opportunity. But Raj's answer had been disappointing.

'Men have more important things to do.'

Michael's mother allowed Raj to run the farm although she did the bookkeeping and took all major policy decisions. They had fought a long and bitter battle over the matter of irrigation. Raj still refused to admit that it had been a good idea even though Claire could see his change of heart. She was pleased that Michael spent time with him. The boy needed adult male company, she knew that. But, after Michael had repeated one or two rather bizarre pieces of information – like the time when he was six and had solemnly informed his mother that he no longer needed toilet paper, he had a perfectly good hand to do the job – she had to explain to Raj with a great deal of diplomacy that his Indian customs were different from her son's and would he please remember that in future.

Raj had accepted the rebuttal with a stiff and formal bow accompanied by stony and outraged silence. As soon as Claire was out of earshot, he retaliated by telling Michael that his mother was a woman and, as women had no say in important matters, he would continue to teach Michael Indian ways. Michael had grinned at him uncertainly, not sure if Raj was joking about his mother or not. However, the tall Sikh rarely joked so Michael had to assume he was serious. While he was happy to accept Raj's advice on most things, on the subject of his mother he made up his mind that the Indian had to be wrong. Claire was the most important person in Michael's life and he both loved and respected her.

Raj put out a sandalled foot to steady the bicycle. 'How was school?'

'Okay.' Michael waved his hand to the cane field on his right. 'When will you burn this block?'

'School,' Raj insisted sternly.

Michael sighed and told Raj of the day's lessons. Then he returned to his question. 'The rains are coming and this field is ready.'

Raj pretended to be surprised. 'So it is, yes indeed. Goodness. We will make a farmer of you yet, Master Michael.'

Michael would not be put off. 'When?'

Raj scratched his chin thoughtfully. 'I am not knowing exactly. Tomorrow perhaps.'

Michael's face fell.

The Sikh smiled. 'Oh, oh!' He clapped his hands. 'Now I am understanding. You wish us to wait for you, isn't it? Perhaps you can tell me when it suits you. Then Raj can decide if we wait.'

Michael held his breath. He'd had many similar conversations with the Indian and found, often to his disappointment, that Raj went ahead and fired the cane when it suited him. Apparently it had something to do with the mill and quotas.

But today was different. Raj finally relented. 'Do not worry, we will wait for when you are here, Master Michael. It is time for you to understand that the fire is not a game. This time you will be responsible.'

Feeling enormously pleased, Michael nodded solemnly. He had watched many times, even helped, and he knew instinctively how to read the weather, where to put the fire in and how to back burn. But this was the first time Raj had allowed him to take charge. 'This weekend,' he decided. 'Unless it rains.'

'As you wish.' Raj bowed low, hiding his smile of pride.

Satisfied, Michael changed the subject. 'Where is he hiding today?'

Raj knew immediately to whom Michael referred. 'I am not knowing, Master Michael.'

Michael frowned at him. The Indian was lying.

Raj let him sweat a bit before adding, 'But I would take care once you are through the cane.'

Michael thumped Raj's bony arm. 'Thank you, Raj.' He said goodbye and raced off up the road, suddenly anxious to get out of the regimented fields and onto his favourite part of the farm.

As sugar farms went, UBejane was large. The flat belt of land which ran parallel to the coast road, nearly 1600 acres, was planted with cane. Behind the cane, where the land rose and became hilly, a further 800 acres had been left uncultivated for cattle. Michael's grandfather had anticipated the demand for sugar but he had been a cattle man at heart and could not bear to be without his herd. Joe King had seen no reason to change. UBejane, as a result, had emerged as a meshing of many different cultures.

Indian sirdars were responsible for transporting the cut sugar cane. They laid the portable lines upon which the mule-drawn trucks hauled it to the main rail terminal. Here the cane was transferred to larger wagons and railed to Empangeni Mill.

Their wives, or 'Toght labour' as they were called, weeded – a job which required constant diligence until the canopy of cane covered one hundred per cent of the ground. It was backbreaking work which they did uncomplainingly. The Indians had been imported into South Africa specifically for work in the cane fields and they worked willingly, grateful they had a roof over their heads and food on their tables – neither a foregone conclusion in their country of birth.

The hardest work of all, the actual cane cutting,

was done by migrant Pondo labourers who came up on one-year contracts from down south. Once a contract was over, they returned to their families and a new crew of workers would arrive.

A few Indians held under-management positions, supervising the labourers. Raj was the only Indian on the farm who was considered to be a manager. He had come to UBejane many years before and old man King had been impressed by his intelligence and willingness to learn. Slowly, he had worked his way up to his current position. But while Indians and Pondos concentrated on the sugar side, their responsibilities did not extend to the livestock. Zulus worked with the cattle, refusing to have anything to do with the Indians, the Pondos or the sugar.

A dour old Scotsman, known to all and sundry as Mac, ran the workshop, taking orders from no-one. He was a mechanical genius and extremely useful with his hands, and could fix anything from Claire's Singer sewing machine to the most complicated piece of farm equipment. He had miraculously survived twenty-six years of old man King's acerbic tongue and was unquestionably a law unto himself. Joe King had no quarrel with that. When he became owner of UBejane he had been quick to make sure Mac would stay on.

'Aye,' Mac had said. 'But if ye come snooping aboot ma workshop I'll kick your bloody arse so fast you'll no ken what hit ye.'

'Deal,' Joe had said, sticking out his hand. 'On one condition.'

'And what would that be?' Mac ignored Joe's hand and scowled ferociously.

'Stay away from the whisky.'

Mac's scowl had deepened. 'I dinna drink whisky, you young pup, I drink scotch, and ye'll no be finding it on ma breath except Sundays and Sundays will no be any of your business.'

The two men had shaken hands. Joe kept his distance from Mac's workshop and, for his part, Mac mainly remained sober from Monday to Saturday.

When Joe had gone off to the war in Europe, Mac displayed an uncharacteristic soft spot for Michael and seemed to welcome his company. Claire often wondered about her son's upbringing. When he wasn't listening to Raj's more bizarre advice his head was being filled by Mac's equally dogmatic ramblings which seemed to draw freely on old Gaelic superstitions. 'Mac's magic' she called it one day when Michael placed a cork on her badly cramped leg and the tension went away immediately. Another time, when Claire could not stop hiccuping, Michael asked, 'Have you seen a white horse today?' She had to think for a second but that was all it took for her hiccups to disappear. Hoping none of this would adversely affect her son's development, Claire left Michael to seek the company of anyone he chose, only stepping in if she felt it really important.

Michael emerged from the cane and stood leaning on a wide wooden gate. Ahead of him, stretching away towards the hills, cattle grazed the lush grass. The farm road lost its grid pattern, climbing through flat-topped acacia trees and out-crops of rock. He scanned the way ahead carefully. From here he could see the house, snug in its enveloping protection of trees, sitting solid halfway up the hill. There was smoke rising lazily from the Zulu compound and, away to the left, the Indian barracks sprawled untidily over an area of almost ten acres.

Beyond the compound and barracks, isolated in an area where no-one cared to visit, was the row of huts for the Pondos. Built from flimsy wood of the kind used to make packing cases, and protected by thatch overhead, at the end of each one-year con-tract period the huts were burned to the ground. It was the only way to get rid of the accumulated vermin and filth. As hard as everybody tried to make them understand it, the inhabitants, year after year, seemed unable to comprehend the need for cleanliness. Screened behind bushes, the area remained a mystery to Michael. It was the only part of the farm he was forbidden to visit but having contact with the Pondos as they worked in the fields was enough. Silent, sullen and unhygienic in every respect, Michael had no desire to visit their quarters.

'Where is he?' Michael muttered, his eyes slitted like he'd seen Mac doing when he was concen-trating hard. Dyson could be anywhere.

The road ran between two massive boulders. They would bear investigation. Between the gate and the rocks, a dry creek ran alongside the left of the road. Michael climbed over the gate, lined himself up with where the gully ended at a culvert, then made a mad dash across open ground and jumped down to the sandy bottom of the creek bed. From here to the rocks at least, he was safe. Crouching low, he ran, carefully avoiding twigs and leaves. He reached the outcrop of rock and cautiously sidled around the first. Nothing. Now to investigate the other side. He had no choice but to cross the open ground ahead. Taking a deep breath, Michael stepped on to the road.

Dyson Mpande grinned. He was observing Michael's progress from the top of the boulder on the right. Flat on his stomach now, he had spent the last half hour in an overhanging tree, tying the lower branches together so that, from the cane fields, they screened the top of the rock. He was gambling that Michael would not notice, and he hadn't. It was getting increasingly difficult to take Michael by surprise so Dyson had found it necessary to become ever more cunning. Now, as Michael moved directly beneath him, Dyson launched himself, screaming like a banshee, straight on to the back of his friend. Both boys rolled together on the dusty road. Whoever managed to straddle the other won the game.

'I am *Mhlathuze*, the forceful one,' Dyson taunted, laughing, as he pushed Michael down and tried to hold him, his mouth stretched open with effort revealing the gap where four milk teeth had recently fallen out, leaving a thin, uneven white line as their replacements erupted through the gum.

'I am *iNdlovu*, the elephant,' Michael panted in Zulu, rolling sideways so Dyson fell on his side and had to scramble away quickly before their positions were reversed.

The two boys grappled with each other, half serious, half in fun, as the game of strength was played. They were friends, close friends, and they would not hurt each other, but honour was at stake.

Michael, with the advantage of being nearly a year older, won the contest. Dyson took it in good spirit. 'One day, *Nkawu*,' he said, using Michael's nickname, monkey, 'I will catch you. You will not always be able to beat me.' He was brushing dust off his shorts as he spoke.

Michael threw his arm around Dyson's shoulders, grinning. 'That is the day I will wear the modesty skirt.'

Both boys giggled.

Dyson looked at Michael's dusty school uniform. 'Your mother will beat you.'

'My mother never beats me.'

'Well, she'll beat you today.'

'Nah!' Michael was unconcerned. He would sneak into the house and give his uniform to Bessie, the Zulu maid. It would be washed, dry, ironed and back in his room by morning.

'How was the school today?' Dyson did not yet go to school, it was the only thing the two boys could not share. A school for African children had

58

been built in Empangeni but it had been over-whelmed with applications. New classrooms were being erected. Until they were finished, Dyson had to wait.

'I learned a new sum.' Michael squatted and drew it in the dirt with his finger.

Dyson studied it. 'How does this work?'

'It's called long division. See, if you have to divide it by more than twelve it's called long division. This is how it's done.' Michael showed Dyson how to do the sum.

Dyson picked it up quickly. Since Michael had been going to school he had passed on his lessons to Dyson in this fashion. Every afternoon, as soon as he alighted from the school cart, Michael would go on to red alert for Dyson. The long walk had any number of places where his friend could hide. They would pretend that Michael was a brave ele-phant hunter and Dyson a fearless Zulu warrior and that they were enemies who had sworn to kill each other. The tension leading up to the ambush was very real to both boys, dissipating immediately afterwards. Then Michael would show Dyson what he had learned.

'I have written down my arithmetic homework for you. It is all long division. Bring it tomorrow and see if your answers are the same as mine.'

Dyson took the sheet. 'What else did you learn?'

Michael pulled a face. 'History.'

'Pah! I do not need your history, I have my own.'

'Spelling,' Michael offered. 'Here is the sheet. I will test you on Saturday.'

'And I will test you also, *Nkawu*.'

Michael turned and squinted towards the compound where Dyson lived. It was like a traditional Zulu village with beehive-shaped huts covered with plaited grass. Most had no windows and the doors were a low arch that required all but the tiniest tot to bend in order to get through. Cooking was generally done outside and each dwelling had its own cooking fire within a circle of stones. The cattle kraals were a short distance away. His grandfather had been fond of quoting Mpande, the third Zulu king who, much to Michael's fascination was an ancestor of Dyson's: 'You cannot rule a Zulu without killing him.' Michael had always taken this literally and could never understand why anyone would wish to rule a dead person, especially since his grandfather usually went on to say, 'The way forward for the Zulu is backwards.' However, he was glad that the Zulus on UBejane lived according to their traditions. It seemed to make them happy and that was all Michael cared about.

Michael loved the compound and the pungent smell of the cooking fires. He loved to sit around the fire and share food with Dyson and his mother, to talk only in Zulu with them and the others. He was equally at home with these Africans as he was with his mother, aunts and cousins. In their open-hearted, hospitable way, the Zulus at UBejane accepted Michael as their equal, an honour indeed if only he had thought about it and one with certain obligations on Michael's part. Not that anything was onerous or difficult to learn. Michael accepted the Zulu ways as easily as he accepted his own. The twin cultures, though poles apart, were part of his upbringing. Moving automatically to the right-hand side of a hut, the men's side, if bad weather forced them to eat inside was as natural to Michael as using the correct utensils when he ate at home. He spoke Zulu as well as Dyson, mastering the language before he was fluent in English. He was also responsible for Dyson's grasp of English, correcting his pronunciation and grammar so that, for a rural farm boy, Dyson's English was only slightly accented and unusually articulate.

When they were together, Michael and Dyson spoke a mixture of English and Zulu, sometimes switching from one language to the other in mid-sentence. The friendship may have been born out of loneliness but, despite Michael now going to school and mixing with others, it continued as strongly as ever. They were best friends, confidants and, the fact that neither of their fathers had yet returned from the war, bonded them even closer. It was often a subject of discussion between them.

They started walking towards the fork in the road, the right of which led to the Zulu compound, the left to the main house. Where the road split, they stopped. Michael picked up a stone and shied it back the way they'd come, startling a family of francolin out of their cover. 'My mother thinks Dad will be home soon.' He watched the scurrying red-beaked birds calling out their harsh cry of alarm to each other then turned back to Dyson. 'I wonder what it will be like. You know, to have a father.'

Dyson sent a stone spinning away after Michael's. 'I do not know. It will be strange perhaps.'

'Yes,' Michael agreed, 'but it will be good too.'

They talked about it for some time, each boy drawing on their imagination as best he could. The prospect excited both of them yet it was scary as well. Fifteen minutes later they said goodbye and parted. As he trudged the last 500 metres to his house, Michael wondered what his father's return would really mean. Aside from Raj and Mac, who provided guidance in their own fields and in their own peculiar ways, he had grown up in the company of his mother, and, to a lesser extent, Bessie. His mother was very special and he loved her deeply. The way she looked, smelled, dressed and even spoke were, to Michael, a source of constant delight. He looked forward to the moment when, just before she went to bed, she would look in on him, bending to kiss his hair, thinking he was asleep. Michael never went to sleep until she had done that. While she was the voice of authority in his life, she was still the comfort zone. There was always an extra sense of wellbeing whenever they were together, a feeling that, whatever happened, it would be all right as long as she were there.

Michael had no real memory of his father. He suspected that the man he called Dad actually had little to do with him before the war took him away. His mother once remarked that farming was a very busy way of life but now that he was older, when his father returned, Michael could help more and they could get to know each other. It was that comment which stayed with Michael, that and the vaguest recollection of fear, or something close to it – apprehension, a need for caution. He could not remember.

His father was a sepia image in a photograph, a laughing, good-looking man, white teeth and dark eyes flashing, thick black hair that curled forward over his forehead, a thatch of dark hair on his powerful chest. Michael tried to emulate the man in the photograph but, for starters, he had his mother's colouring. The buccaneer good looks of his father were beyond him. Sometimes, when he and Dyson played, Michael would smear mud over his blonde hair, pretending to be dark like his father. In other ways too, Michael felt he could never measure up. He was tall for his age and slender. He believed he would never be muscular. His eyes were blue and he had his mother's Grecian nose, or he would have when he matured, that's what they all said. Michael didn't quite know what it meant but he had no-one with whom he could discuss these things.

Michael's teacher was a woman. Two of his uncles didn't return from the war. The one who did was in a wheelchair, both legs missing. He rarely spoke. Michael would never discuss his physique with his mother or aunts. The mere idea of doing so made him blush with embarrassment. His cousins, male and female, were of a similar age to himself, give or take a few years, and not worldly enough to advise him. And anyway, under the circumstances, Michael couldn't have asked them. Six of them no longer had a father and two had only half a father. His best friend, Dyson, was hopeless. But then, Dyson's mother said that Dyson was the image of his father so he had no need to worry. They did talk about it once. Dyson's, 'Why don't you just wait and see,' hadn't been much help and Michael never mentioned it to him again.

He also hesitated to ask Raj or Mac. Raj, he knew, would have quoted Indian gods. He always did that. He'd relate some story about an elephant-man or a swan-girl and end up saying how the gods know best so it would not be a good idea to question their will. As for Mac, he got all soft in the eyes over Claire King and Michael knew that Mac wouldn't understand why he wanted to look more like his father.

He was nearly at the house. A sprawling, one-storeyed building, lime washed white, its dark green corrugated-iron roof sitting low over a deep, paved verandah which ran around three sides. Two Zulu women, working full-time, kept the sprawling two-acre garden immaculate. Shrubs of all description assured vibrant colours all year round. Beds of annuals were specially cultivated for the house. The hedge-hidden vegetable garden was an oasis of succulent treasures through which Michael would prowl, munching on raw peas, beans and anything else that took his fancy. Another favourite destination when he felt peckish was the orchard. Everything grew there, bananas, pawpaw, oranges, peaches, guavas, granadillas, avocados, all his favourites. Planted strategically around the house, mature flamboyants, jacaranda and cassia added more colour, their spent flowers carpeting the lawns before they came into leaf to provide welcome relief from the merciless Zululand sun.

Michael closed the gate, imagining the swimming pool his mother said they might put in when his father came back. Michael hoped they would. Although the sea wasn't far, it was still a long hot walk. He cut across the lawn, jumping a bed of phlox. His mother would be in the office, just off the lounge on the far side of the house. The dogs – two large German shepherds and a ratty-looking little wire-haired terrier that his mother said looked like an animated dishrag but which was the only one allowed inside – would be snoozing outside on the verandah. If he could make it to the kitchen without alerting them, he was home and dry, his dusty condition, as usual, a secret between him and Bessie. Michael skirted the near side of the house, making for the kitchen door. As he drew closer, delicious smells wafted to him, making his mouth water. Roast chicken, freshly baked bread and the unmistakeable vanilla and cinnamon scent of bread-and-butter pudding. Like any other growing boy, he was perpetually hungry.

'What's this? You and Dyson have been rolling in the dirt again.' Bessie's ample frame waddled up to him. 'You get out of those dirty things quick, quick. Your mother will have a fit if she sees you.' Without waiting for his reply, Bessie pulled off his shorts and unbuttoned his shirt.

'Aw, Bessie, I'll do it.'

'You stand still. Tch! What a state. Where are your shoes and socks? Tch! You'd run naked if you could. I swear, you are more a Zulu than I am.' Left in nothing more than underpants, Michael turned to go but Bessie hadn't finished with him. 'Outside, boy. Get out and under the hose.'

Michael bounded outside and pretended shocked outrage while Bessie played the hose on him. The dogs, alerted by the noise, raced around the side of the house, barking hysterically and joining in the fun. It was something they did most afternoons. 'Now you run around till you dry,' Bessie said, turning off the tap and smiling broadly at him. 'Then get yourself into the kitchen. Got something for you.'

Unconcerned at his state of near nudity, Michael stayed in the sun until he had stopped dripping. Then he went to the kitchen. 'You not dried yet,' Bessie said, not even glancing at him.

'I'm dry enough. Anyway, it keeps me cool.'

Bessie shook her head. 'Got an answer for everything, don't you, boy?'

'Yep.'

Bessie laughed. 'Here. Kept these for you.' She handed him three shortbread biscuits. 'Don't go making crumbs now,' she warned as he left the kitchen, cheeks bulging. The wire-haired terrier, officially called Duke but generally referred to as Boet, followed Michael, nose to the floor, licking up the fallout.

Michael popped his head around the office door. His mother was poring over a pile of papers, frowning with concentration. Blonde hair fluffed out, like a halo, around her head. She had recently cut it in a short bob and Michael was still trying to get used to it. Her face was too close to what she was reading. Claire kept saying she needed glasses but never got around to doing anything about it. He bit into a biscuit and she heard him, glanced up, smiling that smile that made her eyes go warm.

'I do trust, young man, that you waited until you arrived home before undressing?'

'Mum!'

'Go and get some clothes on and do your homework. I'll be finished here in about an hour. Then we can talk.'

Michael grinned through a mouthful of biscuit.

'Okay, okay. We'll play cards. Just two games, mind.' She shook her head at her son's departure. Sometimes she worried that he was growing up too wild, that she didn't spend enough time with him. He was always out on the farm, in the Zulu compound or the Indian barracks. Although he had cousins his own age, he seemed to prefer the company of Dyson. Not that Claire minded, but she could see the way South Africa was headed and wondered how it would affect her son. She shook her head again. No! That was the wrong way to look at it. If South Africa went the way it seemed to be going then, heaven forbid, there would be a great need for people like Michael who didn't appear to see different colours.

Claire sighed. Michael was a good child who did well at school and was popular. What would happen when Joe returned? Her husband hadn't exactly shown much interest in him. 'Perhaps it will be different now that Michael is older,' she thought.

'Where is he?' Claire wondered aloud. There had been no news for months. She knew Joe was alive and in England. Why hadn't he come home? Claire had been brought up to believe that a wife did as her husband bade at all times, yet Joe's absence and silence irritated her. She tried to push the anger aside but it wouldn't go away, churning around along with her uncertainty over Michael and the responsibility of running the farm. 'It can't last,' she thought tiredly, turning back to her work. 'Joe must come home soon.'

Michael went to his room and shut the door. When he had turned six and started school his mother announced that he was too big for the nursery and could choose which bedroom he wanted as his own. The house had six, not counting the master bedroom. Michael gave it careful consideration but, in the end, chose the one she expected, next to hers. The room was large with bay windows, one on either side of French doors which led out onto the verandah. In the summer, the doors and windows were left open and a cool sea breeze blew in. His bed was larger than a single – it had been made by his grandfather – and was both solid and comfortable. A bedside chest provided space enough to accommodate a paraffin lamp, his penknife, bicycle torch and a rather noisy Big Ben alarm clock. There were two ornately carved oak wardrobes with a matching chest of drawers between them. In front of one window were a desk and chair, also in oak, and in front of the other a well-padded armchair. A mosquito net hung suspended from the ceiling over his bed, caught up during the day by some mysterious method of Bessie's. Honey-coloured cedar flooring was all but covered by a deep pile Indian carpet, the rich redness of its pattern repeated in long folds of velvet curtain. Outside, on the verandah, his mother had placed two cane chairs and a table which, she said, were for his exclusive use. Unfortunately, nobody told the dogs of this arrangement and Michael usually had to fight them for space.

Michael loved his room. The first thing he did was inform his mother, Bessie and the other servants that they all had to knock before entering. These instructions were taken seriously and it made him feel most important when adults knocked on his door.

Rummaging in a drawer, he found a pair of shorts and pulled them on. That was it. It was early October, the rains were not far off and it was hot and sticky, even in the house. The air seemed to hang in moist and torpid lethargy. Clothes would soon cling with perspiration. Michael finished the biscuits, washed his hands in a small basin, opened his school satchel and pulled out three exercise books. As well as the arithmetic, he had English sentences to write and history notes to study for a test the next day.

Michael enjoyed school. His quick mind and thirst

for knowledge meant that learning came easily. He also looked forward to homework. Sitting at the desk in his room it was a simple enough flight of imagination to pretend that he was the owner of a large sugar estate, an important businessman or a politician – whatever mood he found himself in – working through the endless mounds of paperwork. He bent to his books and was soon lost in concentration.

Half an hour passed quickly. Michael's concentration was broken by the sound of a motor car that had the dogs barking loudly. It was not the old Ford his mother drove, nor was it like any of the other cars that brought neighbours, relatives or friends to visit. The noise was sufficiently intriguing for him to walk out of his room and stand on the verandah, watching the car approach. It was Empangeni's one and only taxi which spent most of its time parked either at the railway station or outside the hotel. He heard a screen door bang and his mother came out to join him, shading her eyes and looking with interest at the dusty black vehicle as it stopped in front of the house.

A painfully thin man with hollow eyes struggled awkwardly from the back seat. The heavy greatcoat he wore made Michael feel hot, just looking at it. The man threw a glance at them, then turned and pulled a rucksack from the seat. Michael heard his mother gasp in shock. 'Joe!' Then she was running off the verandah towards the car. She reached the man just as he turned back towards the house and flung herself at him, nearly knocking him off balance.

Joe! His father's name was Joe. But this gaunt man in the overcoat wasn't, couldn't possibly be, his father. This unshaven old man bore no resemblance to the photograph. Shyly, Michael hung back. He saw the man disentangle himself, wincing as he did, saw him put out a hand to ward his mother off, heard him laugh and say, 'Steady on, Claire.'

As Michael watched, his mother crumpled to the ground.

Michael thought the man had pushed her. Without stopping to think, he leapt off the verandah and ran straight at Joe who was staring at his wife's inert form. Shouting a mixture of Zulu and English, Michael head-butted his father in the groin. To his amazement, the stranger buckled forward and joined Claire on the ground. One of the German shepherds was standing a metre away, its teeth bared. Uncertain what to do next, Michael hovered.

'You little bastard!' The man's face had gone white and he was breathing with difficulty. 'You bloody little savage.'

Michael was unrepentant. 'My mother. What is wrong with her? You hurt my mother.'

The man put out his left hand. 'Help me up.'

The authority in his voice gave Michael no option. He clasped the hand and hauled. On his feet, the man let go and swiftly cuffed him on the side of the head. The dog exploded into action and jumped forward but Joe sent it flying with a kick and the German shepherd fled, yelping with pain. Michael's vision was swimming as a rush of pain went through his head. He barely heard Joe's next words. 'I can see a father's touch is what you need.'

Michael shook his head to clear it. The blow had been viciously powerful. But scared as he was, he would not move away from his mother who was stirring and moaning. 'Joe?'

'Yes, it's me, Claire.'

She looked dazed for a second, blinking as the realisation of who stood before her sank in and she rose, staggering slightly. Michael wanted to help her but his mother was too close to the man. 'Why didn't you let us know? Where have you been? Oh, Joe, it's wonderful to see you again. You're so thin. Let me look at you.'

She stepped up to him and Joe King backed off quickly. 'Don't touch my arm,' he said sharply. 'It's not healed yet.'

'Darling!' Claire was all concern. Then she turned to Michael, her face beaming with happiness until she saw the unshed tears in his eyes, a combination of concern and the blow she hadn't seen. 'Oh, my darling, don't cry. Mummy's all right, I just fainted. See, I'm fine again. This is your father, isn't it wonderful, he's home at last. Come, darling. Come and say hello.'

Michael stepped reluctantly forward. 'How do you do, sir.'

Joe King scrutinised his son. He regretted cuffing the boy like that but he could still feel the numbing pain of that hard little head. He took in the oval face and blue eyes, the wide mouth and straight blonde hair. He was a good-looking lad.

Joe noticed that, of his own genes, there was no sign. His son was all Claire and he was looking at his father with a barely masked aggression. 'Shake, son. Let's start again.' Joe put out his left hand.

Michael hesitatingly extended his right hand then realised his mistake and changed it to his left. The handshake was clumsy and, as soon as physical contact had been broken, Michael stepped back. He needed to get away on his own. 'Excuse me, sir. I must finish my homework.'

His mother gave a tinkling laugh. 'Blow your homework, Michael darling. I'll write your teacher a note.' She took Joe's left arm in her right. 'Is this okay? Just tell me where it hurts and I'll be careful.' Michael could see that, for the moment at least, he had lost her. She was no longer his. A total stranger had come along and his mother's attention, something to which he had enjoyed almost total exclusivity, had wavered. Try as he might, Michael could not prevent the empty and lonely feeling as he saw his mother's happiness. It wasn't supposed to be like this, he knew that, and blamed himself. He had to get away.

'I'm nearly finished,' he told his mother, looking into her eyes, not glancing at his father. 'It won't take long.'

His loneliness increased when she simply nodded, squeezed the arm she held and said, 'Fine. Join us when you're done.' Then she was talking nineteen-to-the-dozen to *that* man, as though Michael had ceased to exist.

As he walked away he heard his father say,

'So, that's my son, not really what I expected,' and his mother's quick response, 'Joe, what do you mean? He's a wonderful boy.'

To make matters worse, Bessie came rushing from the house. 'Master Joe, Master Joe, you're home. Oh thank God. Blessed is our Father in Heaven. Welcome home, *nkosi*.'

'She makes it sound as though the place is falling down around our ears just because he's been away,' Michael thought crossly. 'What does she want to call him a lord for? He's just a bloody man.'

His father was home, and somehow, Michael had disappointed him. His mother was behaving in a way he had never seen before. And he, Michael, felt guilty that he didn't like his father and was angry with his mother. The event he had looked forward to for so long was a crushing disappointment. Rebellion stirred in him, an emotion he rarely experienced. So, his father was disappointed. So what? Michael was disappointed as well. That man looked nothing like his father. An entirely new sensation welled within him – self-pity. The game of cards with his mother was off, something else he blamed on the stranger. There was no doubting that life would be different from now on. Michael had never heard such authority in anyone's voice. His father obviously expected total obedience and wasn't above physical punishment if it were not forthcoming. He hoped the dog hadn't been seriously hurt. All the poor thing had been doing was defending them.

Michael had always imagined his father's homecoming would be a joyous occasion, that his father would become a friend, someone he could look up to. Maybe this man wasn't his real father? But Michael quickly discarded that thought. His mother's happy smile was too real. Sighing, he went and stood in front of the full-length mirror on the wardrobe door. What did his father mean, not really what he expected?

At that moment, his bedroom opened and the subject of his thoughts stood there. 'Leave the door open, son. That way I'll know you've got nothing to hide.' It was supposed to be a joke but it came out wrong. Michael just nodded dumbly. His privacy was precious to him. 'Stop admiring yourself and do your homework. Join us when you've finished.' With a penetrating look at the desk, Michael's father left, leaving the door wide open.

'Join us,' Michael seethed, going towards his desk. 'You're the one joining *us*.'

It was not a propitious beginning.

Dinner that night was a terrible ordeal. His father drank too much whisky which made him difficult to understand, especially when he grew angry, which he appeared to do for no reason. Joe spent most of the meal criticising Claire's running of the farm, the new irrigation system being the first target. 'What was wrong with the old way? Why on earth did you change things?'

Claire answered patiently. 'Because it's more profitable. The mill prefers it. We truck more cane with better sucrose and we save on labour as well.

A fifteen-minute burn does the work that would take fifty men almost two days. I've got all the figures, Joe.'

'Figures!' He scoffed. 'Who thought them up? Figures can be made to say anything you damn well please.'

'I didn't think them up, I drew them up. See for yourself, tomorrow,' Claire responded evenly, though Michael could see a steely glint in her eye. 'They work. The mill burned nearly a third of Colin's quota because the cane was dirty.'

'Colin!' Joe swallowed half a glass of whisky. 'Without legs he's about as much use as you.'

Claire bit her lip. 'It hasn't been easy for him. He's had no-one to turn to.'

'I suppose he'll expect my help.' Joe banged his hand on the table, making Michael jump with fright. 'Where the hell are Bob and Noel? They must have been back for months. By hell, Claire, things are going to change around here. If those lazy brothers . . .'

'Joe!' Claire was shocked. 'I wrote to you. Didn't you get my letters?'

'What letters?' Joe asked belligerently, knowing that he had received many, most of which were never read. He poured more whisky from the decanter that he'd insisted be placed on the table.

'Bob and Noel were both killed,' Claire whispered, tears in her eyes. 'Oh, my darling, didn't you know?'

The news sobered Joe briefly. 'Dear God!' he whispered, rubbing his left hand across his eyes.

Two brothers dead, another crippled. So many fine young lives ruined. All in the name of power. He forced himself to listen to Claire.

'Bridget is selling Kingston. She says that, without Bob, she can't bear to stay. Peg wants to keep Kingsmead going. It's a battle for her. She has also started to irrigate and things are improving. You'll see, Joe. We get one ratoon a year now.'

'One a year!' Joe was startled. A ratoon, the new sprout after cane has been cut, normally took eighteen months to reach maturity. If Claire was getting one a year he could substantially increase his quota.

'We'll go and see Colin tomorrow,' Claire suggested. 'Bridget and Peg too, I know they'll be pleased to see you.'

But Joe was only half listening. His wife had become more forceful, more confident than he remembered, taking charge and doing a good job of it though he'd be damned if he'd tell her so. He should be proud of her, he knew that. But resentment was crowding his masculine pride. He was the boss and Claire, having proved to herself that she could run the farm, was obviously not about to take a back seat. The news that two of his brothers were dead was a shock. They had never been close, old man King had seen to that, always playing one off against the other, but even so, they were his brothers. More to exert his own authority than anything else, he said, 'Why don't we buy Kingston? It's good land.'

'We can't afford it,' Claire said flatly.

'I'll be the judge of that.' Joe spoke sharply. He glanced at Michael. 'What are you staring at? Get used to the fact that I'm back and I'll make the decisions.' He looked back at Claire. 'You can both get used to the idea.' He reached for the decanter again.

'Joe!' Claire's eyes reproached him.

'Joe!' he mimicked. 'So I drink a bit. So what? You would too if you'd been through what I went through.'

He had her there. She had no idea what he'd been through and he wasn't about to tell her. Let her imagine the worst. It might keep her off his back.

'May I be excused please, Mum?' Michael looked imploringly at Claire.

She nodded and he went to rise.

'Sit down,' Joe barked. 'You'll leave the table when *I* tell you.'

Michael had to endure another twenty minutes while his father looked for faults in the way the farm had been run, complained about and criticised most things and even ordered Claire to grow her hair again. When he was finally allowed to leave the table, Michael escaped to his room with a feeling of profound relief. He wished he had the courage to defy his father and shut the door. He didn't want to see or hear the man again.

Joe lay on his back, staring up at the ceiling, a cigarette between his lips. Claire's, 'Darling, do you have to smoke in bed?' had bounced straight off him. Claire was in the bathroom nervously getting ready for bed. He couldn't put it off any longer. He had to tell her that, for the moment at least, her darling husband couldn't get it up. Joe dragged on the cigarette and blew smoke towards the ceiling. He supposed it might even come as some relief to her. From memory, she hadn't exactly been thrilled with the prospect of lovemaking two and three times a night. Joe's appetite for sex was the one thing about him that she had never understood. Once a week would have suited Claire better.

She came into the room and smiled at him tentatively. 'Joe, you haven't explained why it took so long for you to come home. Was it the injury?'

'Yes,' he said shortly. 'It took a while to heal up.'

'My poor darling. How awful for you.'

Joe shrugged and drew on his cigarette. 'These things happen. I don't really want to talk about it.'

'Of course, darling. Forgive me.' She was rubbing cream into her face.

'Come to bed, Claire.'

'In a minute.' She picked up her hairbrush and ran it through her hair vigorously. 'How did you get back here?'

'Milk train. Never again. Damned thing takes forever.'

'The milk train. But, Joe, that gets in at eight in the morning. Where have you been?'

'I had some business to take care of in town.' That was true enough. He'd gone straight to the hotel from the train. 'What the hell are you doing now?'

Hand cream. She was wringing it into her

hands. She looked at him uneasily. 'Isn't it silly? I'm as nervous as a young bride.'

Joe stubbed the cigarette out. 'Come here.'

Claire turned the lamp down on her side of the bed and slid in next to him. Joe left his burning. He rolled onto his side and turned into her. 'Not with the light on, Joe.'

'There's something you should know,' he said, ignoring her protests and sliding his good hand under her nightie. Her skin felt hot. He reached the bush of hair and ran his thumb lightly over it before pushing his hand between her legs, forcing them open a little. He slid his finger into her and she gave a little cry as emotions, so long held in check, flooded through her. She was dry and un-responsive at first but Joe had learned a thing or two in London and, before long, five years of absti-nence had his wife responding more than he had ever known before. 'I'll tell her later,' he thought.

Joe had spoken of his impotence to several doc-tors in London. All but one had dismissed his condition and told him to be patient. The excep-tion, a young doctor he'd seen just before returning to South Africa, advised him to keep trying.

'There's no physical reason, Joe. Not any more. You're like a lot of men. One failure to have an erection and you become convinced you'll never have one again. Don't force it. Once you're home with your wife let nature take its course. Give your wife pleasure – I'm sure you know what I mean – and you'll be surprised how quickly your little friend will respond.'

The Joe who went to war would not have fully understood the doctor's advice but he was not so innocent now.

Claire was squirming under his hand, her legs wider. She was slippery and ready for him. Abruptly, he removed his hand and flung back the bedclothes.

'Joe, the lamp.'

'Leave it. I want to see you.' He slid down in the bed and raised himself over her. Claire immediately snapped her legs shut. 'Open your legs.'

'Joe,' she begged.

He forced her legs apart and lowered his face to her. Soon, her ragged breath told him she had forgotten about the light. She came to him reluctantly, with a long, drawn-out sigh of satisfaction tinged with guilt. Joe understood Claire well enough to know that she would be deeply shocked by what they had just done and by her own reaction to it. He sat up and lit another cigarette.

Claire turned her face to him and he saw tears in her eyes. 'You've never done that before.' There was an accusation in her voice.

'Did you like it?'

She didn't answer, just put her hands over her eyes. 'Aren't you going to . . . you know . . . do it to me?'

He looked at her through a haze of smoke. 'I can't,' he told her flatly. 'I can't get it up any more.'

'What do you mean?' She had never heard the expression.

'My cock doesn't work,' he said crudely. 'It won't get stiff.'

'Joe!' She was terribly offended by his language.

Joe relented. It wasn't Claire's fault. Her innocence had once been a source of pride to him. Could he feel like that again? God knows, she was attractive enough. 'I'm sorry, darling. I've been in the company of men too long.'

To Joe's astonishment, feelings so long dead began to stir. While he didn't exactly have an erection, his old mate was definitely showing interest. He stubbed out the cigarette and lay back, the covers around his knees. Claire still had her eyes shut, convinced they were guilty of some terrible sin. Joe knew she would baulk at what he was about to ask. He had to convince her. This was the closest he'd come in years. 'Darling, look at me.'

Reluctantly, she opened her eyes and turned to him.

'We are married. There's nothing wrong with what we just did.'

'Are you sure? We've never done that before.'

She wanted to believe him, she just needed convincing. 'You liked it, didn't you?'

She nodded slowly.

'You still love me don't you?'

'Yes of course.' She didn't sound too sure.

'I love you too, darling. What we did was perfectly normal.'

'How do you know?'

'Men don't usually talk about these things but, with three years in the camp, we had nothing better to do. We often spoke of our wives. The conversations were, well, quite frank. It shocked me,

I can tell you. But I was the one who was different.'

'Oh.' She was relieved. 'I thought that maybe, that you might have . . .'

'Had an affair? Don't be silly. I love you.'

'I wouldn't blame you if you did. I really would understand.'

'That's nice of you.' He could not keep sarcasm from his voice. *If only you knew.*

She rolled towards him and put an arm over his chest. 'Forgive me, my darling. It's just that you seem different somehow.'

He kissed her cheek. 'Of course I'm different but I still love you. I want to make love to you, but you'll have to help me.'

'How?' The word was filled with dread.

He reached out and picked up her hand. 'Like this.'

She gripped him and jerked his foreskin back and forth so hard it hurt. 'Jesus!'

'Sorry.' She let go of him immediately.

'Try kissing it.'

'What!'

He nearly laughed out loud at her shock. 'Go on, it won't bite.'

Steeling herself, Claire planted a timid peck on his flaccid penis. This was not the Joe she remembered. His lovemaking had been predictable. As soon as they got into bed he would reach out and stroke her a few times, playing with her breasts, before raising himself and entering her. Sometimes in the middle of the night she would wake up with his fingers inside her and, as soon as he knew she was awake, he would take her again. Every morning he used to cuddle up behind her so she could feel his engorged penis. It was always the same, he would roll her over and make love again. She rarely saw him erect, or even naked. She had been brought up to believe that men had urges which they couldn't control and that it was a wife's lot in life to endure their husband's attentions and, if lucky, occasionally enjoy it. Joe used to share these beliefs and, if she had any complaints about him, it was the regularity with which he appeared to need sex. Their lovemaking was always conducted in the dark, under the covers with both of them wearing nightclothes. Now he was lying next to her, stark naked, with the bedclothes around his knees and the lamp still burning. The few times Claire had seen Joe erect she wondered how he ever fitted inside her.

She felt ashamed of what they were doing. It had to be a sin. The things he had just done to her, she'd never felt like that before. Claire King had just experienced her first orgasm and felt embarrassed that she had enjoyed it so much.

'Lick it, Claire. Lick it like I just licked you.' His breathing had become a little unsteady.

Claire stared at his penis, revolted. It was stirring, like a great slug. 'I can't,' she moaned.

'Give me the same pleasure I gave you.'

Slowly, reluctantly, Claire lowered her face to his groin. His moans, and the alarming way his penis grew inside her mouth, told her he was enjoying it. Which was more than could be said for

Claire. Quite suddenly, he grabbed her head, held it firm and ejaculated into her mouth. As soon as he let her go, Claire jumped up and ran for the bathroom, reaching the toilet just in time and vomiting into it. She was shocked beyond belief, nauseous and weak. She rinsed her mouth and, as an afterthought, cleaned her teeth again.

When she returned to the bedroom, he was smoking another cigarette. Joe smiled as though she were a favourite child. 'Thank you, my darling.'

Claire knew then that she did not love this man, that he had changed beyond recognition and that the Joe who had gone to war did not appear to have come back. Her upbringing made it impossible to consider divorce but she knew it had to be made clear to him that certain things would not be tolerated. 'Don't you ever do that to me again.' Revulsion put anger into her voice.

He looked genuinely surprised. 'It's the only way I can do it.'

'Then go and see a doctor. I will not let you do that to me again, it's disgusting.'

He could see she meant every word. He remembered how stubborn she could be. 'I'm sorry, darling. I thought you'd want to help me.'

Her face softened, she came to the bed and sat down. 'I do . . . I will help you, Joe, but if you ever do that in my mouth again I'll . . . I'll bite it off.' She was only half joking.

Joe laughed. 'I promise.'

Claire got into bed and curled into him. She would still be a dutiful wife, there was no other course of action available to her. 'Go to sleep. You've had a long day.'

Well after Claire had fallen asleep, Joe was still wide awake. He had been surprised by his erection. He wondered if his excitement had been caused by Claire's obvious reluctance. He knew what he was doing, that he was playing on her old-fashioned beliefs that she comply with his sexual wishes. It crossed Joe's mind that this would possibly be a way of controlling his wife who seemed to have developed more confidence, at least in the matter of the farm.

Joe already knew that he had ceased to love Claire. The woman he had come home to was a virtual stranger. Her modesty annoyed him. Her lack of worldliness exasperated him. But it was her confidence which got to him most. He was in charge and she would just have to get used to it. He could probably get his sexual kicks elsewhere, that would help.

The son he didn't know, or even particularly like, was another irritation. The boy sat at dinner staring accusingly at his father. His father, damn it! The word used to mean something. The kid would need sorting out. Joe had been raised on his father's belt and it hadn't harmed him. The kid would find out the hard way.

Quite suddenly his mood switched. 'Damn it! Come on, Joe. This is all you ever wanted once. You can't have changed that much. Give it time. Claire's a wonderful woman. Michael's probably okay too, you just have to get to know him.' Joe stared up towards the dark ceiling. 'The old Joe will come back. He's in there somewhere. He'll come back. He's got to.'

It was the closest the new Joe could come to a prayer.

THREE

Wilson Mpande trudged wearily along the track. The going was tough. It was little more than a trail made by the passing of people and animals. It had been all uphill for the past ten kilometres. With each minute his rucksack grew heavier, and the army uniform hotter. Ahead, he could see the jagged peak of Ka Isele, towering above the Amahlumbe Range. Tired as he was, the sight of it cheered him on. He was nearly home. This was the land of kings. His illustrious ancestor, Mpande, after whom he had been named – third king of the Zulus – had ruled for more than thirty years and built his kraal in sight of Ka Isele. Mpande's son and successor, Cetshwayo, established his own kraal nearby. These hills were rich in the history of the Zulu nation but it was more than that. Much more. Zululand was in his blood and Wilson had dreamed of this homecoming for more than five years.

He stopped and breathed in deeply, the pure air a delight, the green rolling hills a balm for eyes that had squinted for so long against the white-hot desert glare of North Africa. The sky was like a painting, a perfectly blue backdrop for the fluffy white clouds overhead and the darker thunder-clouds that boiled up behind distant hills. Soaring effortlessly, a pair of black eagles were lazily riding unseen thermals in their never-ending search for food. Each time one of them banked and turned, the jet colour of their feathers gleamed in the sunshine. As he watched, one suddenly folded its wings and dropped like a stone to the ground, rising again with a struggling dassie firmly held in razor-sharp talons. Calling to its mate, the black eagle quickly became a dot in the sky, powering back towards the far escarpment. The heavy rock rabbit didn't seem to impede its progress at all.

Wilson sighed with pleasure at the sight. His roots were here. That, in fact, was what *Mpande* meant – the root – and he, Wilson Mpande, bore the name with pride, aware that his royal blood was linked to the greatest king of all, Shaka.

It had come as something of a shock to Wilson to learn how little most white South Africans knew about the history of the Zulu royal house. In North Africa, on those few occasions the subject came up, Wilson realised that while all whites had heard of Shaka and most knew his half-brother, Dingane, had assassinated him, their knowledge dwindled at that point.

Right now it didn't bother him. For once, he did not care that the only people who seemed in awe of, or showed respect for, his royal blood were other Zulus. That would change. It had to. The Zulu nation had been too powerful, too magnificent, to simply fade into obscurity. The time was coming when his people would once again pull together and become such a force that all their neighbours would show respect. And that included the white man.

Wilson threw out his chest and took in great gulps of air, feeling the tiredness leave him. His village, his wife Nandi, and his son were just over the next rise. As a child he had played on the very spot where he now stood. Where that line of trees followed the stream, he had wooed and won Nandi. And away to his left, as far as the eye could see, were the valleys, hills and rivers in which the young Wilson had grown into a man. Wilson knew every inch, every nuance, every mood of this land that was his home. It held no surprises other than its beauty and treachery. It could be harsh and unforgiving yet little glades and streams offered water so pure, so sweet, so cold, that his tongue stung with anticipation. The ground on which he walked was no stranger to Zulu sweat, blood and bones – the air he breathed alive with echoes of ancient battles. '*Yebo*,' Wilson said aloud, setting off again. 'I am home.'

The sense of coming home had been slowly increasing since he left the train at Empangeni and began walking north-west. It was good to be finally speaking his own language with people he met along the way. The sight of Wilson in uniform created a great deal of interest. Many people knew nothing about the war, it held no importance to them. Wilson wondered if their ignorance was a good or a bad thing. He didn't know if he envied or pitied them. A bit of both he suspected.

He could have changed trains at Nseleni and ridden all the way to Ulundi but he wanted this experience. He wanted to walk the hills of his home and cross the White Umfolozi River where it swept lazily around the big bend, sandy banks so wide they looked like a beach. On the other side lay the land he knew intimately. As soon as he crossed the river he began to meet people he knew well. He passed places where he had herded his father's cattle, killed his first duiker, met with friends to talk or practise stick fighting. The area was alive with Wilson's memories, his past.

Two days' walking fell away, he felt invigorated and excited. He topped the last hill and there was the village looking almost exactly as he had kept it in his mind. It had grown somewhat in his absence, new huts to accommodate younger men as they came of age and took a wife, new kraals for their cattle and, something that had not been there before, a shop. Garishly painted with dancing figures and advertising, it looked decidedly out of place among the neat beehive dwellings. Wilson frowned with disapproval as he scanned the area below, trying to pick out his father's kraal and the homes within. When he located the dwellings his concern deepened. Much repair was needed to the hut he had built for Nandi. His brothers should have been taking care of it for him. There was something very wrong.

Reaching the village he made directly for his

father's kraal. Built in the traditional, time-honoured way, it was a large circular enclosure of cut acacia trees, the flat and thorny tops inter-meshed and compacted to form an impenetrable wall. Sited on a gently declining slope with the entrance at the lowest point so that, when it rained, dung and other dirt washed through and onto the vegetable garden beyond, within the outer stock-ade was a second enclosure where the cattle were secured at night to keep them safe from predators. Between the inner and outer walls were the huts, fourteen in all. Wilson's grandmother's was the largest and on the highest ground, furthest from the entrance. With her lived the spirits of their ancestors. To the right was his father's hut and to the left, his mother's. Various other family members lived within the kraal's inner and outer walls, the distance from the entrance depending on their seniority. On either side of the entrance were the huts of the unmarried girls and men.

People greeted him, but Wilson did not stop to talk. There would be time for that later. His first priority was to present himself to his father. His heart was beating excitedly as he stepped through the entrance, back to his childhood and the only place on earth he called home. A young man went to challenge his right to enter, recognised him, smiled a welcome and let him pass.

His mother was bent over her cooking fire and did not hear him approach. He watched for a few moments, smiling at the familiar way she fussed over the sticks until they were burning exactly to her liking. Bent almost double, her considerable bulk did not in any way hamper her effortless agility. He had seen her like this thousands of times but never had the sight been so precious, so satisfyingly familiar or such a comfort as it was now. Wilson finally knew he was home. 'I see you, Mother,' he called softly.

Her reaction to her son's unexpected appearance called on several hundred years of dignified Zulu tradition. She straightened slowly and turned, a small smile on her face. Observing him with great care, she did not move until satisfied that he was well. Then, and only then, did she walk towards him, placing a hand briefly on his cheek before saying, 'Your father will be pleased to welcome you home.' She called sharply and a young girl, perhaps seven or eight years old, came shyly from the hut, her eyes averted as a mark of respect.

Wilson looked at the child. She would undoubtedly be his niece. 'Silomo?'

His mother touched the child's head fondly. 'The second born of your older brother,' she confirmed. 'She has grown from the baby you once knew.'

There was a lump forming in Wilson's throat. Silomo and Dyson were the same age. His son would have changed this much too.

'Go and find your grandfather and bring him here. Tell him his son has come home. Tell him,' she called after the girl who was already racing away to do as her grandmother had instructed, 'that his son comes home a man.' She could not hide her pride and Wilson knew that, once she heard how he had rescued the white captain, the story of his bravery would be passed to every woman in the village. Such was the way of the Zulu. If a man returned from battle covered in glory the women would ensure he stayed that way until tales of his greatness passed into legend. Her son's elevated reputation would increase her own standing too. Women could only gain respect through the deeds and the status of their menfolk.

Wilson was anxious for news of Nandi and wondered why she had not appeared to greet him. He felt some disquiet, fearful that misfortune might have fallen on her. His brother's wives had seen him and were approaching shyly, not crowding, keeping a respectful distance until he greeted them. Where was Nandi? Wilson, however, did not ask. He would have to wait for his father to tell him.

Despite his anxiety there was no impatience in Wilson. Important news had to be given with due consideration to its value. And that meant more trivial matters would be discussed first. All the things that Wilson had been happily anticipating would have to wait. Removing, for the last time, the white man's uniform of war. The freedom of his own traditional clothing. Control of his own destiny. He was eager for his father, who had looked after his cattle during his absence, to take him to the kraal and point them out. Wilson had been able to identify each and every one of his beasts before he left. Now he would have to reacquaint himself with them, and any of their issue. He wanted, more than anything, to see his wife and son. But first there was the matter of man-talk with his father.

'I see you, my son. Welcome home.'

His father had put on weight. Wilson was pleased to see that he still dressed in the traditional way and not in the manner of the white man. 'I see you, Father.' A sprinkling of grey in the closely cropped hair. A few wrinkles he didn't remember. A tooth missing, leaving only four that he could see. But still, wisdom shone from the eyes that examined him and dignity surrounded the proudly held head.

His father walked to him, slow and sedate as Wilson remembered, as unhurried as time itself, and clasped Wilson's hand, chuckling gently. He was as delighted to see his son as Wilson was to see his father but there was a protocol and the old man would not dream of breaking with it.

'You return decorated with the white man's symbol. I understand it is for brave deeds.'

'Yes, Father.'

'Hmmm.' His father roughly fingered the ribbon on Wilson's chest. 'There is blood on your spear?'

'That is not their way, Father.'

'Tell me.'

'They gave me this for saving a man's life.'

'Hau! Why would you do that?'

'I was ordered to try.'

His father looked scathing. 'What kind of fool

orders a good warrior to risk his life to save one who is in difficulties? If a warrior is destined to die, then die he must. It is not up to others to help him. If you are not fighting then the enemy will overpower you. How can this thing be?' He shook his head. 'Tsk! The white man fights like old women.'

To his father the only honourable way to fight was up close, with the words of an individual's praise-poem spurring him on to such a frenzy that the thought of death only applied to the enemy. Wilson knew that the traditional old man despised the long-range methods of the white man in battle. He spoke quickly, before his father worked himself up into a rage. 'If I am to learn how the white man thinks, Father, then I must learn how he fights.'

'Ah, so it is.' The explanation pleased his father. 'The war is now ended and the English are well satisfied,' he stated.

Wilson nodded. 'Yes, Father.'

'There are those in this country who have sadness about this.'

Wilson's father was referring to those Afrikaners who had sympathised with Germany and who, at the orders of the British, had spent the duration of the war interned in camps. Wilson respected his father's knowledge of political affairs in South Africa. It had been his father who urged Wilson to join the African National Congress. However, Wilson was not particularly interested in white man's politics. 'They quarrel between themselves like children,' he said dismissively.

'And we do not?' his father asked gently, smiling a little.

Wilson inclined his head. His father was right, Zulu history was littered with quarrels.

'How was the battle?' Fighting and killing was part of a tradition. His father wanted details.

'There were many battles. I do not like the white man's way of fighting. Many die but there is little blood on the spear.'

His father nodded. 'They do not change. There is no honour in killing when you do not stand chest to chest with your enemy.' His father spat on the ground. 'It has always been so. The ways of the white man are sometimes strange. They pretend friendship yet, in their hearts, there is nothing but greed and treachery. They call us savages and treat us like dogs and yet they pray to a god who they say is just and kind. But who can see this god? If he is such a good person, why then does he not teach his people to show kindness? We have shown them nothing but courtesy and where has that led? Pah! We should have killed them all when they first came to our land.'

Wilson knew that his father could go on for hours about the mysteries and misdoings of the white race so he sought to shorten the conversation. 'Tell me, Father, what of Inkatha ka Zulu?' He already knew that when the ANC lost its direction the Zulus had formed their own organisation, naming it after the *inkatha yezwe*, the sacred coil of grass symbolising unity of the Zulu kingdom. But it too appeared to have failed. The aim of Inkatha, to improve the lives of Zulu people through the purchase of land and by developing recognition of the royal house, had been equally corrupted by misuse of funds. Instead of being used to acquire land, some of the money – which had been raised by increasing taxes within the Zulu nation – was spent on a memorial to Shaka but most had been wasted on King Solomon's addiction to alcohol and on his lavish lifestyle.

Before he went away Wilson had grave fears for the continuance of Inkatha. On his return, he learned of its fate. However, his father would expect him to ask and so that is what he did, prepared to wait patiently for a carefully formulated reply.

'Finished,' his father spat out contemptuously, shaking his head. 'Now we have the Zulu Cultural Society.'

Again, Wilson had learned of this in Durban. But he asked, 'What does that do?'

His father hawked and spat again. 'Like Inkatha, they want recognition. They're trying to establish a Zulu identity but it is becoming difficult. Pretoria gives us white magistrates who take power from the chiefs. If a man does not like his chief's decision he goes to a magistrate. If the magistrate's decision does not please him, he goes to his chief. These magistrates do not understand our ways and make bad decisions. The old ways are going.'

His father looked angry. 'Some of us think this thing is being done to divide us. If this is so, even if we win recognition, there will be nothing left to recognise.'

Wilson had resigned himself to a long discussion when his mother, realising how he must be longing to hear of his own family, uncharacteristically intervened. 'Husband, these matters you speak of trouble all of us. Our son will learn of them soon enough. It is likely that the things he wishes to hear of are closer to home.'

His father looked disappointed but, when he saw the smile spread over his son's face, realised a political discussion would have to wait. 'Come, we will sit.' He led Wilson to the shade of a tree and the two of them sat on small, handmade wooden stools. His father spent some time fussing to find the most comfortable position. 'You will not have heard of the Bantu Purity League?' he asked suddenly.

Wilson hadn't, and said so.

'Times are changing. Many *amakholwa* now live among us.' Wilson's father was referring to the Christian converts who had been lured away from traditional values to adopt the white man's ideals. 'There is much trouble among them. The young girls leave and go to find work in the towns. They bring back *isifo sabelungu* – the white man's disease – and they bring back babies before they take a husband. Those of us who respect old traditions have become concerned.' He glanced sharply at Wilson. 'It is yet another way in which our culture is being eroded by the white man. Many of our women have decided it is time to take action and they try to teach the *amakholwa* the old ways. It is a difficult task for the young do not wish to listen. Still, the decent women among us do not give up.

Nandi is one such believer. She has joined those who founded the Purity League.'

Wilson was rocked. Nandi, although as traditional as he, had never had any need to protect or promote the traditional values by which she lived. Things must be bad for her to do such a thing. 'Is she here?'

His father pursed his lips. 'No. She has taken your son and now lives on a sugar farm near Empangeni. She is the local representative for the league.' While he obviously approved of the league's aspirations, Wilson's father undoubtedly disapproved of Nandi's actions. A woman's place was in the home, especially the wife of his son.

To some extent Wilson shared his father's feelings but he was a man standing with one foot planted in tradition while the other took root in progress. The difficulty was trying to preserve the best of the old ways while remaining receptive to the new. It was a necessary juggling act. The purity of Shaka's day, where Zulus ranged far and wide across a land which they had paid for in blood, was gone forever. Not even the most hopeless dreamer could imagine it would ever come back. The trick was, in this era of change, to somehow keep intact what was left.

Wilson had seen enough of the world to realise that the Zulus weren't the only ones trying to deal with this situation. He had listened to Australians, white South Africans, Scotsmen and New Zealanders in the Western Desert speak of change and how the older generations resisted it. But it seemed to Wilson that the matters of which they spoke were of their own making. The Zulus didn't have that luxury.

And now it was his own wife who, despite being motivated by the ideals of traditional behaviour, had broken with tradition herself. It was not up to Nandi to make a decision as important as the one she had and move from her husband's village, irrespective of whether it be right or wrong. In that regard, Wilson was angry with Nandi. On the other hand, he was proud of her as well.

'You will bring her home,' his father stated flatly.

Wilson hesitated. It was a question he could not readily answer. He wanted to more than anything else in the world, but reason told him such a commitment was not possible. In the short years they were together Nandi had proven time and again that she had a mind of her own, and a good one at that. It was a sign of the times that Wilson was prepared to accept this and question only what was for the best. *Someone* had to act, *someone* had to care enough to try and bring back dignity and self-respect to his people, before they lost it altogether. 'I do not know,' he spoke quietly. 'It is too early for me to tell.'

With that, his father had to be content.

The night was spent at his own fire, visited by all members of the family and many friends. Talk ranged from cattle to old clan quarrels and, within a very short time, Wilson felt he had never been away. But when he tried to raise more profound issues, it was obvious that Wilson and his father were the only ones with any interest in political matters.

When the women and children finally left and it was only the men sitting around, Wilson found himself comparing the experience with many during the past five years. Men, in the company of other men, talking, laughing, smoking and getting a little drunk. He remembered a rangy Australian he'd met in the desert saying, in that peculiarly nasal tone which had taken months to understand, 'Yeah, mate. Nothin' like a keg, a few mates and a good yarn.' Here he was now, back home, and while they didn't have a keg they had something better – fine home-brewed beer, milky and bitter-sweet to wash down the dryness of 'a good yarn'.

'We're all the same,' he reflected as the talk flowed over him. 'We're men and we're all the same. Why then are we so different?'

Later, as he rolled onto a sleeping mat, he knew that the silence of a dark Zululand night was the best sound he had heard for five years.

Before he left the next morning to make the long walk back to Empangeni, Wilson paid a visit to the village *sangoma* seeking both spiritual guidance and advice. 'I saw you coming three full moons ago. What delayed you?' were the diviner's opening words.

Wilson dropped to his haunches in front of her. 'I was delayed in Durban.'

She watched his face for a few seconds, a long looped wig, threaded with white beads, framing her face. 'There is nothing there for you,' she said finally. 'Not yet. The day is coming but it is a long way from now. You are not yet ready.'

Wilson was watching her headdress carefully. The loops were said to be strung in such a way that the spirits had somewhere to sit while they were speaking into the *sangoma*'s ears. Surely there would be some movement when they sat down. But nothing stirred.

The *sangoma*'s eyes gleamed approval when he didn't speak. 'The choice is yours,' she said suddenly. 'The spirits offer you two paths. One is littered with the bones of things now out of reach. If you tread that way you will discover peace but you will also find that the way ahead is blocked. The doors of our past have closed and they cannot be opened again.'

Wilson kept his face impassive. The *sangoma* was telling him what he already suspected. The past was the past. 'Tell me of the other path,' he said quietly.

The *sangoma* closed her eyes. She smiled to herself, then jerked and sat still. 'The other is new, strange, with much to confuse and frighten a weaker man. The doors are difficult to open but that does not mean they cannot be opened. If you choose this path you will need to be strong.'

'Strong?' Wilson wondered. 'Or foolish?' The *sangoma* had given no indication of which he would choose, although he suspected she knew.

She opened her eyes and looked directly at him,

though they were glazed and he didn't think she could see him. Her voice was soft and singsong when she spoke again.

'Each day brings with it a gift. It is our choice whether to take it or not. If we accept it, no matter how small it might be, nothing will be quite the same as it was yesterday. If we do not take the gift it will leave with the day. But if we try to take more than the day offers, we break the rhythm of patience. That which grows slowest, lasts longest.' She fell silent, rocking slightly.

'That's all very well,' Wilson thought, waiting for her to speak again. 'But the tortoise only makes progress when it sticks its neck out.'

The glazed look was leaving her eyes. 'What else do you need to know?'

'Please,' he said, careful to be polite, 'can you tell me where to find Nandi?'

She unrolled a springbok skin in front of her and arranged a number of items on either side. They were mainly bones, though there were some human teeth among them and a small ceremonial spear. Placing the smaller items, the bones, shells and stones into a leather pouch, she shook them out onto the skin and studied where they fell for a long time. 'Find the place where the sea and *uBejane* live side by side,' she told him finally. 'It is near to where the people of the bad omen settled,' the *sangoma* added, naming the area known as Kwa Mbonambi. 'There you will find Nandi.'

She continued to look down at the array of items. 'There is much here,' she went on calmly.

'There is death and deception and a great evil. But there is goodness and reward too. You cannot change what the ancients foretell. Whichever path you choose, these things will come to pass. The evil I speak of will touch the lives of two families, yours and one other. There is nothing you can do to prevent it.' A shudder ran through her. 'I have never seen such wickedness,' she whispered.

Wilson went cold. The *sangoma* was never wrong.

'The spirits are already at work. Your destiny is in place.' She looked up at him briefly. 'Remember this. Do not lose your way to sorrow. You have been selected. The third king of the Zulu nation watches you. Use your time well and be satisfied.' She picked up a handful of dirt. 'One speck may not seem much. How would it be if each speck believed itself insignificant and went away?'

Wilson sat spellbound. Consultations with the *sangoma* always both fascinated and frightened him. Her message was clear enough: walk before you run.

She looked back at the skin. 'Inkatha will rise again. You will play a small part. Do not be disappointed. Many will do the same. Remember, one speck of dirt does not make a land but have faith in the strength of many specks for that is the shape of the future.' She picked up the assorted pieces and put them back into the pouch before rolling up the skin and tucking it behind her. When next the *sangoma* spoke, it was with the voice of a friend rather than in the dreamy trance of someone in touch with the spirits. 'You will find Nandi easily. Not today or the next but the one after that. Accept that she has changed. If you can do that, you will be happy. Take time to spend with her, you owe yourself that much.' She nodded briefly to indicate the session was over.

Wilson rose to his feet. 'Thank you,' he said. 'I have listened and heard your words.' He turned to go.

'Your first son is a fine boy,' she called out after him. 'You will be proud of him.'

Wilson kept walking and did not look back. But a smile of joy crossed his face.

The Inyanga, the traditional healer of the village, greeted him as he passed. Wilson briefly considered consulting him too. True, his main function was curing coughs, stomach upsets, and many other ailments with his potions of bark, leaves, seeds and animal parts but he was also skilled in other ways. He had proved many times that his potions could protect against lightning strikes, turn bad luck into good, cast love spells, ensure successful harvests of staple foods such as sorghum, millet, beans, sweet potatoes and pumpkins. Also, if an evil spell had been cast against a village member, the Inyanga – the man of the trees – was capable of turning it away.

Tempting as it was to hedge his bets and ask the Inyanga for guidance and perhaps a magic spell to assist his quest in finding Nandi, Wilson kept walking. The *sangoma* was the one in touch with the spirits and the spirits had sent a clear message. Better not to anger them.

His father was set to say more about bringing Nandi back to the village but, despite his high status within the clan, not even he would dare to quibble with the *sangoma*'s advice. All he could do was shake his head and tut at the changing way of things. Wilson said goodbye to his family and set off towards the coast.

He was still undecided. One part of him yearned to take Nandi and his son home, home to where the spirits of his ancestors still hunted the hills and valleys; home to where the rising sun sent long shadows sliding across valley floors as it burned through the early mist; home to where high cliffs bounced back the voices of his cattle, echoes mingled with the distant cry of the black eagles. It would be so easy to turn his back and go forward into the past.

But could he? The fingers of another world had already reached his village. It was only the beginning. He had seen the white man's cooking pots, store-bought chairs, even a paraffin refrigerator. Village life had changed and Wilson knew it would not stop there. Progress was like a runaway train, and just as impartial. The Zulus would have to take the good with the bad. Would they rush headlong to embrace the ways of the white man only to find they hadn't progressed at all?

Thoughts churned inside him as he walked. He had seen the towns and what they did to his people. He had seen Zulus who wanted what the whites had but who, out of desperation, had found work in kitchens and gardens and answered to the insultingly uniform call of 'boy'. It was clear to Wilson that the Zulus needed direction, but which way? How? Would the proud nation raised by Shaka flounder and disappear? Was that the destiny of his people?

Just as he thought he knew which of the *sangoma*'s paths he must take, Wilson's resolve would waver towards the other. She had said Inkatha would rise again and he would be among those responsible. Could he do it from his rural village or should he stay in a city or large town?

Wilson reached Empangeni the following evening, dropping from the hills just as the sun sank behind them. His original intention had been to travel light with just the clothes he wore, his shield, spears and *knobkerrie*, but his mother had pressed gifts on to him for Nandi and his son, his sisters suggested he take some European-style clothes to wear when he sought work and he also needed something in which to carry the food his father insisted he should take. In the end, it was all packed into his army kitbag.

An aunt lived just outside Empangeni and he made his way there, knowing he would be made welcome. Despite their proximity to the town, none knew of Nandi's whereabouts. Wilson woke early the next morning and set off again, towards the ocean.

The *sangoma* had said to look for a place where the rhinoceros comes close to the sea, just below where the people of the bad omen had settled. Rhinoceros, he knew, did not venture onto a beach. Nor were they to be found this close to big towns. However, the *sangoma* had been quite specific so he stuck to the dirt road which ran along the coast. At a quarter past one in the afternoon he found what he was looking for. UBejane Estate. He went through the arched gateway and set off up a straight road flanked on either side by sugar cane. Reaching the first crossroad, he stopped. Which way? A voice hailed him in lilting English, 'You are on private property, Zulu. What is it you seek here?'

Wilson turned and found himself looking at a tall Indian Sikh. Automatically, he drew himself to his full height, transferred his spears to his left hand and held up the other, palm out, so the approaching man could see he carried no weapon and came in friendship. 'I come to find my wife and son,' he said in English, the only language common to such widely diverse cultural backgrounds.

The Indian stopped in front of him. 'And who might they be?'

'They are Nandi and Dyson Mpande.'

The Sikh's expression changed. 'You would be Wilson, isn't it?'

Wilson nodded.

'Goodness! They will be very pleased to see you are coming. Goodness, yes.' He directed Wilson towards the Zulu compound. 'If you are stopped along the way tell them Raj knows you. That is being myself,' he added gravely. 'Goodness!'

Wilson thanked Raj and turned to go.

'Wait, Zulu.'

He turned back.

'If you see a white man on a horse it would be best if you seek cover. The man who owns this farm is . . . goodness, how do I put it . . . you do not know which way he will jump. Once he was a man who was fair but, ever since he returned from the war . . .' Raj shrugged. 'Try to stay out of his sight.'

Wilson looked at the Sikh. He could see the man spoke from his heart. But he, Wilson, was a Zulu. He would not hide like some whipped dog from anyone. Raj was watching him anxiously and Wilson realised that if the white owner found him wandering on his property it would most likely be the Indian he would blame. So he nodded gravely, thanked the man again and left, following his directions through the cane fields.

While the healthy and neatly planted fields were not as pleasing to the eye as the rows of mealies at home that curved with each gentle contour of the land, they nonetheless were living evidence of the white man's determination and knowledge. Not only were the plants organised into clearly defined sections, they were obviously thriving in the sandy soil and, wonder of wonders, pipes pushed out long arcs of water keeping them alive.

He passed a field where Indian women were hoeing out weeds, backs bent to their task, working methodically, without distracting chatter. Quite suddenly he reached the end of the sugar cane. This was more like it. The undulating land stretched away towards distant hills. It wasn't the dramatic country of home but Wilson preferred it to the flat symmetry of cane fields. He could see cattle grazing and his critical eye noted how fine they were, straight backed and well fleshed, coats a healthy shine in the afternoon sun, a herd to be proud of. Carefully shutting the gate as he had found it Wilson set off up the winding road, passing between two large boulders.

Dyson Mpande, making preparations to ambush Michael, watched the stranger go past, wondering who he was. The man walked with the proud bearing of one who carried ancestral greatness. Dyson was impressed.

Nandi Mpande placed a cover over the Olivetti typewriter and stood up. 'I have finished the letters, Mrs King.'

Claire glanced at the clock on the wall. It was one-thirty. Nandi had stayed back an extra half-hour to finish the typing. She only worked a half day and was usually gone by one. 'Thank you, Nandi. I will post them this afternoon.' She ran a hand through her hair. 'Tomorrow we'll do the accounts.'

'Yes, madam.' Nandi collected up her purse. 'I will see you tomorrow, madam.'

Claire nodded vaguely, returning to her short-sighted examination of the day's mail.

Nandi left the office and stepped off the verandah. When she got home there were thirty letters to write for the Bantu Purity League, food to prepare and, if time permitted, she might spend an hour or so on the heavy, pleated skirt she was making for herself from ox hide. The beadwork was time consuming but each colour had traditional significance and she had already planned a matching headdress. Normally her husband would have created the basic skirt, leaving Nandi to deal only with the beadwork, but Wilson had been away for five years and Nandi had no idea when he would return. Although she wore a dress and shoes in the European style when working in the farm office, she preferred a simple wraparound piece of material or, for more formal occasions, the ox-hide skirt.

It was sticky hot and the sun burned through the thin cotton of her dress as she hurried towards the compound. Nandi often longed for the cooler air of her home in the hill country. What would Wilson think when he arrived to find her gone? There was no such thing as a mail service to the village and, when he left, Wilson did not have an address where letters might reach him. There had been no way to let him know that she was moving. She had no idea where he was but she knew he was still alive because the *sangoma* had told her that he was safe and she would see him again. Nandi expected that her husband would beat her for leaving the village. She accepted that. But what if he insist she return? Although trained from her earliest years to obey her father and brothers, and then her husband and his male relatives, Nandi knew she could not go back.

Her father-in-law had beaten her and demanded she stay in the village to await Wilson's return. Nandi had expected him to do that. She faced her punishment squarely, making no attempt to sneak off. It had broken her heart when, with contempt in his voice, Wilson's father had disowned her, saying he would only 'see' her again when she came to her senses. Wilson's mother had no option but to shun her daughter-in-law but not before Nandi saw sorrow, understanding and even approval on her normally expressionless face.

Nandi made her way along the road towards where it forked. She sighed. Sometimes it seemed that the Bantu Purity League was getting nowhere. Girls still flocked to the towns, seeking work. So did the men, leaving their wives and children at home in the villages. Loneliness brought them together and the inevitable consequence of an unwanted pregnancy was so often the outcome. The league knew they could not prevent men and women lying together so they tried to encourage *hlobonga*. Traditional tribal custom accepted sexual activities from puberty onwards. Young men and women were free to enjoy mutual stimulation, but on no account was a girl to lose her virginity. Girls were instructed in ways to squeeze their thighs together. This technique, *hlobonga*, prevented penetration while, at the same time, giving their partner pleasure.

These days, it seemed, the old ways were not enough. Nandi and her colleagues were fighting a losing battle. It was not only in the matter of sex. Instead of toiling in the fields, many young women preferred to work in the homes of whites, living in servants' quarters, or *kias* as they were called. There they slept on beds rather than mats and cooked their food over paraffin burners in preference to an open fire. The men found them lazy and disobedient, compared them unfavourably with their traditional wives back in the villages but that didn't stop them accepting the hospitality of these more modern girls. Nandi could see that despite their best efforts to keep tribal values alive, members of the Bantu Purity League themselves were adopting more modern ways. They too were less inclined to accept that a man's word was law. Recently Nandi had found herself wondering the same thing.

When a representative of the league first visited Wilson's village and respectfully asked the chief if she could address the women, that in itself was a sufficient break with tradition for the chief to refuse permission. The visitor had simply gone behind his back and spoken to the women one at a time. While most of the women agreed that the breakdown of tribal ways was a terrible thing, their lives were fully occupied. Their menfolk forbade them to become involved in anything perceived as a threat to male authority and, for the life of them, most of the women could not separate in their minds the new-look league representative from those girls she purported were in need of saving.

Nandi had been the woman's only conscript, though she had at first baulked at leaving the village to serve the league in the far off district of Empangeni.

'Why can't I work here?' she asked.

The representative had spent two days convincing Nandi that she would be more useful in a bigger place.

'How will I live?' Nandi worried, wavering a little.

'I will find work for you. The league cannot pay you but I can get you a job that will.'

She had been as good as her word. Nandi arrived in Empangeni two weeks later carrying all her worldly possessions, a three-year-old son in tow and the fading bruises of Wilson's father's fists on her body.

The league representative took her to UBejane to meet Claire King. Thanks to her cousin Bessie who worked in the kitchen, she knew Claire needed help with the office work. When Claire learned that Nandi had been taught English at a mission school, she hired her on the spot.

A whole new world then opened up for Nandi. Mrs King taught her how to use the typewriter, how to answer the telephone and, when she discovered that Nandi's handwriting was a beautiful flowing script, how to enter transactions into the ledger. Nandi had proved an apt and willing student, in four years becoming an invaluable assistant, extending her duties to include writing out orders and preparation of the wages book. Mrs

115

King paid her well and had offered a room in the servants' quarters near the house. When Nandi refused, saying she'd rather live in the manner to which she was familiar, Mrs King provided her with a house in the Zulu compound.

Nandi was lost in thought as she walked. For the past four days Mrs King had not been her normal self. Her husband had come home and instead of being overjoyed and happy, she appeared to be preoccupied and distant. A tension had appeared in her manner and, once or twice, she had snapped at Nandi for no apparent reason. It was obvious that things between Mrs King and her husband were not going well. When she was introduced to Mr King, Nandi could see that the difficulties stemmed from him. He always had liquor on his breath and seemed either distant or aggressive. Talk in the compound among those who knew him before he went away, was that he had become a different person.

Nandi could not make allowances for this. She simply did not like him. Once or twice he had looked at her too boldly and, one time, when Mrs King was out of the office, he had brushed his hand against her breast on the pretext of reaching for something on the desk.

Up until his return Nandi had enjoyed her work. Now she was wary. There was something about Joe King she did not trust. And she could not understand why he seemed so disinterested in the farm, preferring to spend his days drinking or hanging around the office criticising.

Yesterday, Mrs King had obviously asked him

why he wasn't getting more involved in the farm and Nandi heard him shout, 'Give me a fucking break, I've been injured for Christ's sake.' Mrs King had not come back to the office for a long time. When she did, her eyes were red.

Nandi had nearly reached the compound. Busy with her thoughts, she hadn't noticed the man coming towards her. He was a stranger, dressed in the manner of a Zulu. It was unusual, these days, to see a man wearing traditional apparel. 'He is fine looking,' she thought, lowering her eyes so he would not see admiration in them as they drew closer. Nandi was a healthy young woman and lately her body had been telling her it was too long since she had lain with a man. She had remained faithful to Wilson because she loved him but it was increasingly difficult not to have immodest thoughts. Failing to resist one last peep at the approaching man she looked up and gave a cry of unrestrained joy. 'Wilson!'

Wilson stopped in his tracks. He hadn't paid much attention to the woman walking towards him. His mind was on Nandi. When he realised it was she, he dropped the kitbag and, holding his shield and spears proudly, walked towards her with as much dignity as he could muster. Nandi approached her husband with the same restraint. Twenty metres apart both gave up and ran the last of the distance, laughing and shouting. He caught her up in his arms, spun her around and then wrapped her in a bear hug. 'I missed you.'

'I have missed you too.'

'Oh, wife,' he whispered. 'How good it feels to hold you again.'

As they stood in each other's arms, Nandi's memories of him came flooding back: the feel of his hard body against her, his strong arms around her, his hands gentle on her, the smell of him. A shudder ran through her. It was unusual for Zulus to display such affection but, oh it felt good to be with him like this.

Eventually he eased her away from him. 'Where is my son?'

She had felt his need of her but it would be immodest to mention it. 'You did not see a fine boy on your way?'

'No.'

Nandi smiled. 'He waits for his friend, the son of the white *nkosi*.'

Wilson raised his eyebrows. 'My son is friends with the *izilwane*?'

Nandi pushed him playfully. He had referred to the white man in the old way, as a wild beast. 'He will not be home for a few hours,' she told him coyly, encouraged by the fact that he did not seem to be angry with her.

'Come, wife,' Wilson said, smiling broadly, unable to resist the urge to make love to her any longer. 'Come show your husband how much you have missed him.'

Dyson Mpande had a new strategy. He had ambushed Michael for four consecutive days at the place where the road ran between the large rocks, alternating between the right- and left-hand boulders. Yesterday, he had taken care to let Michael see him and had been easily overpowered. Michael commented afterwards, 'You grow lazy. A leopard never returns to the same spot twice.'

Dyson had looked suitably shamed and responded, 'You will not see me tomorrow.'

Michael hadn't seen him but then, he hadn't really been looking for him. The problem of his father was weighing heavily on his mind and he wasn't concentrating on their game as much as usual. Even if he had been, he would hardly have expected that Dyson would be on the same rock as yesterday. Dyson dropped silently and Michael had gone sprawling.

'That's not fair,' Michael protested, scrambling up and dusting himself off as best he could.

'War is not fair,' Dyson told him, laughing with glee. 'And the leopard is wily.'

A horse snorting a little distance off galvanised Michael into action. 'Quick, hide.' He pulled Dyson off the road and the two boys crouched in the dry gully. Joe King rode past, his horse kept at a fast walk. They waited in the gully until they could no longer hear its hooves on the hard track.

'Why do you hide from your father?' Dyson asked, straightening up and staring after the horse and its rider.

Michael scowled. 'Don't like him.'

Dyson was scandalised. 'He's your father.'

'Shaka didn't like his father either,' Michael retorted, stung by the implied criticism.

'You are wrong. Shaka's father didn't like him.'

'Same difference. My father doesn't like me.'

Dyson considered this. 'Perhaps you will be a great warrior like Shaka.'

Michael knew his Zulu history almost as well as Dyson. He was angry with himself for letting Dyson outsmart him, confused by his feelings towards his father and generally out of sorts about life, otherwise what happened next would never have occurred. Michael started it. 'At least my mother did not blame the *itshaka* for her fat stomach. At least I am not named after a beetle. My name means "Who is like the Lord?" I will be a great king, not just a warrior.'

'Shaka *was* a king. He was the first king. All the Zulus took their name from his clan.' Dyson was getting angry too. It was not like Michael to pick a fight.

'Heaven,' Michael scoffed the name of an early Qwabe prince. Translated into English the word Zulu means 'heaven' and it was after this prince that the Zulus were named. 'What a stupid name for a man who called his clan after himself.' Then he added insult to injury. 'You who came from a dog's penis.' It was an old expression sometimes levelled at members of the Zulu clan before Shaka's day, and it was deeply offensive, as Michael well knew, although he wasn't sure he understood exactly what it meant.

Dyson pushed Michael. Michael swung at Dyson. Suddenly they were fighting in deadly earnest. Neither of them heard Joe King returning.

The first Michael knew was a stinging blow to the side of his head. 'Get home, boy. Wait for me in your room.' Joe turned to Dyson. 'Get out of here, you little bastard, before you feel my boot up your arse.'

Dyson turned and fled. Michael, his face dirty, bloody and streaked with tears of rage, bent to gather up his school bag. Without looking at his father, he set off towards the house. By the time he'd reached the fork Dyson had disappeared and he had calmed down somewhat. He regretted taunting his friend and, at the first opportunity, he would apologise. It was hardly Dyson's fault that since the arrival of his father four days earlier Michael's life had been turned upside-down.

Dyson might have raced straight into his hut but was stopped by one of the wives of the *induna*, the headman in charge of all the Zulus on UBejane. 'Stay your feet, boy,' she called sharply. Dyson was so surprised, he stopped in his tracks. True, she was a wife of the most important man in the kraal but she was, after all, only his third wife, and he, Dyson, was a male.

She smiled to soften her sharp words. 'Your mother has company,' she explained. 'Your father has returned.'

Dyson was stunned, excited and afraid all at once. He would have a father at last, something he had yearned for ever since he was old enough to realise that he and his mother were different from everyone else. But since Michael's father had returned, his friend had changed. Perhaps fathers weren't the best thing in the world after all? Not knowing what to do, Dyson sat just outside the hut, waiting to meet his father. He didn't have long to wait. Ten minutes later the man who had so impressed him as he passed by his hiding place emerged from within, followed by his mother who was smiling happily.

'Here,' she said to the man proudly. 'Here is your son, Dyson.'

Dyson stood up, not knowing what to expect.

'Dyson!' It burst from the man happily.

Dyson felt himself being lifted high into the air. Looking down into the stranger's face, he saw only love, pride and happiness. 'My father,' he said breathlessly, clasped briefly to his father's chest before being returned to the ground.

His father dropped to his haunches in front of Dyson. 'My son, I see you. It has been too long.'

Dyson scrutinised his father's face. It was strong and proud. He gave a small sigh of satisfaction. It was all right. His father loved him, he could see it already. Acting uncharacteristically – young Zulu boys did not show any outward affection towards their father, just as their father usually showed none to them – Dyson flung himself into his father's arms, almost knocking him over. Then, remembering his mother's teachings, he stood back and said solemnly, 'Welcome home, Father.'

Wilson Mpande stood and looked at Nandi. 'We are a family again. It is all I have thought about for five years.' His features became stern as he added, 'But I fear my family is not how I left them. It would seem that my wife takes it upon herself to make my decisions for me.'

Dyson held his breath. A steely note of authority had crept into his father's voice. His mother stood, head hanging, saying nothing.

'Come, wife. You had much to say about where you would live to my father. What have you to say to me?'

Nandi peeped up at him. 'There are things to discuss,' she said softly.

Dyson could sense that his mother was uneasy. He was too young to fully appreciate why but understood her well enough to know that she did not wish to leave UBejane. And he was old enough to know that refusal to comply with his father's instructions would, in the old days anyway, have resulted in her death. Although those times were long gone, his mother was still running the risk of being cast aside by her husband and, if this was to be then he, Dyson, would be cast aside with her. He waited anxiously to see what his father would do.

'We will discuss these things tonight, wife. You have shamed me with your actions. You have angered my father and wounded my mother. In the village they laugh and whisper behind my back. "How is it," they ask, "that Wilson Mpande cannot keep his wife at home?" What have you become? Am I to believe that you do not honour my wishes?'

When she did not respond, Wilson added less sternly, 'I see what you are doing and I see why it must be done. Do not think I disagree. But if I say we return to the kraal of my father, then you will obey me.'

'There is much work still to be done,' she protested.

'Then, if necessary, others will do it.'

Nandi looked back at the ground. She nodded slowly. But Dyson knew, by the set of her shoulders, that she was prepared to argue. Wilson glanced at him and Dyson saw a twinkle in his father's eyes as he went on, 'But if I decide that we stay here, wife, then you will do as you are told and you will not argue. That is my final word.'

Dyson saw the small smile touch his mother's lips and just as quickly disappear. He had heard the words but was too young to catch the subtlety of them. However, his mother appeared well pleased and he relaxed.

FOUR

Joe watched his son walk away and wondered why he had been fighting with the African boy. 'Just look at the state of him,' he thought in disgust. Michael was barefoot, his shirt untucked, shorts filthy. 'He might as well be a bloody African himself.' As far as Joe was concerned, Michael was too familiar with the farm workers. He needed to distance himself from them. After all, one day they would be taking orders from him. Saturday was a good example. There was his son making decisions about firing one of the cane fields – okay, the lad seemed to know what he was doing – but he treated the blacks and Indians as friends, as they in turn treated him. It wasn't right. Sighing, he got back onto his horse.

He could not make any headway with getting closer to Michael. The boy seemed so self-contained, as though he didn't want a father. He never spoke unless spoken to first and even then his responses were brief, almost to the point of rudeness. If Michael ever looked at Joe there was accusation in his eyes. Most of the time he went out of his way to avoid his father's company. He wasn't a bad kid, Joe had to admit. Good-looking, well built, spoke impeccable Zulu. If he'd just show a bit more respect, or even interest. Couldn't he see that his father was trying to make amends for their unfortunate reunion?

Joe reached down to the saddle pouch. The hipflask had been full that morning and he gave an irritated grunt when it yielded no more than a sip. He debated whether to go back for a refill but decided against it. Instead, Joe turned his horse past the Indian barracks and dismounted outside the workshop. Claire had been on his back because he had not, as yet, seen Mac. This would kill two birds with one stone.

He found Mac with his head under the bonnet of Claire's old Ford.

'Aboot bloody time ye paid your respects,' the old Scotsman grouched, not looking up.

Joe smothered an irritable response. The man had been around for as long as he could remember and, if Joe stood in awe of anyone, it was Mac. Besides, Joe knew he'd never find a better handyman anywhere. 'I've been busy,' he said, as shortly as he dared.

Mac straightened up, wincing as his back twinged. 'Aye, that'll be right.' He wiped his hands on a filthy rag and stuck out a huge and calloused paw. 'Welcome back.'

Joe shook the grease-stained hand. 'What's wrong with the car?'

'Nought that can't be put right.' Mac jerked his head towards one of the tractors. 'It's that bitch needs a bullet.'

'Yeah!' Joe agreed. 'So Raj said.' He walked over to the tractor and kicked one of its heavily lugged tyres. 'Can you get a few more months out of it?'

'Aye.' Mac followed him. 'But that's aboot all.' Mac reached into a wooden toolbox and pulled out a bottle. 'Looks like you could do with a nip,' he said, unscrewing the cap and passing the whisky to Joe. 'Hear you've taken quite a shine to the stuff.'

Joe snatched the bottle. 'Who says?' he demanded.

'Come on mon, you've been foo since you came home.'

Joe scowled. 'Doesn't stop me working.'

Mac stuffed his hands into the pockets of his overalls and rocked back on his heels. 'Well now, that's as may be.' He was getting impatient. 'Go on, go on, get it down, mon. I haven't got all day.'

'Thanks.' Joe raised the bottle to his lips and took two large gulps before passing it back. 'You joining me?'

But Mac put the cap back. 'I dinna tak a bevy this early.'

'Since when?'

Mac shot Joe a sharp look. 'Since you went away. Mrs King has needed steady heads around her. She's a fine lassie ye ken but it hasn't been easy. She'll be relieved tae have ye back.'

Joe eyed the bottle hopefully but Mac placed it carefully back in the toolbox. 'So, you ready tae pick up the reins again?' he asked, a touch of sarcasm in his voice.

'I have already,' Joe said sharply.

Mac shook his head and returned to the Ford. 'No that anybody can see,' he commented quietly.

Stung, Joe tried to defend himself. 'I've only just got back.'

'Aye,' Mac agreed, scratching his bristly chin. 'And just look at the state of you. You'd better pull yourself together or you'll lose everything that's decent around here.' Mac scowled and delivered one of his little pearls of philosophy. 'When a man is wrapped in self-pity he makes a very small parcel.' He looked satisfied at his words before adding, 'You'd do well to remember that. I'm of a mind there's more of your father in you than is good for you.' He put his head back under the bonnet and his voice floated out to Joe. 'Your wife's a fine young lassie,' he repeated, 'but she has need of a good husband. Wake up to yourself, Joey King, afore it's too late.'

Taken aback at the outburst, Joe waited for Mac to say more but the Scotsman had gone back to his work, dismissing him. Joe left the workshop with Mac's criticism ringing in his ears. As he rode away he was thinking, 'Mac's wrong. I'll never be like that old bastard. And what's wrong with a drink now and then? It's not as if I'm falling down drunk. To hell with him. Who does he think he is talking to me like that? I'll drink when I bloody-well feel like it. There's not one of them around here who knows what I went through.'

Feeling aggrieved, when he returned to the house Joe made straight for the bar, walking quickly past where Claire worked alone in the office. That sassy little Nandi had left for the day, otherwise he might have paid the ladies a visit. She was quite an eyeful, pert little breasts and voluptuous arse straining the tight cotton dresses she wore. It made visiting the office a pleasure. Joe reckoned she'd be up for it too, he just had to get her alone one morning when Claire was in town. Smiling at the thought, he poured himself a straight whisky and tossed half of it down before setting the heavy crystal glass back on the bar.

'Now for you, young man,' he thought, going to Michael's room. The boy had defied him and shut his bedroom door. Joe opened it and went in without knocking. 'I told you to keep the door open.'

Michael looked up from his homework. 'Mum always let me shut it.'

'Your mother let you get away with murder. You'll do as I say from now on, is that clear?'

'Yes,' Michael mumbled.

'Yes, sir.'

Michael stared down at the desk top. He was beginning to hate the man. It seemed that everything he did or said went wrong, that his father went out of his way to find fault. 'Yes, sir.'

Joe's face clouded with anger. The boy was deliberately being cheeky. He crossed to where his son sat and raised a hand. Michael shrank away from him.

'Joe!' Joe turned. Claire stood in the doorway. 'Can I see you for a moment?' Her face was pale but she had fire in her eyes.

Joe spoke to his son. 'I'll be back. In the meantime you might like to spend some time smartening up your manners.' He left with Claire, leaving the door open.

Michael crossed quietly to the doorway and listened. He had never heard his mother so angry. '. . . I will not tolerate you continually hitting and belittling our son. You're not giving him a chance.'

His father's voice was hard. 'He goes out of his way to get under my skin. He needs a firm hand.'

'A firm hand is one thing, Joe, not physical bashing. I saw bruises on his legs this morning. You can't do that to him, he's only young.'

Michael heard his father bang a whisky glass down. 'He's a spoiled brat. You've ruined him.'

'He's a good boy and I haven't ruined him. Please Joe, if you'd just show him some love . . .'

'Jesus!' Joe snapped. 'Love! The kid's up to his ears in love. He needs a bloody good kick up the arse.'

'No!' his mother yelled angrily. 'It's you who needs that. I'm warning you, Joe . . .'

The crash of breaking glass startled Michael. Then his father's voice. 'Shit! Now look what you've made me do. Christ! As if that brat isn't enough. Bessie!' he bellowed suddenly. 'Where the hell is that bloody woman? Bessie . . . oh, there you are. Get this mess cleaned up and bring me another bottle from the storeroom. Come on, girl, come on. Don't just stand there. Jesus! Do I have to do everything myself?'

There was silence for perhaps two minutes, broken only by the sound of glass being swept up.

'Joe!' Michael's mother's voice pleaded finally. 'What's got into you? You've changed so much.'

'Of course I've changed. What did you expect? You try prisoner-of-war camp for three years. You try living with constant pain. You're pushing too hard. Give me time. I'm a bloody human being, not some robot you can turn on and off at will. Oh, for Christ's sake, Claire, will you stop that pathetic crying. It's driving me mad.'

Michael heard his mother run to the master bedroom and shut the door. He ducked back quickly to his desk and waited. Nobody came. Outside, the old Bedford truck roared into life. His father had been particularly critical about its purchase. 'What was wrong with the horses?' he had railed more than once at Claire. Michael suspected his objections had less to do with financial considerations and more to do with his injured arm frustrating his attempts to drive the truck. From the harsh revving and crunching of gears, the only person driving it now could be his father. Michael didn't know what to do. He wanted to go to his mother but he was too scared to leave his room. His father had told him to wait. Eventually, and a little defiantly, he went out on to the verandah and, shooing off one of the dogs, sat in a chair, staring across the garden with unseeing eyes. Everything had changed.

For the past four nights Michael had waited for his mother to come and kiss him goodnight, as she usually did, but she hadn't come. Lying awake, waiting, he had heard disturbing noises coming from his parents' bedroom. Groans and grunts, bedsprings squeaking, and the drawn-out animal moaning of his father. He could not imagine what was happening on the other side of the wall. All he did know was that his mother had changed, that the warmth and tenderness he had enjoyed all his life had suddenly gone. Michael blamed his father. But he was too scared of him to go to his mother's rescue, listening helplessly whenever his father started yelling at her or when the noises started up in the bedroom next to his. Michael had learned very quickly that when his father became angry, he spared himself no energy when it came to punishment.

Never had Michael's mother raised a hand to him. If punishment were called for, she would find other ways, like banning him from the Zulu compound for two days, always careful to explain the reason and that she still loved him. His father was different. A quick, vicious cuff at the back of the head which put tears of pain into Michael's eyes and left him with a headache. Twice in the past four days, his father had taken off his belt and whipped Michael around the legs. The sheer brute force of his father's left arm left Michael in fear and trepidation of what it would be like once his injured right arm recovered. The pain of those whippings stayed with him. He was only just recovering from the first when it happened for the second time. All Michael had done had been to ask if he could leave the table. His father had looked at his plate and snapped, 'Finish your food.'

Michael couldn't. His parents had been having an argument, or rather, his father had been picking on his mother, which upset Michael to the point where food stuck in his throat. 'I'm not hungry, sir.'

'Don't backchat me, young man. Finish your bloody food.'

Michael had tried to eat but knew he would be sick. So he just sat there, pushing food around on the plate until his father jumped up, grabbed an arm and hustled him into his bedroom. When Michael realised his father was removing his belt, he had been paralysed with fear. But, as he advanced, face contorted with rage, Michael burst out hysterically, 'I'll eat it, I'll eat it. Sorry, sir. I'll eat it.'

It fell on deaf ears and Michael had crawled onto his bed, sobbing tears of pain and rage, legs on fire. In the morning, this morning, his mother had found the bruises. She had kissed him gently, a look of great sorrow in her eyes, and whispered, 'Oh, my son, my poor baby. I'm so sorry.'

Michael considered the prospect of running away. Where would he go? Anywhere. Anywhere to get away from his father. His mother said he had changed. Certainly he was nothing like the father she had told him about, the loving picture she had painted for Michael.

The door to his parents' bedroom opened and his mother came out onto the verandah, her face blotchy from crying. Michael leapt up and ran to her, wrapping his arms around her waist and burying his head into her, heart breaking for the sorrow they both felt. She held him and stroked his hair. 'Let's sit down,' she said finally. 'There are some things we have to talk about.'

They sat, side by side, outside Michael's room.

'Daddy doesn't mean to be angry,' she began. 'He was a prisoner-of-war. Do you remember what I told you about that?'

'Yes,' Michael said promptly. 'It means the Germans captured him.'

She nodded slowly. 'They didn't treat him very well. He's still trying to get better. It may take a long time but, you'll see, he will be fine. He really does love you.'

'I don't like him,' Michael burst out.

'Sssh! He's your father. Try to understand, he's been through a very bad time.'

'I don't care,' Michael said rebelliously. 'I hate him.'

His mother was silent for a moment and Michael thought he'd gone too far. Finally she spoke again. 'I wish you could remember him before the war, darling. He was so different then.' Her voice was sad, as though she didn't quite believe her own words.

'Did he hit me before he went away?'

'No, darling. He loved you.'

Her voice gave her away. Michael knew suddenly that his father had never liked him, even back then. 'Why does he always hit me?' he asked, his voice not quite steady.

His mother looked down at his legs and tears filled her eyes. 'I won't let him do that to you ever again.'

But Michael wondered how she could stop him.

★

That night, Joe King ignored both his son and wife. He was more than a little drunk on whisky and the look of reproach on Claire's face was enough to drive him back to the decanter for more. At least the kid ate his food. After dinner, Michael had said goodnight and gone to his room. He left the door open and so was able to hear every sound from the dining room. If he thought his world had already been turned upside-down, his father's almost shouted words now brought Michael out in a sweat of dread.

Joe topped up his glass.

'Do you have to drink so much?' Claire asked.

'Yes,' he said bluntly.

'Why, Joe?'

He looked at her. In the soft lamplight, her hair was a pale halo. Large eyes, like those of a trusting dog, gazed at him reproachfully. 'What does she want from me?' Joe wondered, irritated by Claire's questioning. He was in a vicious circle. The more Claire queried his actions, the more he wanted to upset her. Joe was too angry with his own life to realise that he was taking it out on Claire. 'In case you hadn't noticed,' he said, slurring his words a little, 'I'm in pain.' It was a lie, and he knew it. True, his arm throbbed occasionally, but not all the time.

One thing Joe knew for certain was that the life he'd had before the war was not the life he wanted now. Yet he could do nothing else, nor could he think of anything he might do. Except when it suited him to bring it up, Joe was no longer dwelling on the three years of prison camp. He tended to compare his life now with the heady days in London before he'd been shot down. The prospect of spending the rest of his life on this boring farm with his boring wife filled him with dread. It was this that caused him more anguish than his useless arm, that made him such a bastard to his wife. Yes, Joe admitted to himself that he was being a bastard. Perhaps it was this that drove him into the arms of alcoholic stupor every day? Joe knew he drank too much. He would not, however, accept that he had a problem, not even when his drinking made him hurt his wife in ways he had never done before.

Only a couple of days ago he had suggested they buy out one of his brother's farms. Thank God Claire said they couldn't afford it. A few days home and he already knew there was no way he could spend the rest of his life here. He wanted to sell UBejane and head for Durban. He'd give Claire a fair share and tell her there was no place in his life for her or the kid. She could divorce him or she needn't bother – she probably wouldn't, divorce was a disgraceful word to his wife.

He had loved Claire once. He had cherished her and held her in the highest regard. Now it seemed that he was going out of his way to debase her. That she bore his attentions with quiet dignity, with understanding murmurings and with professions of love only made him worse. Did he want to break her? Did he want to use her as a whore? No. He only wanted to prove that he could. And Joe King didn't know why.

She was still watching him, wary and hurt. 'For God's sake, Claire, say something.'

She shook her head. 'I always say the wrong thing.'

Joe gave a cynical laugh. 'It's a gift you seem to have.'

Claire changed the subject. 'Raj spoke to me this morning. There are some blocks ready for burning.'

Once again, her words prompted an irrational outburst. 'Keep off my back, Claire, I'm warning you. I'll decide when and if we fire the cane. You're getting too damned big for your boots.'

'I'm only trying to help.'

'Then don't,' Joe snapped. He poured more whisky, slopping liquid over the side of the glass. He didn't notice. 'We're seeing the lawyer on Wednesday.'

'Oh! Why?'

'Remember I put the farm in your name in case I didn't come back? The way you're bloody acting anyone would think it really belongs to you. Well it doesn't and now I'm taking it back. I'm in charge here and if you don't like it you can piss off and take that brat with you.'

'Joe!' She was shocked. But she was also getting angry. 'I think you'll find you need my signature.'

Joe's eyes narrowed. 'So?'

'So,' Claire said calmly, 'I'm not signing.'

'You'll do as I bloody-well tell you.'

'Sorry.'

'We'll see about that. I can cut you off without a penny.'

'No you can't, Joe.'

He knew she was right and the knowledge annoyed him. Although he was drunk, Joe was not so inebriated that he was prepared to alienate his wife completely. She could cut *him* off without a penny. 'Give me time, Claire. That's all I ask. I know it's difficult for you but it's hard for me too. We can come through this together. Maybe you're right. We'll leave the farm in your name for now.' He gave an unsteady laugh. 'I must say, my darling, you've surprised me. I didn't expect you to cope quite as well as you have.'

The stubborn look was leaving her face. He had her. Joe winced suddenly and gave a groan. Instantly, Claire was full of concern. 'Is it your arm?'

'Yes.' He grimaced with feigned agony. 'It hits me out of the blue.'

'I'll get you some aspirin.'

Joe wrapped his left arm around his right and hugged it to his body. 'Nothing helps. Don't worry, it'll go away in a little while.'

'Can I get you anything? I feel so helpless. What can I do?'

'You mean that?' Without being aware of it, his expression had changed to one of anticipation.

'Of course,' she said uncertainly.

'You can help take my mind off it. Come to bed, my darling. I need you so much. Come and show me how much you love me.'

The look of dread that passed over Claire's face was immensely satisfying.

A little while later the noises started coming

from his parents' bedroom but, for once, Michael barely heard them. His father didn't like him, it was confirmed. That was okay, Michael didn't like him either. But what did he mean about taking the farm back? Would he throw Michael and his mother out? Where would they go? UBejane was the only home he'd ever known. The great unknown world, something that usually seemed so exciting, now became threatening. Michael had not been fooled by his father's backdown. It worried Michael that his mother had been taken in by it. He was frightened because he knew, with no doubt in his mind, that if his father felt like it, he would indeed throw them out. It was the only thing about his father that was predictable.

Wilson and Nandi were both trying to stay calm in a situation that appeared to have no real solution. Wilson acknowledged that his wife had good reasons for wanting to stay at UBejane. The money she earned was good and her work for the Bantu Purity League was important. He could see all that. Neither was he committed to the idea of returning home. In fact, he was more inclined to head for Empangeni, or even down to Durban, where he knew he could find work. Wilson's main problem was that his wife was prepared to defy him. So he was deliberately testing her obedience and, in all matters but that one, had no cause for complaint.

For her part, Nandi was well aware of what Wilson was up to. What she didn't know was how far he was prepared to push her in order to keep his masculine pride intact. He had always been very fair but she knew his patience was being sorely tried.

Nandi was an intelligent woman and, up until four years ago, she had no outlet for her mental capacity. The thought of returning to a traditional rural way of life held no appeal. And therein lay her own personal conflict. At UBejane she was promoting the old ways and yet she was not interested in returning to them herself. She tried to justify it by reasoning that she still kept her own Zulu traditions alive, she simply did so closer to town. But in her heart of hearts Nandi knew that to some extent she sympathised with the very people she was trying to save.

She could see that the Purity League, despite its best efforts, was running a poor second to the temptations of city life. Zulus, both men and women, were flocking to the larger towns and the cities of Durban and Pietermaritzburg. The floodgates had opened and the voice of the league could barely be heard over the clamour of eager people determined to sample a more modern way of life. If the league could not stop the headlong rush into westernisation then the Zulus needed something else – a voice, a body, to represent them. As far as Nandi was concerned, her husband was the perfect candidate.

Wilson, disenchanted by the African National Congress, was not so sure. 'What would I do if we stay? Where would we live?'

'You could get work here. We could live here.'

'Work for the white man! I am a Zulu.'

'Many do.'

'And is this not what you are trying to change?'

Nandi reached over and lightly scratched her fingernails down Wilson's arm. 'We can never go backwards, husband. We can only try to keep our traditions alive.'

A shudder ran through Wilson at his wife's gentle touch.

'Our son has no future in the village,' Nandi continued. 'That way of life is going.'

'And what is his future in the towns?' Wilson demanded. 'I have seen the young people there. They are nothing more than beggars.'

'Not if he is educated.'

'Hau! And who will educate a black boy?'

'There is a mission school in Empangeni. They are building new classrooms. Dyson can start next year, I have his name on the waiting list.'

'Hau! And how will he get to this school?'

'They have a scotch cart to collect the children.'

'White children.'

'There is another for Africans.'

Round and round they went. For every argument Wilson brought up, Nandi had an answer. For every objection Nandi put forward, Wilson suggested a solution. But while Nandi was committed, Wilson dithered. The thought of returning to their village was certainly appealing. To live the old way, to keep their traditions alive. But was it too selfish? What of others? To be able to help the Zulu, all

Zulus, also made sense. Could Wilson make a difference? Nandi seemed to think so.

'You know the ways of the white man,' she argued. 'If we do not have a voice, our nation will be finished.'

'We have the Zulu Cultural Society,' Wilson argued back. 'I hear what you are up to, wife, but Inkatha is finished.'

'Some whisper that it should be brought back. The time is coming when our people will need help. It is being said that the Afrikaner Malan will not listen to us.'

Wilson cocked his head to one side. 'What is this? My wife speaks of matters that should be left to the men.'

Nandi sat very still. In the darkness of their hut, it was impossible to read Wilson's expression. Nor could she tell from his voice if he was angry. They had been speaking softly so as not to waken Dyson.

She heard him sigh. 'It troubles me greatly. We cannot go back, yet it is what I wish more than anything. I do not like what I see ahead, yet where else can we go? You are right, wife, although it pains me to admit it. There are troubled times ahead.'

Nandi smiled into the darkness, sensing victory. 'You would make such a handsome member of Inkatha,' she said. 'I would be very proud of you.'

Wilson, despite his misgivings, chuckled. 'I would have to wear the white man's clothing,' he protested.

Emboldened by the cover of darkness, Nandi reached under his loin flap. 'You could dress the

Zulu way for me, just for me,' she whispered, stroking him to hardness.

'Where is your modesty?' Wilson admonished, giving himself up to the sensations flooding through him. 'We will discuss this more in the morning. The issue is not settled between us.'

He came awake slowly, reluctantly, a hangover pounding behind his eyes, last night's whisky souring his stomach. 'Jesus!' Joe groaned to himself, remembering the things he had done to Claire in his anger and drunkenness. How could he face her this morning? How could he avoid it? He couldn't, so to hell with it. He vaguely recalled that he had fallen into a drunken sleep with the sound of her sobbing in his ears. He'd gone over the top last night. That would call for yet another ridiculous apology. But first, his little mate was stirring. Good little fellow. Now he was functioning that way again his only friend had not let him down once. Joe rolled over, planning to wake his wife, and was surprised to find she wasn't there. Claire appeared a few seconds later, dressed and ready for work. She would not look at him.

'Come back to bed, Claire. Come and see what I've got for you.' Joe flung the covers down and put a hand around his erection.

Claire walked to the end of the bed, and raised her eyes to his face. Her expression was grim. 'You are moving out of this room today.'

'Like hell!' he said, startled by her tone.

'What's more,' she carried on as though he had not spoken, 'unless you can pull yourself together and start behaving like the man I married, you can forget any kind of intimacy between us. I've had enough, Joe.'

Joe staggered off the bed with difficulty, wincing as his hangover shifted up a gear, and grabbed her arm. 'What in the hell's got into you? You're my wife.'

'True,' she agreed, staring at his face with an expression of distaste. 'Not your possession. Not a prostitute. Not some vessel into which you can deposit any kind of filth you like. I don't like what you've become, Joe, and unless you change, that side of our marriage is over.'

Joe squeezed her arm hard but she didn't flinch. Instead, she reached out her other hand and squeezed back, on his bad arm. Her expression didn't change. It was Joe who backed away. 'You bitch!' he whispered, as the deep ache started up.

'You will not touch me again. You will not hit Michael again. You will get your backside out on the farm, start working and show some interest. If you haven't got anything nice to say to your son, say nothing.' Claire literally spat out the last two words. 'You do not own us, Joe King. You are part of a family and unless you remember that and start acting accordingly you are out in the cold. You've asked for time, you've got it. But while you're sorting yourself out you will not use Michael and me as your own personal whipping boys. Do I make myself clear?'

She had made it perfectly clear. He forgot his guilt over last night as rage swept over him. The bitch couldn't talk to him like that. Joe stepped up to his wife and slapped her face, hard.

Claire, with no apparent sign of shock or pain, slapped him back, raking her nails down his cheek. Her outward calm was unnerving.

Joe lost his temper. Ignoring the pounding headache, he grabbed at her blouse and ripped it open, buttons popping and flying to the floor. He was furious and beyond caring. He'd show her who was boss. An explosion of pain in his testicles doubled him over. She had kneed him in the groin. Joe fell on to the bed. Claire simply stood there, waiting.

When he could speak, Joe grated, 'There are plenty of women who aren't so prim and proper, of that I can assure you. Keep me out of my room and I'll find sex somewhere else.'

'Good,' she said succinctly. 'That suits me fine.' Calmly Claire removed her torn blouse, found another in the wardrobe and put it on. She did not look at him again.

Joe was left lying on the bed feeling slightly ridiculous, seething with resentment. He knew that his wife had come out of their argument on top. But she didn't mean those things. He'd show her tonight just who was the boss around here.

At breakfast, Claire appeared quite normal. Michael, as usual, was silent. 'When you get back from school today, we'll have that game of cards,' she said.

Michael shot his mother a disbelieving look.

She smiled at him.

There was a flurry of activity at the kitchen door and Raj, in a state of great agitation, burst into the room. 'Madam! Goodness, very bad thing. You come quickly, goodness yes. The Zulu *induna* has very bad accident. I am thinking that Moses is not living any more. Those cattle, I am telling you, they have no place on a sugar farm.' Raj had never hidden his fear of cattle, took every opportunity to say so and always avoided them. So his outburst that the Zulu in charge of the cattle had been hurt in some way did not at first alarm Claire.

She remained seated and looked at Joe. 'You'd better see to it,' she said calmly.

Joe was not going to be bossed around. 'I'm eating my breakfast.'

Claire looked at Raj. 'Wait for the master outside.' When the Sikh had gone, she turned to Joe. 'Go and see what the problem is. Now.'

'I said, I'm eating my breakfast.'

As cool as a cucumber, Claire stood and picked up her steaming coffee cup. 'You can go and see to it now, or you can wear this. Please yourself.'

Michael couldn't believe his ears.

Joe saw the look in his wife's eyes and rose from the table, throwing down his napkin. 'I've finished anyway. What the hell are you staring at?' he snarled at Michael. Then he was gone.

Michael sat waiting for the sky to fall on him.

But all his mother said was, 'Better get off now, darling, you'll miss the cart.'

Joe, despite his criticism over the Bedford, had found it infinitely more convenient than a horse. He drove down to the Zulu compound, only half listening to Raj.

'It's that big bull, master, the new one. He's mad I am telling you. Moses is very broken.'

What the hell had got into Claire? Okay, he'd been a bit rough on her last night but, Jesus, she was acting like a madwoman. She couldn't order him about like that, especially in front of the brat. And there was no way the bloody woman could ban him from his own bed. 'Better cut back on the booze,' he thought. But, turning to Raj, all he said was, 'In future, any news you bring to the house you will bring to me. Is that understood?'

Raj looked at him and smiled. 'Of course, master. I forgot myself in the emergency.'

They drove into the compound to find a crowd of wailing women and silent men surrounding the fallen Moses. Raj had not exaggerated. The bull had been thorough. 'Get my gun from the vehicle,' Joe said to Raj. 'The bull will have to be destroyed.' He looked around at the sea of faces. 'Any of you see this happen?'

One man stepped forward. 'Moses was in the pens filling the troughs with water, master. The bull attacked him.'

'What did Moses do to the bull?'

'Nothing, master.'

Joe shook his head. Destroying the bull was the

last thing he wanted to do. 'It must have been provoked. Okay, I know it's new and quite likely unsettled by the truck ride here but Moses was experienced. What happened?'

The Zulu merely stared at him.

'Speak up,' Joe bellowed suddenly, then wished he hadn't as pain shot through his head. 'A bull doesn't attack for no reason,' he added more quietly.

A second man stepped forward. 'Perhaps your bull was sick, or in pain.'

Joe glared at him. He looked familiar. Goodlooking for an African and with an air of quiet authority about him, the man's eyes never wavered. Joe knew they had met before but where? Then it hit him. The African he had met on the train. Joe couldn't remember his name. He looked quite different out of uniform. 'What are you doing on my property?'

'I came for my wife and son.'

'Who are they?'

Nandi and Dyson joined Wilson. 'This is my husband, Wilson,' Nandi said shyly. Joe King intimidated her at the best of times but in this mood he was frightening.

Joe looked her up and down. The office girl with nice tits and a big bum. Claire's educated house ape. Joe had no time for intelligent Africans and he distrusted them. He glanced at the kid standing next to her. It was the boy he'd caught fighting with Michael. Trouble. The whole bloody bunch of them were nothing but trouble. 'Well you can all get the hell out of here. I'm not running a bloody guesthouse.'

Nandi gasped in dismay. She had intended to speak to Mrs King this morning about Wilson's return. If there was no work for him on UBejane then at least Mrs King would allow Wilson to stay at the compound while he looked for employment elsewhere. Now they were all being told to leave.

There was shuffling among those standing nearby. Not many remembered Joe from before he went away. All they had seen since his return was a man with no patience who had a quick and violent temper, especially when he was drunk, which seemed to be most of the time. Those few who did recall an earlier boss had tried to explain that he hadn't always been like this but the majority made their own assessment and found Joe King wanting. And as they had been doing for centuries, ever since the white man came to their land and started to throw his weight around, they banded together against him.

'You will need a new *induna*,' said the man who had witnessed Moses' demise. 'This Wilson has experience.' Whether Wilson had experience or not was irrelevant, he had to be protected. If the job was given to him there were many others who could offer advice. And what of Nandi? The master had just told her to leave. Mrs King might have something to say about that but, then again, she might not. With Wilson as *induna*, Nandi and her son could stay. 'He is a very honest man, master.'

'I'll make my own decision about that.' Joe could see where the conversation was heading. These people were backing him into a corner. He stared at the impassive black faces around him, not recognising many. They were all waiting for his next words. He had to gain the upper hand. There was no way he wanted this man, Wilson, working for him. He was too intelligent, too politically aware, too likely to turn into a troublemaker. 'I'm not taking on someone I don't know.'

Before the war, Joe had enjoyed a good relationship with his men. He spoke fluent Zulu and appreciated the subtleties of their humour and wisdom. The fact that he couldn't seem to get a grip on anything any more, his farm, the workers, his family, even the house servants, made him angry. Joe knew that he was not respected and the knowledge made things worse. The more he tried, the more pronounced his failure to win their respect became. 'I might put Raj in charge.'

Raj, returning with the gun, heard him. 'Goodness, no, master. I am not knowing about cattle.'

Joe's face became red with anger. 'If I put you in charge, Raj, then you will fucking-well learn about cattle.'

Wilson had wondered if Nandi's employer were married to the Joe King he had met on the train. He hoped not. He hadn't liked him on the train and nothing he had been told about the man since arriving at UBejane gave him cause to change his mind. The man was a bully with a chip on his shoulder, Wilson had sensed that when they first met. Yet his wife and son, according to Nandi, were good people. It was obvious that Joe King had once been a successful farmer. War did strange things to people – Wilson had seen it before.

Three things happened at once to cement Wilson's destiny. Raj backed away from Joe's anger, shaking his head and saying, 'I am sorry, master, Raj does not like cattle.' The Zulus were muttering about taking orders from an Indian. And Joe King, eyes bulging with rage, grabbed the Sikh's loose-fitting robe and jerked him forward.

That was when Wilson realised that things had to change, that the white man could not be permitted to behave as if they were the only ones who mattered any longer. Change had to start somewhere. Wilson put a tentative foot on the *sangoma*'s second path and pushed gently at the first closed door. 'If you are willing, master,' he said softly, 'I would be honoured to work with such fine-looking cattle.' He knew, as he spoke, that the path would be long and rocky and the doors would be many. But, as the diviner had said, his destiny was already in place.

Joe was stuck, and he knew it. The solution to his problem was staring him in the face. The man was intelligent and would bear watching but the others would take orders from him. After all, they had offered him as a replacement for Moses in the first place. It was obvious that Raj would be useless. Although that fact angered Joe, Raj was too good a farm manager, too well respected by both the coolies and the Pondos on the sugar side, to lose. There was no apparent successor to Moses among the Zulus who already worked for Joe. The problem seemed to be how to accept Wilson without losing face.

'Very well.' He nodded curtly to Wilson and tossed him the rifle. 'Go and shoot the bull, hotshot soldier boy. I take it I can trust you with a gun? Try not to shoot yourself in the foot.'

Wilson caught the rifle and immediately checked whether it was loaded. It was and he removed the bullet, an expression of disapproval on his face. But even as he disapproved, he could see why Joe King had done what he had. Putting a loaded weapon into the hands of an African was not something many whites cared to do. The action had the potential to backfire on them. The assumption that he, Wilson, could be trusted with the weapon was not lost on the surrounding men, cementing Wilson's position as *induna*. His face impassive, he asked, 'The meat, master?'

'Cut it up and bring it to the kitchen. You lot can have the offal.' Joe turned on his heel and headed towards the truck. 'You've got one bullet,' he yelled back. 'That's all I want it to take. Bring the rifle to me after you've cleaned it.' The problem of a new *induna* had been solved, though not as much to Joe's liking as he would have hoped. Still, the man had been put forward by the others which he supposed was some kind of plus.

As he drove back to the house, Joe's mind was busy with the problem of his wife. She had steel in her, he'd give her that. She was not the timid little mouse he remembered. The war had changed her too.

Claire's threat not to sign the transfer of ownership back to him was serious. Joe had made sure her tenure of UBejane was watertight. It had been his way of ensuring that should something happen to him and he failed to return, she would not have to be bothered with the legal processes involved in transferring the farm to her own name. It crossed his mind now that he needn't have worried. She'd shown how capable she really was. Having the title deeds back in his name would help keep Claire off his back until he could sell. Right now she was using the situation against him and he was stuck. 'Christ!' Joe thought savagely as he pulled up at the gate. 'Better get this whole mess sorted out. Just stay off the sauce for a few days. Claire will come round.'

He intended to take a couple of aspirin but, on entering the house, Joe found two servants moving his clothes out of the master bedroom. 'Put those back,' he bellowed.

Startled, the girls froze. The madam had told them to put these things into the blue bedroom. Now the master wanted them back in the big bedroom. Their relief was evident when Claire appeared. 'Go on. Take the clothes to the blue room.' The girls hurried away.

'I will not be thrown out of my own bedroom,' Joe thundered.

'Fine,' Claire said calmly. '*I'll* move into the blue room.'

'Jesus!' Joe ran his left hand through his hair. 'What's got into you?'

'We spoke of it this morning,' Claire told him. 'There's no point in repeating myself.' She turned towards the office, then stopped. 'What's the story with Moses?'

'I thought you wanted me to deal with that. It's fixed.'

'I'd still like to know.'

'He's dead,' Joe said flatly, knowing she'd be upset and not caring.

Claire closed her eyes briefly but all she said was, 'I'll go and see his family this afternoon. They'll need help to bury him.'

'I'm not running a fucking charity,' Joe said cruelly. 'They can pay for the funeral themselves.'

Claire was tempted to point out that he didn't seem to be running anything but the girls re-appeared so she said nothing. Joe took advantage of her silence.

'We are not sleeping in separate bedrooms.'

'We'll discuss this in private if you don't mind. Come into the office.'

Claire shut the door behind them and turned to him, waiting, her arms folded, her eyes calm.

Joe had already realised that of the two of them, his wife was the stronger. 'Look, maybe I've been a bit of a bastard.' He smiled tentatively. 'I apologise, okay? Let's make a fresh start.'

Claire moved to the desk and sat down, leaning forward on her elbows, her hands clasped. She looked up at him. There was a hard note in her voice when she spoke. 'I know you've had a rough time, Joe, but it hasn't been easy for me either. I've kept the farm running, we're in profit, and I've handled all the bookwork. I've reared our son and run the household. The last thing in the world I need is a stranger for a husband. It's difficult enough, trying to adjust to you being home, without having to cope with your moods, temper and perverted sexual demands. This doesn't have to be for long, Joe. We've both got to make adjustments. If you'd stop drinking it might help. As soon as you start you turn into someone else, someone that, quite frankly, isn't very nice. We have to work this through, Joe. That's all I'm asking.'

'Dammit, Claire. I've been three years without a woman.'

'Three years, Joe,' Claire said softly. 'But you've been away five.'

'Three, five, what's the damned difference?' he blustered, knowing she was not fooled.

'Forget it, Joe. I know you think I'm a prude but I don't need sex as often as you.' Claire was blushing. 'The things you've made me do in the last few days are . . . too much.' She was finding it hard to even speak of but carried on, determined he know that she meant every word. Last night her husband had become savage and cruel. It wasn't modesty to which she referred although, God knows, that too had been viciously violated, it was disgust. Willing as she had been to accept her husband's demands, Claire would not tolerate another night of humiliation and abuse. 'You hurt me, Joe. I will not allow you to touch me like that again.'

'All right, all right, I won't touch you like that again.' His headache was killing him. Would she ever shut up?

'You won't touch me at all. Not until you show that the Joe I remember has returned. Not until you start taking an interest in our son. I warn you, Joe. If you harm that child in any way I will call the police.'

A single gun blast in the distance stilled the angry response Joe was about to make. 'I've got work to do.' He left the office, furious with his wife, furious with the need to kill a bloody good stud bull even before it had been with the herd, furious with life. Passing the bar he thought, 'To hell with all of it. A hair of the dog is what I need.'

Moses had been UBejane's *induna* for seven years. As such, he was an important person and Zulu tradition demanded that certain rituals take place. His home was Kwabhekithunga, near Empangeni. His spirit had to be returned.

Word had been sent to his family who, in turn, sent a delegation to bring Moses' spirit home. Michael was at the Zulu compound when they arrived, carrying with them a small branch cut from a buffalo thorn acacia tree. He watched, fascinated, as they went to the exact spot where Moses died, laying the branch on the ground. After allowing time for the spirit to enter the branch, it was picked up by the leader of the group who immediately began speaking to the spirit, bringing it up to date with all manner of events from home.

Michael had never seen this ritual performed before but he knew that the flow of conversation from this person would not cease until reaching Kwabhekithunga, that the branch bearer was not permitted to speak to anyone else until then and that any lapse of concentration might result in the spirit slipping away. He also knew enough of Zulu tradition to be aware that if the return journey had necessitated a train trip, or the purchase of a meal – which, on this occasion, it did not – then a ticket or food would also be provided for the spirit.

Once home, the branch would be placed in the cattle enclosure, eaten, and thus Moses' spirit would forever reside in the kraal matriarch's hut where regular offerings of food and praise would be presented to him. In return, his spirit was expected to act as guardian angel, along with all the others who had predeceased Moses, thereby ensuring good health and prosperity.

It was knowledge like this, and his acceptance of such things, that bonded Michael to the Zulus, broadening his mind far beyond most boys of his age.

FIVE

Nine weeks after his father's return and two weeks before Christmas, Michael celebrated his eighth birthday. Bessie had been busy in the kitchen for days preparing cakes and biscuits and homemade sweets for the event. All Michael's cousins were invited, all his friends from school, and Dyson, who had readily forgiven Michael for their fight.

Joe King marked the occasion by getting roaring drunk and frightening some of the children so badly that Claire moved the party outside into the garden and put Bessie in charge of keeping her husband inside. It hadn't been difficult. Bessie simply plied Joe with more whisky until he passed out.

Joe's drinking had rapidly escalated into a real problem. Despite pleas from Claire that he see a doctor and try to get help, Joe steadfastly refused to accept that he needed it. The slightest upset in his day, of which there were many since he was argumentative and aggressive most of the time, sent Joe to the bar. In sober moments, he would cringe with embarrassment at some of the things he remembered doing or saying. Then he would reach for the bottle for 'a hair of the dog'. He believed he could stop any time he wanted but was never inclined to try.

Increasingly, Joe spent more time in town than on the farm. His absences were a relief to everyone. At home, if sober enough to eat, he usually had food sent to his room. He rarely spoke to Claire or Michael, and on those occasions when he did, he was invariably too drunk to make any sense. However, his presence was still very much felt, mainly because he was so unpredictable. Irrational temper tantrums were terrible displays of accusations and threats. Though physical violence was seldom evident, Michael gave his father a wide berth and Claire kept a small pistol in the drawer of her desk. There was no doubt in her mind that she would use it if necessary.

Michael's cousins knew that their uncle Joe was often drunk and difficult. Dyson too was aware of the problems within Michael's home. His school friends had no idea. If Michael didn't like his father before his eighth birthday, the sight of him swaying, yelling incoherent nonsense, and the looks of disbelief, disgust and even fear on the faces of his party guests left him in no doubt. He detested his father.

It was the same for Claire. The realisation that her husband had changed; that he was probably never going to be much use on the farm again; that their marriage was, to all intents and purposes, over; and that she was stuck with a drunken, loutish bully for the rest of her life was hard enough. But on Michael's special day, when she had implored Joe to stay sober and then watched him, at nine in the morning, deliberately head for the whisky bottle and get inebriated, any residual feelings she might have had for her husband died. She hated him.

Which made the suspicion that she was pregnant that much harder to accept.

Claire needed to tell someone and decided to confide in her sister-in-law Peg that she was five weeks overdue.

'Oh, my dear, how do you feel about it?' Peg, like all of them, was appalled by the changes in Joe.

Claire smiled at one of the children, separated two others who were having an ownership struggle over one of Michael's presents, shooed the German shepherds away from the food table, and said softly, 'Terrible. It's the last thing I need.'

'Does Joe know?'

'No. I'm not certain myself yet. It might just be stress or something, the last few weeks haven't exactly been fun.'

'What will you do?'

'What can I do? Have it, I suppose. Poor little mite. What kind of a family is this to come into?'

Peg placed a hand on Claire's arm in sympathy. 'Bridget and I often wonder if Noel and Bob had come home . . . Well, what they'd be like. Other men are back and they're just the same as when they went away, or at least, they seem to be. It's just the King family. Look at Anna. Colin never speaks to her, never speaks to anyone. Just sits in his wheel-chair all day staring into space. And you? My poor darling Claire, look what you've got back.' She sighed. 'It's this family, Claire. The war brought out the worst in both Colin and Joe, they weren't like this before. Dear God, it must have been terrible.'

Claire nodded. 'Joe said something like that when he first came back. But he's become worse, Peg. Much worse. Sometimes I think it must be my fault. He'd been through hell and somehow I approached him the wrong way. Maybe I expected too much.' She ran a hand through her hair. 'I just don't know. There are times when I wish he were dead.'

'No,' Peg said softly. 'Don't even think that. For all his faults . . .' she left it hanging.

'I'm sorry,' Claire said quickly. 'That was thoughtless.'

Peg smiled. 'Come on, let's get these children organised. Anna's drawn a beautiful donkey. Where's the blindfold?'

Claire and Michael spent ten days over the Christmas and New Year period with Claire's parents in Durban. Joe said he had too much work to do to go away but no-one was fooled. Michael caught his mother deep in conversation with her parents and, judging by his grandparents' grave expressions, knew she was telling them of her difficulties with Joe.

On their return to UBejane it came as no surprise when Bessie informed them that, 'The master has not been here very often.' Michael could tell by her tone that when his father was at home he had proved to be a bit of a handful, even for the normally imperturbable Bessie.

Late in February, Claire told Joe and Michael that she was pregnant.

Joe had stared at her blearily, then asked, 'Are you sure it's mine?'

But Claire was used to dealing with Joe by now. She said calmly, 'It's yours,' and left him to mull it over.

Joe didn't take long. He found her in the office. 'Just keep it quiet, you know I can't stand their squawking.' He had winked at Nandi lewdly. 'You'll be on your own for a while. Perhaps I'll come and give you a hand.'

Claire had seen the stricken look on Nandi's face. After he'd gone, she said, 'You're expecting a baby too, aren't you?'

Nandi nodded and smiled.

'When is it due?'

Nandi had no idea. Women got pregnant and had babies. They didn't bother themselves too much with the expected date of birth. 'I do not know exactly, madam.'

'About the same time as me I expect,' Claire guessed. 'That means you'll be off on maternity leave.'

Nandi looked relieved, especially when Claire added, 'Don't worry, Nandi, I'll see to it that you are not left alone with him.'

Michael was excited at the prospect of a baby

brother or sister and asked all kinds of questions relating to exactly how the baby would get out of his mother's stomach. Claire told him as much as she thought he should know, never dodging his questions but only elaborating if he insisted.

In May, Claire had to tell both Joe and Michael that she was expecting twins. It seemed to her that under the circumstances, one baby was punishment enough. But twins? Outwardly calm and unflappable, she went about all her daily business and still found time to prepare the nursery for two babies.

Unlike Claire and Joe, Nandi and Wilson were delighted that a baby was on the way. 'It will be a boy,' Wilson predicted. Nandi knew it was. The *sangoma* had predicted a second son.

Dyson and Michael discussed the imminent arrivals with a deal of impractical speculation.

'My mother says we won't be able to play with them for a long time,' Michael said.

'My mother says I will have to look after it sometimes,' Dyson told him.

'How?'

'I don't know. Watch it I suppose.'

'Why? What's it going to do?'

'I don't know.'

'How long do you think it will be before we can play with them?' Michael asked.

'Maybe months.'

'Months! That long?'

'Well, weeks at least.'

At school, Michael got into a fight with a boy who commented, 'I saw your mum in town yesterday. She's going to have a baby, hey? Jeepers, Mike! Your old man's a drunk. How did he ever get it up?'

Michael hadn't minded the comment about his father, though he didn't really understand it, but he took exception to what he suspected was an implied slur on his mother.

Mac spent about an hour telling Michael how much Claire would need his help. 'I'll not beat around in the bushes, laddie. Your father is useless. It's up to you.'

Michael nodded, though he wasn't sure what Mac was talking about. What was up to him? He knew nothing about babies.

Mac went on. 'Aye. It's a fine kettle full o' fish. You get yourself away with Raj now. You've much to learn.' As Michael left the workshop in search of the Indian, Mac added under his breath, 'You poor wee bugger.'

Nandi gave birth to a strapping baby boy at three o'clock on a cool August morning. It was an easy birth and the child was healthy. As was traditional, Nandi gave the baby the first of perhaps half-a-dozen pet names he would collect during his life. She called him Phalo. And, as was expected, the name had significance to an important event taking place at the time of his birth. Ancient Zulu custom regarded the birth of twins as ominous and the father was expected to kill one of them. But, late in the eighteenth century, history recorded that the then chief of the Zulu clan, a man called Jama, had refused to do this when his wife gave birth to twin girls. It was whispered among the clan that evil spirits were at work and had caused the death of Jama's son a year earlier, a boy called Phalo, by mysterious and supernatural means. In that Claire was expecting twins any day, the name Phalo was considered to be of monumental significance.

Wilson, as was the custom, gave the child his official name. He decided to call him Mapitha, after one of Mpande's key advisers, then added, 'He will be known as Jackson.' It was a practice now adopted by most Africans – to give a tribal name but also a Christian name, one usually taken from the Old Testament.

Nandi was happy with her husband's decision. 'Jackson,' she said softly, brushing the baby's downy head with her fingers. 'Come, Dyson,' she added. 'Come and meet your brother Jackson.'

Feeling proud, happy and anxious all at once, Dyson stared down at the helpless little baby and revised his earlier speculation about how long it would be before they could play together.

'Leave your mother to rest,' Wilson Mpande told his firstborn son.

Wilson had slotted into farm life with ease. He was a natural leader and the other Zulus accepted his authority. The bull that had killed Moses was found to have a large tumour in one leg, cutting off circulation. Moses should have seen it. Joe should

165

have seen it. Someone should have seen it. When the pain must have been unbearable, Moses was just in the wrong place at the wrong time. Wilson, who knew cattle, made a practice of inspecting each and every beast on UBejane at least once a month.

Inkatha, as Wilson quickly discovered, while being on the lips of many as a voice which should be heard again, was an issue to which most were reluctant to commit. Except for an enlightened few who could see the way South Africa was heading, there appeared to be a certain lassitude among the Zulus for taking any action at all. Jan Smuts' United Party, while pandering to the white population, at least lent an ear to problems facing South Africa's other races. Elections were two years away. The people Wilson spoke to were inclined to adopt a 'wait and see' policy.

Life on UBejane was pretty good. Wilson was working with cattle, which he loved. Adequate food and lodging were provided and the wages he was paid, combined with Nandi's, allowed him to buy more beasts for his own kraal, which his father happily cared for. Dyson was, at last, going to school. Because of Michael's teachings, he quickly caught up and passed others of the same age. Wilson found himself easily slipping into the same 'wait and see' mode and was content to do so. With the arrival of a second son, he felt a certain smugness about his life.

Claire went into labour three days after Nandi. Her waters broke at ten in the morning and Mac drove her to Empangeni. Joe was drunk. Leaving her at the hospital in the hands of starched efficiency, Mac drove on to Michael's school to collect him, where he told a rather astonished teacher in his own inimitable brusque way, 'The wee laddie needs to understand what he is responsible for.' She let Michael go, having convinced herself that Mac must have meant something else.

Michael and Mac paced outside the labour ward for six hours before a nurse popped her head around the door. 'It's a girl.' An hour later she was back. 'Another girl.'

All three were well and Michael was allowed five minutes with his mother. 'Do you want me to tell him?' he asked, not comfortable with the word father.

'If he's sober,' Claire said wearily. 'Otherwise, keep out of his way.'

Driving home, Mac offered to put Michael up in his own house until Claire returned. Michael refused. 'I'm not scared of him. Anyway, Bessie will be there.'

'If you need me, laddie, just yell.'

Two hours later, Michael dragged himself to Mac's door, bleeding and sobbing. 'He was waiting. Asked where Mum was and then just beat me, for nothing.'

Michael's savage beating shocked the old Scotsman to his very core. From the looks of it, Joe King had let fly with the buckle end of his belt as well as either a whip or a cane. He had also used his fists. Mac wrapped Michael in a blanket and drove back to the hospital.

The doctor, deeply shocked by the vicious lacerations and bruising, tended to Michael's injuries. He took Mac on one side. 'Look, this is very serious. I don't want to worry Mrs King right now but her husband must be reported.'

'Dinna worry about that,' Mac said. 'He'll be punished. Can you keep the laddie in for a night? I'll look after him after that.'

'I'd keep him in anyway. I suspect he's slightly concussed.'

'Aye,' Mac muttered to himself as he left the hospital. 'And he's not going to be the only one.'

Mac came from the Clyde shipyards. Reserved and antisocial most of the time, when his blood was up, Mac never shied from a fight. The fact that Joe King was drunk meant nothing. Mac handed out as good, if not better, than Joe had given his son. But Mac was an old man and the exertion took its toll. He said nothing to Michael, hanging stubbornly on to life until Claire returned. The night Michael moved back to the main house, Mac succumbed to a heart attack. He slipped peacefully from sleep to coma and from coma to death, leaving this world as privately as he had lived.

'Good riddance,' Joe slurred. His face still carried bruises.

So did Michael's body and legs. Claire took one look at her son and, weakened as she was, organised for Joe's belongings to be moved yet again, this time to a room at the end of the verandah which had access to the house only from outside. Joe King had effectively been kicked out of his own house and there was nothing he could do about it. Claire also contacted the police who warned Joe that if he went anywhere near Michael again he would find himself in jail for criminal assault. The threat worked. Drunk or sober, Joe kept well clear of his son after that.

The babies were called Sally and Tessa. Michael came to the same conclusion as Dyson. It would be a very long time before he could play with them.

Life settled down. Joe's absences from the farm became more and more prolonged. A series of women took his attention and he wasn't fussy about who they were, where they came from or even who they might have been married to. Anyone he could get to listen was up for a long, rambling diatribe about how his wife didn't understand him, how the war had ruined his life, how unfair everything was. Nothing was ever Joe's fault. He could always find an excuse, something to blame, for the way his life had turned out. He had his cronies too. Other men who were drunk by ten each morning for whatever reason they cared to give, if any. Joe had a roof over his head when he felt like going home and money in his pocket. The allowance Claire handed out was enough for booze and she seemed willing enough to keep on paying, as long as he stayed out of her way.

Occasionally Joe would show his face around the farm. More often than not, the running of UBejane was left to Raj, Wilson, Claire and, with increasing regularity, Michael.

Michael's uncle Colin became more morose and less interested in his own farm. He appointed a manager, an Englishman called Peter Dawson, who knew a lot about sugar cane. Although he was of a similar age to Joe, Peter became Michael's close friend and, at an age when most boys were discarding childhood toys for the mysteries of puberty, Michael and Peter would spend long hours discussing farming techniques. Peter was appalled at the heavy load of responsibility Claire King carried and took it upon himself to assist her whenever possible. He spent almost as much time on UBejane as he did working for Colin at Kingsway.

He got into the habit of having dinner with them several times a week. Lying in bed at night, listening to the murmur of his mother's and Peter's voices, hearing his mother laugh, Michael sometimes reflected that this was how his life should be. The sounds from the lounge were happy ones and filled him with a sense of security.

Over the next few years, with just the occasional burst of irrational interference by Joe, Michael could almost convince himself that his life was normal.

He might have known better.

Michael and Dyson were walking together on a back road through the cane fields. The games of ambush they played as boys were a thing of the past. At fourteen and thirteen respectively, each now shouldered a share of additional responsibilities. Dyson helped his father with the cattle, his mother with the other children and still found time to do his homework and study hard. Nandi had produced, in addition to Jackson, another son and then a daughter.

The dire predictions that if the former clergyman Daniel Malan and his Nationalist Party won the 1948 elections then life would become even more difficult for the Africans, had come true. Malan wasted no time instigating a policy of separate development. It was called apartheid. Life had become so difficult in fact that Michael and Dyson could only show their friendship once they were out of sight of others. The mule-drawn scotch carts had been replaced by school buses and, since it had been decreed that black and white children must not travel in the same vehicle, whoever arrived at UBejane's gate first would wait for the other to arrive, hiding in a pre-arranged place in the cane fields. To be seen together as friends would have brought unwelcome attention from the Security Police.

With indecent haste Malan's Nationalist government had passed the Mixed Marriages and Immorality Acts, prohibiting marriage, or any sexual contact between the races; the Population Registration Act, which classified all people by the colour of their skins; and the Group Areas Act, which dictated where different races could live. To cover up many examples of wanton cruelty or mindless persecution, the Suppression of Communism Act quickly followed. Anyone not toeing the line could be classified as a communist and incarcerated for as long as the government saw fit. Most of the black population were simply too frightened to protest against this rampant racism.

Friendships formed between blacks and whites were rare enough before Malan took office, cultural differences saw to that. A few, like Michael, who perceived no barriers, were horrified by the new restrictions. He could not understand why the majority of whites seemed to accept the changes, not noticing that every benefit or privilege was at the expense of South Africa's other races.

Life for the Mpande family, and indeed, for all the Africans and Indians on UBejane, was one of increasing hardship. Not on the farm itself, since Claire would not tolerate the new laws of South Africa changing the way things were run. But the separate development policies affected everyone as soon as they set foot outside UBejane. Anyone not classified as white was treated as a second-class citizen.

Nandi's involvement with the Bantu Purity League went underground because all organised meetings of African groups had been outlawed. The perception of the new regime was that any black organisation, irrespective of whether or not they had political leanings, was a potential threat to law and order. Eventually, the league ran out of steam. Meetings were too difficult and dangerous to organise and anyway, no-one was listening to them.

By this time, and with Nandi's persistence, Wilson had come to believe that the Zulus desperately needed a coordinated voice of their own rather than the Xhosa-dominated African National Congress. Despite the fact that the Xhosa and Zulus were all descended from the Nguni tribe and were closely related, time and distance intercepted until the only similarity between the two was their language, and even that grew progressively more remote. Wilson, like most Zulus, while acknowledging historical connections with the Xhosa, regarded them as a different tribe. And, indeed, it did seem to him that his own people were treating an escalating policy of suppression by Malan's Nationalist Party with alarming lassitude which set them apart from every other major tribe in South Africa. So absorbed were his people with clan infighting that when the ANC organised a defiance campaign supported by all South Africa's black population groups, to protest against government injustice, the Zulus were conspicuous by their lacklustre response.

Wilson became convinced that what the Zulus needed was a Zulu-focused organisation, run by Zulus, for Zulus. The fact that the Natal branch of the ANC was headed by a Zulu, Albert John Lutuli, didn't count. The ANC was simply too fragmented. Wilson held secret meetings with some of the most influential chiefs in Zululand but they were either preoccupied with whatever blood-feud was current or they were content to do nothing.

His staunchest ally was his son. Dyson was naturally bright and because of his long-term and deep friendship with Michael, he was not overawed by the white man. Inevitably, the boy's keen intelligence had become known to the Security Police who regarded any educated African, even if he were only thirteen, as a potential troublemaker. Michael felt that in all probability the Security Police resented the fact that Dyson was demonstrably better educated and more clever than most of their number. That, and the fact that he tended to speak to them as equals, an unpardonable aberration and one which had him earmarked as someone to watch out for.

Michael worried for him. Dyson, like his father, was outspoken about apartheid. All it would take was one word by someone with a grievance and the two of them could disappear forever. This was obviously a situation about which Dyson was aware. He grew less open with Michael, less willing to criticise the white regime, even to his oldest friend. It was this they now spoke of.

'I do trust you,' Dyson said hotly. 'It's just that . . . Well, it's better if you do not know certain things.'

'Why? Who do you think I would tell?'

'No-one. I know you would say nothing.'

'Then what is happening? I talk to you about secret things.'

'That's different.'

'No it isn't. I could get into trouble too.'

Dyson stopped and faced Michael. 'It's not just me. I am forbidden to speak to you by others. They are scared.'

Michael knew what he meant. Speaking Zulu,

he pledged his loyalty to Dyson, the Mpande family and the entire Zulu nation, ending by saying, 'I am a friend. If that is not good enough for you then I am sorry.'

Dyson began walking again, his head bowed. 'You are a friend, we know that. But, *Nkawu,* for how much longer will this thing be allowed? It is better that you know nothing.' He scuffed his bare foot on the sandy road. 'And you must stay away from the compound. If the police come and you are there . . .' He shrugged.

Michael could not blame his friend but it hurt. They parted at the fork in the road and Michael went on up to the main house, his mind busy not only with homework and jobs that needed doing on the farm but also with things he did not completely understand and which seemed to be coming between Dyson and himself. He was nearly there when Peter Dawson's Land Rover rushed past him, heading away from the house. Michael had to jump to the side of the road to get out of the way and stood, staring after the vehicle, wondering what had caused Peter to drive like that.

He found five-year-old Sally crying silently on the verandah and picked her up. 'What is it, monkey face? No, don't tell me, let me guess. Tessa's teddy bear came to life and ate all your ice-cream.'

Normally his sister would have laughed but not this time. Through her clothes, Michael could feel the slight body shaking with fear. Holding her close, he went inside and stopped dead. The lounge looked as though a tornado had hit it. Chairs over-turned, vases and lamps broken, the glass-fronted display cabinet smashed. Bessie and another servant were trying to clear up the chaos.

'What happened?' Michael asked.

Bessie shook her head and answered in Zulu. 'Big trouble, Mr Michael.'

Tessa came into the lounge, her face smeared with jam. 'Mummy's going to have a baby and Daddy is very angry,' she informed Michael import-antly. Tessa had a knack of knowing everything.

'How do you know that?' Michael was dumb-founded. To the best of his knowledge, Joe hadn't been anywhere near his mother's room in years. The mysteries of how babies were made had been solved for him years ago by a friend at school. It wasn't possible that his mother was pregnant.

'I heard him yelling at her,' Tessa said, licking jam from her fingers. 'Mummy's crying. Uncle Peter was crying too and he and Daddy had a fight but he's gone now.' She looked smugly up at him. 'Daddy broke everything with a poker.'

Peter! What did Peter Dawson have to do with this? 'Where is your father now?' he asked Tessa. Michael still could not refer to Joe as his own father.

'In his room.' She looked almost excited, as if it were some kind of secret game. 'He's drunk.'

Michael gently put Sally down and went to go outside.

'No, Mr Michael. Do not go there.' Bessie heaved herself up from where she was sweeping

176

broken glass from the floor. 'There is someone with him.'

Michael nodded curtly. Now that he lived outside the house, Joe King made no bones about his mistresses, often installing them in his room for days on end. So Michael went to his mother's room and knocked tentatively on the closed door. He found her sobbing into the pillow. 'Mum! What's wrong? What's this about a baby?'

But she would not look at him. She just shook her head and cried harder.

'Mum, please.'

When his mother finally turned to him, he saw that the lounge was not the only thing Joe King had trashed. Claire's nose looked broken, her lip split, one eye closed and black. 'I'll tell you about it some day,' she whispered. 'Just not now, okay?'

A few weeks later, on one of his rare appearances out on the farm and only slightly drunk, Joe King shed some light on the situation by telling Michael and everybody else within earshot, 'If she thinks I'm paying for her little bastard then she's got another thought coming.'

Michael, from long years of practice, ignored him.

'That's right,' Joe yelled. 'Say nothing as usual. Act as though your shit doesn't stink. Well, what do you think of your precious mother now? She's nothing but a whore.' He stepped up to Michael and cuffed him. Michael's fists curled but he did nothing, just stood waiting for his father's rage to subside. 'Say it,' Joe demanded, cuffing him again. 'Say it. Say, my mother is a whore. Go on, say it.'

Michael would be damned before he would. Instead, he looked squarely at his father, hatred radiating from his eyes and said clearly, slowly and distinctly, 'Your mother is a whore.' He stepped back smartly, turned and ran as fast as he could to the sanctuary of the African compound. If Joe King tried to hurt him there the Africans would probably kill him.

Gregor King arrived in the spring of 1952. He was a sickly baby and Claire spent a lot of her time taking care of him. Michael, now nearly fifteen, looked carefully at Gregor and decided, with a degree of satisfaction, that he could not possibly be Joe King's. The twins, now six, were less concerned with the baby's appearance. Sally couldn't wait to cuddle him and treat him like a doll. Tessa gave the new arrival a quick glance and said, 'Erk! He's all squirmy.'

Claire's eyes met Michael's over the baby's head and she smiled. 'He's very much loved and wanted. That's the main thing.'

'Yes, Mother,' Michael replied softly. 'And what about you?'

It was a question for which Claire had no answer.

PART TWO

1960

SIX

She was five years old and this was her territory. Her history was one of disruption and fear. At two, just after parting company with her mother, she had been darted, placed in a crate on the back of a vehicle and transported to Umfolozi Game Reserve where she was kept in a high security enclosure with other black rhinos. She hadn't liked that. To make her displeasure abundantly clear, she didn't wait for the men to let her out of the crate. She wrecked it. She then went on to put a half-metre tear along the side of one of their brand new vehicles, opening it up like a tin of sardines. She remained unpredictably temperamental until, two months ago, she had been taken from the enclosure and given the freedom of the reserve.

All of 164 centimetres at the shoulder and weighing close on 1000 kilograms, as lady black rhinos went, she was in her prime. Coming on heat for the first time, the hormone in her urine led the big bull into her territory. She allowed him to stay for two days before the familiar need to be alone over-rode her need to mate and she kicked him out.

Placid and plodding when left alone, she would, at the drop of a hat, charge anything that startled, frightened, annoyed or confused her; running full tilt at trees, rocks, elephants, vehicles and men. Her policy was kill first, ask questions later. Not even fellow rhinos escaped this treatment since, like all of her species, she had terrible eyesight and was guided largely by smell and sound. Besides, she didn't like other black rhinos any more than she liked anybody else. She was solitary, happily bad-tempered, abruptly aggressive and concerned more about filling her bulk with food than winning friends.

Her territory was clearly marked by her toilet, a flattened mound of droppings, to which she returned for several months before starting another elsewhere. This midden was a sign to any would-be intruder: enter here at your own risk.

The man had walked eight kilometres from his village, carrying a rifle and a battered suitcase containing the tools of his trade. He saw the sign and trod warily. Big as the cow was, he knew she could hide within five metres of the well-worn track. She could charge with the speed of a galloping horse, toss him to the tops of the trees, catching him expertly on the point of her upturned horn before throwing him high in the air again. It was an experience he'd prefer to live without.

He'd found the cow about four months ago, quite by accident, and had been greatly impressed by the size of her 'horn'. This hard, fused mass of hair was at least sixty centimetres long and probably the same around its base. He knew it would fetch a good price. He considered it a great pity that she was protected by a high and electrified fence. However, six weeks ago he saw her in the main part of the park and so he'd begun to make plans.

In his right hand was what had once been a military issue .303 rifle. Now, cut back for easy concealment, the weapon was so loose it was held together by braided copper wire and the wet thigh skin of an impala had been stretched over a cracked stock, drying hard and leather-strong to prevent it breaking further. In his suitcase were eight home-made nooses. Constructed from high tensile steel cable which he'd heated in a fire to reduce springiness, these rusty old snares were deadly efficient, strong enough to stop an elephant, easily concealed and one of the cruellest poaching aids known to man. In addition to the snares his suitcase contained an axe, some short lengths of fencing wire, a small hand shovel and a skinning knife. The only other thing was an over-ripe and bruised orange. His lunch.

Over the last weeks he'd learned a lot about this cow. He knew where the path ran from her feeding ground to where she drank. He knew she'd be resting under a tree at this time of day. He knew that, as the day cooled, she'd start to browse again, pulling with her pointed upper lip at twigs, leaves, the bark of trees and bushes until she'd had enough. Only then would she make her way along the well-trodden path to drink at the stagnant waterhole. It would be sundown or later by then, which gave him six hours to lay snares. Plenty of time.

Even so, he kept a sharp lookout. Aware that she had just mated he didn't want to run into her lover. Nor did he wish to encounter the cow herself. She could easily have decided to cut her rest period short in favour of a mudbath, or a wallow in the dust. Having so recently been in oestrus, chances were she would still be in a highly volatile frame of mind. He kept close to trees in case of a charge, his ears alert for the distinctive puffing snort which always preceded an attack.

He was making for a place just above the water-hole where she regularly drank. The intention was to set his snares where the path dipped sharply to the water, knowing that the cow, once she reached this point, would be concentrating more on the scent of water and less on any lingering smell of man that he would unavoidably have left behind. Four neck nooses and four foot snares, set at strategic points, should be more than enough. The chance of snaring the wrong animal was minimal since the rhinoceros's bad temper while she was on heat had driven most others away.

The dry and thorny scrub country was quiescent in the intense heat. He listened carefully for the shrill warning cry of tick-birds, the constant companions of rhinoceros. Feeding on parasites which infested their host's hide, in return they warned of approaching danger. All he heard was the far off *whip . . . whip . . . wheeoo* of a Piet-my-vrou, and then, much closer, the sharp warning *waa-hoo* bark of a baboon sentinel, which set the troop off for five minutes of hysterical shrieking, barking and grunting. Savage as the sound was, the poacher was less concerned about the baboons than he was about their reasons for such alarm. Such displays generally meant the presence of leopard.

The man was also listening for the sound of a vehicle. He knew he was breaking the law. If the park rangers found him, he'd go to prison. That was the penalty for poaching in a game reserve. But he'd been helping himself for years in this so-called protective haven for animals. He was good at it and his family ate well as a result. He had never, however, attempted anything quite so daring as this.

Reaching the game path he turned east, towards the waterhole. The track seemed to run at random, not fitted to contours of the land but rising and descending sharply in places. The trail smelled of animal dung, dust and leaves as well as an indefinable quality which was manifestly African bush. Nothing stirred in the energy-sapping temperature. Sweat ran freely down the man's face and bare back, the odour of it clashing with bush smells. The poacher ignored his discomfort. He was too busy listening for any sounds that might indicate danger.

He walked nearly two kilometres along the game path until he reached the spot he'd chosen. Then he set to work, doing what he knew best, toiling for the reward the white Baas would pay him when he delivered the rhinoceros horn. The money would keep him and his family in food for the next two months.

There was nothing other than financial gain in the man's heart and mind. No conscience for the cruelty he was about to inflict on the unsuspecting animal, no awareness that the black rhinoceros was perilously close to extinction. These issues were alien to a man who relied on self-taught skills simply to feed and clothe his family.

He lashed the foot snares to trees beside the trail. Then, taking his axe, he chopped down several others just off the path, wiring their thick trunks tightly to the neck nooses which he carefully concealed in surrounding bushes. Each log was approximately two metres long and weighed around 200 kilograms. Having satisfied himself that the snares were correctly positioned and could not be easily detected, he packed up his suitcase and moved along the trail towards the waterhole, where he would wait for the big cow to come for her evening drink.

No more than a kilometre away, the black rhinoceros cow browsed happily in the cooling afternoon, stripping twigs and leaves off the acacia trees and munching contentedly, untroubled by the wickedly sharp thorns which, on lesser beings, cut through skin, flesh and muscle. As evening fell, she found the game trail and, in her usual fast walk, set off for the waterhole. On her back, undisturbed by the faster pace, picking at ticks and other parasites, were two tick-birds and an egret.

Nearing the waterhole, anticipation caused her to pick up speed. Looking forward to a cooling drink and a wallow in the mud, confident in her great thick wrinkled hide and considerable bulk, she trod mightily along the familiar path. Quite unexpectedly her hind foot picked up a ground snare and, in turning to investigate, her head went through one of the neck nooses. She felt the sudden drag and tried to shake them off, impatient to get to water, not yet alarmed.

The high-tensile wires tightened and the cow, characteristically, lost her temper, lunging forward in frustrated annoyance. The nooses bit deep. Steel cables cut through her hide and the cow started to panic. She bucked and thrashed, lunging and heaving against the snares and with each powerful movement the cables cut deeper. They cut through sinew and flesh. The neck noose tightened against her windpipe and began to strangle. There was blood everywhere and the cow, still too angry to feel much pain, reared and pulled until the rusty, jagged steel reached bone. Then, nearly one tonne of exceedingly angry rhinoceros, with one mighty jerk, snapped the tree anchoring the foot snare and lurched forward up the game trail, dragging the heavy log attached to the snare around her neck.

Choking and wheezing for air, the now frantic rhinoceros plunged blindly along the track, shaking her head in a vain attempt to lose the tree trunk which bounced crazily in her wake. Eyes wide with fear she ran, mindless with terror until, crashing down a steep and rocky part of the game trail, she lost her balance, slid and rolled off the path and into the scrub beyond, thrashing and bellowing. And the log attached to her neck noose caught between two rocks.

Then the agony started. As she lay there with flanks heaving, eyes wide and staring, mouth open and desperate for air through her tortured windpipe, the sharp, searing, throbbing pain hit home knocking the fight from her tortured limbs. The steel cable rubbing against bone in her leg sent shock waves up through her hip and spine. The snare crushing air from her lungs sent thumping, rolling surges of pain into her head and down her spine fusing with the agony coming up from her near severed leg.

She lay trembling, hurting, and very, very afraid. With less and less frequency she thrashed and fought against the snares, but the movement sent blackness to her numbed brain. Some time around midnight the foetus, that had just begun to grow inside her, died.

The poacher found her without difficulty. He was indifferent to her suffering. Death meant access to the horn which, in turn, would bring much money. He sat patiently, several metres away, waiting for her to die.

The black rhinoceros cow didn't die that night, or the following day, or even the following night. The ants and flies, the infection which set in, the loss of blood, thirst, slow strangulation, the cheeky vultures and hyena, all contributed to her death. Half the time, during her last twenty-four hours, she was mercifully unconscious. When she was aware of what was going on the pain was unbearable. The poacher didn't shoot her. Bullets cost money and a shot might alert the rangers. Instead, having retrieved the snares still hidden in the bushes, he occupied himself collecting fruit to eat and by fashioning a small bow and arrow for his youngest son.

Some time around midnight on the third night, after enduring more agony than any man or beast should ever have to face, the rhinoceros took one last shuddering breath, heaved her flanks painfully, and sought refuge in the silky blackness of death. She went gratefully. If she could have understood the reason behind her brutal and horrifying death, she might have reacted characteristically. With a full-blown, lusty, joyful, head-down, fifty kilometre an hour charge. But no-one could explain to her why she had to die.

When Michael King found the cow, or what remained of her, he let forth a stream of obscenities. It was not only the death of one black rhinoceros which upset him – though God knows, the reserve had so few that this loss constituted a twenty per cent reduction in their numbers – it was the death of this particular animal which rocked him.

For the past three years Michael's work at Umfolozi Game Reserve had included a project which was attempting to save black rhinoceros from the very real possibility of extinction. In neighbouring Hluhluwe, similar Parks Board operations had already come far towards saving the white rhino from the same fate. The authorities were not alone in their attempts. Indian rhinoceros were now protected by both the Indian and Nepalese governments while a number of South-East Asian countries were trying to increase the population of the Sumatran rhinoceros before it suffered the same fate as its already extinct cousin, the Javan rhinoceros.

The catalyst for this scramble to save the rhino had been publication of the *Red Data Book* by the International Union for Conservation of Nature and Natural Resources, in Switzerland, which listed all rhinoceros as endangered. Around the world the rhinoceros had long been hunted for its horn, a fused mass of hair, rather like that of a finger-nail, which was prized as a material for ornate Oriental dagger handles or powdered to yield a supposed aphrodisiac.

Michael's project was small by comparison with some. The reason was due in part to the nature of the very animal he was trying to save. As many who had come into contact with this highly volatile beast found out the hard way, *uBejane* does not like people, especially those intent on darting and transporting him for anything up to 1000 kilo-metres in order to save his life. Even if it were possible to make him understand that it was for his own good, *uBejane* would most likely still try very hard to kill those attempting to help him. Such was his nature.

Many willing hands went up for the more docile white rhino but volunteers to capture and transport the black were few. Michael had only five beasts in his care. The project now had three cows and two bulls. To protect them, a high-security enclosure spreading over several square kilometres of the reserve was built. There, they had as much to eat as they wanted, an abundance of clean water and several mud wallows. There, the snares, pits, arrows and rifles used by poachers couldn't reach them. The only trouble was, there, in their sanctuary, the animals wouldn't breed.

'We've given it our best shot, it's just not working,' one ranger voiced the opinion of the rest at their monthly meeting. 'They need more space. I vote we give them the freedom of the park.'

'They'll be poached,' Michael warned.

'What's the difference?' another asked. 'Poached or without offspring, the outcome is the same.'

He had a point. 'Two then. One bull and one cow,' Michael conceded. 'We can let the rest out once we've finished upgrading the fences.'

Once released into the main park, Michael watched over the two animals like an anxious mother hen. The rhinos didn't make it easy for him since they could usually be found at opposite ends of the reserve. But every Monday, on his day off, he searched the 50,000 hectare reserve in his Parks Board vehicle and, where the land was too hilly, on foot, until he was satisfied that his charges were safe. During the rest of each week he kept a watchful eye open for them as he went about his more routine duties.

One other kept a watch on them too, and, in the course of doing so, became aware that every

Monday one of the rangers drove or walked all over the reserve until he had located both animals. So he set his snares on a Tuesday. And the barely pregnant black rhinoceros died in unspeakable agony on Thursday.

Which was why Michael now stood in the African bush, tears in his eyes and a cold rage in his heart. 'Bastards!' he finally spat out.

Dyson Mpande, his tracker, assistant and best friend, pursed his lips and whistled silently. 'Only one, *Nkawu*.' Dyson indicated the ground. 'This is the work of one man.'

Michael wiped sweat from his forehead with the back of a hand. 'Bastard then.'

'They do not understand.'

'Yes they do,' Michael gritted. 'Maybe not when it's for food but they know this is wrong.'

'The money comes from white men.'

'I know,' Michael said. 'That doesn't make any difference.'

'The white man is never caught.'

'Only because he's had more practice at breaking the law. The poor bastard who did this probably had no option. The money is irresistible.'

Africa doesn't leave much behind. Hyena, jackals, vultures and ants had all but removed the evidence. Another few days and the cow's existence might never have been. Michael stared down at the pathetic remains. The taut snares were still there. Scattered rocks, broken bushes and trees told of the cow's attempts to free herself. 'Fuck this,' Michael yelled to no-one in particular.

Dyson understood Michael's frustration. For three years they had known this particular cow. She even had a name. Betty Black. When the decision had been made to release two rhino into the main reserve, Michael had deliberately chosen Betty Black. She was the most volatile of the cows, by far the most aggressive and, he thought, the most likely to survive. But nothing wild could stack up against the cunning of man – not when he's thinking about his back pocket.

Michael had been elated when Betty Black accepted the bull into her territory. At last, the breeding program was under way. And not a moment too soon. Government funding for the project was running low, and without financial support from somewhere, the program, like so many others, was likely to die.

'Come on,' Michael said harshly. 'Let's see if we can track the bastard.' His anger was less directed at the man responsible than it was at the plight of the black rhinoceros. Once, these mighty beasts had roamed all of Zululand. Now, with farms taking up their habitat, the only place they remained was in a couple of game reserves. And even there, they weren't safe. Michael didn't actually blame the poacher. He didn't even particularly want to catch him, knowing that if he did, it would inflict more hardship on a family who, most probably, already had difficulty making ends meet. But he knew that unless an example was made of this man, others would copy his deeds. The Zulus had to understand. They could not be exempted from the world's growing concern that the animal population was becoming extinct at the rate of one species a year. So what if the Zulus once measured manliness against hunting prowess? The world was changing and the population explosion would see to it that it continued to change. Traditional hunting had become poaching. And the Zulus had to adapt with it.

Michael clamped down on any feelings of sympathy for a race of people who, in the main, were bewildered by their altered lifestyle. Whoever poached this cow had done so dishonourably and for the wrong reasons. As he climbed back into the Land Rover he felt the crackle of paper in his shirt pocket. The letter! He hadn't opened it. It was from his mother. He'd read it later.

Dyson swung in next to him. 'He'll have cut the fence.'

'Yeah.' Michael started the engine. 'Right next to his village if we're lucky.'

Thirty minutes later they found where the diamond mesh perimeter had been breached. 'Bloody fool,' Michael muttered. The hole had not been repaired and was large enough for a lion to pass through. 'He'd be the first to scream if a cat climbed into his cattle.'

'Lots of spoor,' Dyson pointed. 'And close to the village.'

Leaving the vehicle, Michael and Dyson slipped through the gap and walked the last kilometre to the village. The poacher had been easy to find. An empty bottle of cane spirit at the door of his hut, a brand new bicycle leaning against the wall and two full five gallon tins of paraffin in front proclaimed the hut owner as someone who had just had a financial windfall. They found the man inside, dead drunk. His wife and children watched fearfully, knowing they were about to pay a terrible price for their new-found wealth. Dyson spoke to the chief, who was adamant that none of his villagers had gone into the reserve and returned with the horn from a rhinoceros. But when Michael told him in fluent Zulu that unless he told the truth, before nightfall the village would be crawling with members of the South African Police, the chief had a change of heart.

'Was that using or abusing the system?' Michael asked after the poacher had been arrested.

Dyson shrugged unhappily. 'A bit of both.'

'I don't like it any more than you,' Michael admitted. 'I feel like a bully.'

'You've said it yourself many times, *Nkawu*. There can be only one set of rules.'

'But there isn't, is there? Oh sure, if it's convenient but, more often than not . . . Look, I was wrong back there. I used a threat against which the chief had no defence.'

'Don't wear yourself out worrying about it. The chief will be used to it.'

'That's not the point, dammit,' Michael burst out, angry with himself. 'I should know better.'

'What else could you do? You wanted to punish the culprit, make an example of him. If you'd done things the tribal way, sure, you'd have a culprit, the witchdoctor would have given you someone to blame. But we both know it wouldn't be the *real* offender. He'd give you a troublemaker or the least productive man, someone the village wanted to get rid of.'

Michael glanced at Dyson and smiled slightly. His friend was right. 'Sometimes you think like a white man.'

'Thanks,' Dyson said dryly. 'You sure know how to make a man feel good.'

They laughed, totally at ease together while, all around them, the system fed on its voracious appetite of colour-based hatred. Both were part of a tiny percentage of black and white South Africans who ignored the system, but it was increasingly difficult to be like that. On both sides of the racial fence, reason had been replaced by justification. Dyson's acceptance of Michael's actions was a case in point. They had often tried to work out where it would all end. They never could. The issue was too big and too complicated.

Michael and Dyson repaired the fence before driving back to camp to file a report. The two men parted company after that, Dyson heading for the African compound, Michael to his room in the staff quarters.

Tired and frustrated, Michael stripped off his clothes and threw them on the floor. With a towel wrapped around his waist, he went to the ablution block and took a long, cold shower. Dripping wet, he returned to his room, stopping to collect a Lion beer from the refrigerator in the staff dining room.

Drinking straight from the bottle, Michael sat on the bed and picked up his shirt, fishing out the crumpled letter. He opened it, anticipating the usual rush of nostalgia his mother's words invariably caused.

It was full of news from home – the farm had been granted a bigger sugar quota; cattle were fetching good prices; Aunt Anna was worried about Uncle Colin's health; old Raj was sick again and his eldest son, Balram, was shouldering more and more responsibility; Wilson and Nandi's second son, Jackson, was proving a bit of a handful. Claire made no mention of Joe. She never did. Her letters read as though he didn't exist. But she was full of news about the twins and Gregor. She ended by mentioning that Tessa was getting very difficult to deal with.

Michael folded the letter and dropped it on to the bed. 'Dear God!' he thought. 'She's acting as though it never happened.'

Eight years younger than Michael, Tessa and Sally were now fourteen. Identical in appearance to such an extent that only those who saw them every day could tell them apart, their personalities were so contrasting they could have belonged to different species.

It had been clear right from the start that Sally's nature was gentle and Tessa's hard. Where Sally cried for attention as a baby, Tessa screamed. As they grew into toddlers, Tessa dominated Sally, commandeered all the toys and, when she thought no-one was looking, was not above inflicting a furtive pinch or bite.

With age, the differences between them became more marked. Sally asked, Tessa demanded. Sally gave, Tessa took. Sally relented or apologised easily, Tessa never did, even if she were patently in the wrong. Sally was honest, Tessa sneaky.

The twins were six when Gregor arrived. Sally adored her little brother and spent hours with him reading and playing games. Tessa, when she wasn't ignoring him, teased Gregor to the point where he would scream with frustration.

Tessa entered puberty early. She was barely eleven when her breasts began to develop and body hair appeared. According to Claire's letters, Sally was nearly fourteen before her body began to change.

From the time his sisters were born, Michael had found it hard to get a handle on Tessa. It was clear that Gregor didn't like her much. But Sally, who bore the brunt of her sister's taunts, tricks and sometimes acts of downright cruelty, always tried to defend her. For her part, Tessa seemed to expect her twin's loyalty, though she saw no reason to reciprocate.

Tessa was the only one in the family who had any time for Joe. Despite his alcohol dependence, his mistresses and his violent temper, she seemed to be fascinated by him, often seeking out his company. When her father ranted and raved, Tessa would giggle delightedly. When he was drunk and talking aggressive rubbish, she hung on every word. She appeared drawn to his excessive, often irrational behaviour and, as she grew older, it was Joe she tried to emulate despite it being obvious that her father was generally regarded as a complete social outcast.

Joe responded to his daughter's obvious devotion. A bond formed between them. Not that he loved her. He didn't. But in a household where no-one bothered to hide their disgust for him, Tessa's total acceptance, irrespective of his actions, was a balm on his severely bruised ego. It also gave Joe something to bargain with. He could reach Claire through their daughter. Not that he used this for any good purpose. Joe knew that Claire worried about his influence over Tessa and actively encouraged her to be disruptive and disobedient.

Tessa thought she was being singled out as special. She proudly boasted to Sally that she was the only one who could control Joe. She was too young to see that he was deliberately using her to hurt Claire. As far as Joe was concerned the children were Claire's only Achilles heel. Nothing else touched her.

Over the years, Joe King had not bothered to hide the fact that he was bedding any woman who was willing. At first it had been to hurt his wife but he quickly realised that she couldn't have cared less. Now he was hooked. He wasn't fussy. Black, white, old, young, married, single, pretty, ugly, Joe's libido was in overdrive and he accepted whatever was on offer.

And that, as Michael discovered three years ago, included Tessa.

The memory of that day would stay with Michael forever. Sometimes he wondered why he hadn't seen it coming. The wildness in Tessa could not be contained. She challenged and disrupted everything, argued all the time and refused to do anything for anybody except Joe. Her puberty was a nightmare of mood swings spaced with screaming matches with Claire. Michael was glad he mainly experienced them through his mother's letters. At twelve, she had wanted to wear high heels and lipstick. At thirteen, she threw a tantrum when Claire refused to buy her a revealing black sheath dress. More and more, Tessa seemed to be rushing into situations far above her physical and emotional years. It had been going on since she was eleven.

Michael was only nineteen when his life, which had been only loosely stitched together ever since his father's return from the war, burst at the seams. He'd heard of incest. For some reason he thought it only happened in the backwoods of America. Not in Africa. Not in Zululand. Not here at home. Not with an eleven-year-old sister.

It was like a recurring nightmare, it would not go away. And while other memories blurred around the edges, this one remained sharp and clear.

Claire had gone into town and expected to be away for most of the morning. Michael, out on a cane burn since before dawn, saw her car leave at around nine o'clock. The twins and Gregor had left the house much earlier to catch the school bus. Joe King was, presumably, sleeping off last night's whisky, that is if he bothered to return to the house at all. Michael didn't know.

Tired, dirty, it was ten-thirty when he went back to the house for a shower and late breakfast. He was free for the rest of the day and planned to meet a group of friends at the beach.

As usual, Michael entered the house via the kitchen and was surprised to find the servants – gardeners, housegirls and Bessie – clustered together in a huddle, their expressions ranging from fear to disgust. 'What's this?' he teased. 'Are you lot on strike?'

Bessie had shaken her head. 'No, *Nkosaan*.' She appeared unwilling to look at him.

Michael glanced at her sharply. 'What's the matter, Bessie? Has someone been hurt?'

She shook her head again. 'No, *Nkosaan*,' and glanced fearfully beyond Michael to where the verandah led to Joe's room.

Michael heard a giggle. It was a childish sound and seemed uncoordinated, out of control somehow. 'Who's in there with him?'

Bessie had a dishcloth in her hands and was wringing it with jerky, nervous movements. 'Tessa,' she whispered, tears sliding down her cheeks.

'Why would Tessa . . . she's at school . . .' A warning screamed in his head as Michael looked wildly at Bessie. The realisation had nowhere to go and burst from him in a cry of anguish. 'Christ! The bastard! Not Tessa!'

Bessie stared at the ground, sobs shaking her ample frame.

Michael spun on his heel and ran from the kitchen, along the verandah. He flung open the door to Joe's room. They were on the bed. Joe had his arm around Tessa who was leaning against him. In her hand was a bottle of scotch. Both Joe and Tessa stared at Michael defiantly and, as he stood in the doorway immobilised by the scene, Tessa slowly raised the bottle to her lips. It wasn't the drinking, though God knows, that in itself was shocking enough. It was the fact that Joe wore no shirt. It was the absence of Tessa's shoes and socks. There was an intimacy in the way they sat together that said there was more here than met the eye.

'Go to your room,' Michael snapped at Tessa.

She giggled, and he could see from her glazed expression that she was drunk.

'Bessie,' Michael bellowed. He needn't have shouted. Bessie was already halfway along the verandah. 'Take Tessa away.'

Joe struggled off the bed. He was equally as inebriated. 'Get out of here. Go on . . . the lot of you. Get out. This is my room.'

Bessie ignored him, grabbed Tessa's arm and pulled her, none too gently, off the bed. Joe staggered forward to stop her and Michael stepped between them. Joe swung at Michael and connected with his ear. Considering his condition, it was a surprisingly powerful blow. Michael pushed and Joe fell backwards onto the bed. Following Bessie and a wildly struggling Tessa, Michael did not see the bottle coming. Fortunately, Joe's aim was off. The missile went wide, smashing against the wall. 'Have another drink,' Michael gritted, before slamming the door.

They propelled Tessa to the bathroom. 'Stick her under the shower, a cold one. Keep her there until she sobers up. I'll send one of the girls to help.'

Bessie nodded grimly and turned on the cold tap. Tessa, still clothed, slid down the shower wall and sat, almost trancelike, under the cascade of cold water. The fight had gone out of her. 'I feel sick,' she mumbled, before her system rejected the alcohol and she vomited.

Michael returned to the kitchen and told one of the housegirls to help Bessie. He was too upset to eat. He went back outside, uncertain what to do next. Was it only the whisky or had something much more sinister taken place in Joe's room? What should he do?

Joe King appeared on the verandah suddenly, belt in hand, eyes glittering with the staring intensity of madness. 'You're going to get a lesson you won't forget,' he snarled at Michael. 'You've had this coming for a very long time.'

It had been years since his father last threatened him with a belt. Something snapped in Michael as he looked at the man, at his red-veined face, blood-shot eyes, alcohol-wasted body. Michael curled his hands, beckoning. 'Come on then,' he said softly. 'Come and get me, you sick bastard.'

Belt raised, buckle ready to strike, Joe King lunged towards his son. 'You little bastard. You prudish little prick.' Joe swung the belt at Michael's head.

Michael rocked backwards, turning sideways, but the buckle just made contact, drawing blood from his cheek. It was a vicious blow and could have inflicted serious damage. Joe's eyes were wild and Michael realised suddenly that he was in a fight for his life, that Joe was beyond reason. If he could, Joe King would kill him. The belt swung again and Michael shot out his right hand, grabbing the hard leather and jerking his father towards him. Joe had wrapped the belt around his left hand to swing it since he still had very little use of his right. When Michael pulled him forward he was effectively trapped. He tried to protect himself but Michael delivered a rapid succession of punches, straight into his father's face, only stopping when Joe sagged and fell, his face a bloody pulp. Disgusted, Michael stepped back from his father's fallen body. He was panting from exertion and rage. He wanted to lash out and kick the breath from Joe's body. He wanted to pummel that chest until the black heart stopped beating. When Joe moaned then rolled to a sitting position, it took every ounce of willpower for Michael to walk away. Before he did, however, he had one last message for Joe. 'If you ever go near Tessa again, I'll kill you.'

Michael went back inside. He could not bear to be under the same sky as his father. Bessie was just coming from Tessa's room. 'She's nearly asleep, *Nkosi*.'

Michael noticed that Bessie had called him Lord, rather than the diminutive, *Nkosaan*. 'Did she say anything?'

'No, *Nkosi*. Only that she felt sick.'

After Bessie had gone to the kitchen Michael paced in the lounge. 'Now what?' He needed to get away and think. But he couldn't focus, his mind was a scrambled mess of uninvited images and questions. 'What do I tell Mother?' Claire, he knew, was not blind to Tessa's faults but if she ever found out what happened here today it would ruin her life forever. 'Would Tessa say anything? What about the servants? How do I keep this quiet?'

Michael knew he couldn't. By evening every person on UBejane would know, there was nothing he could do about it. He could go to the police, have his father arrested. But then the entire area would hear of it. The situation had to be contained. But how?

He ran trembling hands through his hair, ignoring the pain of raw and bleeding knuckles. 'Think! For Chrissakes, think!'

Bessie came back into the lounge. 'Mr King has gone.'

'Good riddance. I hope he stays gone.'

She nodded, went to say more but thought better of it and turned away.

Michael stopped her. 'Bessie, what do I do?'

'I do not know,' she said softly. 'I have never seen anything like this.'

'No,' he agreed savagely. 'Neither have I. Has this happened before?'

'Two times before.'

'Why the hell didn't you tell me?'

Bessie hung her head. 'What could we do? When I try to talk to Miss Tessa she tell me to

mind my own business. She say where is proof.'
Bessie looked up at Michael. 'There is evil inside
that one, *Nkosi*. She is bad, just like her father.'

Michael could not have agreed more. 'I'll talk to
my mother, Bessie. Tessa must go away.'

'Yes. That would be best. But what will you say
to Mrs King?'

Michael closed his eyes. *Yes, what can I say?*

Bessie went back to the kitchen, Michael, deep
in thought, looked up some minutes later to see
Tessa standing in the entrance to the lounge. 'Please
don't let Mother send me away,' she sobbed. 'Please,
Michael. I couldn't stand being sent to a convent. It
won't happen again. He made me do it. It wasn't
my fault.'

'God!' Michael thought watching her. 'She's
only a child.' Tessa was rubbing her eyes, crying and
hiccupping.

'Please help me,' she begged. 'I know it was
wrong. I'll never drink that stuff again.'

Michael's heart softened slightly. *Is that all? Joe is
more than capable of getting Tessa drunk for his own
insatiable craving for revenge. Oh, God, I hope that is all.*

But Tessa's next words confirmed the worst of
his fears. 'I didn't want to do those things. He made
me do them.'

A rush of pure rage and hatred swept over
Michael. His voice shook with the effort of trying
to keep it normal. 'What things, Tessa?'

However, his sister had said all she was going to
say. Her face closed and she shrugged. 'Silly things.
Nothing really.'

Michael knew he'd get no more from her. 'You must *never*, *ever* go to his room again. Do you understand?'

She nodded. 'Don't send me away. Please, Michael.'

After she had gone, Michael rubbed a hand over his eyes. Had he done the right thing? He was very conscious of being totally unqualified to deal with such a situation. Had he just swept it under the carpet? Tessa seemed genuinely upset but Michael suspected that was more to do with the threat of being sent away. Could he trust her?

Did she really understand the enormity of her actions? Tessa had always done everything to excess, anything she liked was taken to the limit and beyond. Michael had seen her eat chocolate until she was sick. Her body was maturing. Could this be another example? Was she really incapable of seeing how wrong it was?

He desperately wanted to talk to his mother but she would be in town for hours. He peeped in on Tessa. She was sound asleep, curled into a ball, a picture of childish innocence. Suddenly, he had to get away from the house. Telling Bessie to keep an eye on Tessa, Michael drove to the beach. He needed to be in carefree, normal company, the kind that had no dark and dreadful secrets. He wanted the warm Indian Ocean to wash the filth of his father away. He didn't wish to speculate on the unthinkable any more. He was only nineteen – he wanted to feel nineteen.

The long sweep of beach was empty, save for his friends, a few of their dogs and two horses tethered on the grass. Michael parked the Land Rover, took off his shoes and shirt and, throwing a towel over his shoulders, made his way down to where everyone was gathered around a fire. People greeted him but he barely heard them. One girl, Jennifer Bailey, who had been occupying his thoughts rather a lot lately, saw him coming. She smiled and waved. Normally he'd have gone directly to her. She was leaving for university soon and he cherished their time together. Now he felt too unclean to sully her with his company.

'Hey, man. What kept you?'

'We're cooking up some sausages. Plenty to go round.'

'Hi, Michael.'

Michael greeted them absently, tossed his towel on the sand and ran down to the water. He plunged into the waves and struck out strongly, swimming beyond the breakers. Treading water, alone in the ocean, Michael gave way to the tears of shock and disgust which had been building up for the past half-hour. His sister and father shamed him beyond belief. He felt dirty, as though their actions had somehow rubbed off on him. The way they'd been sitting together, behind a closed door, drinking. It had been too cosy, too intimate, too secretive to be innocent. *Oh, God, I want it to be innocent.* But he knew it hadn't been.

On the beach they were waving him in, holding sausages up to entice him back. And Michael was out in the sea, on his own, blubbering like a kid.

He returned to the beach twenty minutes later, composed, clean again, red eyes the only telltale sign that anything was amiss. No-one took any notice. Most of them had red eyes from the salt water. Jennifer Bailey handed him a fork with a sausage impaled on it.

'Thanks.'

'We thought you were never coming in.'

Michael looked up at the wide blue sky. 'It's a beautiful day. I was hot.'

Someone handed him a bottle of soft drink.

Jennifer drew him aside. 'What's wrong?'

'Nothing.'

'Something's wrong.'

He looked at her fresh-faced innocence. Blonde ponytail, clear hazel eyes shining with wholesome pleasure at being alive. What would she think of him if he told her? 'I said nothing's wrong. Just leave it will you.'

He moved away but she followed. 'You're upset about something, I can tell.'

Oh, Jesus! If only I could tell you.

'Come on, Michael. We're friends.'

He turned on her then. 'Can you drop it? It's none of your bloody business.'

Her face showed hurt. 'Fine.' She tossed her head and left him standing alone.

He was in no mood for company but no shape to be on his own. He checked his watch a little later and decided that his mother must be home by now. Saying a curt goodbye to everyone, he left the beach. As he trudged up the sand to where his vehicle was parked, he heard one of the girls asking Jennifer what was wrong with Michael.

'How should I know,' Jennifer had snapped back. 'Maybe he got out of bed on the wrong side.'

Claire had just arrived back. Michael walked into the kitchen just as Bessie was telling her that Tessa had come home because she wasn't feeling well and was in bed, asleep.

'Mother, I need to talk to you.'

'In a minute, darling. I want to check on Tessa.'

'Tessa's fine. Now, Mother.'

Claire glanced at him, surprised. 'Come into the office then.'

'No. Nandi is still there. Outside.'

Michael waited until they were well away from the house. Claire held her silence. Whatever was bothering her son, she knew he'd tell her in his own time.

'I came back to the house this morning and found Tessa in Joe's room. They were both drunk.'

'What! How could he? She's only eleven.'

'That's not all.'

Claire's trembling fingers found her lips. 'What?' she whispered.

'I think something else is going on between them.'

'Don't be ridiculous,' Claire snapped. 'What a terrible thing to say.'

Michael put his hands on her shoulders and looked into her face. 'I have no proof,' he said quietly. 'It was the way they were sitting. If it hasn't happened already then it will happen soon. You've got to keep her away from him.'

Claire pulled back from him angrily. 'I will not

listen to this disgusting filth. How could you even suggest it, Michael? Tessa's only a child.'

'She's maturing. You know what she's like.'

His mother put her hands over her ears. 'Stop it. Stop it at once. Your father is a drunk, not a child molester. Joe would never stoop to such a thing. Never.'

Michael pulled his mother's hands away. 'For God's sake, Mother, listen to me. You can't ignore this. Anything's likely to happen when they're both drunk. You've got to take action now, before it goes any further. Tessa should be sent to a convent.'

'I will not send my daughter away,' Claire said stiffly. 'I suggest you listen to yourself. These things . . . these terrible accusations . . . how could you, Michael? I know you hate Joe but this is beyond the beyond.'

Michael knew then that he had to get away from UBejane for a while before he went mad. The responsibility of the farm and now this. He wanted the freedom to be young. He could just about cope if his mother was on his side, but now? 'Pull your head out of the sand, Mother.' He was angry with her. 'I don't like it any more than you.'

'Then forget it,' she shot back, angry herself. 'Do yourself a favour and go on holiday for a while. I can handle things perfectly well.'

'Tomorrow,' he said curtly. 'I'll leave tomorrow.'

'Fine. And, Michael, don't come back until you get this nonsense out of your head.'

Michael knew they would never speak of it again. Not ever.

Before leaving the farm he had to say goodbye to Dyson. The look on his friend's face told him that news of Tessa and the fight had already spread.

'My bag is packed,' Dyson said matter-of-factly. 'I am coming with you.'

'You can't.' Michael was just as pragmatic. 'You're black.'

Dyson threw his bag into the Land Rover. 'I thought we could try Umfolozi. The Parks Board is always looking for experienced rangers and trackers.' He got in next to Michael.

Michael rested both arms on the steering wheel and looked at Dyson. 'You couldn't track an elephant across ice-cream.'

'I know that.'

'You couldn't tell a rhino from a hippo.'

'This thing is true.' Dyson was staring dead ahead.

'You couldn't . . . Christ, Dyson, you're scared of lions.'

'So?'

The crushing weight of shock was lifting. It felt good that his oldest friend wanted to come with him. 'So,' Michael said, grinning. 'That makes two of us. We'll just have to convince someone otherwise.'

'I'll leave that to you,' Dyson said comfortably. 'You're the white man.'

The memory was still so vivid, especially when he received letters like this. Until now he had not been able to confront the reality of that day, even from a distance. Michael drained his beer. 'Maybe it's time I went home.' For the first time in three years, it was an appealing thought.

He picked up the letter again. Claire never once so much as hinted that Michael should return. So why was he suddenly filled with guilt? 'Hell,' he thought. 'I'm nearly twenty-three, the project is broke and likely to collapse, and yes, I miss UBejane. It's time I pulled my fucking head out of the sand and got moving. If Tessa is still playing up she can bloody-well go to a convent.'

Michael found some shorts, pulled them on and set off to find Dyson. The two of them made their way down to the river where, on a flat rock shaded by trees, with the muddy water rolling slowly past, they had more than once rearranged all that was wrong with the world.

'I think it's time I went home for a while.'

Dyson smiled. 'Good. I miss my family.'

Michael threw him a sour look. 'Lucky you.'

'Tessa?' Dyson inquired. He and Michael had never discussed that day.

'Yeah. She's giving Mum a hard time.'

'Fourteen isn't she? Same as Jackson. He's got my parents worried sick. He's running with a bad crowd.'

'Okay.' Michael squinted away up the river. 'I'll hand in my notice on Friday.'

'What about your work here?'

'What about it? It's all but finished. There's no more money.'

'So when do we leave?'

'You don't have to leave.'

Dyson simply looked at him.

'You're right. You have to leave.'

'When?' Dyson repeated.

'I imagine the sooner the better. End of the month. The project virtually died with that cow.'

'There are other rhino in the reserve.'

Michael sighed. 'Sure. And if we let them out to breed they'll be poached. The new fences won't be finished for two years and anyway, the bastards will cut their way through just as easily. I'm supposed to be saving the black rhino from extinction and I can't even provide a habitat they'll breed in. It's a farce.'

'What about suggesting a bigger security area?'

'I can just see the response to that. The trouble always comes back to our lack of funds. The government wants it to be seen that they're doing something but they sure as hell aren't prepared to spend the money on it.' Michael stared glumly at Dyson. 'How much worse does the situation have to become before they take this seriously?'

'You did your best.' Dyson was pragmatic. 'There'll be other projects.'

'Then they'd better get a bloody wriggle on. There won't be any black rhino left soon.'

Dyson picked up a pebble and tossed it into the river. 'That is not what troubles you.'

'No,' Michael admitted. 'It's my wonderful, happy family.'

'Go back and try it. Your father might have changed.'

'Yeah! And the leopard loses its spots. Some hope.'

There was no arguing with Michael. Dyson switched subjects and languages. 'The one with hair that shines like the moon, does the *hlobonga* progress?'

Despite his mood, Michael punched Dyson's arm lightly and laughed. 'White women do not practise *hlobonga*.'

Dyson knew this already but pretended to be shocked. 'Hau! The white woman lets you go all the way, as if she is your wife?'

'All the way or none of the way. No middle ground.'

'And on which side of the middle ground do you stand?'

Michael grinned. 'What about your meetings?' He changed the subject suddenly.

'What meetings?'

'Come on, Dyson. The ones you go to twice a month. Do you think I don't know about them?'

'I do not,' Dyson said seriously, 'know what you're talking about.'

Michael leaned towards him. 'Oh yes you do. You know exactly what I'm saying.' He placed a hand on Dyson's arm. 'Be careful, my friend. It's easy enough out here but if you join a group in Empangeni the police will know.'

Dyson gently shook off Michael's hand and eased to his feet. 'Do not worry about me, *Nkawu*, I do what I must but I am always careful.'

Michael rose too. 'You are playing with fire. The

African National Congress *and* the Pan African Congress have been banned organisations ever since the State of Emergency was declared after Sharpeville.'

'I am not a member of either,' Dyson said softly.

'Aren't you? Way I hear it, they've branched out, introduced more radical groups,' Michael replied. 'Some of them are pretty hairy.'

They started walking back to the compound. 'You're not into anything violent are you?' Michael asked.

Dyson stopped. 'What are you worried about?'

Michael thought before saying, 'Look, if you try to free yourselves with violence, how then do you ensure that it doesn't turn back on you? Apartheid cannot last. Economic sanctions must come soon. Be patient.'

Dyson gave a cynical laugh. 'Then why are there are no signs of it? For how long must we suffer?'

'All I'm saying is be careful. If you are arrested no-one can help.'

'I know.' Dyson started walking again. 'And it is as I said. I am always careful.'

Michael knew he could not change Dyson's mind. He just hoped that his friend would not come to the attention of the Security Police. Sharpeville should have chastened the South African police. It had been a disgrace. Sixty-nine people, including women and children, dead. Most of them had been shot in the back as they fled a hail of bullets outside the police station. Instead of being embarrassed, the police later went to the hospital where some 150 people were being treated for a variety of wounds and arrested all of them. The police, presumably with Pretoria's backing, seemed to be out of control.

They parted at the camp. Michael went in search of the one with hair that shines like the moon. She was the daughter of a senior ranger, twenty years old, very attractive. She was killing time until she went overseas. She wanted no involvement, lusting after life and Michael's body in that order. She suited Michael admirably.

SEVEN

Two weeks later, on a Sunday, they drove through the gates of UBejane Estate.

'Told you,' Dyson said, when Michael commented on how good the farm looked. Dyson had been back on a number of occasions during the past three years. 'This place runs itself.'

'Just as well,' Michael observed dryly.

Dyson made no comment. He was too busy being pleased to be back.

Michael's keen eyes took in everything. The dirt roads were well maintained, their grassy verges recently cut. The gate between the cane lands and open cattle pasture had been replaced by a grid. There were new plantings, wide irrigation channels with gate weirs to control water flow, huge Rain King gantries for overhead irrigation. In the distance, the house looked as though it had been repainted. Michael had been uncertain about coming home but it sure felt good to be here.

Before resigning his job with the Parks Board, Michael had considered the possibility of specialising in wildlife management. It would mean furthering his education – a university degree most probably – and he was prepared to do that. He spent an interesting couple of days weighing up the pros and cons of two very different lifestyles. It was an important time, the rest of his life would depend on this decision. The idea of game conservation was certainly tempting. He enjoyed the work and believed in its importance.

However, two things decided him to return home. It was not difficult to see that South Africa was heading for trouble. There was no way the country's majority would continue to accept rule by a white minority. The government was crazy if it thought it could continue to act solely for the benefit of the white population. If they'd gone about things in a different way . . . but they hadn't. World pressure for change had been ignored. Unrest was coming, it was inevitable. When that happened, the already dwindling funds for wildlife projects would, more than likely, dry up completely. The other deciding factor was simply the lure of working for himself, taking decisions, acting on them and standing or falling by them.

Claire had turned UBejane into a company. She held fifty-five per cent of the shares, the bank five per cent and each child ten per cent. Joe King was a director, as was Michael, his mother holding a proxy on his behalf. The twins and Gregor would probably be invited to join the board when they turned twenty-one. Michael knew the girls had no interest in sugar cane or cattle. Tessa would probably head for the bright lights just as soon as she could. Sally had only one burning ambition. To become a ballet dancer. As for Gregor, he was too young to know what he wanted. He still had ten years of schooling ahead of him and, according to Claire's letters, preferred to spend his time listening to radio plays or reading rather than learning about the farm.

It could be a good life and, if Joe King kept out of the way, an enjoyable one.

Michael turned onto the road that led to the African compound and Dyson directed him to his parents' neat brick house which had been built for them two years earlier. The compound was unrecognisable. Gone were the beehive huts and kraal walls of neatly woven sapling sticks. Gone were the traditional cooking fires and woven grass grain stores. The only thing left was a central meeting place but even that, surrounded as it was by wooden benches, had lost its traditional appearance. The compound now resembled the Indian barracks and Michael wondered aloud if the Zulus preferred it.

'Of course,' Dyson said, surprised by the question. 'Why wouldn't they? It's more comfortable.'

'Okay. I'm just old fashioned, I guess. I liked the compound as it was.'

'You, my friend, didn't have to live in it.'

'Was it that bad?'

Dyson laughed at the wistfulness in Michael's voice. 'No. We miss some of it too.'

'Progress!' They said it in unison, and Dyson added, 'A necessary step forward is not necessarily a step forward.'

Michael grinned. Dyson was fond of such expressions.

'There is my father.' Wilson had emerged from his house at the sound of the vehicle.

Michael pulled up and watched, smiling, as Dyson and his father greeted each other. Wilson Mpande approached the vehicle. 'I see you, *Nkosi*.'

Michael laughed as he got out of the Land Rover to greet the farm's *induna*. 'Do not call me *Nkosi*. I am neither a chief nor a king.'

'Not in your heart perhaps, Master Michael, but in ours you are chief of UBejane.'

'I'm back to stay,' Michael told him. 'Let me at least earn the title.'

Wilson nodded in approval. 'That day will come soon enough, *Nkosi*. Spare us the inconvenience of two names.' His eyes twinkled as he turned back to Dyson. 'And you, my son. Do you also return to this place?'

Dyson's eyes found a point on the ground. 'For the moment, Father.'

Wilson pressed his lips together, then said briefly, 'We will speak of it later.' He looked over at Michael. 'Would you care to inspect your cattle, *Nkosi*?'

Through the formality, Michael detected pride. Wilson loved the cattle on UBejane as passionately as he loved his own. 'My cattle are in the hands of one who treats them as his own. I would not insult that man by rushing to check on his work. It is true, I am anxious to examine the cattle but I am also impatient to greet my mother. I would prefer to wait until tomorrow.'

'Thank you, *Nkosi*,' Wilson said warmly. 'Will you take some beer with us?'

'Another time, Wilson, it would be a pleasure.'

'Quite so. Your mother has waited long enough.'

A tall young man walked up to Dyson and greeted him with very little enthusiasm. Dyson, on the other hand, was delighted. 'See,' he said to Michael. 'See how my brother has grown.'

Michael looked at the powerfully built Zulu who stared back at him with an almost blank expression in his eyes. 'Jackson? Look at you! You are a man now.' The boy must have been the same age as the twins but, in the three years since Michael had last seen him, he had grown from a pot-bellied child into a strapping teenager. He held out his hand in greeting.

'Time does not stand still to await your return,' Jackson said coldly, ignoring Michael's outstretched hand.

Michael remembered that he had never been able to get close to Dyson's brother. 'That is true. I must hasten home before my sisters turn into old women.'

Dyson and his father laughed. Jackson did not. He looked Michael up and down insultingly then turned and sauntered off.

'I must teach my young brother some manners,' Dyson said quickly, trying to disguise his embarrassment.

Michael clapped him on the shoulder. 'Your brother's hot-blooded and proud. A true Zulu.

Surely that is no shame. Don't be too hard on him, my friend.'

But he saw the worry in Wilson's eyes as they followed Jackson's departing back.

When Michael left home, Gregor had been a small boy of five. The rangy, barefoot youngster who swung off the verandah to greet him was not the brother Michael remembered. He had been something of a sickly child. Now he was the picture of health. Dark blonde hair hung down over his eyes, his lithe body tanned, sturdy arms and legs fleshed out. Michael went to pick him up, thought better of it and held out a hand instead. Gregor responded by flinging himself at Michael, wrapping both arms around his older brother's waist. 'I knew it was you, I just knew it.'

'Ho, little brother. I see a man must not stay away too long. You are growing so fast I hardly recognised you.'

Gregor smiled happily at the compliment. With no father figure in his life, Michael was the substitute Gregor had always looked up to and tried to please. 'Have you come home for good?'

'Depends. I hope so.'

The look on Gregor's face told Michael that his brother knew what Michael had meant. He would stay as long as he could stand his father.

The screen door banged and Claire King came out onto the verandah. 'Michael! I don't believe it! What a wonderful surprise. Why didn't you let us know you were coming?'

Michael jumped the steps and hugged his

mother. Holding her shoulders he looked closely at her. She had aged. Calm grey eyes smiled a warm welcome but in their depths he also saw a great sense of relief. 'How long can you stay?'

'I'm back for good if that's okay with you.'

'About time too,' she said briskly.

Although Claire's manner was matter-of-fact, Michael could see how pleased she really was. His mother had carried the responsibility of UBejane for over twenty years. Fine lines had appeared around her eyes and mouth. She looked tired. 'Have you got glasses yet?'

Claire laughed. 'Not yet. I must do something about it now you're back.'

Michael shook his head. 'Where are the girls?'

'Sally is over at Kingsway. Tessa spent last night with a school friend in Empangeni. They'll both be back this evening.'

Michael looked for some clue, any innuendo in his mother's words, but found none. 'I'm looking forward to seeing them,' he said.

'Sally will be overjoyed,' Claire added, giving Michael the hint he sought.

'Good.' Michael braced himself. 'And Joe?'

Gregor answered with the succinctness of one who has run out of patience. 'Pissed, no doubt. Probably entertaining his latest. She's black.'

'Gregor!' Claire admonished, but not very vehemently.

'Some things never change,' Michael remarked. It came as no surprise. In the past he had often wished that Joe would get caught with one of his

African women. It was a crime for which he might be sent to prison. Then again, who would know? Being a member of the elite white club might simply mean a slap on the wrist while the unfortunate woman paid the more severe price.

'Come inside,' Claire said. 'Tea should be ready.'

'I'll get my things. Which room?'

'Same one,' she smiled. 'It's just as you left it.'

As he unpacked, Michael's thoughts wandered. His mother's outward tranquillity was a rare gift and one she had come to master. Whether out of necessity or she had been born that way he wasn't sure, but he was glad she had it. A more emotional woman would have gone to the wall years ago. The way his mother coped with unpleasantness was to pretend it didn't exist. For years she had acted as though Joe simply wasn't there. On those rare occasions when she absolutely had to speak to him, drunk or sober, Joe received nothing but polite indifference from Claire. Her letters made it seem that she was doing the same thing with Tessa, ignoring the truth and acting as though all was well with the girl. Michael had never decided if his mother was weak or incredibly strong. Could she possibly be as serene as her outward manner suggested, or did unspoken anxieties churn inside, invading each and every day of her life?

Joe King woke up with a terrible hangover and an erection. Opening one eye, he observed daylight.

He'd been at the club when? Earlier today or yesterday? He remembered leaving and going . . . oh yes, to see some friends on the pretext of having a Sunday drink with them. Anyway, that's what he had told his cronies. In truth, he was going to see one of their servants.

'Fool!' he thought. 'You'll get caught one day.'

Joe had no idea why, but having sex with African women, or with someone else's wife where the chance they might be caught together was a real possibility, was far more exciting than screwing someone who was free, white and over sixteen. Bringing women back to UBejane was another buzz. Claire might *think* her distress didn't show but Joe could see it in her eyes.

The woman at his side stirred. Joe glanced at her with disinterest but the throbbing of his loins would not be denied. Once spent, he rolled off her and sat on the side of bed. 'Get dressed and get out,' he said curtly, bored with her. It had been exciting at first, the illicit intimacy of their coupling the stimulant on which he thrived. But Lena, once the thrill of breaking the law had waned, and in the cold light of whatever time of day it was, had since become as interesting as humping a sack of potatoes.

It was always like this. Alcohol made the glorious chase appear attractive. Hangovers revealed life's raw reality. Lena was nothing special, not worth the risk and, not to put too fine a point on it, a drag. What Joe glimpsed through his self-imposed suffering reminded him that she really hadn't had much choice. Joe vaguely recalled threatening to tell the police that she had no pass. It was a threat which usually worked since, without that all-important document, all Africans would be forcibly returned to his or her government decreed homeland and a lower than subsistence lifestyle.

The bed heaved as Lena rose and then Joe heard the rustle of her clothes. 'Tomorrow?' she asked, timidly.

'No.'

Her face showed no expression. 'You no want?'

Joe shook his head. 'It's finished.'

The woman shrugged and left his room. She had to go along the verandah and past the lounge where Claire might be. Joe smirked. He hoped his bitch of a wife was there. A screen door banged and he heard a man's voice speaking Zulu. 'Wait, young woman. Who do you seek?'

Lena's soft response was unintelligible to Joe.

'It's Bessie's day off,' the man said.

Joe wondered who it was. He heard footsteps on the verandah and then the voice again, hard with anger. 'Why do you put up with this, Mother? I'm going to stop this, once and for all.'

Michael! Joe scowled. He lurched to his feet, legs pressed against the bed for support as a wave of dizziness swept over him. Then, moving to the dressing table, Joe peered at himself in the mirror, grunted with self-loathing and ran a hand over the stubble on his chin. *Jesus Christ! What a mess!*

He stumbled back to the bed and sat down

heavily, head in hands. *Oh God! What have I become?* This was a familiar scenario, the inevitable alcoholic remorse. It hit him with every hangover. 'I've got to stop drinking,' Joe groaned into his hands. 'Get a grip before it's too late.' He reached out a trembling hand and fumbled under the bed for the bottle. 'Just one. Just to get rid of the shakes.' The spirit warmed his belly and immediately quelled the nausea. 'That's better.' In fact, he felt so much better he drained the bottle. 'I'll stop tomorrow. Fresh start. Get up early and see what's happening on the farm.' He reached into the bedside cabinet and brought out another bottle. 'Last day,' he muttered aloud, removing the top. 'Might as well enjoy it.'

Joe King was lost in a vicious circle, though he honestly believed he could break out of it at any time. When drunk, life offered excitement. When sober, it only gave him a headache. Still, he persisted with the fallacy that he was in control, especially after a couple of drinks to quell his shaking hands.

By the time Joe made it to the shower he was thoroughly plastered and in excellent spirits, singing loudly and off key. Not that it bothered anyone. A storeroom had long ago been converted into an en suite bathroom and Joe's whisky-enhanced musical talents could be heard only by a handful of chickens in the henhouse.

The water sobered him slightly. He padded, naked, back into his bedroom. Sunday – the afternoon had that kind of feel to it. In alcoholic limbo,

Joe's mood was hovering between aggression, self-pity and defiance.

He stood in front of the wardrobe, selected crisp white knee-length shorts, a short-sleeved white shirt, long white socks and brown shoes. The skin showing between socks and shorts bore very few scars from the burning when he'd been shot down, just enough to look interesting. Joe learned long ago that women found battle scars intriguing. Dressed, he looked at himself in the full-length mirror and nodded, satisfied. That would do. He'd just cut along to the club and see what was what. Devlin Rattigan's wife had given him the eye a couple of times. They were usually in the bar on a Sunday afternoon. She was a bit plump but what the hell. It wasn't her looks he was after.

Dressed, he went back to the bathroom and splashed aftershave on his cheeks, though he hadn't bothered to shave. With a final pull at the whisky bottle, Joe stepped outside.

Claire, Michael and Gregor were sitting on the verandah. Joe ignored them, making his way to his car with the slow deliberation of one trying to appear sober. Halfway across the lawn he stopped, turned and shouted, 'If you've come home to make trouble you can piss off right now. As of tomorrow, I'm running this farm.'

'Forget it,' Claire said as Joe drove off. 'He's been saying that for years.'

'I'm surprised he hasn't killed himself,' Michael remarked. 'Driving in that condition.'

'He's got the luck of a pox doctor,' Gregor said,

grinning, knowing his words were daringly close to naughty but not really understanding their meaning.

'Where on earth did you get that expression?' Claire reacted as he hoped she would.

'Mac.'

Michael and Claire stared at him, not knowing if they were being wound up.

Gregor explained. 'It's true. Someone called Mac taught it to Raj and he taught it to me.'

'Dear God,' Claire said quietly. 'A woman-hating Sikh is bad enough without him quoting dubious Scottish wisdom.'

'Come on, Mother. You know you love it,' Michael teased.

'What, from an eight-year-old!' But she was smiling.

They heard the motorbike before it came into view. 'That'll be Sally,' Claire said.

'Sally!' Somehow, Michael could not picture gentle Sally on a motorbike.

'It was Colin's. She's allowed to ride on the farm roads. She's very careful, doesn't speed or try anything foolish.'

'Not like Tessa,' Gregor put in. 'She tried to jump it across a corner of the pool. Landed in the deep end. It took four men to get the bike out. Mum won't let her ride it now.'

A heavy old BSA 250 came into view. It looked far too big for Sally but she brought it to a careful stop. 'They said you were home,' she cried, running up the steps. 'Gosh, Michael, it's great to see you.'

Michael was nearly bowled over. 'Who are *they* who seem to know my every move?'

'The servants.' Sally stepped back and looked up at him. 'They know everything way before we do. Have I grown? Please say I have.'

Michael looked her up and down critically while Sally hopped from one foot to the other waiting for his verdict. Finally he grinned. 'Grown and grown up. My goodness, what a delightful young lady. A pleasure to behold.'

Sally giggled.

'Got a boyfriend?'

She flushed. 'No.'

'Tessa?'

Sally looked down at her feet. 'Hundreds.'

Michael shuddered and did not glance at his mother.

'Is Tess back yet?' Sally asked.

'Not yet, darling.'

'Fab! That means I get the bathroom first.' She rolled her eyes at Michael. 'You wait and see. Tessa always leaves such a mess.'

'She'd better not leave one for me,' Michael tried to look serious, 'or I'll be using her as a mop.'

Sally giggled, but there was no mirth in her voice when she said, 'I don't think Tessa would like that.'

It was after dark when Tessa returned. She breezed into the dining room where the rest of them had just finished their usual Sunday curry. 'Sorry I'm late. Not my fault, Janet's stupid mother lost the car keys. Had a super weekend and I've already eaten. Must finish my homework. Got an English assignment I'd completely forgotten about.' Her eyes flicked over Michael as she turned to leave.

'Tessa!' Claire said sharply.

'What?' Her voice was sullen.

'The very least you could do is greet your brother.'

'Why?' she asked spitefully. 'He doesn't like me any more than I like him.'

'She's got a point there,' Michael thought, wondering how Tessa could look so like Sally and yet be so totally different. Their features were the same but Sally still retained the softness of youth. Tessa's face was hard, angular and much older than her years.

She tossed her head and left the dining room, still ignoring Michael.

Claire raised her hands in helpless apology. 'Sorry.'

'That's our Tessa,' Gregor muttered.

'It doesn't matter.' Michael found it didn't. 'She'll come round.'

'Don't hold your breath,' Gregor warned darkly.

Later that night, with everyone else asleep, Claire and Michael sat on the verandah talking quietly and sipping their brandies. 'I'm so pleased you're staying, Michael. Raj and Wilson do their best but farming is changing and we can't afford to fall behind. They're content to do things the old way.'

'The farm's looking very good. Do you still get actively involved?'

'Not really. Sometimes I must but you can imagine how Raj feels about that. I worry about him. He's getting on a bit and it shows. I've told him to let Balram do more but you know how he is – won't take orders from a woman. Balram is virtually running the sugar side but Raj just will not let go. He's out there every day, in all kinds of weather, making sure everything is being done properly. The man is driving everyone nuts. He even sticks his nose into the workshop. I've had three mechanics in three years and the latest, Derek, is threatening to leave because of Raj's constant interference. I've tried to stop it but . . .' She shrugged. '*You* tell him, Michael. Raj will listen to you.'

'Does Joe *ever* raise a finger to help?'

'Hardly. Oh, he threatens to every now and then, like he did this afternoon . . .' Her voice tailed off.

'What's wrong with the man, Mother?'

He heard his mother sigh softly. 'I wish I knew, darling. All I can tell you is that when he came back from the war, he had changed. I thought that, given time, he'd get back to normal. Instead, he became worse.'

'I remember the day he returned as though it were yesterday. He arrived confrontational and stayed that way. You tried to be loyal but no-one could blame you for giving up on him. The problem must have been evident before.'

233

'I suppose so.' Claire sounded uncertain. 'But he worked hard. The men liked him. And he hardly ever drank more than a couple of beers. Your father was always kind and considerate. I adored him.' She took a deep breath. 'I admit, he never had much time for you, but a lot of men are like that with babies. If only the war . . .' Again her voice faltered and the sentence remained unfinished.

'Why don't you stop shelling out money? He only spends it on booze. You're making the problem worse.'

'I can't. Don't you see? Everything we have, the lifestyle we enjoy, if it weren't for Joe . . .'

'That's rubbish,' Michael cut in sharply. 'If you must thank someone for UBejane, thank Grandfather. All Joe ever did was get born.'

'I can't help it, Michael. It may be a company now but this place rightfully belongs to Joe. That's the way I feel. It was good enough for me before the war. If he hadn't been so badly treated . . .'

'Stop making excuses for him, Mother. I know he had a rough time of it, but that was fifteen years ago.'

'Can we talk about something else please?' Claire wouldn't be drawn. 'It has happened and I deal with it. Let's leave it at that.'

'Okay.' Michael hesitated. 'Then let's discuss Tessa.'

'Must we?'

'You're still having problems with her. Every letter you wrote had some reference to her antics.'

'She's difficult, I admit.'

Michael had to ask. 'Has she stayed away from Joe?'

Claire's voice went hard. 'I've made sure of it. I'll never forgive Joe for giving an eleven-year-old whisky.'

She did not refer to Michael's other fears but then, he hadn't expected her to. 'And now?' he asked.

She let her breath out slowly, dissipating the rush of bottled-up emotion. 'Tessa's wild. I know she smokes, I can smell it in her room. Sometimes there's liquor on her breath. She answers back, is rude to everyone. You saw how she was earlier. That's tame by comparison. She seems to hate us all. I don't know.' Claire spread her hands helplessly. 'I've tried talking to her but she just walks off.'

'Can *anyone* get close to her?'

Claire shook her head. 'Not even Sally.'

'Friends? She must have friends.'

'She doesn't really. Janet, the girl she stayed with this weekend, is the closest but Tessa only uses her to get away from here. I'm quite sure that if I phoned Janet's mother to find out why Tessa was so late getting back it would have nothing to do with lost car keys. Tessa would have deliberately delayed coming home. I know what she gets up to, Michael. I just don't know how to prevent it from happening.'

'How about a convent?'

'I've thought of that. It would certainly make life easier around here but, Michael, she's my daughter. I love her. A convent would make Tessa desperately unhappy.'

'Okay, she's my sister and while I don't like her

very much, I suppose I love her too. My point is, Mother, if she steps too far out of line then unhappy or not, you and I will have this convent conversation again. Given the choice between her unhappiness and the disruption to all our lives, there really is no contest.'

He felt her fingers on his arm. 'I'm so terribly pleased you're back, darling. UBejane has been without you for too long. Things can only get better now you're home.'

Michael heard the wistful note in her voice and hoped she was right. All he said, however, was, 'Sorry I stayed away so long.'

'That was my fault,' she said quietly. 'I sent you away.'

It was the closest his mother would come to referring to that afternoon three years earlier.

Word had spread that Michael was back. He went to the workshop first and met Derek, who was on the verge of resigning. 'Give me a couple of weeks and I promise, Raj won't interfere with your work any more.'

By nature an agreeable man, Derek nodded acceptance and went back to work, saying only, 'You've got it.'

Michael found Raj supervising the loading of newly cut cane on to rail trucks. 'Goodness, Mr Michael, goodness. I see a man before me.' Raj's shrewd eyes observed him critically. 'You stay away too long I am thinking.'

Michael clapped him on the shoulder. 'You are right, my friend, but I am home now and also see passing years in the one who stands before me.'

Raj took no offence as none was intended. 'It is true, Mr Michael. Old Raj should be at home with his feet up.'

Michael knew that the old Sikh was more than ready for retirement. 'So what of your eldest, Balram? Let's see. He'd be nearly thirty. Surely it is more than time for him to take over your duties?'

Raj smiled, welcoming the suggestion as though it had never been mentioned to him before. 'Goodness yes, Mr Michael. My boy is very ready.'

'Then let's arrange it. It should have happened two years ago. Why didn't you listen to my mother?'

Raj looked haughty. 'She is a woman.'

Michael laughed. 'Is she indeed? I hadn't noticed.'

Raj did that Indian thing with his head, shaking it from side to side in a figure of eight which looked like a negative but was actually quite the opposite. 'She is very good and, I am thinking, better than a lot of men.'

This was high praise from Raj.

'But,' he continued, 'a new manager will be meaning more work for some, isn't it? At least until they are sure that this man can be trusted.'

Michael put an arm around the old Indian's bony shoulders and hugged him briefly. 'Thank you, Raj. Your loyalty to this family has not gone unnoticed. Before long you will be complaining of boredom and begging for your job back.'

'No, no,' Raj said, smiling a little. 'Raj will be too busy sticking his nose into Balram's work.'

'You will stay here then?'

'Where else would I go, Mr Michael? This is my home.'

'Then we must find a good spot for your retirement house,' Michael said, smiling. 'Somewhere high up where you can spy on the whole farm.'

Raj's thin face split wide with pleasure, revealing stained red teeth from the betel nut he chewed incessantly. 'I know the very spot, Mr Michael,' he said. 'The very spot.'

Michael laughed. 'I'll just bet you do,' he said fondly. 'I imagine it was selected the day you arrived.'

Raj fiddled with one end of his red sash, a gesture which told Michael that the old man had something else on his mind. 'Something troubles you, Raj. What is it?'

'Let us walk, Mr Michael. There is much to show you.'

They left the men loading cane and walked down past the Indian barracks towards the cane fields. Michael could see that Raj was searching for the right words. Finally, he burst out, 'It's Miss Tessa, Mr Michael.'

Michael's heart sank. He nodded curtly. 'What of Miss Tessa?'

Raj stopped. He looked acutely miserable. 'You will be angry.'

'Probably,' Michael admitted. 'What has she done this time?'

Raj hung his head. 'It is my youngest son, Mr Michael.'

Oh sweet Jesus! What next?

Raj continued. 'He has the hot blood, oh goodness yes. He is only eighteen, Mr Michael. For how much longer can he hold off against her? I am terrible afraid for him, Mr Michael. The young do not listen any more.'

'Well he'd better listen to this.' Michael had turned steely serious. 'Tell him if he so much as lays a finger on Tessa he jeopardises his entire family's future on UBejane.'

Raj looked shocked.

'Perhaps,' Michael went on in a gentler tone, 'that will give your son the strength to resist.'

Raj's head went in a figure of eight as he understood that Michael was angry with Tessa, not his son. But he needed to make his point. 'My son,' he said quietly, 'should not have to resist. Life is hard enough as it is.'

'I do not blame your son, Raj. I have met him a few times, he's a good boy.'

'But what can you do?' Raj asked. 'She is . . . she has . . . Miss Tessa does not seem to . . .' he stopped abruptly. 'Forgive an old man, Mr Michael.'

'I hear what you say, Raj. My sister has the morals of an alley cat.'

'It is not that she is bad, Mr Michael. I am just thinking she does not understand the things that most of us are born knowing, isn't it?'

Michael thought that summed up Tessa better than anything else he had heard. He started walking again. 'Leave it with me, Raj. I'll talk to her. If all else fails, she'll go to boarding school.'

The expression on Raj's face was one of profound relief.

It took Michael and Raj most of the day to examine the sugarcane operations. Towards three in the afternoon, they stood discussing the problem they were experiencing with a plant variety known as 310. While it yielded a much higher sucrose content, 310 was susceptible to a black fungal disease known as smut. Michael noticed his father heading towards them. *What the hell does he want?*

Raj saw him as well. Judging by his expression, it was a sight he found very surprising.

Joe King started shouting while he was still some distance from them. 'Don't think you can come back to my farm and just take over.'

'Shit!' Michael swore softly. He waited until his father reached them. 'Someone has to help,' he said.

'I want you off this property,' Joe ranted.

Michael could smell the whisky. 'Have another drink,' he suggested sarcastically.

Joe pulled a flask from his pocket. 'Don't mind if I do.' He tilted it to his mouth, staggered slightly, then stared belligerently at Raj. 'You still take orders from me.'

'Yes, sir.' Raj touched his forehead in a gesture of respect.

Joe nodded, satisfied. 'Good.' A long pause followed. 'Carry on then,' he said finally. His gaze came back to Michael. 'You'd better remember it too. This is *my* farm.'

Michael simply stared at him.

Under his son's unwavering look, Joe ran out of words. He turned and walked unsteadily away.

'How often does he come into the fields?' Michael asked once his father was out of earshot.

'Never, Mr Michael. Goodness, I do not remember the last time.'

Michael nodded slowly. 'Since it's highly unlikely that he'll remember, we too will forget that my father was here today.' He started walking and Raj hurried to catch him. 'Come, Raj. We must find Balram and tell him that *his* father is too old to work any more.'

Raj permitted himself a short laugh. 'Mr Michael,' he said, 'you make too much fun of such an old man.'

'Mr Raj,' Michael said, only half-joking, 'you have worked with the English for long enough now to know that we only make fun of those we love.'

They went in search of Balram and found him supervising the cutting of newly burnt cane. It was hot, heavy and dirty work but, once the fire had gone through, they only had seventy-two hours to get the cane cut, stacked and delivered to the mill, before the sucrose levels dropped and the crop's value fell dramatically. Balram joined them, casting a worried look at the sky. Rain was threatening. A shower would not be a problem, might even clean things up a bit, but anything prolonged could prove disastrous. 'Welcome home, Mr Michael.'

Michael acknowledged the greeting but could see the man was busy. 'Come to the house when you've finished this evening. I have something important to discuss.'

Balram responded with an enthusiastic side-to-side wagging of his head.

Michael grinned back at him. 'I see you are ahead of me, Balram, as a good manager should be.'

Balram's smile grew wider but then he looked anxiously at the cane field. 'If you will excuse me please, Mr Michael.'

Michael let him go. 'A good man and a son to make you proud,' he told Raj.

'Balram will not let you down.'

Out on the road they could see the school bus stopping at the gate. 'I'll speak to Tessa now,' Michael said to Raj. 'I suggest you make yourself scarce.'

The old Sikh looked at him anxiously. 'This will not make trouble for my son?'

'No,' Michael assured him. 'But it's sure as hell not going to sit well with my sister.'

Tessa saw her older brother walking towards them. As usual, Gregor and Sally were some way ahead, discussing school, friends or anything else that took their fancy. Tessa could not imagine what Sally found interesting in their eight-year-old brother. He was far too young to be of any consequence. Come to that, Sally's conversation was also boring. She had only just become aware of boys and the mere mention of one had her stuttering and blushing furiously. Tessa sometimes wondered what Sally's reaction might be if she told her sister even a fraction of her own experiences. Miss Goody-Two-Shoes would probably die of shock. She frowned at Michael's approach. There was something purposeful in his walk and Tessa knew, way before he reached them, that he had come to speak with her.

'What does *he* want?' she asked herself. Perhaps he'd found the bottle of cane spirit in her room, or the cigarettes she kept hidden in a drawer. Maybe he'd discovered the magazines she'd stuffed under her mattress. Tessa hoped not. They contained the most sexually explicit photographs she had ever seen. Just looking at the graphic illustrations made her wildly excited. She'd come across them years ago while snooping in her father's room. He had lots in the back of a drawer. It was a laugh at first, the people looked so undignified and silly. She borrowed a couple, intending to show them to Sally. Instead, Tessa took them to her own room. Turning the pages, she was at first scared, then excited, as unfamiliar sensations gripped her. Acting instinctively, Tessa had put her fingers at the centre point of these pulsating feelings, crying out in amazement as they immediately strengthened. Without fully understanding what was happening, she masturbated herself to an orgasm. It was better than anything she'd ever known.

All her life, Tessa had overdone experiences she enjoyed. Whenever the feelings started up, Tessa could always find somewhere private to oblige them. Her young mind made some of the connections, that the things she saw in the magazine promised to yield even better sensations. Tessa had understood at an early age that men and women were built to do such things to each other. The magazines merely confirmed it. And Tessa was more than ready to try them.

She particularly associated these things with her father, and the string of women he never bothered to hide. One steamy Sunday afternoon, when her mother had taken Sally and Gregor to the beach and Michael was away fishing at Cape Vidal, Tessa crept to her father's window and watched, spellbound. It wasn't him who fascinated Tessa. It was the ecstatic look on the woman's face that held her attention. The things Tessa did to herself were terrific but this was obviously better. And her father had it in his power to cause such rapture. Without being aware of it, Tessa began to flirt with him.

At first, Joe had reacted with amused indifference. Of all his children, Tessa was the only one who ever took notice of him. Her sudden coquettishness was put down to being quite normal in a young girl on the threshold of maturity. He had no idea his daughter was aching with desire and had no way of controlling it. One Thursday afternoon, however, during the school holidays, when there were only the two of them in the house, she had come to his room and woken him from an alcohol-induced sleep. Joe had, as usual, woken with an erection. Things just got out of hand.

Joe blamed the whisky. If he'd been sober nothing would have happened. In the back of his mind, however, he was aware that Tessa knew exactly what she was doing that day.

The memory of that afternoon, or the little of it he could recall, burned him with shame. The old Joe resurfaced long enough to force him to confront the fact that he had sunk as low as he could go. He'd vowed never again and avoided Tessa as much as possible. He'd almost managed to convince himself that he'd imagined the whole thing when she, once again, came into his room at the wrong time. Up until then, he'd been sober enough to be wary but on this second occasion he'd been blind drunk.

When Michael burst in on them three years ago, nothing had taken place except for the whisky. But Joe knew where they were heading because he had consumed enough alcohol to lower his inhibitions.

For all his disgust at his actions, Joe still found excuses. She didn't seem like his daughter; he was not part of the family; she was like a stranger; she certainly didn't look eleven, sixteen more like. And one abiding certainty. Tessa knew what she was doing.

Tessa had known and she hadn't. Wilful, always ready to buck the system, full of aggressive feelings of not fitting in, when puberty and all the confusing emotions that went with it came calling, Tessa was too young to deal with it. She got her wires crossed. To her mind the erratic and antisocial behaviour of her father was synonymous with the freedom of adulthood. Her father's approval of her was vital. And then there were all those fires sending messages she couldn't control. She knew what she was doing up to a point, beyond that she was as helpless as a moth drawn to flame.

The word incest meant little to Tessa. The word *fuck* did. She would become aroused just by saying it. However, when Michael raised the threat of a convent, she knew he was serious. She never went near her father again. But Tessa saw no reason why her enjoyment should stop. Word soon went around the school. Tessa King was a sure thing.

Michael reached Gregor and Sally and fell in beside them. Behind them, Tessa's lip curled when she saw Sally's hand seek his. *Stupid girl*! She idolised Michael.

'You two go on ahead,' Michael prompted Sally and Gregor. 'I need to have a chat to Tessa.'

Tessa heard him. 'I don't want to talk,' she shot back. 'You can't make me.'

Michael silenced her with a look over his shoulder. Sally and Gregor, with a glance of smug satisfaction between them, kept walking. Tessa's steps slowed, then stopped. Michael left the road and sat on the short grassy verge. 'Here.' He patted the ground beside him.

Reluctantly, she joined him. 'I can leave any time I want.'

'Sure,' he agreed. 'But first, listen for a minute.'

He looked at her face. The twins were beautiful, of that there was no doubt. Dark curly hair which Sally kept up in a ponytail and Tessa allowed to flow around her face and shoulders. Dark eyes.

In Sally's a deep compassion and intelligence, Tessa's were hard, calculating and distant. Both had flawless complexions, wide and well-formed lips, high cheekbones and their father's aristocratic high-bridged nose. Michael sighed inwardly. What was it that made them so different?

'Raj is worried that you are flirting with one of his sons.' There was no point in beating about the bush with Tessa. 'You will stop it immediately. It's unfair.'

Tessa tossed her head. 'Raj is a stupid old man who should have retired years ago.'

'Raj,' Michael told her softly, in a voice hard with authority, 'is not a stupid old man. He's the man who has been running UBejane for the past three years with no help from anyone. He's the man who puts food on your table and clothes on your back. He's a man for whom you will show respect or, by Jesus, you'll know about it from me. Is that clear, Missy?'

If Michael had lost his temper and shouted Tessa could have handled it. She had very quickly learned that men were at their most vulnerable when they were emotionally off balance. She glanced at Michael's face, looking for a weak spot. She saw none. His eyes were steady and calm.

'Right or wrong, it is against the law of this country to have a relationship with a person of a different colour. I'm warning you, Tessa. Leave that boy alone.'

'Tell that to father,' Tessa shot back. Then wished she hadn't.

'You, of all people, should know that our father has no scruples or common decency,' he reminded her quietly. 'I will not speak of this again but you're on very thin ice, young lady. One more complaint about your behaviour and it's off to a convent. No more warnings. Do you understand?'

'Mother would never agree.'

'I wouldn't count on that, little sister. I believe I could convince her.'

The threat was made with no inflection. He was stating a fact and she knew he would follow through.

Michael rose and stood looking down at her. 'Believe me, Tessa, I've had enough of your non-sense. I will not allow you to bring disgrace to this family. Keep your bloody hormones under control. There'll be plenty of time for that later.'

'And just who do you think you are?' she spat back. 'You don't control this family. Stop acting like you're my father.'

Something dark stirred in Michael's eyes. 'That,' he said with deadly seriousness, 'is the last thing I would do.'

Tessa scrambled up and stood, hands on hips, eyes blazing. 'What do you know?' she cried out, losing control. 'I can't help the way I am.' She turned and ran up the road, leaving her school bag lying in the dust.

Michael picked it up and stared thoughtfully after her, his heart full of sadness. What she had said was true. She probably couldn't help herself. 'What should I do?' he asked himself. But no answer came.

EIGHT

Dyson could see that his father was anxious to speak with him and he thought he knew why. Word of his involvement with a new wing of the African National Congress, Umkhonto we Sizwe, a division that proposed violence as a means to end apartheid, would have reached his father's ears. The tried and trusted word-of-mouth network, used for centuries as a means of spreading information, would have seen to it. Wilson Mpande was opposed to violence and tended towards the same views Michael had recently expressed, that apartheid would fall under the weight of economic sanctions. Dyson disagreed. He did, however, draw the line at some of the more revolutionary organisations, like the armed wing of the Pan African Congress, POGO, which promoted uncoordinated attacks on whites with its catchcry 'One settler, one bullet'. Dyson believed, as did the Umkhonto we Sizwe, that the way to bring apartheid down was to render parts of South Africa ungovernable. These were the meetings he attended twice a month, secret gatherings to discuss how best to bring about unrest in the townships. These were the meetings he could not discuss with Michael. Nor did he wish to speak of them with his father.

When they finally sat down to talk, his father's opening words came as something of a shock. 'The king is dying.'

'I have heard nothing of this.'

'It is not generally known.'

'What ails the king?'

Wilson clucked his tongue with disapproval. 'That which comes in a bottle.'

King Cyprian's addiction to alcohol was well known among his subjects and it had become increasingly clear to the Zulu nation that unless he stopped drinking, the king would soon go the way of his father, Solomon, who had died of drink-related illness in 1933 at the age of forty. If Cyprian died, the heir apparent was too young to assume his royal responsibilities. This meant that a regent would be appointed. While this in itself was not a problem, the most obvious man for the position, Prince Israel Mcwayizeni, was no friend of Cyprian's main adviser, Chief Mangosuthu Gatsha Buthelezi. With anarchy and chaos high on the ANC agenda, a rift in the royal house was the last thing the Zulus needed.

'How bad is he?'

'He is sick here.' Wilson touched just under his right ribcage. 'It is his liver. The doctors call it cirrhosis. He may live for a few years but our king is already too ill to rule.'

'And no-one can take over until he dies.'

'Which means our people are virtually leader-less and likely to face even greater hardships,' Wilson said bitterly. 'This could not have come at a worse time.' He leaned back against the trunk of an avocado pear tree under which they were sitting. The slight movement caused an overripe fruit to drop near them. The outer skin split on impact and soft flesh, almost black with age, exploded from it.

Dyson gazed at it, waiting for his father to speak again, his mind busy with the implications of what he had just learned. The president of the ANC, Albert Lutuli, although a Zulu, had been born and raised in Rhodesia. Nelson Mandela, commander-in-chief of Umkhonto we Sizwe, was Xhosa. It seemed to Dyson that within the larger framework of a fight for equality in South Africa there was one glaring omission – the Zulus had no champion.

'Tell me of the royal house,' Wilson Mpande eventually asked his son, smiling a little. 'Let me see if absence has affected your memory.'

Dyson screwed up his forehead as he turned his mind backwards, over nearly 150 years. As a boy, his father had often quizzed him on Zulu history, explaining that it was only through knowledge and discussion that Zulus could hope to retain their pride and sense of identity. Without this, they would revert to clan rivalry and the great nation forged by Shaka would cease to exist. It surprised Dyson that his father still felt the need to test him. But he was happy enough to oblige.

'We come from the Qwabe people,' he began

251

slowly. 'We take our name, Zulu, from the second son of the great Malandela, our illustrious ancestor. The word Zulu means that which the white people call "heaven". Our first king was Shaka. Before this, he was chief of the Zulu clan. It was he who ordered the stamping of the thorns.'

Wilson Mpande nodded. The stamping of the thorns. Shaka had ordered his warriors to remove their sandals and stamp on *nkunzana* thorns which had been scattered over a gathering place. Shaka believed that men were impeded by footwear on the battle ground. To avoid this the soles of their feet had to become hard. It was the very beginning of the Zulu nation. In 1816, when Shaka became their chief, the Zulu clan had not been particularly large, numbering no more than a couple of thousand. Ten years later, Shaka's kingdom spread over some 50,000 square kilometres and the population was thought to be in the vicinity of 100,000. Shaka encouraged other clans to join his. Most of the smaller ones saw the sense of strength through unity. Those who resisted were quickly defeated in battle.

'Who were Shaka's parents?' Wilson asked.

'His father was Senzangakona and his mother one they called Nandi.'

'Why was their son named Shaka?'

'Nandi and Senzangakona had *hlobonga* but,' Dyson allowed a small grin, '*kwehl' itonsi.*'

His father frowned at his brevity. Pregnancy, before a man takes a woman as his wife, was still considered to be scandalous. 'A drop descended is

252

not a laughing matter,' he said severely. 'Senzangakona was a chief, Nandi the daughter of a chief. Their behaviour was unseemly.'

'Sorry, Father. When Nandi discovered she was pregnant she pretended to be suffering from *itshaka*. That is where the great king's name came from.'

'What is *itshaka*?'

'It is a stomach illness, Father. It is caused by a beetle.'

Wilson nodded. His son remembered well. 'Why was Shaka such a great king?'

Dyson replied promptly, 'Because he merged many small clans into one mighty Zulu nation. Before Shaka, the clans numbered in their hundreds.'

'How long did he reign?'

Again, Dyson answered without hesitation, 'Twelve years.'

'How did he die?'

'Dingane, his half-brother, assassinated him.'

'And what was said of Dingane?'

'He had the heart of a dog and the nature of a witch.'

Wilson Mpande broke off his questions to light a pipe. When it was burning to his satisfaction, he resumed. 'So why did Dingane become the second king? Why not his brother Mhlangana? You will remember, it was Mhlangana who jumped over Shaka's body, not Dingane.'

'A man may not rule when his spear is red with blood,' Dyson quoted the old taboo. 'It was said that Dingane had not taken part in the actual stabbing.'

'Ha!' Wilson scoffed. 'And did Mhlangana kill Shaka on his own?'

'Probably not, but Dingane had him assassinated too, possibly to hide the truth.'

'Who broke the rope?'

Dyson had been waiting for this question. 'Mpande, after whom our family was named.'

'Tell me of him,' Wilson Mpande commanded.

'Mpande was Dingane's half-brother. When the new king had all his brothers killed so that his right to the throne could not be challenged, Mpande went into hiding, eventually crossing the Tugela River to seek protection from the Boers. It was not Mpande's intention to divide our people. He fled south to save his own life. By this time many were sick of Dingane who was constantly forcing them into battles against the Boers, battles they could not win. When Mpande went south, 17,000 people followed him, breaking the rope that had bound the clans together as a single Zulu nation.'

'What happened then?'

Dyson couldn't understand why he was being tested like this. He knew the Zulu history backwards, so what was his father's purpose? However, he answered the question patiently. 'The Boers didn't want him on their side of the Tugela but they saw him as a chance to get rid of Dingane who was friends with the British. At first they treated him with respect, even giving Mpande a grand title – Reigning Prince of the Emigrant Zulus.' Dyson shook his head. 'That was the only sweet plum in their basket of fruit. The Boers told Mpande they could spare him no land south of the river, at the same time warning that as soon as Dingane was defeated they would also take the land to the north. If he wanted his own kingdom he had to join the Boers in defeating Dingane and the English.'

'Which he did?'

'Yes. There was little choice. But the Boers had no intention of losing more men. They sat back and allowed Mpande to challenge Dingane on his own.'

'Our ancestor proved to be a great warrior.' Wilson's face shone with pride.

'As you well know, Father. Mpande's *impi* defeated Dingane's in the hills near Magudu.'

'And he became our third king?'

Dyson nodded slowly. 'But the Boers tricked him. Claiming the spoils of war, they drove almost half of the Zulu cattle back to their lands, took our children as slaves, then tried to seize more land north of the Tugela.'

'And did they succeed?'

'No, Father. They were too busy arguing with the English. In the end, it was the Boers who left.'

'Quickly now. How long did Mpande rule?'

'Thirty-two years.'

'Who succeeded him?'

'The slandered one, Cetshwayo.'

'To be followed by?'

'The satisfier of the Zulus, Dinuzulu.'

'Then?'

'Then Solomon. And now Cyprian.'

'And Cyprian is dying,' Wilson stated flatly.

Dyson bowed his head. The death of a king, especially one who had ruled for twenty years, was very bad news. 'What are those close to him saying?'

Wilson Mpande considered his answer for some minutes. 'They are saying it is time to bring back the *inkatha yezwe.*'

'Here it comes,' Dyson thought. 'This is where we're heading.' His father had referred to the sacred coil of grass that had perished in 1879, when the English set fire to Zulu military barracks in the valley where the kings were buried. The Inkatha ka Zulu movement, started in 1921 and fallen into decline by 1937, had been named after this symbol of Zulu unity.

His father puffed on his pipe. 'Which would you prefer?' he asked quietly. 'To somehow buy back our own land and live peacefully? Or to encourage disruption so that your children know nothing else? When the day comes, as it surely will, that this country achieves majority rule, how will it be possible to govern a people who know nothing but violence? Armed confrontation would spread across South Africa like a plague and all it touches will remain forever affected. Is this the future you advocate? A land of law-breakers? A land of people who know only anger? We must think beyond today. Learn from our history. Shaka proved that strength comes from standing together in unity.'

'Inkatha has been tried before, Father. It didn't work then and it won't work now.'

Wilson shook his head sadly. 'Try to see, my son. Before it is too late.'

'I do see, Father. I see that unless we act now, tomorrow and the next day and all the days after that will remain as they are today.'

'If you are caught . . .'

'I am a Zulu,' Dyson interrupted. 'If necessary, I will die like one.'

Wilson sighed and remained silent. Although he did not agree with his son's beliefs, his eyes registered their silent approval of the proud words.

Jackson Mpande watched his father and older brother deep in conversation, jealousy burning a fire deep in his gut. Since Dyson had returned the day before, his father had made it plain that he regarded Dyson as a man but Jackson was still a boy. Before his brother came back, Jackson had been treated as the elder. He resented being demoted.

The world had turned and Jackson and his friends turned with it, catching a glimpse of the future. Their parents, however, seemed reluctant to go forward, preferring to stick with the familiarity of tradition. Even though his father had consistently tried to instil an understanding and respect for the old ways, Jackson could see that these were changing. As far as he was concerned, they couldn't go fast enough. Traditions could not rebuild the Zulu nation.

Jackson was fiercely Zulu. He was one of an emerging new breed who carried not the glory of past battles in his heart but rather the dream of an independent Zululand, free from the choking restraints of the whites, free to rule themselves and free to demand that they be treated as equals. He did not see himself as an idealist. To Jackson, freedom and independence were attainable. All that stood in their way was apartheid.

It was common knowledge that many young men were leaving South Africa, heading for countries further north to undergo training in guerrilla warfare. The best, those with leadership potential, were sent on to Russia and China for specialised training. An armed struggle was coming and Jackson wanted to be a part of it.

Excited as he was by the idea, Jackson knew he first needed an education. It was hard for him, only fourteen and filled with all the impatience of a young man. So, while accepting that he had to hang around for at least another two years, Jackson grew frustrated and difficult to handle.

He left the compound and wandered aimlessly down the road as far as the two large rocks. He scrambled onto one and sat staring, without seeing, off towards the Indian Ocean. Here, he often came to brood on fate's fickle finger. As far as Jackson was concerned, if things had turned out differently all those years ago, then his life, and that of his family, would now be one of luxury and eminence.

Jackson firmly believed that it should be *his* family in the royal house. *His* father as king. And Jackson a prince.

He knew his Zulu history as well as Dyson. His forefather, Mpande, had taken at least twenty wives and sired nearly one hundred children. Although Mpande had not named a 'great wife', she who would bear the next king, Nqgumbazi, his first wife, was a chief's daughter and her firstborn son – Cetshwayo – was considered to be heir apparent. However, Cetshwayo fell from Mpande's favour and he named another son, Mbuyazi, as the next king. Cetshwayo's reaction had been swift. He declared war on his brother.

The Tugela River, scene of so much fear and slaughter in the past, once again ran red with blood. Mbuyazi and five of his brothers were among the fallen. When Cetshwayo was shown Mbuyazi's body, he jumped over it. It was a symbolic act which declared that he was now, in his eyes and those of every Zulu who witnessed the event, the rightful heir to the royal throne.

Jackson's lip curled. He remembered the stories of how Cetshwayo had returned in triumph, expecting his father's acceptance. Regally dressed, his loin cover the skin of a silver jackal, his buttocks hidden by the skin of a genet, around his head a band of otter skin hung with tassels of blue monkey's fur and, as proclamation of his royal status, a single crane feather tucked into it. He also carried a gun. When Mpande heard that his favourite son was dead he refused to see Cetshwayo.

Seemingly unperturbed by this rebuttal, Cetshwayo was content to bide his time, knowing that his reputation as a leader was growing all the time. He was even praised in verse for his prowess on the battle field: *The wild beast which looks up at its father's sons and they bow down.* As time went by, his patient acceptance of Mpande's rejection caused a new line in his praise-poem to be written: *The one who remains silent and provokes quarrels with no-one.* A more impatient heir-apparent might have assisted fate to hasten the day he became king. Cetshwayo was content to wait.

In time, Mpande's grief subsided and he fell deeply in love with the youngest of his wives whom he affectionately called Somapa – the thighs that become the centre of attention. She bore him a son named Mthonga. It was this child who was Jackson's direct blood link with Mpande. However, when the royal court realised that their ruler was showing signs of favouritism towards the young Mthonga, they became uneasy. Cetshwayo, without doubt, would defend his position to the death. More feuding and blood-letting was the last thing anybody wanted so they gave their blessing that Mthonga be assassinated. But the boy escaped, seeking protection from the Boers. Delighted that such a high-born Zulu had come to them, they set about grooming him to be the next king, confident that he would become their puppet.

Cetshwayo could see what the Boers intended and made his own deal with them. He guaranteed Mthonga's safety and offered a stretch of land in north Zululand in return for recognition of himself as heir to the royal throne.

Jackson's proud, young face reflected his bitterness. But for Cetshwayo, he might have been a prince, or even a king.

Voices interrupted his thoughts and he quickly flattened himself on top of the rock. It was the young white boy from the big house and one of his twin sisters. Jackson couldn't tell the girls apart except that one usually wore her hair long and flowing. The two went past where Jackson lay, oblivious of his presence. Jackson's English was excellent. They were discussing the other girl, the one called Tessa, and he heard the boy say, '. . . and if Michael finds out half of it she'll be sent away. Even the Standard 10 boys say she's easy.'

'Gregor,' Jackson heard the girl protest. 'Don't say that about your sister.'

'I don't care,' he said hotly. 'She's as bad as our father. I'll bet Michael won't put up with it. I hope she's sent away. I hope . . .' His voice faded as they walked away.

Jackson lay immobile. His sympathies were very definitely with the twin called Tessa. She was obviously a rebel like himself. He was about to sit up when he spied the other sister. She was coming up the road, arms held tightly around her body. Jackson watched carefully. There was something angry in the way she walked, as if she carried a great sorrow or resentment. Or perhaps, as Jackson did, rejection. Tessa disappeared between the boulders. Jackson waited, listening carefully. When she spoke, he jumped with fright, not expecting her to appear behind him.

'Why are you spying on me?' She stood on top of the boulder, arms folded, looking down at him.

'I wasn't.' He met her eyes defiantly. Just because

she was white was no reason for him to be fearful. Besides, she didn't look cross.

'Yes you were.' Tessa jumped down next to him, hitching her skirt over her knees and pointing back towards the cane fields. 'I saw you from way back there.' She stared at him, a small frown on her face. 'You're Jackson aren't you?'

He nodded.

'I'm Tessa.'

'I know who you are, Miss Tessa.'

She smiled and bit a knuckle. 'I said Tessa, not Miss Tessa.'

'I'm supposed to call you Miss Tessa.'

'I know.' She was scrutinising his face. 'You're very black,' she said candidly.

'You're very white,' he responded quickly.

Tessa laughed. Then scowled. 'Oh shit!' she said, shocking Jackson. 'There's that pompous arse Michael. Quick, down.' She flung herself flat on the rock and Jackson did the same.

They lay like that for several minutes, listening. Michael passed between the boulders and on towards the main house. When he was well out of earshot, Tessa sat up again. 'What do you do here?'

'I live here.'

'Yes, but don't you work?'

'I go to school.'

Tessa pulled a face. 'So do I. How come you aren't at school today?'

'I was. We get out earlier than you.'

'Lucky you. I wish I didn't have to go at all.'

Jackson relaxed. This girl was different from

other white people. She was treating him as an equal. 'Don't you like school?'

'No. Do you?'

'It's okay.'

She was still studying his face. 'Do you have *hlobonga*?' she asked suddenly, causing him to blush.

'Yes,' he stammered.

'Do you like it?'

'What kind of a question is that?' Jackson was becoming acutely uncomfortable. Her eyes had narrowed. He was suddenly suspicious of her motives.

'It's a perfectly ordinary question. I asked if you like *hlobonga*? Do you?'

She was wriggling as she sat. Jackson didn't have much experience but he suddenly realised where the conversation was going. This girl really was different. 'Yes,' he said, watching her squirm her bottom against the hard boulder.

'How do they do it?' Tessa asked. 'Show me.'

Jackson threw her a sharp look but he didn't think she was setting him up. 'Like this.' He shut his legs firmly together and tensed his thigh muscles.

Tessa reached over and pushed a finger between his clamped legs, feeling the flesh quiver at her touch. 'Is that it? You put your thing here?'

'Yes.' Jackson's voice was unsteady.

She rubbed her finger slowly up and down. 'It can't be much fun for the girl.'

He shrugged. *Hlobonga* was designed for a man's pleasure, not that of a woman. Tessa's hand lay on his leg. He was becoming aroused. She would notice. He knew he should get up and go, but he didn't want to.

'That's not fair,' Tessa said, her voice soft and dreamy. 'You have all the fun. The girl should like it too.' She had a small smile on her face. Very deliberately, she brushed her hand against the front of his shorts, enjoying his obvious discomfort.

Jackson knew that she had felt his erection. He felt a hot flush of embarrassment rise to his cheeks. He had no idea what to do or say. Suddenly, she took her hand away and leaned back on both arms, staring at him, her firm breasts provocatively thrust forward in a well-practised display.

'I've never had *hlobonga*,' she said.

Is this an invitation? He remained silent.

'I don't think I would like it.'

Jackson said nothing.

'Do you think I'd like it?'

He shrugged, miserably mute.

She gave a light tinkling laugh. 'You want to do it to me don't you?'

She was playing with him. His earlier bravado collapsed. The calls were all hers and she knew it. He would tell her to go to hell. Instead, he heard himself meekly say, 'Yes.'

Again the little laugh. 'You're honest. I like that.' She leaned towards him. 'I've heard that Africans are bigger than white men.' She put her hand back on his bare leg. 'Is that true?'

Her skin burned into his flesh. 'I do not know, I've never seen a white man's . . .' He didn't know what to call it in English.

'Dick,' she said, staring into his eyes.

'Deek?'

'Can you keep a secret?' She seemed to change the subject.

'Of course.'

'Do you know what fuck means?'

Jackson had heard the word and knew what it meant. To hear it come from a girl's lips was shocking. 'Yes.'

He nearly fell off the boulder at her next words. 'Would you like to fuck me?'

His penis was straining painfully against his shorts. His heart was beating wildly as an uninvited wave of butterflies took over his stomach. 'Yes,' he said hoarsely. 'But it is against the law.'

She pouted. 'It's a stupid law.' Her nails scratched his leg. 'You have a dick and I have a hole. They don't care what colour they are. Why should we?'

Jackson's head was spinning. Her words were too direct for him to know how to deal with them. She seemed devoid of any shame. Then he thought, 'What if this is a set-up?' He looked wildly around, half expecting to see policemen.

'Are you afraid of me?'

She was watching him intently, that half-smile back on her face. He knew, suddenly, that she was deadly serious. 'Show me your hole,' he burst out, made bold himself by her deliberate vulgarity.

Tessa unbuttoned her school blouse and cupped one lace-covered breast with her hand. Jackson was unmoved. Breasts were an everyday sight. It was what she had between her legs that fascinated him.

She'd offered more than just *hlobonga*. As he watched her face the small pink tip of her tongue darted out to wet her lips. Sitting opposite him on the rock, she spread her legs and, taking his hand, placed it against her panties. He could feel her warmth through the thin material. Reaching out, she felt the front of his shorts. 'My,' Tessa breathed. 'What a big boy you are.'

All Jackson's reason told him he was playing with fire. White girls were off limits. Especially the daughter of his father's employer. But she drew aside the elastic of her panties and guided his finger into her. He had never been this far with a girl before. She felt soft and moist. 'Would you like to put your dick into there?' Her breathing was unsteady.

Jackson simply nodded.

'Show it to me,' Tessa demanded.

Using one hand, he tried to unbutton his straining flies. Impatient, she knocked his fumbling fingers away and drew him out. He groaned as her hand closed around him.

Tessa's eyes were wide with carnal interest. 'My God, you are huge.' She pushed his hand away from her panties and jumped up. Jackson looked bewildered, his penis sticking straight out of his shorts like a staff. 'Down here,' she panted, jumping off the rock.

As he watched, she pulled off her panties, hoisted her skirt and lay on the bare ground, legs spread. Thick black pubic hair glistened in the sun and plump pink lips parted invitingly. She was playing with herself, half-shut eyes watching him. 'Come on,' she beseeched.

Jackson realised that she was gripped by the same kind of need that sometimes came over him. He could wait no longer. Jumping down, he stepped out of his shorts and fell on her. Tessa gave a cry of shock as she took the full length of him and then, raising her legs around his waist, not paying any heed to the rough surface of the ground against her back and shoulders, she rocked with him, exhorting him to go deeper, faster, rougher.

When Jackson came inside her it was truly the best moment of all his fourteen years. But he pulled back almost immediately, fearfully expecting her to cry or scream, somehow to blame him. She did none of those things. She lay very still, smiling. Then she breathed, 'Yesss!' and reached for him.

Tessa went straight to her room via the French doors off the verandah, avoiding both her mother and Michael. She stripped off her clothes and stood naked, looking at herself in the full-length mirror on the door of her wardrobe. She could smell Jackson's sweat, and his semen. She could feel the soreness from his large penis. Her gaze travelled up to her face and she saw the small smile of satisfaction there. It had been better than anything she had ever had before. She'd heard that Africans were huge down there. It was true. Jackson was enormous. She shivered at the memory of him thrusting into her. She was becoming aroused again. Crossing to the door, she locked it. Her school bag was on the floor just inside the room but she ignored it. Instead, she went to her bed and lay down, fingers seeking the little bud of pleasure. This time she did not need the pornographic magazines from under the mattress. This time all she needed was Jackson's promise to come to her room later this evening. It was a promise he'd given readily.

Tessa gave a sigh as release flooded through her. For a few minutes she just lay there, savouring the languid peace that always followed. Finally, humming a little, she rose, pulled on a robe, picked up her wash bag and headed for the bathroom. She passed Sally's room. As usual, the door was open and, as usual, Sally's head was bent over her homework. Tessa lounged against the door. 'Hi!'

Sally looked up. 'Hi!' she responded, surprised. Tessa rarely went out of her way to speak to her. 'Are you having a bath already?'

'Yes.' Tessa reached one hand behind her head and fluffed and shook out her dark curls, arching and stretching so that the robe fell open revealing her nakedness. She made no attempt to cover up. 'I smell like a kaffir.'

'Tessa,' Sally admonished. 'That's not very nice.'

'Yes it is,' Tessa said smugly. 'It's very, very nice.'

Sally looked at her, puzzled.

Tessa laughed and turned to go. 'Don't worry about it, sis. Just take my word for it.' Then she was gone.

Sally shrugged. Half the time she was at a loss to know what Tessa was talking about. A faint smell hung in the air. It was not unpleasant, just earthy and noticeable. It took her a moment to identify it. It was the odour of African sweat, quite different from white people's. Sally stared at the doorway where Tessa had stood. *She wouldn't . . . she couldn't. Not even Tessa would go that far, surely?* Sally shuddered. She was under no illusions about her sister.

As Tessa lay in the warm scented water, she experienced a radical mood swing. It had happened before, after she'd been with one of the boys at school. A sudden switch from euphoria to despair. *Why am I like this? None of the other girls are. What's wrong with me?* Tears welled in her eyes. At times like this, Tessa felt so much hatred for Sally she could almost imagine killing her. *It's not fair. Why me and not Sally?*

For most of the time Tessa honestly believed that she carried an exciting secret no-one else knew, and that she was daring and sophisticated. When a boy singled her out for special attention, especially one of the seniors, she convinced herself that she was popular. Never for one moment did she suspect that practically the whole school knew of her antics and were laughing behind her back. Tessa wanted acceptance and so, when the inevitable hand crept up her skirt, she gave in because she thought it was a way of getting it. And yes, she liked it too.

But once or twice, like now, when she questioned why she was so different from others her age, she would cast around miserably in her mind, trying to find a reason. Inevitably, it always came back to her father. He was flawed. So was she. The thought left her weak with self-pity.

By the time she returned to her room, however, Tessa's mood had swung again. Jackson was coming to see her tonight. And Tessa could hardly wait.

At dinner, Claire noticed that her usually fractious and surly daughter was almost amenable. Sally was unusually silent. Claire wrongly deduced that the two had had an argument from which, judging by her good humour, Tessa had emerged as the winner.

Gregor chattered, oblivious of the mood reversal in his sisters.

Michael ate quickly and excused himself, his mind on other things. The weather had held, there was no wind and they had two blocks of cane to burn off that evening.

Joe came awake reluctantly, his mind blearily anticipating the inevitable hangover. It was pitch dark and it took a moment for Joe to register that he was not in bed. Groaning, he sat up, willing his mind to work. Blindly reaching out a hand, he felt the bamboo-like stalk of sugar cane. So, he was in the fields. *That's right.* He could recall stumbling into one after his earlier encounter with Raj and Michael. It wasn't the first time he'd been incapable of making it back to his room. 'God!' Joe muttered, as a familiar surge of guilt hit him. 'I'm supposed to be on the wagon.' It was then that he smelled the smoke.

Not unduly alarmed, Joe took his time. He was still trying to stand when he heard the distinctive sound. He tried to work out where exactly the fire was but, having no idea which field he was in, his senses were completely disoriented. He knew that they would start lots of small fires along one whole side of the block but from where he stood, with the plants towering over him, Joe had no way of telling which way that was.

He was becoming slightly worried. He had never forgotten the agony of burning flesh on his legs and had developed a pathological fear of fire. Turning slowly, he could see nothing. The crackling roar of the fire grew louder, the sound like a tornado. Once the small fires caught and combined, an unstoppable wall of flame would race from one side of the block to the other. He should run. But which way? 'Stay calm,' he told himself. At this time of year there was usually a breeze coming off the sea which meant that the fire should go in on the western side and back burn towards the coast.

As Joe worked this out the sky above suddenly exploded into an eerie red. Which way was east? How far into the field had he gone before falling asleep? 'Jesus Christ,' Joe yelled in a panic. The fire, fed by the air it sucked towards it, gathered speed.

To the east would be darker. Joe stumbled and cursed. The cane, planted along ridges, formed a wall, difficult enough to get through even by day.

In this particular field the rows appeared to run from north to south. Joe knew he'd never get out alive by running along the furrows – the breadth of the fire at his back told him he was smack in the middle of the northern and southern boundaries. The only way out was away from the flames.

Years of abuse had robbed his body of stamina. He blundered blindly on, stumbling and falling, forcing his way through the rigid stalks.

Flames were leaping thirty metres into the air. Sparks and burning trash were carried even higher by the swirling vortex of heat. Joe could see the way ahead now. Sugar cane, row after row of it, lit by the fire at his back. *Where's the fucking road?* He risked a look over his shoulder and a chill of horror froze his adrenalin-charged body. The flames were just behind him, roaring, reaching out, sucking in the air, greedy and eager. His air. 'Nooooo!' he screamed. At that moment, Joe knew he was going to die.

Feeling the hair on his head start to singe as the overwhelming heat closed in, Joe faced the fire, his fists bunched and a snarl on his face. Impartial to this gesture of defiance, the fire swept on. There was an instant of searing agony, a wild scream of anguish, and Joe King was no more.

A soft scratching at the flyscreen announced that Jackson had arrived. Tessa had been pacing her room, excited and anxious, convinced he would not come. She opened the door and drew him inside.

'No,' he whispered, as she went to close the door, 'I might have to leave quickly.'

Tessa shut the door. 'You won't,' she promised. 'Sally and Gregor are asleep. Mother thinks I am too. She's listening to the radio. Michael's out on a cane burn.' She reached out in the darkened room and found his arm. 'Come,' she murmured. Closing her fingers around his wrist, she led him to her bed.

Jackson went willingly, anxious as she to repeat this afternoon's experience. He had never known anything like it, nor anyone like Tessa. It was better by far than *hlobonga*. That they were both under age, that the laws in South Africa forbade sexual contact between the races, that she might fall pregnant, of these things he did not care. Her hands were reaching for him, demanding, hot hands. Jackson pulled his T-shirt over his head, unbuttoned his pants at the waist and, hooking thumbs under both shorts and underpants, pulled them down and stepped free. Naked and ready, he turned to her.

'Oohhh!' she breathed, fingers closing around him.

Jackson's hands slid under her nightdress. Tessa spread her legs a little so he could feel her. She wore no panties and his probing fingers found her moist and eager.

'Wait.' She stepped back, raising the flimsy garment over her head and flinging it impatiently away. She moved towards him in the darkness until his erect penis was touching her belly, then slowly, turning slightly, she swayed from side to side. The sensation of her soft skin rubbing against him was exquisite and he throbbed with desire. Neither of them could wait. Tessa was trembling from head to foot. 'Now,' she demanded. 'Do it to me now.'

He heard the rustle of bedclothes as she sat and reached up to his shoulders, drawing him forward and down as she lay back. He slid into her and she raised herself to meet him, legs going up and around his waist.

'Harder,' she breathed into his ear. 'Harder.'

Jackson pumped at Tessa with everything he had. He felt his climax gather, felt the liquid release running through his lower belly and genitals, there was a roaring in his head as a low groan escaped him.

'Sshhh!'

He rolled off her, suddenly aware that they were naked together and that he, Jackson Mpande, was in the house and the bed of the white *Nkosi*'s daughter. He, who only slept on a mat, was lying between the crisp white sheets of a white girl. He, who the government classified as little more than an animal, could reach over and put his hand on her private parts and she, who belonged to the untouchable ruling class, would open her legs and let him.

It was heady stuff to a fourteen-year-old boy. The chances of it happening were so remote, so impossible to even contemplate, that Jackson gave a grunt of genuine amusement.

'What is it?' Tessa hissed.

'I was just thinking,' he whispered into her ear,

'what our God-fearing government would do if they could see us now.'

The mental image of self-righteous outrage was more than Tessa could bear. She got a fit of the giggles. 'Fuck them,' she said, once the amusement passed. 'Who cares what they think.' And to prove it was of no concern to her, she reached for him again. Jackson responded eagerly. If she'd been older and thought about it, Tessa might have concluded that she'd met her sexual equal.

They found Joe King half an hour after the fire had gone through. As the flames raced towards the eastern side of the block, the Pondos positioned themselves along the roads. Carrying stout sticks with a heavy knob carved at one end, and holding flaming torches high, they waited, eyes darting to investigate every rustle, to follow every dark scurrying shadow. Deep within the fields resided all manner of delicacies. Snakes, cane rats, duiker, even larger buck. As all panicked and ran mindlessly before the wall of heat and noise, they proved easy victims to a well-aimed blow from a *knobkerrie*.

Once the fire had burned itself out, the Pondos ventured into the smouldering aftermath to look for any animals caught by the blaze. It was there they found Joe, although at the time no-one knew it was him. A runner was sent to find Michael. 'You come quickly, master.' The African was in such a state of agitation that Michael knew something was seriously wrong.

He could smell the charred flesh before he reached the body. Someone had been caught in the blaze. 'Get a torch up here,' he yelled.

It was the watch which gave Michael the first inkling of the identity of the corpse. Even then, he thought that his father could have lost the distinctive Rolex and that someone else might be wearing it. But the torchlight had also picked up a dull glint of something else on one of the charred fingers. It was a square gold signet ring. His father's.

Raj moved closer and saw the look of disbelief on Michael's face. 'This is very bad business, Master Michael, goodness yes.' He crouched next to Joe's still burning body. The Sikh had often seen bodies cremated on a funeral pyre but their spirits were always long gone. Raj stared for a long time at what was left of Joe King. Michael suspected he was praying. Finally, the Indian rose. 'It was not your fault.'

'I know.' Michael felt inexplicably angry with his father. An accident like this unsettled everyone.

'It would have been quick,' Raj said quietly.

'No,' Michael disagreed. 'You and I both know that even a couple of seconds in that kind of heat would have seemed an eternity. Look at him. No-one sleeps in that position. He must have been trying to get away.'

'Perhaps now he has found the peace which deserted him so long ago,' Raj suggested.

'Perhaps.' Michael shook his head. 'Though what the Almighty will make of him is anyone's guess.' He glanced towards the silent ring of awed

Pondos. 'Go now. There will be no more fires tonight.'

'And you, Master Michael?' Raj asked. 'What will you do?'

'Tell the family. Report it to the police. Phone the undertaker.' Michael's mind was busy with practicalities. It might have been a stranger lying there.

'I will arrange for the body to be taken to the sheds,' Raj offered. 'Do not concern yourself with that.'

Michael stared down at the horribly burned body of his father. There was no pain in him, no grief, only pity. He had hated his father. But he wouldn't have wished a death like this on anyone.

Claire heard the Land Rover pull up and went outside to ask why he was back so early. She knew something was amiss when Michael put his hand on her arm and drew her back into the house. 'There's been an accident,' he stated quietly. 'Joe is dead.'

Claire's hand flew to her mouth. 'Dead! What happened?'

'He was caught in the first fire we put in.'

She sat down heavily. 'Gracious! The poor man.'

Michael poured his mother a brandy and sat next to her. 'He was falling down drunk this afternoon. Must have been sleeping it off.'

'Do you think he suffered? Oh dear! I hope he didn't suffer.'

Michael remembered the twisted, charred remains, the smell of burning flesh. 'I should think the smoke got to him first. He would have passed out. Hard to tell.'

'I hope he didn't suffer,' she repeated, sighing a little. 'Where is he now?'

'Raj is taking him to the sheds. The police will have to be called. I don't think you should see the body, Mother.'

'You're probably right, darling.' Claire rose and cleared her throat. 'We've got things to do,' she said, suddenly brisk.

Michael nodded and stood up. 'I'll wake the others. They should be told immediately.'

Claire agreed. 'While you're doing that, I'll call the police.'

Michael stepped quietly into his young brother's room. Gregor would be the easiest to tell. He had often borne the brunt of Joe's ire and he, like Michael, hated Joe King. Gregor woke with Michael's light touch on his shoulder. He sat up immediately. 'What's happening?' he asked sleepily.

Michael sat on the bed. 'Bad news I'm afraid. Joe was killed tonight. We think he was sleeping in a cane field. The fire got him.'

'Oh!' Gregor sounded more surprised than anything.

'I've got to tell the girls. You can either join us in the lounge or go back to sleep.'

Gregor settled back under the covers. 'I think I'll sleep. I've got an English test tomorrow.'

Leaving the room, Michael reflected that, as

grief-stricken responses went, Gregor had probably dealt with the situation as well as could be expected.

Sally cried a little. 'What a horrible thing to happen. How's Mum taking it?'

Michael put his arms around her. 'She's fine. It would have been quick,' he assured her. 'He was probably asleep.'

'What's going to happen now?'

'About what? The funeral you mean?'

'No, the farm. Will we have to move?'

'Of course not. This is our family business. Things will go on as normal.'

Sally absorbed his words, smiled a little, then looked serious. 'I feel quite guilty, Michael. As if I should be more upset. After all, he was our father.'

'He was indeed,' Michael agreed. 'But only in a biological sense.'

Sally lay back against the pillow. 'I'm glad we don't have to leave UBejane. I don't want to live anywhere else.'

Michael squeezed her hand and sat for a few minutes with his own thoughts. 'Can you hear them, you old bastard? One is more concerned with school and the other about where she wants to live.'

He approached Tessa's room with reluctance. He could never predict how she would react to anything. The door opened silently and it took Michael a moment for his eyes to readjust. The moon had risen and its light filtered through the windows, throwing a silvery candescence onto the bed. Tessa appeared to be having a dream, she was moving restlessly in her bed. Michael took a step forward and stopped in disbelief. What he'd taken as shadow lay on top of his sister, thrusting violently between her raised knees. And Tessa was rising to him just as roughly.

Michael snapped on the light. 'Jackson?'

Dyson's brother flung a look over his shoulder, fell sideways and landed on the floor, reaching frantically for his clothes. Michael lunged forward and tripped on Tessa's school bag and Jackson, abandoning his search, in one fluid movement dashed towards the French doors, shaking them frantically until they burst open. He jumped from the verandah and was gone.

Tessa pulled the sheet up under her chin. 'Don't you ever knock?' she asked coldly.

Michael shook his head to clear it. 'That was Jackson Mpande! Bloody Jackson!'

'So what?' she challenged him. 'It's got nothing to do with you.'

'You're both under age.' Michael knew he sounded ridiculous. In truth, he was having a hard time assembling any coherence at all.

His sister's eyes were darting around the room as if seeking a reason, an excuse, anything to get her off the hook. 'It was his idea.'

'No,' Michael said stonily. 'Not this time. This time you've gone too far.'

'And I couldn't care less.' She was turning sullen. 'You have no right to burst into my room. Who do you think you are?'

'How long has this been going on? Jesus, Tessa!

Right here in our own house with your sister in the next room. Is there a shred of decency in you anywhere?'

'Just go,' Tessa shouted at him. 'Get out of my room.'

Her temper got Michael's thoughts back on track. 'There's been an accident,' he said tightly. 'I came to tell you Joe is dead.'

Tessa raised a hand to her mouth, eyes suddenly wide and staring. She forgot to be defensive. 'What happened?'

'Fire,' he said shortly.

'Fire!' She mouthed the word, then found her voice. 'Cane burn don't you mean? You killed him. You bastard!'

Michael had half expected this. He ignored the outburst. 'Joe must have been sleeping it off in the block we fired. It would have been quick.'

For one moment he thought Tessa was going to burst into tears. She stared at him in silence and bit her lip.

'Here we go,' Michael thought. 'She's going to get hysterical.'

But instead of tears, Tessa threw back her head and howled and howled with laughter.

Most of the Zulus on UBejane Estate witnessed Jackson's shame. In blind panic he rushed, naked, into the compound, yelling incoherently. Convinced that Michael would come after him with a gun, there was only one thought in his head. He had to get away. His hysterical shouting woke everyone and people began to appear, blinking sleepily, trying to work out who was making such a noise and why. Before Wilson could get any sense out of him, Michael's Land Rover burst into the compound, scattering sleeping animals in all directions, stopping in a cloud of dust, headlights blazing on the open door of Wilson and Nandi's house.

'Where's Jackson?' Michael yelled, even before getting out of the vehicle.

The polite greeting on Wilson's lips died as he stared at Michael.

'I said, where's Jackson, dammit?' Michael shouted.

There was a rustle of movement at the door and Nandi appeared clutching a sleeping blanket around her. 'Please, Mr Michael,' she said fearfully. 'What is wrong?'

Michael strode closer. 'Jackson, get out here,' he ordered. Arms folded, he waited until the still naked figure of Jackson appeared reluctantly at the doorway, followed by Dyson. 'Right out,' Michael snapped. 'There will be a meeting.'

Jackson emerged, hands cupping his genitals.

Dyson had never seen Michael so angry. 'Please,' he intervened, 'allow my brother to cover himself.'

Michael looked contemptuously at Jackson's nakedness. 'Quickly then,' he said curtly. 'Get dressed.' Someone threw Jackson a blanket and he wrapped himself in it.

By now others were converging on the scene. Wilson stepped up to Michael. 'You call a meeting,' he said quietly. 'It will be done.' He clapped his hands and ordered that a fire be built up. People settled themselves around it, murmuring to each other. 'What is happening?' 'What has Jackson done?' 'Why is the *Nkosi* so angry?'

Michael pushed Jackson forward. 'I come here tonight with the gravest of complaints,' he said in Zulu. 'It is not something that can wait until tomorrow, it must be dealt with now, tonight.'

The murmuring increased. 'I take it,' Wilson said, standing erect and looking directly into Michael's eyes, 'that it has something to do with my son Jackson. What has he done, *Nkosi*? Was he stealing from you? Whatever his crime, he will be punished.'

Taking in the honesty in this honourable man's eyes Michael also saw bewilderment, fear and a genuine desire to put to rights any misdoing on his son's behalf. The anger left him and he took a deep breath. 'It is not as simple as that,' Michael said. 'Yes, he must be punished but the question is, how?'

Jackson, reassured that Michael had no weapon with him, cut in and he spoke contemptuously. 'Yes, white man. Do not, for one minute, think of punishing your sister. She is white.'

'Be quiet, child,' Wilson hissed at him. 'Do not insult the *Nkosi*.'

Michael closed his eyes for a moment. 'He is right. My sister will also be punished. She will be sent away from this place.' He took two steps forward which brought him face to face with Jackson. 'What were you thinking?' he asked in despair. 'What made you do it?'

Wilson joined them. 'What is it that they have done? I beg you, *Nkosi*, tell me.'

'They were together as man and wife in my sister's bed.'

An audible gasp went through the listening crowd.

'No!' Nandi cried. 'No! He would not be so foolish.'

Michael stared Jackson down. 'Well,' he said. 'Tell them.'

Jackson hung his head. 'It is true. I had my deek in her hole.'

Michael's fists bunched until he realised that Jackson probably got his terminology from Tessa. 'You have to punish this one in your own way. That is only fair. Do whatever you decide, I will not interfere. Let me say only this. I know that my sister is as much to blame, if not more so, than Jackson. I am fully aware of her . . . unacceptable ways. She will be dealt with. That does not excuse your son. I expect you to consider the crime and act accordingly.'

His eyes raked the hushed circle around the fire. 'You have probably heard by now that Joe King was killed tonight. There has been great evil on UBejane for too long. The time has come for change. I leave Jackson in your hands.' He turned to leave.

'Wait, *Nkosi*.' Wilson looked fearfully at Michael. 'Will you tell the police of this thing?'

Michael shook his head. 'How can I? But if the two of them so much as talk to each other again I will throw the whole Mpande family off UBejane.

That is my promise to you. I make it with a heavy heart but it is no empty threat.'

Dyson stared in disbelief and horror after the retreating figure of his only white friend. 'Wait.' He ran after him. 'You can't mean that. You know it was more your sister's fault.'

Michael climbed into the vehicle and leaned his elbow through the open window, staring straight ahead. 'I mean it, Dyson. Keep him away from her.'

'Because he's black,' Dyson stated bitterly. 'I expected more from you.'

Michael did look at Dyson then. 'No, not because he's black. Because they're only fourteen and it's against the law.'

'And if Jackson were white?'

'My actions would be the same.' Michael started the engine and, without another word, drove away.

Dyson did not believe him.

Two sets of rules, as Michael had so aptly put it not long ago. No-one was under any illusions about Tessa, not even Dyson. Jackson had been duly punished, his back lacerated by a *sjambok*, the heavy rhinoceros hide biting deep so that he would carry the scars forever. Wilson himself had administered the punishment while Nandi quietly wept in shame. Dyson felt no sorrow or pity for his brother. He had committed a crime and paid the penalty like a man. What hurt was Michael's threat to throw the family off the farm. Michael knew the Zulu way as well as any but yet seemed unaware, or uncaring, that he'd dished out a double discipline.

NINE

Joe King died on a Monday night. Because of the unnatural nature of his death a coroner had first to establish that the fire had been the cause, and so they could not arrange the funeral before Friday. On Tuesday morning, Michael found his mother on the telephone making an appointment of some kind. She put down the receiver and said, 'I've arranged for Tessa to see a doctor.'

'Why?'

'To see if there's anything we can do.'

'Are you talking about a psychiatrist?'

Claire nodded.

'Where?'

'Durban.'

'That's a hell of a long way.' Michael did not have a high opinion of psychiatrists. He tended to regard them as fallout from the American fad of shrink mania. However, the set of Claire's mouth told him she was not prepared to listen to any argument. She drove a reluctant Tessa to Durban that same morning.

Eight hours later they returned. Tessa was red-eyed and uncommunicative and went straight to her room. Michael followed his mother into the office. 'Well?'

'She wants to see you.'

'Tessa does?' He was surprised. Tessa usually went out of her way to avoid him.

'No. Dr Lewis.'

'Why? There's nothing wrong with me.'

'She says it sounds as though a lot of Tessa's problems stem from you. The doctor thinks that . . .' Claire hesitated, then went on with a rush. 'You're a kind of father-figure. You set standards that Tessa doesn't believe she can live up to.' Claire shrugged miserably. 'I don't know, Michael. Anything's worth a try.'

He took some convincing. As far as he was concerned, Tessa's problems were of her own making. But finally, because his mother seemed to think it was important, Michael agreed to the three-hour drive to see Dr Lewis the next morning. He kept the appointment with about as much enthusiasm as Tessa had the previous day.

He didn't know what to expect but he hadn't expected a woman in jeans and T-shirt who looked to be the same age as him, who smoked incessantly, who sometimes used language that would make a trooper blush and who didn't have a couch anywhere near her office. She had pale blonde hair, wildly curly, caught up by a rubber band and allowed to cascade every which way. She led him into her office, closed the door, crossed to her desk, picked up cigarettes and lit one. Blowing smoke lustily towards the ceiling, she said, 'I'm Annie

Lewis. Have a seat. Let's get acquainted.' Her voice was throaty.

Michael scrutinised her. She wore not a scrap of make-up, her skin was flawless, eyes clear and direct. She looked absurdly young. 'Are you fully qualified?'

'Of course.'

Michael crossed to her desk. 'You look as though you should be at school.'

'Next time I'll wear my grey wig.' She was smiling. 'Come on, Michael King. Sit down and let's get on with it. I'm too bloody expensive for us to discuss my age but, if it makes you feel any better, I'm twenty-five. Okay?'

She was only three years older than him.

Feeling self-conscious, Michael sat down.

Annie Lewis got straight to the point. 'Your sister needs help. Do you honestly believe that sending her to a convent is the answer?'

'It's the answer for the rest of us.'

Anger flitted across her face. 'That's convenient.'

'You haven't had to live with her.'

'She needs patience and understanding, Michael.'

'At thirty Rand an hour, I'll just bet she does.'

Dr Lewis leaned forward and stubbed out her cigarette. 'There's a lot of anger in her. Something has affected her a great deal. It's more than her father's death.'

Michael smiled grimly. 'Nothing affects Tessa a great deal, certainly not that.'

'You really don't like her, do you?'

'Not much.'

'Why?'

Michael stared directly at her. 'Is that any of your business?'

She held his gaze. 'If I'm to help her, yes.'

Her eyes were deep blue, almost violet. 'She's been disruptive since the day she was born. Rude, disobedient, wilful, argumentative, sneaky and a liar.' *Damn but those eyes are beautiful.* 'I'll bet she didn't mention why we're sending her to a convent.'

'She was caught *il flagrante delicto* with an African boy.'

Michael blinked at her bluntness.

'It's a crime on two counts. She's under age and he's black. Does that tell you anything?' she asked.

'Yes. Tessa has no morals.'

'Morals!' She dismissed the word with a wave of a hand.

'I also suspect . . .' Michael choked back his words. What happened between Tessa and Joe was none of this woman's business.

'Suspect what?'

'That she's promiscuous at school.'

'Many girls are.'

'Not like Tessa.'

'No. I admit Tessa is different.'

'What are you saying?'

'I don't know yet. It's too early to tell. Certainly, your sister does not appear to feel any embarrassment or shame. That's unusual in one as young as Tessa. And, from what she told me yesterday, her father's death has left her without a friend. She feels that no-one else in her family likes her, especially you.'

Michael sighed. 'Look, Dr Lewis . . .'

'Annie.'

'Okay, Annie. All her life Tessa has had to blame someone or something else. Nothing is ever her fault. She has no . . .' he cast around in his mind for the right word, '. . . self-control. If you've fallen for that "nobody understands me" routine then you've been had. She doesn't behave the way she does because nobody in the family likes her. That's bullshit.'

Annie Lewis grinned at him. 'Good. I'm glad you said that.'

'Why?'

'Because if you hadn't, I would have. I agree. I rather got the feeling yesterday that I was watching a very good play.'

'We've all had enough.'

'It can't be easy, I understand that. But she needs help.'

'She needs controlling.'

Annie shook her head and curls flew. Michael watched them, fascinated. But her words made him question her experience. 'If you try to control Tessa she'll react badly. She's like a time bomb. She has to be steered towards self-control. Don't you see, Michael? Tessa needs care, not banishment. And you, of all your family, are the one who needs to care most.'

'Why me?'

'Believe it or not, she respects you.'

Michael gave a short laugh. 'Tessa doesn't know the meaning of the word.'

Annie ignored the interruption. 'You are the father-figure, the one she needs approval from. I gather her real father had a drink problem. Tessa needs to have a man in her life, someone she can look up to.'

Michael rose and glared at Annie Lewis. 'Tessa needs a man in her life all right. You haven't a clue what you're talking about. She's off to a convent where there isn't a bloody man in sight. Now, if you'll excuse me, I have a funeral to arrange.'

'Wait.' Annie rose as well. 'All I'm asking is for more time. I can help her, I know I can but, before that, I need to break through the fact that she's using her father's death as an excuse.'

Michael shook his head. 'No more time, no more consultations. She's off to a convent before she brings disgrace to the entire family. As you pointed out, doctor, she's under age and has some kind of fascination for Africans. A lethal combination in this country, wouldn't you say?'

'Stop being so bloody moralistic. It doesn't help at all. Surely you can see that a girl as young as Tessa who deliberately goes out of her way to break the rules is crying out for attention.'

Michael had had enough. 'Where do you get this stuff, Dr Lewis? Anyone with half a brain could see that Tessa is simply obsessed with sex.'

Annie reached out and angrily snatched up her cigarettes. 'Bugger off then. I can see it's useless try-ing to appeal to your better judgment.' She lit one.

'God help your sister and God help the rest of you when she turns eighteen.' She waved her hand impatiently. 'Go on then, go and arrange your bloody funeral.'

Michael left her office without another word.

Annie sank down in her chair staring at the space he'd left. 'You fool, Lewis. You damned fool. You could see he was anti the moment he walked in. You were supposed to get his confidence, not get his back up.'

They came from miles around for Joe King's funeral, a tight-knit community who had only one thing in common – sugar. Some came to socialise, others out of curiosity, even those with no other reason than a day off work. Two separate individuals took Claire to one side and made an offer on the estate. Both said virtually the same things: 'Quick sale, get it off your back, fresh start, I'll give you a fair price, no need to go through the agents, you can trust me.' To each of them Claire smiled vaguely and said, 'I'll let you know.'

The service had been held in Empangeni. Afterwards, everybody made their way to UBejane where Joe was the first and last King to be buried in a family plot, which he'd established a few years earlier in one of his more maudlin moods. A lonely cadaver on a lonely hill in a lonely land. No-one cared. Looking around at the assembled throng of people on the lawn in front of the house, Michael wondered just how many had actually come to mourn. Sober for a change, one of Joe's drinking buddies wiped the back of his hand across his eyes once or twice. A cousin cried copiously. Michael discounted her. She also wept at weddings. Sally shed a couple of tears, not from grief but from pity.

Guests were standing in groups, eating, drinking, talking, laughing. 'Quite a party,' Michael thought. *Thanks, Joe King. Great piss-up. I'm sure you would approve.*

A stunningly beautiful girl with a natural blonde bob, hazel eyes, lightly tanned skin and a figure that turned men's heads, irrespective of their age, made her way through the crowds seeking out Michael. 'I'm so sorry,' she said quietly.

He couldn't place her and it showed.

'Last time I saw you we had a kind of fight.' She smiled. 'You had a bee in your bonnet over something.'

'Jennifer! Jeez! Look . . . I'm sorry.' Michael ran a hand through his hair, distracted. 'You look wonderful.' Three years ago she'd still carried a little puppy fat and worn her hair in a ponytail. The way it was cut now did stunning things to her cheekbones and gave her a sophistication far removed from the teenager he remembered. 'I was going to call your parents, find out how I could contact you.'

'I heard you were back.'

'Jen. I'm sorry. That last time I saw you . . . Well, I had some things on my mind.'

She smiled slightly. 'You're forgiven.'

'How's Varsity? Zoology, wasn't it?'

'Still is.'

She had an economic way with words which he liked. 'Not finished yet?'

'Not quite. Just over a year to go.'

'You didn't come home just for this?' Michael waved a hand towards the assembled throng.

When she shook her head, sunlight shimmered, like spun gold, through her hair as it bounced around her face. 'I'm on study leave.'

'Here for long?'

'Another month.'

'We should get together, catch up on old times.'

'That would be nice.' Her eyes were steady, looking directly into his.

Michael took the plunge. 'Are you doing anything tomorrow night?'

'Nothing.' She came straight out with it. No stalling, no pretence that the question needed thinking about.

'My cousin's having a birthday party at Kingsway. Like to come?'

'Love to.'

'Pick you up around eight, if that's okay?'

'Super.'

'It's casual.'

She had seen someone in the crowd. 'Excuse me, Michael. There's my aunt. I must speak to her or she'll never forgive me.' A quick smile and Jennifer was gone.

Michael watched her go. He watched the way her straight black skirt fitted perfectly over jutting buttocks, how the split at the back exposed long and lovely legs. He watched the way she held her shoulders, the way her hips swayed, ever so slightly, as she walked. She was tall, nearly as tall as Michael. She walked with a long, slow stride, her almost feline grace reminding him of a stalking leopard. She managed to convey both friendly charm and a natural reserve, though Michael sensed that a man lucky enough to push the right buttons would end up with an armful of smouldering passion. He watched the look in other men's eyes as she passed. 'Wow!' he muttered.

The afternoon passed into evening and suddenly Jennifer was gone. When she kissed him on the cheek in a brief goodbye he couldn't help but notice her perfume, woody and natural, with a touch of spice. It was perfect for her.

Tessa had attended the funeral but baulked at the wake. 'All those boring people.' She wrinkled her nose. 'I'll stay in my room.'

Much to Tessa's surprise, Claire had said, 'Fine,' and left it at that.

As the noise swelled from the lawn outside she knew her mother and Michael would be busy. She intended sneaking out to find Jackson. But, when she tried her door she found it had been locked from the other side. On the French doors, a padlock dangled from the normally open hasp and staple security latch. The windows too had been modified, blocked so they could only open a fraction.

'They can't do this,' she raged. 'It's barbaric. It's

. . . illegal.' She was frightened. Everything had gone wrong. The day after Michael found Jackson in her room Claire informed Tessa that she had been booked into a convent near Durban. Michael would take her down two days after the funeral. Tessa had wept, begged, made promises she would never keep. Her mother remained unmoved and stubbornly determined.

Tessa decided to run away with Jackson. Typically, she gave no thought to the impracticalities of the idea, nor did she consider the possibility that Jackson would refuse. She had planned to tell him during the wake for her father. Before then it had been impossible. Someone was always there watching her like a hawk – her mother, Michael, even Bessie.

And now she was locked in. 'God,' she cried silently. 'Don't let them send me away.' But Tessa knew she would have to go. Michael would give her no opportunity to run away.

The prospect was terrifying. She'd heard of the strict discipline, the rigid rules, the reputed cruelty of the nuns. To Tessa, the thought of living like that was worse than death. She was a free spirit and should be allowed to remain as such. Locked away in a convent she would surely die. Tessa had already made up her mind. If she could not avoid going, she would be so disruptive they would have no alternative but to send her home.

Still she was petrified. To one so self-indulgent and undisciplined, the spectre of convent life brought visions of nothing but misery. Not to see

Jackson, do the things she craved with him, how could she bear it? Feminine company had never made her comfortable, women and girls were boring, they lacked challenge. And now she was going to live with nothing else.

Locked in her room, Tessa sobbed out her fear and frustration.

Outside, Claire, Michael, Sally, even Gregor, were going through the motions. The one remaining King brother, Colin, sat silent and staring in his wheelchair, only saying, 'Thank you,' whenever condolences were expressed.

Raj and Balram had attended the burial only, citing pressure of work as a reason not to stay for the wake. Michael suspected that the old Sikh and his son were relieved to see the end of Joe. While prepared to pay their respects, they would not be hypocritical enough to stay for the wake and pretend to be sorry.

Likewise the Zulus. Dyson, knowing full well the extent of Michael's hatred for Joe, simply clasped his hand and looked him deeply in the eyes. The look that passed between them said it all. 'Free at last.' Then both men nodded slightly and Dyson returned to the Zulu compound.

Wilson, while not in any way sorry Joe King was dead but nonetheless shocked by the manner in which he died, offered an awkward kind of solace to Claire. 'It was God's will. If it had not been, He'd have sent a storm to put out the fire.' To

Michael, Wilson was more practical. 'Untimely death is the work of evil spells. There is a clever *sangoma* near here. I will pay her a visit.'

Michael thanked him, knowing that Wilson was trying to protect the family from further mishaps.

That evening, Dyson Mpande was in two minds whether or not to attend the meeting due to start at nine-thirty. So much had happened over the last few days that he felt he should stay at home, if for no other reason than to help his parents with Jackson who was being surly, uncooperative and rude. In the end, however, he decided to go. This particular meeting was too important for him not to be there.

As he drove into Empangeni his mind was busy with the events that had rocked UBejane Estate, events which shamed and terrified his parents to the point where they were considering leaving the farm and returning to their village.

Michael's threat to evict the Mpande family was extremely hard to swallow. It emphasised the line drawn between white and black, a line that Dyson would have sworn was invisible to Michael. Now he wasn't so sure. Dyson wanted to believe his friend had acted out of a need to protect their two families from the authorities learning what had transpired between Tessa and Jackson. Maybe he had. But the threat made was the act of an employer to employee. Michael had the longer arm in that regard and had used it. When the chips were down it seemed, friendship took second place. Dyson could accept that, just. But were Michael's two sets of rules on a level playing field? Did colour come into the equation after all?

There were times when Dyson was honest enough with himself to see that dual standards were the rule, rather than the exception. Like everybody else, he had them. His own involvement with the African National Congress was a perfect example.

Before he went to Umfolozi with Michael, Dyson tended to agree with his father that the ANC could not be all things to all tribes and that the Zulus needed a voice of their own. He had, many times, witnessed Wilson's frustration about Zulu inertia: their reluctance to revive Inkatha which they claimed did not work the first time so what made anyone think it would be successful this time. Like his father, Dyson was in favour of a peaceful end to apartheid. Unlike his father, however, the prospect of freedom from the hated system was too enticing for Dyson to exercise Wilson's kind of patience.

At the end of each day in Umfolozi, with Michael gone to the whites-only accommodation and Dyson to the African compound, the talk around the fire each night quickly revealed that despite banning orders against such meetings, the ANC was alive and active and frustrated by what they saw as virtual containment of a situation that favoured the whites to the detriment of South Africa's majority. Wherever Zulus lived, small groups formed branches of the ANC's armed wing, Umkhonto we Sizwe – The Spear of the Nation.

Dyson was invited to join.

For a while he thought that Umkhonto was no more effective than any of the other groups meeting in secret around the country. They met, they made plans, but it was all hot air. With their hands effectively tied by the State of Emergency there was little else they could do. Regular raids on such meetings by the Security Police, raids which were always covered by a blare of publicity, ensured that distrust of each other ran high among the dissidents which, in turn, rendered them nothing more than a whispered protest.

But, before long, Dyson caught sight of a small miracle. True, the protest was timid but each time it was voiced the whisper grew stronger. It was like a far-off trade wind. It could not yet be felt but they all knew it was coming. So the meetings continued, plans were made, and Dyson knew that when the trade wind finally reached them, not only would it be of hurricane force but they would all be ready to fly with it.

His only problem was that he could see chaos, violence and bloodshed ahead, which would visit on the Africans well before it touched white lives. And when it finally impacted on the whites it would be carnage. And his best friend in this world was white. So where the hell did that leave him?

The meeting was to take place in a private house owned by the uncle of a respected ANC member. The venue changed each time to avoid alerting the ever-vigilant Security Police. The State of Emergency, declared after Sharpeville, was about to be lifted. When that happened the ANC could legally hold meetings but, for the time being, any gathering was assumed to be political and therefore banned.

There had been alarming rumours that the prime minister was about to cut all constitutional ties with Britain, declare a republic and withdraw from the Commonwealth. If that were true and British influence removed, the measures of repression, increasing all the time, would spiral out of control. Before that happened, Pretoria had to be made aware that things would not go all their own way, that the majority of South Africa's population had had enough.

Their agenda this night was to discuss the best way to announce that an armed struggle was about to begin. They had already decided on a series of bomb explosions. The question was, where? Some still wanted to avoid harming anyone, give a warning only of things to come. Others argued that it was necessary for whites to die in order to get Pretoria's attention. The conversation was becoming heated with little or no consensus of opinion. Dyson favoured the idea of one bomb going off in a predominately white shopping complex. He didn't relish the idea of innocent people being killed but desperate situations required desperate measures. After all, Nelson Mandela himself had declared, 'Violence is inevitable. It would be unrealistic and wrong for African leaders to continue preaching peace and non-violence when the government meets our peaceful demands with force.'

In the hubbub of raised voices, no-one heard safety catches being snicked off in the darkness outside. Some later recalled hearing a crash as the front door was kicked in but their arguing had become so volatile that it took all by complete surprise when heavily armed white policemen burst into the room and fanned out, blocking all escape. The sudden silence was profoundly, almost painfully, loud. Fear put a sheen of sweat on faces which, a few seconds earlier, had been confident and aggressive.

No-one moved. There were voices outside and the policemen at the door stepped aside to admit an unarmed man wearing the uniform of a commander. He stood just inside the door, slowly scrutinising faces. Several of the men he knew by name. 'What are you doing?' he barked suddenly.

They were prepared. Beer and crisps evident for just such an intrusion. 'A party, *Nkosi*.'

A sneer crossed the officer's face. 'Where are the women?'

'It is a beer drink, *Nkosi*. No women.'

The man stepped further into the room, turning slowly on one heel as he looked around. 'You were shouting hilltop to hilltop just now. We could hear you from the end of the street.'

'Sorry, *Nkosi*.'

'What was that word we kept hearing? Umkhonto, was it?'

Several of the policemen smirked, nodding their heads.

The commander looked directly at Dyson. 'What is this Umkhonto that has you all yelling and arguing, eh? Tell us. We would like to know too.'

Dyson remained silent, his eyes not meeting those of the policeman.

'Speak up, kaffir.' The friendliness suddenly gone, the commander's voice was hard. 'What is this Umkhonto?'

Another's voice responded timidly, 'It is nothing, *Nkosi*. We were recalling a great battle in the days of Shaka, that is all.'

The commander narrowed his eyes. 'Umkhonto we Sizwe,' he said softly. 'The Spear of the Nation.' Turning slowly around the room he jabbed a finger at various men. 'ANC, ANC, ANC, ANC,' he repeated, selecting at random. 'This is a political meeting.'

'No, *Nkosi*. It is only a beer drink.'

The speaker was knocked flying by a vicious backhander. 'Liar!' the commander screamed. 'Arrest them all,' he snapped. Then he was gone.

Not one man resisted arrest. There were no illusions over their fate. They would be bashed and mocked. A few tortured. The police could keep them locked away indefinitely while they tried to find evidence that would prove them guilty of treason. They might be detained without trial for days, weeks, months or even years. The ANC could not help them, no-one could.

Dyson, handcuffed to another man, waited impassively for his turn to climb into the police wagon. A policeman, for no reason at all, pushed him painfully hard with the barrel of his pistol. 'Get in, kaffir.' There was no reasoning with them. Pointless to explain that he was unable to move until the man in front was inside the vehicle. Dyson shuffled forward, hoping to appear willing and avoid another blow. On the outside, he was cowed and submissive. Inside, terror and rage competed fiercely with each other.

He heard the man cuffed to him whisper, 'I am sorry, Father.' His own personal apology for the trials he had visited on his family. The police would not stop at simply arresting those at the meeting. They would pull in whole families for questioning. Dyson knew that Wilson, Nandi, Jackson and even the two younger children would be interrogated mercilessly. If the police were not absolutely satisfied with their answers, they too would be imprisoned. He broke into a sweat of dread. In the course of their investigations, the police might accidentally discover what had taken place between Jackson and Tessa.

Jammed into the back of the wagon, packed so tightly they could barely breathe, the door slammed shut behind them. Dyson took a despairing look at the relative freedom outside. He wondered how long it might be before he saw it again, if indeed he ever did.

★

News of Dyson's arrest reached UBejane the next morning. Nandi and Wilson had been frantic with worry when their son had not come home after his meeting. Police wagons, six of them, drove up to the main house where Claire was working at her desk in the office. The commander was all smiles and respect. 'Good morning, Mevrou King.'

'Good morning, officer.' Claire could not tell one rank from another. She called them all officer.

'Ah . . . I am sorry about your husband.'

'Thank you.'

'We come here today on a different matter.'

Claire raised a sardonic eyebrow. 'With six vehicles, I rather thought you might have.'

'Ah . . . yes.' The commander looked at Nandi. 'What is your name?'

Nandi looked up fearfully. 'Nandi, master.'

'Nandi what?'

'Mpande, master.'

The policeman shook his head and winked at Claire. 'Nandi Mpande. Sounds like Andy Pandy.'

Claire treated him to a frosty stare. 'Would you mind stating your business please, officer.'

The man took a deep breath, all puffed up with self-importance. 'Last night we arrested twenty-two men who were conducting an illegal political gathering. Dyson Mpande was one of them.' He ignored Nandi's sudden gasp of shock. 'We are here to pick up his family.'

He looked ridiculous, like a pouter pigeon. Claire was getting irritated. 'And just how big a family do you think that is?' She waved her hands at the vehicles and the armed police lounging against them.

'We will take all the Africans for questioning. They will be allowed to return once we are satisfied they are innocent.'

'Innocent of what?' The commander didn't know Claire very well or he would have heard the steel creeping into her voice.

'Treason.' He made the word sound terribly important.

Claire blinked slowly and rubbed the back of one hand across her forehead. 'Tell me, officer,' she said mildly, 'what would you call it if someone deliberately sabotaged the production of one of this country's major exports?'

The commander scratched his head. 'That is treason too,' he said at last, not getting her drift.

Claire rose and leaned on her knuckles until they turned white. 'If you take all my workers, how am I to meet my quota?'

Her meaning suddenly clear, he stood ramrod straight and ignored the question. 'Mevrou,' he said quietly and threateningly, 'I am trying to do my job. Do you refuse to cooperate?'

'I know my rights,' Claire replied just as forcefully. 'You may take the Mpande family in for questioning but I assure you, you'll be wasting your time. I expect them back on UBejane by tonight. If they are not I shall go over your head. The police commissioner in Durban is a personal friend. You will *not* remove any of my other African employees. Do I make myself clear?'

'Madam,' he said heavily, 'if I wish, I can remove every man, woman and child from this estate.'

'I know,' Claire replied, 'but I do not think you would be such a fool.' He was a bully. She was wishing Michael would come in from the fields but she was not about to cave in under his tactics. 'I have heard about you. Women and girls are raped by your men. Young boys tortured. I'm not saying you condone these things or even that the rumours are true, but I wonder what your superiors would have to say about it.'

His face went red with fury. 'How dare you,' he spluttered.

Claire, who had absolutely no idea about the man's personal and private inclinations, smiled sweetly. 'I'm sure these stories are greatly exaggerated, officer, but you must agree that rumours do start in the most mysterious ways, do they not?'

He snapped his fingers at Nandi. 'You. Come with me.'

Nandi, with a frightened look at Claire, followed him outside. She was bundled into the back of a wagon and the entire convoy left.

'Dear God,' Claire said to herself. She knew that the Mpande family were likely to experience threats, physical abuse or even worse before being released. She had not been making idle conversation with that officer. Tales of his cruelty, and those of his men, had been circulating for years. There was no guarantee that Nandi would not be sexually used, or her twelve-year-old daughter for that matter. Wilson and the little boy could expect to be beaten. As for Jackson, God help them all if the events of Monday night came to light. Claire could do nothing more to help them. That brutish man might well have a superior officer in Durban but she had no idea who he was.

Michael drove into the yard minutes later, unaware of the police visit or what had brought it on. Claire quickly told him what she knew. 'The fool!' he exploded. 'I've told him time and again that he was playing with fire.'

Claire's face was drained. 'How can we help them? They're our friends. The police can't just detain them for no good reason.'

'We can probably help all of them except Dyson.' Michael thumped the bonnet of the Land Rover. 'If he was at that meeting, then he's done for.'

'Michael, you know what the police are like. We must do something quickly.'

He put an arm around her. 'Be patient. If they're not back in the morning, I know someone who might be able to pull strings.'

'First Joe, then Tessa, and now this.' She turned and faced him. 'What else can go wrong?'

'Is Tessa still . . .?'

'Yes. But I don't like locking her in like that, Michael. She's not a dog.'

'It's only until tomorrow, Mother. You know it is for the best.'

'I just wish I knew what makes her so difficult, that's all.'

'She hears a different rhythm from most of us.'

Michael looked wry. 'Sorry. It's the best I can do. I don't know either. Whatever it is, let's hope the convent cures her of it.'

Michael collected Jennifer to take her to the party. He was not the best of company. Worries over Tessa and Dyson weighed heavily. An argument with Claire over the psychiatrist didn't help. She wanted Tessa to go one more time, Michael said there was no point. In the end, Claire did take Tessa back to Annie Lewis but Tessa was frustratingly non-cooperative and the session was cut short.

Halfway through the evening, Jennifer asked him what was wrong. Michael said, 'Nothing.'

'I think we've had this conversation before,' she commented, and dropped it.

They left the party early. On the way back to her place, Michael apologised for being such bad company. 'I'll tell you about it some time,' he said.

'Only if you want to.'

So he told her about Dyson.

'I'm sorry,' she said softly. 'You two were such good friends.'

'I tried to warn him.'

'You didn't really expect him to listen, did you?'

'No. It's just that I feel so helpless. There's nothing I can do for him.'

'He knows that, Michael.'

'Yeah.' He sighed. 'It doesn't stop me feeling bad though.'

Jennifer made no comment. They drove in

silence for a few minutes. Then, 'That's not all that's bothering you, is it?'

'No.'

'I can wait.'

'You're going to have to. I can't tell you yet.'

'Why not?'

'Because,' he said, pulling up in front of her house, 'I want you to have a good opinion of me first.'

She leaned over and kissed him lightly on the lips. 'I already have that. Goodnight.' And she was gone.

PART THREE

1964–1967

TEN

Tessa shrugged off her mother's, 'Well done, darling.' The fact that she had cleaned up matriculation awards for English, Geography and Business Studies and come overall top of her class was of little importance to Tessa. After three and a half years at the convent, the only thing on her mind was that she was free of the hated place at last.

They had been desperate years. Routine, ridiculously rigid rules, incessant prayer meetings, punishment meted out for the slightest thing, stupid giggly girls with whom she was forced to share dormitories, and a complete lack of freedom and privacy. Despite disobedience, disruptive behaviour and open aggression on her part in an attempt to be expelled, nothing had worked. What Tessa didn't realise was that Michael had paid for the entire three and a half years in advance and that the money had been spent on some much needed renovations on the convent's roof. As much as the nuns would have loved to see the back of her, they were stuck with her. As she waited her turn to be officially released into the world, Tessa could hardly contain her excitement.

'Ah good morning, Mrs King.' Mother Frances, the Mother Superior of the Sacred Hearts Convent of Mercy, allowed her eyes to flick to Tessa but they quickly returned to Claire. 'Your daughter has done well.'

Tessa could see how much the admission pained the good woman.

Claire responded enthusiastically and Mother Frances was obliged to spend five minutes discussing the merits of the most difficult pupil the convent had ever had the misfortune of trying to educate. Finally, the Mother Superior turned to Tessa. 'Congratulations, child. You are free to leave.'

As they walked away Tessa could have sworn she heard Mother Frances aspirating loud relief.

In the car on the journey home Tessa was silent, barely responding to Claire's attempts at conversation. After a while her mother gave up and concentrated on driving. Tessa was free to let her thoughts wander.

She remembered the day she left UBejane for the convent. If it hadn't been for Sally she wouldn't be sitting here today. She had been in the bathroom, desperate and rebellious. Her mother had just told her there was no way out, she had to go. When Tessa demanded an explanation, Claire had said, 'Because I don't trust you.' Even though she knew her mother was right, the comment had stung.

Standing in the bathroom, she had picked up Michael's razor. 'I'll kill myself,' she thought. 'Then they'll be sorry.' She placed the blade against her skin where the veins showed, bluish and raised.

Sally had experienced premonitions about her twin on a number of occasions and, each time, they had proved to be true. Michael was about to put Tessa's suitcase in the car when his sister gave a sharp gasp of fright. 'Quickly, Michael. Tessa's in trouble.'

Michael didn't hesitate, he'd seen this inexplicable telepathy before. He dropped the case and sprinted inside. 'Where's Tessa?' he shouted to Claire.

'In the bathroom. What's wrong? What is it?'

Michael shouldered the door with such force that the lock tore clean out of the wood. The sudden intrusion startled Tessa so much that she dropped the razor, but not before Michael had seen it pressing against her wrist.

'What the *hell* are you doing?'

'I'm not going, I'm not going, I'm not going, I'm not . . .' Claire's sharp slap on her face stopped the hysterical babbling and Tessa had crumpled to the floor, sobbing uncontrollably.

Tessa supposed now that she was grateful to her twin but there had been many times during her years at the convent that she had wished she were dead. In the space of a couple of weeks the other girls stopped trying to make friends. She was too moody and too rude for them to bother. As Tessa's subsequent sense of isolation deepened, she hid behind a mask of indifference. She was deeply unhappy but she was damned if she'd let anyone know.

Holidays were a nightmare. Tessa blamed

Michael and Claire for her unhappiness and took her anger out on them. Sally, who sensed Tessa's misery, had tried to include her in her own group of friends but quickly stopped inviting her when it became obvious that her sister had nothing but contempt for her female friends and was embarrassingly flirtatious with the boys. Much to Tessa's anguish, coinciding with each holiday Jackson was sent to his grandparents' thereby removing that temptation.

Perhaps if the two of them had been able to see each other during holiday time Tessa's interest in Jackson would have simply remained just that. Instead, her feelings for him went skyrocketing out of perspective. So much so that now, at eighteen, Tessa believed that Jackson was the only man in the world for her. For the past year as a senior she had enjoyed the relative privacy of her own room. There, in the darkness, as she tried to relieve the sexual tensions building within, the face that swam above hers was Jackson's.

The Immorality Act meant nothing to Tessa. She accepted that it existed but, in her fantasies, the problem was solved by her and Jackson moving to a different country. She had convinced herself that he wanted to be with her as desperately as she wanted him. And now, at last, she was free to be with him.

'Nearly there, darling.'

'Good.' She stirred in her seat, pushing memories of the convent into the back of her mind where, she hoped, they would fade away forever.

The first thing Tessa did when she arrived home was to have a blazing row with Michael. He had convinced Claire to send her away with Sally to finishing school in France. 'Like hell,' she snapped at him when he told her. 'I've had enough school. You can't order me around.'

'Okay. You tell me what you intend to do.'

'Stay here of course.' She sounded surprised.

'And do what?'

'I don't know.' Tessa hadn't given her future a single thought. Freedom was what she craved. 'Can't I just stay here?'

'How do you plan to live?'

Money had always just been there. What was he getting at? 'I can help Mother in the office.'

'Nandi does that.'

'Then I'll get a job in Empangeni.'

Michael sighed. 'In case you hadn't noticed, we're a fair distance from town.'

'I can borrow Mother's car.'

'Tessa,' he said, exasperated, 'try to think about others. You can't have Mother's car because she needs it.'

'You are deliberately going out of your way to put obstacles in my path,' she blazed. 'UBejane is my home too. What's wrong with me working here?'

'This,' he grated. 'This is what's wrong. You've been home five minutes and already you're disrupting things.'

'That's right. Blame me. All I've done is offer to work here.'

'Darling,' Claire intervened, 'there's just not enough work.'

'Then get rid of Nandi.'

'Jesus!' Michael ran a hand through his hair.

Tessa stamped her foot. 'You don't want me around, either of you. I'm not going to France, and you can't make me.'

'No,' Michael agreed. 'You're eighteen and I can't. But the farm will not support you.'

Claire tried a softer approach. 'Perhaps we can afford an old car. That way you could work in Empangeni.'

'If you have to worry about buying me some wheels, how come you can afford to send Sally and me off to a poncy finishing school in Europe?'

'I've been putting money away for that.'

'Then send Sally and give me my share. I'll buy a car with it.'

'Tessa,' Claire tried to explain, 'it's taken me eighteen years to save enough to send you to France. I'm not simply going to hand it over. If you don't wish to go to finishing school that's up to you but don't think the money's yours. It isn't. I'm prepared to look around for a second-hand car. Michael can check it out to make sure it's okay.'

'I don't want a heap of junk.' Tessa glared venomously at Michael. 'Not some clapped-out old bakkie.' She turned and marched to her bedroom, slamming the door noisily.

Claire shook her head and sighed. 'What on earth do we do with her?'

'Varsity?'

'I've suggested that. She's bright enough to get in but she refuses to entertain the idea of a university course.'

'Why? She'd get the freedom she wants there.'

'Tessa equates learning with discipline.'

'Of course it's a discipline but it's her own. Surely she can see that. Look, Jennifer will be home next month. She had a wonderful time at varsity. Perhaps she can talk to Tessa.'

'She can try.' Claire was doubtful. 'But if Tessa's reaction when I spoke to her about it is anything to go by, Jennifer won't get to first base.'

Michael was frustrated and it showed. 'Drug the bloody girl and stick her on a plane with Sally.'

'Michael, please! This is your sister. If she refuses we can't force her. What's *wrong* with the girl? Any normal child would jump at the chance to go to France.'

'If I know my dear sister, her current priority is to get back with Jackson.'

Claire buried her face in her hands.

'Don't worry, Mother. I've already had a word with Wilson. Jackson's being sent to his grandparents again. He'll be gone in two days.'

Claire looked up at him. 'A lot can happen in two days.'

Michael nodded. 'I'll make sure it doesn't,' he said grimly.

Dyson Mpande, with no warning, was abruptly set free at 1.45 a.m. on the morning of the same day that Tessa left the Sacred Hearts Convent of Mercy. For the past two years he had been held prisoner just outside the inland city of Pietermaritzburg, having first spent three weeks in Empangeni's local jail and a further eighteen months in Durban.

It hadn't been an easy time but then he hadn't expected it to be. He knew what he was up for, in the event of capture, when he joined Umkhonto. Prisons for Africans were overcrowded and basic. Some officers were fair but, in the main, they were sadistic, uneducated and prejudiced. A lethal combination, especially when they believed right was on their side. Dyson, as with all the others taken that night, had been severely beaten many times, routinely starved, taunted, insulted and nearly worked to death. Life was a never-ending nightmare of pain, fear, filth, and sleep and food deprivation.

News of the outside filtered through with each new intake of prisoners. Two years earlier, just after Dyson had been moved to Pietermaritzburg, a series of bomb explosions outside government offices around the country had heralded Umkhonto's presence and future intentions. No-one had been hurt but the incidents drove a wedge between Nelson Mandela who approved and Albert Lutuli, the African National Congress's president, who did not. However, six months later, when Mandela was arrested and sentenced to life imprisonment, even the peace-loving Lutuli stated, 'No-one can blame brave just men for seeking justice by the use of violent methods.'

Dyson and others, avidly devouring any news, no

matter how insignificant, took comfort in the fact that at last the struggle for equality had nudged up a gear. The knowledge revived their flagging spirits.

And then, at 1.45 a.m. in the morning, they came to his cell. Keys turning in the lock and the metallic clang of his door being roughly opened broke through a thin veil of fitful sleep. The light was snapped on. Blinking against its harshness, Dyson made out one of the regular police guards looking down at him.

'Get up, kaffir.'

The two other occupants of the cell stirred and opened their eyes. Seeing it was Dyson who was the object of the guard's interest, they rolled away from the intruding light and went back to sleep. There was nothing they could do for him.

Presuming he was in for yet another of their sporadic interrogation sessions, Dyson braced himself for the barrage of verbal and physical abuse. Instead, he was led out of the building and up to the main prison entrance. A small door set into the heavy timber gates opened silently and he was shoved through, out into the night. No words were exchanged. He expected the policeman to follow. Dyson could hardly believe it when the door banged shut behind him and he was on his own.

This was a trick. Nothing stirred outside the prison, no barking dogs, not a sound. He went to move, then froze. Realisation made his scalp crawl. It was the middle of the night and no African was supposed to be at large unless they had a permit. He could be shot on sight. He could be dead and buried within an hour, disappear with no trace. The more his mind raced, the more convinced he became that police were out there in the darkness, just waiting for him to move.

Dyson strained to see into the darkness beyond the security lights. He had to get away, couldn't stay here, a perfect target illuminated for the convenience of the police marksmen. But how? Where to? He'd only once seen outside the walls and that had been two long years ago. The prison was in a rural area, Pietermaritzburg being several kilometres away. That much he did know. It was starting to rain. Fat drops splashed on to the dirt road. Thunder. A storm was coming.

Realising he was damned if he stayed and damned if he moved, he opted for the latter. Shoving both hands deep into his pockets, head down against the sudden deluge, he walked slowly along the perimeter road, expecting at any moment that a bullet would take his life. If the intention had been to release him then he would surely have been given back his own clothes. Sometimes, at night, he had heard shots from outside the walls and, inevitably, a face would be missing the next day. The guards would smugly announce that a prisoner had been apprehended while trying to escape. It was invariably someone held without charge or trial long enough for questions to be raised over the legality of their continued internment. Only yesterday, one of the guards had taunted him, 'You have friends in high places, kaffir. Looks like your day in court is coming.'

Dyson had been excited. *Michael!* It had to be his influence. At last, a trial. He was under no illusion that the courts would exonerate him but at least it meant some publicity, all fuel to the growing fire of protest sweeping through enlightened South Africans and around the world.

God! What a fool to think he'd be allowed a trial. This was how the system dealt with anyone considered likely to pose a threat to authority. *For God's sake, think! The shots outside the walls, they were always some distance away. They're not going to shoot you here. The police want sport. Keep it slow. They want you to run. They're playing with you.*

A rustle in the long dry grass nearly panicked him but he forced himself to maintain his steady pace, relaxing slightly when a mountain reedbuck darted across the road in front of him. If the guards were out there, and Dyson was damned sure they were, they would wait for him to run. *The rain is getting harder. They might get sick of waiting. Think!* The games with Michael. The only way he'd ever taken his friend by surprise was to do the completely unexpected. Sometimes that meant doing something blatantly obvious.

Run! His mind screamed at him. *For God's sake, run.* He was approaching a corner of the prison. Then he saw it. A thin corridor of shadow where the security lights did not quite overlap. *Run. Do the obvious.*

Lightning flashed, long jagged tendrils that slammed into the earth frying anything in its path. Dyson didn't consciously make a decision. He was a dead man anyway. Far better to have a bullet end his life than spend the rest of his days in prison. If he ran or didn't run, the outcome would be the same. A dead man couldn't tell anyone he hadn't tried to run. Instinct took over. He did not know he had started running. Thunder exploded and rolled away. Something tugged at the seam of his shirt and, a split second later, he heard the crashing report of a high-powered rifle. A volley of shots rang out. Then silence.

'Where is he? The bastard's gone,' a voice called to his right.

'He's out there. Bring the dogs.'

More voices joined in.

'Hold your fire, men. He won't get far.'

Dyson heard the high excited whine of one of the German shepherds. 'Here, boy. Smell him out. Good boy.'

'Fuck this, man. Let's get it over with. I'm soaked.'

Dyson was beyond the security lights before he stopped. He had no idea of the terrain. His eyes had not adjusted to the dark. He was frozen where he crouched, unwilling to move in case he made a noise.

'Hey, Kurt. This looks like a good one, hey?'

'Ja, Hennie. Bottle of brandy to the man who nails him.'

'Fuck this rain.'

'It's only water. What's the matter, Fanie? Scared you'll wash away?'

'Should we release the dogs, sir?'

'Not yet, man. Let's have some sport.'

There was hearty laughter.

'Fan out, men. The judge will need a body with bullets in it, not someone shredded by teeth. Only if I blow the whistle let the dogs go.'

Dyson recognised the voice. Captain Eksteen sounded confident, almost amused, that Dyson had disappeared. *I can't stay here.*

'He can't get far. You, Kurt, take three men and cover the other side of where he disappeared. Fanie, take another three and stay this side. The rest of you, follow me. Don't veer off. The last thing we need is an injured policeman. Shoot to kill but make damned sure it's the kaffir.'

'Sir? What if . . .'

Dyson didn't wait to hear any more. They were going to advance in formation in his direction. The dogs would let them know where he was. A tree was no good. He had to get away. He turned and took a tentative step. He was still night blind. Another step. Another. The rain was coming down with increasing intensity. He took another step and there was nothing there. Dyson dropped like a stone.

It wasn't a long fall but it winded him slightly. Sand under him. He must be in a dry river bed. Lightning showed he was. No time for caution. Dyson sprinted for the other side and scrambled up it. Thunder. Or were they shooting? *I'll never get away. Dear God, help me.* Behind him were bobbing lights. Torches. *Don't look at the lights.*

Running blind, Dyson headed away from the prison, instinctively trying to veer west where he knew he might find sanctuary in the peaks and valleys of the misty hills of Mpendle. Then he heard the whistle. They were releasing the dogs. And Dyson knew, with agonised certainty, that he would never get away.

Still he ran, not so much blinded by the darkness any more but by the torrential rain as the storm spewed its overburdened clouds on to the land below, indifferent to the drama being played there. *They're gaining, they're gaining.* He was frantic with fear. More afraid of the dogs than a bullet.

A corner of his mind told him the dogs should have reached him by now.

Shots. A dog yelped and cried. *Behind me. They're well behind me.* Dyson ran and ran. Adrenalin pumped through him. He did not feel the straining of his leg muscles, nor the whistling of his breath as he fought for air. He dare not risk a glance behind to see if the torches were there. Shouts. Way back. Distant and muffled by the pouring rain. But he heard their anger. The rain had washed away his scent.

And Dyson dared to hope.

He ran until he was completely blown, until his flight for safety was nothing more than the staggering shuffle of a man well past his endurance level. Tortured lungs screaming for air. Legs trembling with exertion. Heart threatening to burst. Head pounding as blood thumped through. Brain registering nothing. Until he could not take another step and he fell, face down, sobbing with exhaustion as the pounding rain which had saved him poured from the sky and pummelled the man on the ground until he resembled nothing more than the muddy earth on which he lay.

Reason returned slowly. The dogs had lost his scent but, if the rain stopped, they could easily pick it up again. It took all his willpower and every last ounce of strength to rise. He stood, swaying, and looked back towards the prison. He could see the glow of the perimeter security lights. *Is that a torch?* If it was it was several hundred metres away and heading south. Turning away, Dyson moved slowly westward. If they came for him now he had no more reserves. One foot after the other, each step taking him away from his pursuers. It was all he had left and it would have to be good enough. And the rain cascaded down.

He was still not safe but the odds were stacked more in his favour than they had been. *Why didn't they shoot while I was in the light?* There had been excitement in the voices he'd heard. Anticipation. How many had they hunted down in the past? They had wanted him to make it hard. It was a challenge. Man. The last frontier for a hunter. Only they'd lost him, panicked and set the dogs loose. Dyson kept walking. With luck, it would rain all night. With luck, when the rain stopped, he could have further hidden his scent in a stream or, better still, a river. With exceptionally good luck!

As he walked, his mind was working overtime. He could not return to UBejane, that'd be the first place the police would look. In fact, he'd do well to get out of South Africa. 'Worry about that later,' he thought feverishly. 'First get the hell away from here.'

Four hours later, as Tessa King awoke from her last sleep in the convent, Dyson Mpande was on a little used back road heading towards the towering Drakensberg Mountains and the tiny British protectorate of Basutoland. Along the way he had stolen some clothes that had been left draped over a bush to dry, abandoning his prison garb to the swirling waters of a swollen Umkomaas River. With luck, they would end up in the Indian Ocean. He was calling on a lot of luck, he realised that.

The further from the prison he went, the more relaxed he felt. Although still in South Africa, in the English-dominated province of Natal, the hill country was Zulu where he could be certain of unquestioned hospitality.

Among the news of the outside world that had reached him in prison, Dyson knew that the Union of South Africa had become a Republic and that the ANC was now directed by Oliver Tambo from his exiled base in London. The name Mangosuthu Gatsha Buthelezi, Chief of the aristocratic Buthelezi clan, well educated, well connected and related to two previous Zulu kings, was being whispered as the man who could lead the way out of the apartheid era. His following had grown rapidly, especially after a cameo appearance in the film *Zulu* where he played the part of his own great-grandfather, Cetshwayo.

Dyson knew he was out of touch. 'One thing at a time,' he told himself, watching a new day lighten

the peaks of Mpendle. He did not know this country. The terrain was very different from that north
of the Tugela River. Gorges, ravines, wild rivers and
towering rocky peaks. He'd learned of this place at
school and could see why it had been named
Mpendle, the exposed place.

'First, get to Basutoland. Then worry about
where the fight for freedom is heading.'

He was cold. Mist shrouded the valleys. The
majestic beauty of the mountains reaching no further than his eyes. Would he be welcome in
Basutoland? The Sotho were traditional enemies of
the Zulu. Should he try to make it further north to
Bechuanaland? At least there he'd have access to
other countries. Basutoland was surrounded on all
sides by South Africa.

'One thing at a time,' he repeated to himself. 'At
least you're still alive.'

Tessa could barely contain her excitement. She was
home. Jackson was here. She would sneak out
tonight and meet him. God how she longed for
him. She had fantasised to such an extent that all
reason had flown. He was taller, more handsome
than any man had any right to be. He burned for
her and loved her as much as she did him. They
would go to England or somewhere far from
South Africa and live happily ever after.

Dinner was agonisingly slow. Afterwards Sally,
who had also done well in her final exams, wanted
to chat. Gregor, now twelve years old, insisted that

the entire family listen to and help him rehearse his role as Puck in Shakespeare's *A Midsummer Night's Dream*, which was to be staged at his school in Empangeni.

Tessa wondered if the family would ever go to bed. At ten she yawned and stretched. 'I'm tired. It's been a long day. See you in the morning. Good night all.'

Through the closed door of her room she listened until all sound in the house had ceased. She waited for nearly another hour in the total darkness to be sure that everybody was asleep and to give the dogs a chance to settle down in their baskets on the other side of the house. With a wildly beating heart and carrying her shoes, she carefully opened the French doors and stepped on to the verandah.

'Going somewhere?'

Her brother's voice startled her so badly she fumbled and dropped the shoes. 'None of your business.'

She heard his chair scrape as he stood up. 'Oh yes it is.' She could make out his silhouette as he moved towards her. 'Inside, missy.'

Tessa stood her ground. 'I'm eighteen. I can do what I like.'

'Fine.' He kept coming. 'I'll call the police.'

There was something in his voice that told her he meant it. Still, she pushed. 'You wouldn't dare.'

'Try me.'

Tessa nearly howled with frustration. Michael followed her and snapped the padlock shut.

Tessa made a rush towards the inside door but Michael was too quick. Stepping into the passage beyond, he pulled it shut and she heard the lock turn. 'You've brought this on yourself, Tessa,' he called. 'You can't be trusted. You may be eighteen but you will not break the law and run the risk of total disgrace while you're living under this roof. Good night.'

'Wait,' she called in panic, 'I need to go to the bathroom.'

'There's a pot under your bed. Use it.'

His footsteps faded away. She turned to the window and tried to open it. It was still wedged so that it opened only a crack. The other window was the same.

In the morning she was swollen-eyed from crying tears of rage. Claire unlocked the bedroom door. 'I'm sorry, Tessa. I had hoped this would no longer be necessary.'

Tessa made no comment.

Her mother stepped into the room. 'It's for your own good, darling. Men boast about certain things and people talk. If the police ever found out . . . We're only trying to protect you.'

Tessa turned sullen eyes on her mother. 'You have no idea,' she said softly. 'You just have no idea what you are doing to me. I love Jackson.'

'No,' Claire said sadly. 'You may think you do but it's not love.'

'How would you know?' Tessa challenged.

Claire flushed at her daughter's implication. The scorn in Tessa's eyes left her in no doubt that Tessa had been referring to her mother's somewhat celibate existence. 'What are we to do with her?' she thought in despair.

'Do you intend to keep me locked up all day and all night?' Tessa asked coldly.

'No. You are free to do as you please. But I beg you, darling, don't go looking for Jackson. We don't want any more unpleasantness. Jackson is leaving UBejane tomorrow.'

'Why? Where is he going?' Tessa had half expected this but hearing it was like a pronouncement of the end of the world.

'I don't know,' Claire lied. 'Join us for breakfast,' she said, leaving the room.

'I've got to see him,' Tessa thought feverishly as she dressed. 'I must.'

Everyone else was already at the table. Her mother, calm and kind, acting as though everything was normal. Gregor, between mouthfuls, still reciting his lines. Sally embarrassed and silent. Michael had his head in the previous day's *Natal Mercury*. He nodded curtly to her and went back to it. A few seconds later he gave a gasp of shock.

'What?' Claire asked.

'It's Dyson. He's escaped. The police have instigated a manhunt up near Bulwer.' Michael rattled the newspaper in agitation, then read the entire piece.

Forty-five policemen and ten tracker dogs are combing the hills around Bulwer for escaped prisoner Dyson Mpande.

In the early hours of Thursday morning, Mpande broke out of the high security prison near Pietermaritzburg. Possible sightings on the R617 to Bulwer have been confirmed by the discovery of prison clothing in the Umkomaas River.

Police from Howick, Deepdale, Bulwer and Himeville have set in motion one of the biggest manhunts ever seen in the area.

According to a spokesman from South African Police Headquarters in Pretoria, Mpande is a known member of Umkhonto we Sizwe, a wing of the banned African National Congress which has claimed responsibility for a number of terrorist bombings in recent years. Mpande may be armed and is considered highly dangerous. The public are warned not, under any circumstances, to approach him. All sightings should be reported to the police anti-terrorist unit in Himeville.

Mpande is described as five feet, ten inches tall, stocky build, dark complexion and has a disfiguring scar over his right eye.

Michael flung down the newspaper. 'They don't say anything about being held without charge or trial for three-and-a-half bloody years do they? They implicate him in the bombings but conveniently forget to mention that he'd been inside for two years when the first one went off. And what about the scar? He sure as hell didn't have it when he was arrested. It's all too convenient. After pulling God knows how many strings I finally get word two days ago that a trial date is to be set. Now this. It stinks. It's as if he was deliberately allowed to escape so they can justify killing him before he ever reaches a court.'

Tessa looked up from her plate. 'If he came here would you help him?'

'What kind of question is that? Of course I would. He's my friend.'

'But, Michael,' she said sweetly, 'it's against the law.'

'I would . . . it's not . . . dammit, can't you see?' He glared at her. 'This is different.'

'How?'

Michael glanced at Claire. The expression on her face was clear. 'Your call.'

On the surface, Michael had to concede she did have a point. He rationalised that his concern for Dyson was based on a friendship going back over twenty years whereas Tessa's fixation on Jackson was wilfully, defiantly and completely carnal.

Abruptly, he rose from the table. 'I've got work to do.'

Claire had to take Gregor into Empangeni for rehearsals. Sally, who had her learner's licence, asked if she could drive. Tessa said she'd stay home and was surprised when Claire raised no objection.

On the way into town Sally said, 'She'll try to find Jackson.'

'Most probably,' her mother said calmly. 'If she finds him she'll also discover that Wilson is watching his every move.' Claire had her fingers crossed.

Tessa wasted no time when they left. She kept close to the fences along which shade trees cast an intermittent shadow. She could not risk being seen, either by Michael or any of the farm employees. Having no idea where Jackson might be made it more difficult but, since he had recently finished school and would not be considered experienced, chances were he'd be working somewhere where others could advise him.

All she could think of was that Jackson was going away tomorrow. The news had devastated her. She was totally convinced of her love for him and her heart was breaking.

She stopped, scanning the open pasture. Cattle grazed but no people were in sight. Turning, she looked towards the stockyards further up the hill. There. Figures moving, too far away to see who they were. Tessa made her way forward, heart pounding with anticipation.

Jackson saw her coming but only because he'd been watching for her. He knew she was home and was convinced she would come looking for him. Last night he'd sneaked out of the compound and waited on their rocks but she hadn't come. He glanced around at the others. No-one else had seen her approaching. They had finished work on that section of the fence and were preparing to move further along.

Jackson was glad his father wasn't there. The news brought by Michael this morning that Dyson had escaped had stunned Wilson and Nandi with fear for their eldest son's safety. They were under no illusions that he would be returned to prison. He would be shot on sight. Michael had advised Wilson to stay at the compound. 'The police will be around sooner or later,' he told them. 'Stay here.' In his own anxiety over Dyson he'd forgotten all about reminding Wilson to keep an eye on Jackson.

Jackson called to the others. 'I'm going to see if there's any news of my brother.'

He set off down the hill, hoping that Tessa would have the good sense to stay in among the trees. Jackson saw her look in his direction. Her steps faltered but she quickly lowered her head and kept walking. Next time he looked, she had completely disappeared. He thought he knew where and changed direction slightly, heading for the solitary grave, set inside its own fenced-off garden, of Joe King. There, sandwiched between the large headstone and bushes behind it, he found her. She was stark naked, lying on the ground, discarded clothes spread under her.

Jackson caught his breath. For a white girl she was beautiful, of that he had no doubt. Right now it was not her looks that interested him. He'd been making do with *hlobonga* since they'd last been together. The memory of complete sex with her had burned him as much as it had Tessa. With a quick glance to make sure they had not been seen, Jackson dropped down beside her.

'I waited for you last night.'

'They locked me in.' Her hands reached for him. 'Don't talk. Fuck me. Fuck me as hard as you can.'

And there, on the ground that covered Joe King, his daughter and the son of UBejane's Zulu *induna* quelled the fires which raged within them.

Much later, physically sated, Tessa asked, 'Where are they sending you?'

'To my grandparents. It is to keep me from you.'

'I don't want you to go. I love you. Nobody understands.'

Her words surprised him. He never imagined any deeper feelings from her. It was sex, pure and simple.

'Why don't we run away?' Tessa had already decided there was no other way for them to be together.

'Where to? Where would we go?' For some time now Jackson had also been thinking of running away, but not with Tessa. He intended making his way north to the newly independent Zambia where, he'd been told, many South African blacks were being trained in guerrilla warfare.

'Bechuanaland,' Tessa said promptly. She'd already worked it out. 'We could live there, save money and then, if we wanted to, move to England.'

Jackson considered it. He could easily get into Zambia from the sparsely populated British protectorate which consisted largely of the Kalahari Desert. Having Tessa along would be no hardship. He would simply dump her when he felt like it.

'We would have to leave now,' he said. 'Right now.'

Tessa reached for her clothes, thinking of nothing but the pleasure of being with him again. 'Wait for me here.' She kissed him on the lips, not noticing his distaste for such a gesture. 'I'm going down to the house. I know where Mother keeps some money.'

While he waited, Jackson wondered idly what would happen first. Would he get sick of Tessa or would she tire of the hardships of which she obviously had no clue? He knew he shouldn't take her with him. It was madness. If they were caught the consequences didn't bear thinking about. But the lure of her willing body was too powerful for him to think straight.

Tessa arrived back twenty minutes later carrying a knapsack stuffed with food. 'I found nearly a hundred Rand,' she said proudly. 'Here, you keep it.'

As he pocketed more money than he'd ever seen in his life, Tessa added, 'I also took these,' and held out her hand. Glittering in her palm lay her mother's engagement ring, a diamond-encrusted brooch and a gold necklace studded with sapphires. All gifts to Claire from the lonely man who lay under their feet.

They were about to leave when dust on the road below caught their attention. 'Police,' Jackson hissed. 'Looking for Dyson. Come on. We must get away before my father sends for me.'

Before he turned away, Jackson allowed himself a last lingering look at the compound. He noticed that Tessa felt no similar moment was required. She took his hand and led him away from the grave, only saying, 'We should head for the railway line and follow it as far as Breyten.'

'Where's Breyten?'

'In the Transvaal. I've got a map. The line goes through some pretty deserted country. I'll show you later.'

As they set off the only thing in Tessa's heart was that she was happier than she'd ever been in her life.

Tessa had been unable to resist leaving a note but it wasn't found until much later in the day when Claire became worried about her daughter's on-going absence.

'She might be at the beach,' Gregor suggested.

'I can just see Tessa walking all that way,' Michael said.

Sally, having one of her premonitions, found the note propped against Tessa's pillow. Acting more on knowledge of her twin than any divine messages, she suggested they check to see if anything of value was missing.

Claire took the loss of her jewellery pragmati-cally. 'I never wore the stuff anyway.' But she was tight-lipped about the petty cash.

'Good riddance,' Michael said, screwing up Tessa's note and throwing it into the wastepaper basket beside Claire's desk.

A sob at the door announced a very distressed Nandi. 'Madam, Jackson has disappeared. The police wish to question him.'

Michael groaned inwardly. Life had been testing enough for the Mpande family without this. 'Come in, Nandi. There's something we have to tell you.'

Nandi took the news with outward calm. 'Perhaps he will take her to our village.' Trembling lips gave away her true feelings.

'Show her the note, Michael.'

He retrieved the crumpled paper and spread it out for Nandi to read:

You have made my life unbearable. I am running away to live with Jackson. Do not try to find us, I will refuse to return. I love Jackson and he loves me. Neither of us will be missed. We will make our life somewhere else.

Nandi lifted her eyes. 'She is wrong. Already we miss our son.'

'What do we do?' Claire strode around her office. 'Should we contact the police?'

'No!' Michael and Nandi said in unison.

'Think, Mother,' Michael continued. 'They're both eighteen. The police would throw them both in prison.'

Claire sat down behind her desk. 'We can't just forget about them,' she said despairingly.

'Tessa's made it abundantly clear that that's what they want,' Michael countered. 'Personally, I believe it will all fizzle out. The road they've chosen is a hard one. Give them a couple of weeks, they'll be back.' He went to the door. 'I have work to do.'

Claire watched him go. 'Nandi,' she said softly. 'Michael's right. It's the best we can hope for.'

Nandi sighed and turned to leave. 'Forgive me, madam, but Miss Tessa has led my boy astray.' She stood stiffly, expecting a rebuke.

But Claire knew she was right. 'I have never been able to reach her. If this is the life she has chosen then I pray with all my heart that Jackson knows the dangers and treats her well.'

Nandi, so deep in sorrow over Dyson, was beyond caring. 'The danger is your daughter herself,' she said sharply. 'If your girl cannot keep her legs together there will be others, many others, and that has nothing to do with my son.'

Michael drove to the compound to find Wilson. The Zulu was still badly shaken by the news of Dyson and trembling with rage at the bullying tactics of the police who had just left. 'More bad news, I'm afraid,' Michael said.

'What could be worse?'

'Jackson and Tessa have run away.'

Wilson closed his eyes as if to shut out the world.

'We cannot call the police,' Michael went on. 'All we can do is hope they know where they're going and reach there safely.'

'Bechuanaland,' Wilson said suddenly. 'Jackson will go there. Then into Zambia.'

'To get guerrilla training?'

'Yes.' Wilson shook his head. 'He is hot-headed,

my son. He has no patience for slow change. He would rather fight than talk.'

'Then he is a dead man,' Michael said flatly. 'And my sister is likely to die with him.'

'I do not think they will stay together. They are both too selfish. What she offers him is, for now, irresistible but later . . .' He shrugged.

'My sister is a whore,' Michael said harshly.

'Then, *Nkosi*, I am very much afraid that, in the Zulu tradition, she will be treated as one.'

'That is probably the only thing that will make Tessa happy,' Michael said bitterly.

Wilson placed a hand on Michael's shoulder. 'We cannot always understand what is in the hearts of others, even if they are joined to us by blood. The things that drive my son and your sister were there when they were born. All we can do is try and steer them to a safer path. If they fail to take it,' Wilson shook his head, 'then we can only hope they remain safe. Their destinies have already been shaped. All they do is follow.'

'Yeah!' Michael replied, suddenly switching to English. 'Straight to hell.'

'Come. We will walk, you and I.'

They left the compound and walked to where Wilson could see the cattle. The sight always calmed him, left him feeling that though his ancestors must be displeased with him in some way, the sleek, healthy beasts were living proof that the spirits were not angry enough to send disaster to them too. And that, as far as Wilson was concerned, was cause enough to carry a little optimism in a heart full of sorrow.

Michael broke the silence that had fallen between them. 'What did the police tell you about Dyson?'

'Pah!' Wilson dismissed the visit contemptuously. 'They say if he comes here I must tell them. Do they think my son is a fool? Do they think they can frighten me? Do they imagine I have forgotten this?' He pulled up his shirt.

Michael had seen the scars before. Three years ago the police had used truncheons to get through Wilson's silence after Dyson had been captured. The broken ribs had healed but his body would carry the marks for the rest of his life. It had been Michael who had half-carried Wilson from the police station the day after the entire Mpande family had been arrested. Nearly fainting with pain, Wilson refused help to get out of the car once they'd reached the compound. He emerged slowly, then stood erect and dignified. Slowly, with hands that trembled, he took off his shirt, turning so all could see his injuries. Around him, exclamations of shock and anger erupted. Then Wilson moved forward and went into his house, shutting the door behind him. He did not set foot outside for a week. When he returned to work he made no mention of the beating.

Nandi, Jackson and the two younger children had been interrogated but otherwise left alone.

Michael had not been able to take Wilson to the hospital. If Africans needed treatment as a result of violence, doctors could do nothing for them unless they were accompanied by the police. That was the law. Michael knew there was no point in asking so he took Wilson home. Colin's wife, Anna, had been a nurse and generally dealt with injuries. It was Anna who put ointment on the broken skin before taping Wilson's ribcage.

Wilson pulled his shirt down angrily. He was still trembling.

Michael could only guess at the emotions running through this man. Indignation, anger, fear, sorrow.

'I'm sorry,' he said and they both knew he was apologising, not commiserating.

'Thank you,' Wilson responded quietly. He looked away over the land where cattle grazed. 'It is too late to stop. It has gone on too long, gone too far.' He turned back to Michael. 'I have a great fear of what happens next. If a man's right to live like a man is taken away there is only one thing left. He has no other choice. If respect for his life is gone, then he will look to his death.'

'The death of a warrior? Glorious in defeat?'

'It is better to die fighting than to live in fear.'

'When will it end, for God's sake? How much longer can this madness last?'

'It will last for as long as minds are not the same.'

'Then it will never end.'

'Yes. Look at my own family.'

He was right. Wilson, Dyson and Jackson, all seeking the same thing, all seeking them in very different ways.

'Jackson has the hot blood of youth. He disobeys

344

everything we taught him.' He smiled wryly. 'He thinks we are fools. He is too young to know what we know. The only fool is Jackson.' Wilson fingered a leather thong around his neck before stretching it so much it snapped. 'He goes too far.' He held out the piece of leather. 'See what happens.'

Michael said nothing.

'And Dyson,' Wilson continued. 'If he lives he will be like the reed. When the wind blows, he will bend. When the wind stops, he will stand straight and proud.'

'And you?' Michael asked.

'Ah!' Wilson chuckled. 'I am a man of the land and I have learned that the mealie needs rain and time before it is ready to be eaten.' He pointed to some newly born calves. 'Jackson would eat them now. Dyson would wait, but not for long. Me? I am content to wait.'

'I wish I had your patience, Wilson. For now, it appears to be in short supply.'

'You are welcome to my patience, *Nkosi*. But you would not wish for my anger.'

Driving back to the house, Michael wondered, as he had so many times before, how people like Wilson were able to control their emotions. It was a facade, he knew. One borne from necessity. Even so, it was a remarkable show of restraint.

ELEVEN

Tessa was having the time of her life. The sense of freedom was almost overwhelming. She could live like this forever. Life on the run with Jackson was a wonderful adventure. Being summer, though the days were uncomfortably hot, the nights were blissfully balmy, a gentle kiss on their skins as they lay curled together.

The map taken from the house showed that the railway line ran through virtually uninhabited land. This was not strictly true. Although there were no towns as such, tribal trust land and African villages covered most of the area. Tessa could not understand why Jackson avoided contact with these people. In her mind, she was someone to be made welcome, treated like a princess. After all, hadn't she given up a life of pampered luxury? Hadn't she shown that she was not like other whites? Didn't she deserve their acceptance and respect? She was a heroine, a champion of the Zulu cause, to be praised and feted, not treated like some embarrassingly shameful secret. But Jackson knew that Tessa would not be made welcome by his people. The knowledge of what Tessa and Jackson were doing would only make them afraid, fearful that their own lives might be touched by this sinful act. The few they did encounter raised eyebrows at the sight of a young white woman in the company of a young black man but any conclusion they might have drawn was so bizarre that they did not dwell on it.

Each evening Tessa and Jackson sought a sheltered, out-of-the-way place to bed down for the night. There, under the stars, they enjoyed each other to the fullest extent, performing the one and only act that bonded them together, the only thing that intertwined their destinies. It was such a powerful force that neither of them realised that when the music stopped and the stars went away there would be nothing left.

They skirted the village where Jackson's grandparents lived. Jackson knew it well. He'd been coming here for holidays all his life. And, as his father experienced all those years ago when he came back from the war, the sight of the village filled Jackson with nostalgia. He looked with longing at the neat beehive huts. Down there were his kin. Down there he could find the sanctuary of food, shelter and friendship. An uninvited melancholy settled like a cloak around his shoulders. He didn't mention his connections to the village which, nestled in a fold of the foothills, caused Tessa to exclaim, 'That looks like something out of a fairytale. It's beautiful. Oh, Jackson, wouldn't it be wonderful if we could live there.'

Very quickly, Jackson had realised that he was

making a terrible mistake. How could he have been so stupid? Without Tessa in tow all he would have been doing was running away from home, not breaking the law. He could have travelled openly to Bechuanaland. Instead he was living rough, a fugitive, always alert for prying white eyes. Some girls might have coped but Tessa was too different. She was arrogant and demanding and prattled almost non-stop. She was also white. He delighted in her body and using it was fine by him. But within a couple of days, Jackson knew that Tessa could never accept the African way of life. For all her rhetoric, she was too pampered, too totally European and far too giddy in the head to see much further than his deek. She expected him to wait on her hand and foot. It was Jackson who had to find wood when it was safe to build a fire. It was Jackson who prepared a bed of sweet grass for them to lie on. It was Jackson who collected up wild fruit and berries for them to eat. Tessa would simply sit and wait for him, accepting his offerings as her due.

Jackson was caught between two worlds. His tribal, traditional upbringing told him that the woman was supposed to be doing these menial tasks. The system in South Africa had conditioned him to the fact that Tessa was the master and Jackson the slave. The signals were confusing and further complicated by the illegal nature of their relationship.

By the end of the third week, the strain was beginning to tell. As they moved further north it was harder to stay out of sight. Once they crossed the Balelesberg Range, the land flattened out, providing little cover. They had left Natal behind and were in the Transvaal, Afrikaner country, dour individuals who barely tolerated Africans or English-speaking South Africans. Jackson decided it would be safer to travel at night and hide up during the day until they were well north of Johannesburg.

Just for a change, Tessa accepted his decision without an argument.

He looked at her closely. She'd been unusually silent all day. For the past week she had done nothing but complain about the heat, lack of decent food, sore feet and how much she hated sleeping on the ground. Jackson grew thoroughly sick of her. Two nights ago a violent storm caught them without shelter and then it rained all night. Tessa had clung to him shaking with cold and sobs. Her silence today made him think that she too was having second thoughts.

'Are you all right?'

'No.' Tears formed and rolled down her cheeks.

'What's wrong now?' He was unable to hide his irritation.

'I feel sick.'

'You look okay.'

She brushed at her cheeks. 'I've missed a period.'

It was not an expression he knew. 'What do you mean?'

She took a shuddering breath. 'I think I might be pregnant.'

Tessa had been dreading this moment. Jackson was not in love with her. At first she had pushed the thought aside, blaming her imagination. But then, as she started to look for signs that he felt the same for her as she did for him, she realised that not only did he not love her, he made no attempt to hide the fact. He never showed affection, never touched her unless they were having sex, spoke only when he absolutely had to and was obviously irritated by anything she had to say.

Last night, when he reached out and put his hand between her legs she had been unable to stop herself from asking, 'Do you love me, Jackson?'

'Don't be silly,' he'd laughed. 'I am a Zulu. How could I love a white woman?'

The response had stunned her. Tessa realised he had not been referring to the apartheid laws of South Africa. In Jackson's heart, she was simply not good enough for him.

She watched his face now as he absorbed her words. His eyes were cold, expressionless. 'You fool,' he hissed finally.

It was all going horribly wrong and she grew very afraid. He was all she had. 'Jackson!' she pleaded.

'This is the last thing I need.'

'*You* need!' She was suddenly furious. 'What about me?'

'What about you?' he challenged, haughtily Zulu. 'You are a woman.'

It was like a slap in the face. He was no different from all the others. A woman's place was either on her back or bent to one of so many endless tasks. Her fear grew. She'd burned her boats, there was no going back. 'It won't be born for ages,' Tessa tried to placate him. 'We'll be settled in Bechuanaland by then.'

'You might be,' Jackson sneered. 'I'll be in Zambia.'

'But what about us? You will take me with you, won't you? You can't just abandon me. I thought you loved me.'

'Well I don't. And pregnant you're no good to me at all.'

His words pushed her too far. How dare he when she'd given up everything for him?

'I didn't get this way on my own you know. You are equally to blame.'

'If we practised *hlobonga* you wouldn't be pregnant.'

'You were always pleased enough to fuck me properly,' she threw back at him.

'Don't say that word. I hate it when you use that word.'

'Fuck,' Tessa yelled.

That was when Jackson snapped. The backhander was so powerful that it knocked Tessa off her feet. He was surprised. He'd seen African women absorb beatings much worse. Tessa's susceptibility to his blow showed a weak spot. She was all mouth. The knowledge gave Jackson a new power over her. She lay whimpering on the grass as he stood over her. 'Get up.'

'You hurt me.' It was more than just physical.

Tessa's pride had been crushed by his rejection of her.

'I'll hurt you again if you don't get up.'

The threat worked. Tessa rose slowly to her feet, the right side of her face already swollen and discoloured. Again, Jackson was surprised at how this haughty girl had suddenly become vulnerable. 'I want to go home,' she said in a small voice.

There, it was out in the open. Having said it, Tessa's resolve grew. 'This was a mistake. I want to go home.'

'You can't. You've got a bastard black baby in your belly. How do you expect to keep that a secret?'

Tessa began to cry.

Jackson turned and walked away. 'Do what you like. I'm going to Bechuanaland.'

He was several hundred metres away before the realisation finally hit her. While she desperately needed him, Jackson had no need of her. The power she believed she had over him was nothing more than his taking what she had so freely offered. He had used her and now she was trapped, suddenly terrified that he would discard her somewhere to fend for herself. 'Wait.' She began to run after him. 'Jackson, please don't leave me here. Wait for me.'

He didn't stop. Tessa had to run for several minutes to catch up. 'From now on, you'll pull your weight,' he said when she drew level with him. 'See that tree over there. Go and fetch some fruit.'

'You'll wait here?' she asked in a small voice.

'Yes.'

As she plucked the wild apples, Tessa's calculating mind was already looking for a way out. 'When we get to the next town I'll go to the police and tell them he abducted me. They'll believe me. Mother will take me back, I know she will. In the meantime, I mustn't let him suspect. He must think I want to stay with him.' She took the fruit to Jackson. 'Here,' she said softly. 'I'm sorry. I won't use that word again.' She hated him now. *How could I have thought I loved him?*

Jackson was having thoughts of his own. 'I could kill her and bury the body. No-one would ever find it. Travelling alone would be quicker and safer.' But he discarded the idea as soon as he had it. Killing a white girl, if he were ever caught, would mean an automatic death sentence. Far better to take her as far as Bechuanaland and then dump her.

That night, it was Tessa who collected up the grass for their bed. That night, it was Jackson who insisted they have sex. Tessa didn't want to but she was afraid to say no. As he guided himself into her, the fires which she couldn't control burned in open betrayal. Tessa's body responded eagerly although her mind rebelled and her heart was revolted. For the first time, Tessa understood. She was powerless to stop the cravings, a prisoner inside her own body.

About two months after Tessa's disappearance, Michael realised he was happier than he had ever been. He hummed under the shower, smiled all the time, and had a lightness inside him that had never been there before. He did not have to look far to see why. Jennifer Bailey.

Over the past four years he hadn't seen a lot of her. She'd been away at university and, after graduating, went on a working holiday in Europe. In France, she put her degree to good use, joining a team of scientists who were studying the effects of cramped and totally unnatural living conditions under which many European zoos housed and displayed some of Africa's largest animals.

Jennifer had come home a couple of times. Whenever she did, the two of them were inseparable, going to parties or the beach together. Their relationship, however, remained platonic. Both of them felt they were too young for commitment but there was an unspoken understanding between them that when the time was right, they would put their feelings to the test. There was a risk of course that one or the other might meet someone else. Indeed, Michael had found the psychiatrist, Annie Lewis, attractive and might have been tempted to pursue a relationship with her if they hadn't argued over Tessa. He told himself it just wasn't meant to be.

Now Jennifer was back in Africa. She was waiting for Dr Emil Daguin, the head of the research project in France, to arrive for a major breeding habit study of black rhinoceros recently introduced into the Okavango Delta in Bechuanaland and other undisturbed areas nearby. It was an ambitious scheme, scheduled to take five years, and Jennifer had been offered a position on the team.

Fundraising difficulties and the death of Dr Daguin's wife in a tragic car accident had delayed commencement of the project. Fate, it seemed, was giving Jennifer and Michael the opportunity at last. Michael slipped easily into the habit of seeing her three or four times a week. And last night, as naturally as breathing, their relationship soared into intimacy, leaving Michael in no doubt that he was in love.

The evening had started as usual, Michael dropping in for a drink around six. 'Fancy a movie?'

She screwed up her nose. 'Seen it.'

'Dinner?'

'Made it.'

Michael, comfortable on the sofa, stretched his legs. 'Where are your folks?' Then he remembered. They had gone up to their mountain holiday cottage in Himeville for a week to get away from the summer heat. 'Just you and me, huh?'

'You got it.'

The timbre of her voice had deepened. Michael immediately sensed the change. There was no need for more words. They met in the middle of the room, eyes locked, the only outward sign that their minds, hearts and souls had, with no warning, meshed. As their lips met a jolt like an electric shock ran through both of them. And, as his arms tightened around her, the kiss deepened and Michael knew he was holding his future.

Lying together later, Jennifer had talked about

Emil Daguin and his project. 'He'll be looking for someone to coordinate it.'

Michael's head was still spinning from their lovemaking. 'Bit out of my league.'

'Not at all. You'd be perfect.'

'Jen, I'm a cane farmer.'

'You've worked with black rhino, though.'

'Yes but I've got no scientific background.'

'Emil will handle that side of things. What he needs is someone with good organisation skills, not another academic.'

The more she talked about it, the more excited he became. It was not just the prospect of working side by side with Jennifer that appealed to him, though God knows, the thought was about as pleasing as they came. He was honest enough to acknowledge that while he was content to run UBejane, the Umfolozi black rhino project had whetted his appetite for a different kind of future.

It was around two in the morning when Michael returned to the farm. The euphoria was still with him. He knew he wanted to spend the rest of his life with Jennifer. Emil Daguin's project was the icing on the cake. Everything was suddenly falling into place. But, in all fairness, could he expect his mother to yet again shoulder the full responsibility of UBejane? The quandary played on his mind, offering no obvious solution.

Claire commented on his mood at breakfast. 'You're looking very preoccupied this morning. Could it have something to do with Jennifer?'

Gregor paused, spoon halfway to his mouth. At

twelve, he had the annoying habit of knowing everything. 'He's in love.'

Michael cuffed him playfully on the back of his head.

Dramatically, Gregor allowed his face to fall onto the fresh pawpaw he was eating.

Claire was laughing. 'Go and wash your face, you idiot child.'

Gregor left the table saying, 'Don't tell her anything till I get back.'

Michael shook his head. 'Always the entertainer. He belongs on a stage.'

'It's probably where he'll end up. Now, what about you?'

Michael grinned. 'Okay, I admit it. I'm twenty-six and ready to settle down. Jennifer is . . . well, just bloody marvellous.'

'That's great.' Claire threw down her napkin, rose from the table and hugged him. 'I must write to Sally.'

'Hold on.' Michael pushed his chair back and stood up. 'Let's not rush this.'

Claire gave him a shrewd look. 'Rush what? You and Jennifer have been seeing each other regularly since she returned. You've known her most of your life. You may have only just realised that she is the one for you but, I can assure you, Michael, the rest of us have seen it coming for ages and Jennifer has known what her feelings are for some time.'

'You think so?' Michael smiled widely.

'Try asking her to marry you.'

Michael looked anxious. 'What if she says no?'

'She won't.'

'What makes you such an expert?'

'I'm a woman.'

Michael folded his arms. 'So?'

'Women know these things.'

Gregor returned. 'What have I missed?'

'Nothing,' Michael told him airily.

Gregor sat down and resumed his breakfast. 'Must be an interesting nothing,' he observed to his plate. 'The poor man looks like a beagle. All droopy and soppy.'

'Do shut up,' Michael laughed. 'And hurry up. You'll miss the bus.'

When Gregor had gone Claire said, 'Come into the office. We must talk.'

Michael wondered what was on her mind. He was totally unprepared for her words.

'How would you feel about putting UBejane on the market?'

'Sell!' He was incredulous. This place was her life.

Claire looked fondly at her firstborn. 'If Gregor were more interested, I wouldn't think of it. Sally may well stay in Paris. She's overcome her disappointment about being too tall for ballet and wants to concentrate on fashion design. Tessa . . .' Claire bit her lip. 'That leaves you, Michael. You're here for me, I know that, but your heart isn't in it.'

Michael narrowed his eyes at her. 'You haven't been speaking to Jennifer by any chance?'

Claire attempted wide-eyed innocence but Michael wasn't fooled. 'You know, don't you?

About the rhino project. Dammit, Mother, thanks a bunch . . .'

'I needed to know how you felt about Jennifer. I wouldn't even suggest selling if I thought you wanted to carry on here. When Jennifer first mentioned the project . . . well, we both agreed . . . Look, I'm sorry if you think I'm interfering but you do play things rather close to your chest.' She was flustered, thinking he was cross.

Michael decided it was her turn to stew but a traitorous smile betrayed him. 'Did you ask her to marry me as well?'

'Michael! Of course not.'

He fixed eagle eyes on her.

'Ah . . . April's good.'

'Good for what?'

'Month,' Claire babbled. 'It's a good month. Weather is wonderful. If we sell . . . I mean, you'd want the reception here . . . April is . . . oh shit!'

Michael burst out laughing.

'You're not mad at me?'

'How could I be? You suggest selling the farm out from under me, by the sounds of things the wedding is arranged right down to the carnation in my buttonhole, and, if that's not enough, a career change seems to be down to you as well. Really, Mother. What makes you think I'm mad at you?'

'Michael!' she pleaded.

He gave her an enormous hug. 'Now scat out of my life. I'd appreciate the reins for a while. Anyway, what about you? If UBejane is sold, what will you do?'

'Me?' It was Claire's turn to hide a smile. She failed. 'I might go to England.'

'Uh huh! England.' He was grinning at her sudden embarrassment. 'Well, well. You accuse me of not saying much. I don't suppose this has anything to do with one Peter Dawson. Nah! Course not.'

Claire blushed. 'Do you mind, darling? You know we've stayed in touch all these years. He's never married. He's asked me to go to England often enough to see . . . well . . . if things could work out between us.'

Michael hugged her again. 'I think it's wonderful. I always liked Peter.'

'You do know, don't you, that Gregor . . .'

'Yes.' Michael cut her off. Not because he didn't want to hear her say it but because he knew how hard it would be for her to do so. 'I know. Does Gregor?'

'Not yet. But if I go to England he'll obviously come with me. That would be the time.'

'I should think the news would come as some relief to him. He hated Joe.'

'I know,' Claire said softly. 'I've been tempted so often to tell him the truth.'

'Peter knows, of course.'

'Yes. He has met Gregor once or twice on visits. It's been very difficult for him.'

'Why don't you put in a manager? You might want to come back here with Peter.'

Claire shook her head. 'I could never share this place, and all its unpleasant memories, with Peter. It wouldn't be fair to either of us. We need a fresh start. Besides, the way this country is going . . .'

'Not you too! It's all I hear these days. People have been saying, "I give this country no more than five years" for the past ten years.'

'You have to admit, South Africa is headed for a confrontation.'

'I do agree. But a little bit of optimism wouldn't go astray.'

Claire smiled. 'You're young. You have time for optimism.'

Michael could see she'd made up her mind. 'I hope it comes right for you, Mother. God knows, you deserve some happiness.'

Michael left instructions for the day with Balram, then went to find Wilson. 'Any news?'

Wilson knew what he meant. 'No, nothing. I would tell you if I heard anything.'

'Thanks. I have to admit though, I'm not sure I want to hear.'

Wilson nodded gravely. 'It is said by our people that bad news rides the winds of even worse news. I am like you, *Nkosi*. Even though I hunger to hear of my sons, my heart is heavy with fear. Even so, every day I ask Nandi if a letter has arrived.'

'You think they'll write? Can't see that happening.'

'No,' Wilson agreed. 'Jackson will not write. But Nandi's sister who lives in Bechuanaland is aware of the situation. She will write. Each day we expect news.'

'You're convinced that's where they went?'

'Jackson will head for Bechuanaland. He has talked of little else for years. He wishes to join the freedom fighters.' Wilson's eyes searched Michael's. 'But perhaps I tell the *Nkosi* too much.'

'You know you do not,' Michael reassured him quickly. 'I do not think violence is the answer but there are many who believe that dialogue alone will never work. Dyson and I . . .' he broke off at the sudden pain on Wilson's face.

'We fear he may be dead.'

'He's not.' Michael was adamant. 'If the police had recaptured or killed him they'd waste no time boasting about it. No, Wilson. In Dyson's case, no news is good news.'

'But even if he is alive, he can never come home.'

'Not yet admittedly, but he's my friend and I'd like to help him.'

'How can you?'

'Money. I'm as helpless as you because of the way things work in this country but cash is one thing I can provide. He should go to London, join someone like Oliver Tambo. Please tell him that if you hear from him.'

'I will tell him. It would gladden our hearts to know that he was pursuing a peaceful solution from a safe distance.' Wilson smiled suddenly and clapped his hands together softly. 'Eh heh, but I am forgetting. It is being said that on this day the *Nkosi* is to raise the white flag outside his house.'

Michael laughed. 'I won't ask how the hell you know. Is nothing private around here?'

'Private!' Wilson scoffed. 'How can it be private

when this thing is written on your face for all to see? But I am wondering, *Nkosi*, who will speak for you?'

'I will speak for myself.'

'Hau! What if she calls you a dog?'

I'll probably bark. 'I have it on very good authority that the lady in question is more likely to call me a dog if I don't speak for myself.'

Wilson put a hand on Michael's arm. 'Come,' he said, proud as any father. 'If the *Nkosi* is to speak for himself he should do so with courage, a clever tongue and a wise head. I have the very thing.'

Michael's heart sank a little. He was not overly fond of African beer and knew, from experimenting once or twice with Dyson, that it could be awesomely potent. However, he would not insult Wilson by refusing.

And so it was that when Michael proposed marriage to Jennifer Bailey, the girl he had gone to school with, the girl whose silky blonde locks and hazel eyes, whose infectious laugh and straightforward intelligence had captivated his heart, he was more than slightly drunk. Jennifer, a Zululand girl through and through, who spoke Zulu as fluently as Michael, who had practically lived in the kia of her nanny when she was little and who, when she was of a mind, could match the best of them drink for drink, accepted without hesitation. Having sealed the arrangement with a lusty, lingering kiss, she opened two quart bottles of Castle lager, and passed one to Michael saying, 'Cheers. Here's to us.'

Michael drank. 'I take it April will suit you?' he asked.

'Your mother is a blabber mouth.' She grinned at him. 'What took you so long?'

Michael tipped his bottle and drank a quarter of its contents before responding. 'Abject fear,' he admitted candidly.

Jennifer laughed and put down her bottle. 'Enough booze for you, my lad. You're already legless.'

Michael put down his. 'True.'

'Not much point in suggesting you take me out to celebrate.'

'Not much.'

'We could always stay here and, you know, honour the occasion.'

'We could.'

She wound her arms around his neck. 'Your conversation is slipping.'

He put his arms around her waist and kissed her. 'I'm practising to be a husband.'

Her hand found the zipper on his shorts. 'I'm practising too.'

He groaned as her fingers reached him. 'Practise away. I'm all yours.'

'Too bloody right and don't you forget it!' She grinned at him.

Michael knew, with absolute certainty, that he would love this girl forever.

Dyson knocked softly at the door of the darkened house on the outskirts of Gaberones. A few minutes went by before a voice called timidly, 'Who is it?'

'Dyson Mpande. Your nephew.'

The door opened immediately. 'Come inside.'

Dyson had never met his mother's sister. She had married outside the Zulu tribe – a Tswana – and moved to his home in the British protectorate of Bechuanaland. Despite misgivings over their daughter's defection to a different tribe, her parents were pleased that at least one of their children had escaped the repression of South Africa. Letters were frequent, so Dorcas Sobona was well aware of Nandi's difficulties with two of her children.

'You must eat.' She was horrified by Dyson's condition. Gaunt, haunted eyes, clothes in tatters, he appeared to be on the brink of collapse. The way he wolfed down her hastily prepared meal told Dorcas how desperate he must have been.

Her husband, having greeted his hitherto unknown relation, left them in the kitchen and returned to bed saying only, 'Don't Zulus *ever* sleep?'

'He is tired,' Dorcas excused him. 'You are safe now. The South Africans cannot reach you here.'

Dyson shook his head. 'They can request extradition. I have to get further away.'

'Nobody knows you are here. Stay with us a while. Get your strength back. Now come. I will prepare a bed for you. Take off those filthy rags. You can wear something of my husband's until we get some new clothes.' As she quickly made up a bed on the floor using cushions from the sofa, she spoke softly and reassuringly, seeming to sense how wound up and frightened he was. She wasn't his mother but she was the next best thing and Dyson felt himself relax. 'There.' She patted the blankets and fluffed up the pillow. 'Sleep now, Dyson. Sleep deep and well. You are among your own family.'

How good it felt. Food in his belly, pyjamas, a roof over his head, people who cared for him.

He had been on the run for nine weeks, coming close to capture three times. When they brought in the helicopters he thought he was done for. How they missed seeing him as he dived for cover was nothing short of a miracle. He'd been on the edge of the small town of Underberg, heading north towards Sani Pass, the only road into Basutoland in the whole of Natal, when two helicopters swept up from behind a hill. Had the men in them been looking his way they would most certainly have seen him. Perhaps their attention had been momentarily diverted as the towering peaks of the Drakensberg came into view, the full majestic vista unfolding as the choppers rose clear of the Umkomaas valley. They wouldn't be the first to lose their breath at the sight of a seemingly endless escarpment rising from a sea of grass, an impenetrable wall of basalt climbing to 3500 metres above sea level, dramatically sculptured by centuries of erosion, snow capped over high green plateaus swept smooth in an ancient ice age, water tumbling clear into deep dark gorges.

Watching the helicopters, Dyson realised that they too were heading towards Sani Pass, obviously expecting he would do the same. The single track dirt road, climbing, twisting, snake-like for twenty heart-pounding kilometres to the mountain sanctuary of Basutoland, was his only way up. Experienced climbers might tackle the cliffs and crevices but

Dyson knew he could not. Resigned, frightened, hungry and alone, he swung northwards, skirting below the high peaks. There was no alternative. He'd have preferred to lie low for a while, until the man-hunt had been scaled down, but now the only choice was to head as quickly as possible for Bechuanaland.

Twice more, on that seemingly endless journey, he'd nearly blundered into discovery. In an African township just outside a place called Heilbron he'd been unlucky enough to get caught when the police, in a routine 'let's hassle the locals', arrested a group of people drinking at a *shebeen*. Dyson had been passing the illegal but usually tolerated drinking house, his steps slowing as he listened wistfully to the merry-making inside, wishing he had the money to join in. Lost in his longing, by the time he realised the vehicle that pulled up behind him was the police, it was too late to get away. Rounded up with the people from inside, just before being bundled into the wagon he felt something being pushed into his hand. 'Bring it back when you can,' a woman whispered and was gone. Dyson knew what it was, a passbook. He hoped the photograph looked sufficiently like him. There was no way to examine the document, even to register a name. He could not assume he was among friends. If someone saw him studying the passbook, they could very well inform on him in order to save their own skin.

'Where did you steal this from hey, kaffir?' the policeman asked in Afrikaans, staring at Dyson. He had pale blue eyes, full of ice. 'Do not try to tell me this is your passbook.'

'Yes, sir, it is my passbook, sir.' Dyson deliberately spoke in broken and badly accented English.

'Speak Afrikaans, boy. This is not your photograph. What do you take me for?'

'Ah, sir. But I have been very sick.' Dyson responded in Afrikaans. His heart sank when he saw the photograph. The man in it was twice his weight and looked nothing like him.

'Sick,' the policeman sneered, his long bony nose turning down.

Dyson, frantically trying to read the upside-down name, nodded. 'Yes, sir. I am having the shitting sickness.'

'Heh! You bloody kaffirs.' The policeman was not amused.

'Yes, sir. All day I am shitting and all day I am vomiting.'

The passbook was pushed across the desk. 'Get out of here, you dirty bugger. Go on. Out. Jesus!' The policeman's distaste was palpable. He turned to a colleague. 'Probably got cholera. Better have a good scrub when you get home, Dirk.'

Dyson had been tempted to keep the pass but, in the end, returned to the *shebeen*. As it happened, the woman who gave it to him was the owner. 'How did you know?' he asked, handing the book back.

She shrugged. 'I saw you standing in the street. You have the look of a desperate man. I have seen it many times.'

Dyson thanked her for helping him and turned to leave.

'Wait, Zulu.' She handed him a bottle of Carling

black label. 'You are an honest man. Many would have kept that pass.'

'Who does it belong to?' The beer was probably the best he had ever tasted.

'Hau, Zulu! You drink like a man dying of thirst.' She narrowed her eyes. 'Or fear perhaps.'

'Perhaps.' He put the bottle down. 'Thank you,' he said quietly.

The compassion in her eyes as he left the bar would have made him weep had he seen it. As he made his way through the township he realised she had not answered his question. Whoever owned that passbook would remain a mystery. Dyson thought that strange, the man had probably saved his life.

At Zeerust, not far from the Bechuanaland border, he was, once again, in the wrong place at the wrong time. Fortunately for Dyson the entire white police force, all six of them, had been celebrating the birth of the sergeant's fourth child. After some vigorous questioning about why he wasn't carrying his pass . . . 'Please, sir. It is in my home. Very sorry, sir'. . . and some rough handling . . . 'This is just a warning, kaffir. Don't let us catch you without it again'. . . he was driven fifteen kilometres along a bush track and told to walk back. The police drove off in high humour, chortling about 'Teaching these cheeky kaffirs a lesson.' As the vehicle was swallowed up by its own dust, Dyson threw the men a sardonic salute. They had taken him closer to Gaberones. 'Thank you, gentlemen.' He left the sandy road and was soon out of sight in the bush.

That was two days ago. Now, in the relative safety of his aunt's house, he reviewed his options. Rhodesia was out of the question. He could try to reach Zambia, join the freedom fighters possibly, but Dyson had little taste for some of their methods which often caused more problems than they solved. He could just forget the whole South African mess, change his name, and make a life somewhere. Maybe go to Nyasaland, which was heading towards independence. He could . . .

Dyson fell asleep.

Driving back to UBejane, Michael's thoughts were of practical things. Such as buying an engagement ring, who to invite to the wedding, joining the rhino project. Good thoughts, all to do with Jennifer and the rest of his life. He pulled up in front of the house and got out, whistling softly. Wilson materialised out of the darkness. 'I see you, *Nkosi*.'

'I see you, Wilson.' His good mood evaporated. For Wilson to be waiting up for him at this hour could only mean bad news.

'Will you be raising the white flag?'

'First thing tomorrow.'

'That is good. *Nkosi* has spoken well for himself.'

Michael swallowed his impatience. To hurry Wilson would be very rude. However, no harm in a slight nudge. 'It is a fine night but the hour is late.'

'Indeed. A very fine night but it will rain in the morning.'

'We need rain.'

Silence stretched between them. Wilson broke it reluctantly. 'There is a letter. It is not good news.'

'Are they in Bechuanaland?'

'By now, only Miss Tessa will be there. Jackson has gone to Zambia.'

'So he dumped her.' Michael was not surprised.

'It was always going to be. They were not destined to stay together.' It was the closest Wilson could come to censuring Tessa, even though he was probably aware that Michael agreed with him.

'Where is she? I suppose she expects someone to fetch her?'

Michael heard Wilson sigh. 'It is not as simple as that. You will be very angry.'

'Try me. I do not know if my anger can get any worse.'

Wilson said softly, 'I think it can get much worse, *Nkosi*. It is very bad.'

'What are you telling me? Is she dead?'

'No, but perhaps that would be better.'

The Sobona family rose with the sun and Dyson was soon the object of much interest by his younger cousins. After they had gone to school and his uncle to work, Dorcas suddenly announced, 'Your brother, Jackson, he was also here.'

'Jackson! When? Where is he now?'

She pulled up a chair and sat down at the chrome and laminated kitchen table. 'Sit. We have things to talk about.' His aunt looked so serious he knew that whatever Jackson was up to it certainly did not meet with her approval. 'Jackson stayed here two weeks ago. He has now gone north, to Zambia.'

'To join the freedom fighters.' Dyson nodded. 'I'm not surprised. It was all he talked about.'

Dorcas looked down at her hands. 'He was not alone.' She was cleaning a bit of dirt from under a fingernail, unwilling to meet his eyes. 'He had a girl with him.'

Dyson grinned. 'Trust my brother.'

She looked up quickly. 'A white girl.'

He went cold. 'Tessa?'

Dorcas nodded.

'The fools! What were they thinking?' Dyson gave a groan. 'I'll have to let Michael know.'

'Michael?'

'Tessa's brother. He is a friend.'

'I have sent a letter to my sister. Your friend will know soon enough.' She shook her head and tutted disapprovingly. 'Your brother went north alone. He did not take the girl with him. She is here.'

'Where?'

'Working for Mama Naledi.'

'How can I find her? Who is Mama Naledi? You must take me there.'

'Dyson.' She leaned towards him. 'Mama Naledi keeps a place where men go to be with women.'

'A brothel!' He was stunned. 'Tessa's here? In a brothel?'

His aunt nodded.

Dyson rose abruptly, his eyes glittering with anger. 'Jackson left her at a brothel! Tessa King! The sister of my best friend!'

'That is not all,' Dorcas whispered. 'The girl is pregnant.'

It was like a series of hammer blows inside his head. Dyson sucked in air, trying unsuccessfully to stay calm. Where would Jackson's audacity end? Dyson felt no pity for Tessa. He'd had hardly any contact with her for years and, from what he knew of her, she'd probably brought this current situation on herself. But that Jackson could treat the daughter of his father's employer this way, a woman whose kindness had been demonstrated in thousands of ways, showed just how cold his brother really was.

And Michael? Dyson knew of Michael's problems with his sister. Presumably, in the last three years while Dyson had been in prison, Tessa hadn't changed. But she was Michael's blood relative. Michael was Dyson's best friend and that made her Dyson's sister too. Therefore, she was Jackson's sister as well. Complicated by colour, Tessa was nonetheless considered to be part of the Mpande family. There wasn't a Zulu alive who would leave his sister in a brothel. Except Jackson.

'Take me to Mama Naledi,' he said to his aunt. 'We have to bring Tessa back here.'

'She will not let her go. I have heard that the girl is popular.'

'Jesus!' Dyson closed his eyes. 'Then I will go as a customer. I have to get her away from there.'

Jackson had given Tessa no opportunity to get away from him on that long walk to Bechuanaland. He avoided towns completely, perhaps aware that at the first chance she would give herself up and accuse Jackson of abducting her. He was under no illusions about who the authorities would believe.

Using a combination of her fear that he would abandon her, together with the desires she seemed unable to control, Tessa was easily managed. By day, she followed, silent and obedient, though her eyes were full of panic and resentment. Strangely, she did not appear to hate him. Jackson knew she was terrified of losing him, though he supposed that had more to do with her own selfish needs than any remaining illusions of love. At night, though she must have been bone weary, as soon as he reached for her she responded eagerly. Finished, he would roll away. Inevitably, her hand would creep around his waist as she snuggled into him. The proud young girl who had once seemed so sure of herself was, he had discovered, vulnerable and full of complexity. It gave him the power he sought.

She kept her misery to herself, never voicing it. She had been a fool, she knew that now. Lying in the open, staring up at the stars, Tessa had finally faced the reality of what she was. As Jackson slept next to her, she wept silent tears of self-pity and fear. It was not this boy she loved, it was his body and the things he did to her. The knowledge brought cold comfort. Carrying an illegitimate black child in her womb, living in the open like a wild animal, craving for a man who made no effort to conceal his contempt for her, breaking the laws of South Africa – none of that mattered as much as the word that kept spinning in her head. Nymphomaniac.

For the first time in her life Tessa felt deeply ashamed. Little did she suspect that worse was to come.

They skirted well to the north of Johannesburg, avoiding Rustenburg and swinging west into the harsh scrublands near Groot Marico. It was terrible country, desiccated, red dirt, littered with rocks, scorching air so dry it hurt to breathe. Tessa's clothes, halfheartedly washed in streams along the way, were torn and falling apart. Her hair, normally washed and conditioned twice a week, did not take kindly to cold rivers and drying sun. It was dry and wildly curly. She was badly scratched on both legs. Her hands rough, the nails dirty and bitten to the quick.

The closer they came to the Bechuanaland border, the more isolated and desperate the land. Only a handful of hardy Afrikaners lived here. Even the African villages, which they relied on for labour, were few and far between.

They walked into one remote village just on dusk. Tessa looked around, aching for the sight of a white face, but, naturally, there were none. Curious children ran alongside them, women clucked their tongues and men stared at her boldly. Jackson spoke to the elders who agreed to provide them with a bed for the night. Tessa listened with horror. In return for a bed Jackson was offering her to the men of the village.

'No, Jackson,' she pleaded with him. 'For the love of God. You can't do this to me.'

He had smiled cruelly. 'It is our way. Don't tell me you won't enjoy it. It's all you think about.'

Apartheid and racial segregation meant little to the isolated groups in the Groot Marico. By the end of that long night, Tessa knew it would be impossible to sink any lower.

Cowed, desperate, and in terrible pain, knowing she was about to lose her only link with home, when they reached Gaberones her worst fears became reality. They went first to the home of a woman who Jackson said was his aunt. After a lengthy discussion and some resistance on the woman's part, which Tessa was able to follow perfectly since they spoke in Zulu, she was taken to a curtained-off cubicle, given a pail of water and a cake of soap and told to wash. She could hear them talking in the next room. It was clear that Dorcas Sobona had been expecting them and she was making it abundantly obvious that she disapproved totally of Jackson's actions and plans. However, it was equally apparent that, as close family, she was honour bound to assist her nephew in any way she could, despite any personal misgivings she might have had. As Tessa listened to the conversation, the misery of the past weeks fell away. She could not believe her ears as the full horror of Jackson's intentions left her trembling with fear.

'Please,' she begged him, stumbling into the room. 'Don't do this. I'll write to my mother, she'll help me. Or let me come with you. I won't be a nuisance, I promise. Please, Jackson, I'm begging you. Don't . . .' Her eyes grew wide with fear as he stepped up and grabbed her arm. 'Nooooo!' she screamed. 'Help me, for God's sake, don't let him do this.' Tessa's pleading fell on deaf ears as the stony-faced woman turned away.

She pleaded with him as he propelled her through dusty streets. He kept a vice-like grip on her arm, not even bothering to answer. Jackson could hardly wait to be rid of her. He doubted she would last long at Mama Naledi's, she simply did not have the mental or physical resilience of African women. That was good. Alive, she posed a threat to him. Dead, her lips could not accuse him or tell where he was going. The beauty of his plan was that he could not be held responsible for anything that may happen to her.

He was indifferent to Aunt Dorcas' disapproval. As a male relative, he was entitled to her loyalty. It was perfect.

They reached the address his aunt had given him, a redbrick dwelling indistinguishable from those around it but for its larger size. Jackson rang the bell. The door was opened by a mountainous woman who wore a flowing caftan. 'Yes?' The woman's eyes flicked to Tessa, then back to Jackson. Any surprise she might have felt was well concealed.

'Are you Mama Naledi?'

'Who wants to know?'

'Jackson Mpande.'

She had shrewd eyes and they assessed the two before her, accurately deducing why they were there. Reaching out a pudgy hand she grasped Tessa's free arm and literally pulled her into the house. Jackson followed and the door slammed shut behind them, swallowing up the terrified white girl.

'Her name?'

'Tessa.'

Mama Naledi shook her head. 'From now on it's . . .' she studied Tessa's face carefully, '. . . it's Opal.' She smiled slyly. 'Anyone asking for Tessa will not find her here. You want her, ask for Opal.'

'I have finished with her,' Jackson said coldly.

A sob came from Tessa. Her legs were shaking so badly she could hardly stand.

'She's pregnant,' Jackson told Mama Naledi curtly.

'She won't be for long.' The woman was matter-of-fact. 'She's no use to me with a big belly.'

Jackson shrugged indifferently and turned to leave.

'Jackson!' It was wrung from her. Tessa lurched at him. 'Don't leave me, please.'

Mama Naledi was a good judge of human nature. She had to be, her business depended on willing girls and being able to quickly assess if a customer could prove difficult or violent. She could see that despite this girl's fear and desperation there was pride and defiance just under the surface. Stepping between Tessa and Jackson with surprising agility considering her size, she delivered a ferocious smack across Tessa's face. 'This way,' she snapped at Jackson.

Between them they dragged the wildly struggling girl into a room and locked the door. Tessa's screams became heaving sobs. As a final gesture of his lack of regard for her, Jackson took the jewellery Tessa had stolen from her mother. Where she was heading, she wouldn't need it.

After Jackson left, having extracted a disappointingly small payment from the deal, Mama Naledi considered how best to capitalise on a white whore. She could only use the girl for, at best, a few months. The authorities would be bound to hear of her and come to investigate. The brothel was tolerated provided she broke no other law.

'First, we get rid of the baby,' she decided. A prostitute with morning sickness could not give of her best and Mama Naledi, using her infallible instinct, had already sensed that Opal had passion to burn.

'A week to recover then put her to work. Two months. If she's as good as I think I'll make a lot of money. If she's still alive after that, who knows.'

Mentally calculating the profit from, conservatively, ten customers a day, and well satisfied with the total, Mama Naledi sent one of her girls to fetch the midwife. She had performed many abortions for the brothel and Mama Naledi knew she could be trusted to keep her mouth shut.

Dyson realised that he couldn't just walk up to Mama Naledi's and ask for Tessa. The woman would be cautious of strangers, protecting what was, for her, a valuable property. He needed a name, someone known to the brothel owner who might recommend that Dyson try the white girl. He also needed to act fast. Tessa had been taken to the brothel two weeks ago. Pampered all her life, having walked to Bechuanaland, pregnant and undoubtedly very frightened, she would be at a very low ebb. It took two days of drinking at a nearby bar before someone mentioned a white prostitute called Opal.

'White?' Dyson asked, his pulse quickening. 'Are you sure?'

The man looked drunkenly wise. 'As white as chicken meat.'

'What's she like?' Dyson deliberately slurred his words.

'My friend, she's hot enough to burn your cock off.'

The man laughed at his own wit and Dyson joined in.

'Try her. See for yourself. Tell Mama Naledi that Toffee the taxi driver sent you.'

Dyson bought the man a beer and, after some more crude exchanges, left the bar. He made his way unsteadily towards the brothel. It was not all put on. He had been drinking for most of the day.

Mama Naledi took one look at him and thought, 'Good. The word is spreading.' He had the same sheepish yet excited look as all the men who wanted to try the white girl.

'Toffee the taxi driver said you have a white girl.' Dyson fumbled in his pocket. 'How much?'

The price was high, five times the normal rate. Dyson panicked that he didn't have enough but just made it, counting out all his small change, the last of the money loaned to him by his aunt. 'She'd better be worth it,' he muttered.

'Every cent.' Mama Naledi stuffed the money, coins and all, between her more than ample breasts. 'Twenty minutes only. This way.' She led him through the house, stopped outside a closed door, produced a key and unlocked it. 'Twenty minutes,' she reminded him. 'Then I'll be back.'

Dyson stepped into the room, the door closing behind him. One dirty window, barred and shut, curtains hanging limp, admitting just enough light to make out a single bed. The only other furniture was a chest of drawers and two straight-backed chairs. Tessa sat on the bed, head bent. She did not look up. Dyson crossed the room and knelt in front of her. 'Tessa,' he whispered.

She raised her head reluctantly and he was shocked to see the lacklustre eyes hollow with fear and fatigue. 'Dyson?' He placed a hand gently over her mouth, fearful she would make a noise and alert Mama Naledi. Her skin was hot to the touch and clammy. She was burning up.

'Ssshhh! I'm going to get you out of here.' He had no idea how. The bars on the window were solid, welded to a metal frame. Overpowering Mama Naledi would not be too hard but she was bound to have a few strong men around in case of trouble.

'She doesn't lock the door when I'm with someone,' Tessa whispered, her mind recovering from the initial surprise.

'Can you stand?'

She nodded, rising with difficulty and obviously in great pain.

Slumped against him, he could feel her whole body shaking. She smelled unpleasant, of disease or something rotten.

They were halfway across the room when the door burst open.

Michael King had driven into Gaberones that same afternoon. Following directions given to him by Nandi, he found Dorcas Sobona's house with no difficulty. Initially, she was reluctant to tell him anything but then, knowing of Dyson's high regard for Michael and making her own assessment of the troubled man in front of her, she unburdened all the events of the past two weeks – Tessa, Jackson and Dyson. Michael listened with increasing rage over Jackson's cold-blooded treatment of Tessa.

'Dyson crossed the border illegally. He cannot go to the police. My husband wants no trouble and has forbidden me to report Tessa's whereabouts. Each day Dyson goes to a bar near the brothel hoping for someone to tell him about a white girl. This way he can use their name as an introduction to Mama Naledi. He plans to rescue your sister.'

Glad as he was to hear that Dyson was alive, all Michael could think about was getting Tessa to safety. 'Bugger that,' he said roughly. 'I'm going in myself.'

'Then take this with you,' Dorcas said, handing him a *knobkerrie*.

Michael gripped the smooth wood in one hand,

hitting the other with the rounded knob at one end of the stick. It was perfectly balanced and satisfyingly heavy. He had practised traditional Zulu stick-fighting many times with Dyson when they were boys, and although the sticks they'd used had no weighted end there was little harm in having some extra insurance on this occasion. 'Thank you.'

'If you are successful bring her here. She will need rest.'

He was just plain lucky. Being a weekday afternoon, Mama Naledi had only one of her strong men on duty. She called him immediately when Michael forced his way into the house. He came at a run, crouched low, skinning knife held ready to use. Michael steadied himself and swung the *knobkerrie*. The blow was aimed to just miss the man's head. Michael saw his attacker's run falter but the figure of eight action was aimed for the man's knife hand. It struck home, snapping the wrist with an audible crack.

'Which room?' Michael demanded.

Mama Naledi pointed, her face white with shock. Her bouncer was lying on the floor, clutching his broken wrist and groaning.

Michael sprinted down the passage and flung open the door. Dyson and Tessa were halfway across the room. In two strides Michael reached them and swept up his sister. She was alarmingly light. 'Let's go.'

Dyson took the *knobkerrie* from Michael. 'Follow me but don't get too close.' The lounge was deserted. Mama Naledi and her bouncer had vanished. 'Come on,' Dyson yelled urgently. 'Before anybody else gets here.'

'Michael,' Tessa murmured. 'I don't believe it's you.'

'Later, Tess. We can talk later.'

'I'm sick, Michael.'

Dorcas Sobona clucked and tutted with horror and sympathy over Tessa's condition then set about mixing and boiling traditional herbal remedies to draw the sickness out.

Michael and Dyson spent most of the next two days sitting together catching up. Dyson already knew of his father's treatment during interrogation since most of it had taken place just a few cells away from where he was being held. He told Michael of his shame that he had been responsible and of the frustration and anger, but also the pride that not once did his father cry out or utter any sound to give his tormentors satisfaction.

Michael was able to put Dyson's mind at rest about the remainder of the family. 'My mother threatened to report the commander to his superior officer in Durban if they were badly treated. She told him that the man was a friend of hers.'

'Knowing your mother, she'd have done it too.'

'Not really.' Michael grinned. 'She doesn't know him.'

Dyson expressed regret that UBejane was to be sold. 'It's the only home I've ever known.'

'Me too. It will be strange without it.'

Dyson shrugged. 'Perhaps it is not UBejane that matters.'

'What do you mean?'

'In these troubled times, we must live where we are understood.'

Michael saw the depths of sadness in Dyson's eyes. 'One day, my friend.'

'I don't know. It may never be possible for me to return to Zululand.'

'Don't say that. It *must* be possible.'

They were closer than brothers, their relationship cemented by mutual respect and understanding, by memories of games played on hot afternoons, by teenage worries and hopes shared, and by their love of a land they called home.

On the second day, Michael worried aloud that Tessa was not getting better. 'If she's like this tomorrow I'm not waiting around.'

Dyson agreed. 'Our medicines are good but perhaps she needs something more.'

'I can never thank you enough for trying to save her.'

Dyson grinned. 'What else could I do? She is my sister.'

Michael knew he was speaking metaphorically, the Zulu way, but he laughed and said, 'You know what they say, you can choose your friends but not your relatives.'

'Is that an English expression?'

'Yes.'

Dyson thought that over. 'See my aunt's cooking pot.'

'I see it.' Michael could guess what was coming.

'It has one burned spot she cannot remove.'

'So?'

'Every cooking pot has one. A black spot. But we do not throw away the pot.'

Tessa was sicker than anyone realised and did not respond to the traditional treatment administered by Dorcas Sobona. Since Tessa had entered Bechuanaland illegally, Michael did not want to bring attention to her by taking her to a doctor. The following day he decided to risk smuggling her out so that she could return home and see the family doctor. With Tessa lying on the back seat of his car covered by a blanket, Michael chose a time of day to exit Bechuanaland and enter South Africa when the border posts were busy. His caution was unnecessary. No-one was interested in looking in his car anyway.

Before leaving he spent a last few minutes alone with Dyson. 'I wish we had more time, old friend.'

'One day, *Nkawu*, one day.'

Michael handed him a cash cheque. 'I don't know how you're going to organise a passport but this should get you to London and keep body and soul together for a while. Stay in touch.'

Dyson looked at the amount. 'This is too much.'

'I'd give everything I had,' Michael told him with feeling, 'if it would see our country come right.'

Dyson gripped Michael's hand. 'Stay well, Michael King,' he said quietly.

'Go well, Dyson Mpande.'

TWELVE

Claire had wept brokenly when Michael brought Tessa home from Bechuanaland. The infection, brought on by an unclean abortion, lingered in her body. She also had syphilis. Practical as ever, once Claire recovered from the shock, she picked up the telephone and called her own doctor in Empangeni, sparing no details when he arrived at the farm.

Dr John Cane, although classified white and, indeed, with his sandy coloured hair and pale blue eyes he epitomised the appearance of a typical white South African, had a secret he fondly imagined no-one knew. He was in fact a descendant of, and had been named after, an earlier adventurer who arrived in Zululand during Shaka's reign. A deserter from the merchant navy, turned trader and coloniser, the first John Cane had been a rough-and-ready individual who despised authority and whose only interest appeared to be enjoying life to the hilt. While doing this he was not averse to lining his pockets any which way he could. Historians, if they mentioned him at all, tended to paint him as a man of atrocious manners and deeds. However, he spoke Zulu fluently, regularly made himself available to do battle for the second Zulu king, Dingane, and adopted a tribal lifestyle that included the taking of numerous wives.

The current John Cane was under the illusion that no-one knew his history. But such things were gleefully discussed around dinner tables. Most whites were aware of his ancestry. Claire hoped that his pedigree would make him sympathetic to what she was telling him. It did not. In fact, almost the opposite occurred. When South Africa first decided to classify individuals into racial groups, the scramble of Dr Cane's parents to prove they were as white as the next family led them to adopt extremes of racially prejudiced views and behaviour. Hence, Dr John Cane, whose maternal ancestors were as black as the ace of spades, became highly agitated and morally outraged by Claire's frankness.

Realising that the good doctor's shock could well cause him to forget any oath of patient–doctor confidentiality and report the conversation, Claire panicked. She packed herself and an extremely sick daughter onto the first available flight to London. There, with Peter Dawson's assistance, she managed to book Tessa into a private clinic. By the time she was admitted, Tessa was delirious with fever. When her condition had been stabilised the doctor in charge angrily demanded that Claire provide a full and frank explanation of the situation.

Taking a deep, steadying breath, Claire began.

The floodgates opened and Claire, who had denied certain things in the past, found she could deny them no longer. As she poured her heart out, telling of Tessa's promiscuity, from the suspected incestuous relationship with her father through to being rescued from a brothel, Dr Benjamin Greenberg, himself the father of two small girls, for the first time found himself wishing he had fathered sons.

When Claire at last fell silent, the relief of pent-up anxiety still coursing unchecked down her cheeks, Dr Greenberg's earlier anger had been replaced by a desperate need to help the grieving woman before him. However, he wasn't certain that he could.

'You use the term nymphomaniac. It's not one we favour.' He didn't mean to but it sounded as though he was rebuking her.

'Don't play word games with me, doctor,' Claire snapped, sensing a brick wall. 'I don't care what you choose to call it.'

Dr Greenberg leaned forward over his desk. 'Hold on. I'm not lecturing you or being pedantic. I'm trying to put your daughter's situation into perspective. Nymphomania has some pretty nasty connotations but it isn't a medical term. Tessa's problem is not a physical one.'

'Are you saying my daughter has a mental problem?' The steel was still there. Claire didn't like what she was hearing and it showed.

The doctor grinned suddenly, disarming her. 'It's not an accusation, you know. I am trying to help.'

Claire stared at him for a long moment. He was an odd-looking man. Without the white coat and stethoscope she'd have taken him for one of the hippie-types so prevalent in London at the time. His hair was long and curly and he made no attempt to tame it except for an absurd-looking baseball cap jammed on backwards. He wore huge glasses that practically covered the top half of his face. His nose had been broken at some stage and leaned to the right. For all that, his face was boyish and soft. His eyes, kind and sincere, met her stare with a frank one of his own. She decided she trusted him. 'Speak to me.'

He nodded and sat back. 'Okay. We can fix the toxins in her system. Might take a little while but the new antibiotics are a real breakthrough.' He picked up a pencil and tapped it on the desk. 'Syphilis is a bit of a bugger but we'll get on top of that too. Physically we can make Tessa well again.'

'And mentally?' Claire frowned. 'What *do* you call nymphomania then?'

'Sex addiction.'

Claire snorted. 'What's the bloody difference?'

The doctor grinned again, this time ruefully. 'Okay. I'll try to explain. The word nymphomaniac conjures up visions of sex-starved women prowling the streets looking for men to jump on. They are perceived as little more than ravaging animals, driven by a need to copulate. They are scorned and joked about but no-one makes any attempt to understand what drives them. In short, Mrs King, they are regarded as society's dregs, not so?'

Claire nodded hesitatingly. This doctor was not pulling his punches for which she was grateful.

'Sex addiction is exactly what the name implies,' Dr Greenberg went on. 'It's as much of a reality as drug or alcohol dependency. It provides the same kind of high and is sought for exactly the same reasons. Tell me, Mrs King, why does an alcoholic drink?'

'My husband was an alcoholic,' Claire said slowly.

Dr Greenberg nodded. 'I rather thought he might have been.'

'He drank because he was unhappy.' Claire realised that talking to this stranger was bringing to the surface a new level of understanding. She had, many times, tried to work out why Joe drank but this doctor was leading her further than she had gone on her own, closer to a truth that had always been denied. *It's about time.*

'What made him unhappy?'

'War was exciting,' Claire said, feeling her way. 'He was a hero, a glamour boy. There would have been women . . .' She bit her lip.

'Go on,' the doctor prodded gently.

'Before the war there had only been the farm and me. Those days in London were a high point in his life. Then he was shot down over France. I suppose what kept him going as a prisoner-of-war was to remember those times. I don't think he gave much thought to his wife and son. Coming home meant facing reality. Life was no longer an adrenalin rush. It was a farm he didn't want, a wife he'd practically forgotten and a son who was a stranger.'

The words were pouring out as the extent of Joe's unhappiness became clear.

'I did everything wrong. I pushed his son at him. I loved Michael, so why didn't Joe? I expected him to go straight back into farming and when he wouldn't, couldn't, I showed him how good I was and made it impossible for him to sell the place. And because I found his personal attentions too adventurous, too distasteful, I . . .' Her voice faltered. 'Oh God!'

'Don't be too hard on yourself. It can't have been easy.'

'It wasn't, but I made no attempt to understand.'

'I'm fairly sure you did, Mrs King. Someone you had loved and cherished returned a changed man. Whatever the reasons, you were not to blame. He *could* have rolled up his sleeves and got on with his life. Instead of that, he lost himself in alcohol, became an addict.'

'Like Tessa?'

'Some people have addictive personalities. Not all of them become addicts. Depends on what life dishes out. Growing up as she did in a dysfunctional family, Tessa found a way to escape her fears or unhappiness. She discovered that having sex hid, momentarily, all those feelings of longing for a normal family life. I'm guessing a bit here, Mrs King, I won't know for sure until I've had a chance to talk with her, but if you're right about Tessa and her father I'll lay odds right now that her addiction started with a simple desire to bond with him.'

Claire blinked. 'That's it?'

'Human nature is the last word in weirdo. All of

us get crossed wires. Addiction is the vicious circle when we fail, for whatever reason, to undo them. Your husband most probably wanted to stop drinking. He would not have been happy the way he was. Trouble is, he drank because he was unhappy and he was unhappy because he drank. Like I said, a vicious circle. I assure you, Tessa doesn't want to be the way she is either. Her addiction makes her unhappy. Unhappiness is eased by giving in to her addiction.'

'So what can we do?'

He regarded her soberly. 'I'll only be able to answer that after I get to know her.'

'You mean there's no cut-and-dried treatment? No wonder *muthi* to make her better?'

'Muthi?'

'Sorry. Medicine.'

Dr Greenberg shook his head. 'Afraid not.'

'Our options then,' Claire quizzed, 'what are they?'

'A self-help program is worth trying. There are a number of them around. But success would really depend on Tessa's determination to get better.'

'Or?' Claire pressed.

'Keep her on drugs for depression. That usually pole-axes the libido.'

'What else?'

'Any chance she'd agree to becoming a nun?'

Claire just looked at him.

'Give it time, Mrs King. Let's get her physically well first.'

★

Tessa stayed at the clinic. Claire visited every day to fuss and fret over her. Fed intravenously, bathed twice a day, and medicated to the hilt, she responded to treatment almost immediately. The syphilis infection took two weeks to bring under control.

'She'll never have children, I'm afraid,' Dr Greenberg told Claire once Tessa was on the mend. 'There's too much damage.'

Claire wept a little at that. 'What exactly is her future?'

'It's a bit early to tell. She's not being very co-operative I'm afraid.'

'Give her a break. She's still drugged to the eyeballs.'

The doctor looked at her sympathetically. 'I don't know how to put this delicately, Mrs King, so I won't even try. Many sex addicts don't actually enjoy the sexual act. Tessa, to quote her, loves it. So what we are dealing with here is a young lady who has an addiction, who is headstrong and rebellious and who doesn't really wish to stop. The combination is lethal. A self-help program would be a waste of time. We're taking her off the sedatives tomorrow. Expect some fireworks.'

'Dr Greenberg, the fireworks are easy compared to the rest of it. What can we *do* for her? There must be something. I can't take her back to South Africa and run the risk she'll re-offend. She'd end up in prison. She's eighteen now so I really can't force her to do anything she doesn't wish to. She refuses point blank to join her sister in France and won't entertain the idea of university. I can't just leave her on the streets of London.'

The doctor was silent for a long moment, seemingly lost in thought. Finally he heaved a sigh and said, 'There is one more thing I can suggest.'

'What?'

'You're not going to like it.'

'Try me.' Claire was prepared to listen to anything. Anything but the doctor's next words.

'There is a woman in London who runs a . . . boarding house for girls with Tessa's problem. She also operates a companion agency. Now, I know what you're thinking, that the term is a euphemism for a high-class brothel but it isn't. Please . . .' he held up his hand as Claire was about to interrupt, 'let me finish.'

Claire nodded, tight-lipped. Without being aware of it she had crossed her arms, subconsciously distancing herself from the doctor's words.

'Her name is Judith Murray-Brown. She comes from a good family, has had an excellent education and is a lovely lady. She was also addicted to sex. She went right off the rails, finally ending up on the streets. Drugs, prostitution, the works. Then one night she was beaten so badly she had to spend ten days in hospital.' Dr Greenberg frowned at the mental image. 'Judith is intelligent. She could see that she was in a downward spiral. And she could see she wasn't the only one. There were others just like her who were unable to help themselves. She began the long climb back.'

'No,' Claire said stonily.

'No?' he quizzed gently.

'Absolutely not.'

'Hear the rest of it first.'

Claire pressed her lips together and said nothing.

Dr Greenberg took that as an affirmative. 'My father was practising at this clinic at the time. He was recognised as one of the leading sexual therapists in London and he was also doing research into the reasons for addiction. Judith came to see him. She cooperated with all the tests he did and, between them, they reached the conclusion that while most girls suffering from sex addiction benefit from a more conventional self-help program, a small percentage would not. Girls like Tessa, difficult personalities; addicted and not wishing to stop. These were the girls Judith wanted to help. My father completely agreed. He'd seen too many of them end up in the morgue.'

Claire closed her eyes for a long moment.

'With financial backing from her parents, Judith bought a house in Wimbledon. She opened a small and very exclusive companion agency.' He leaned towards Claire. 'It is *not* a brothel. I cannot emphasise that enough.' He leaned back. 'It's quite amazing to see the change in these girls. All their lives they've been square pegs in round holes. When they go to Judith they're confused and angry. She teaches them it's okay to be different. And we've noticed something quite exciting. Many of these girls recover and lead perfectly normal lives.'

'So this clinic is involved.'

'Heavens, yes. My father is retired but the research goes on.' He gave her a quick grin. 'The girls are probably unaware of it but this, compliments of Judith, is as much of a self-help program as any of the others. It's just . . .'

'More unconventional.'

He inclined his head. 'It works. That's the main thing. What are your options?'

Claire took a taxi to the address in Wimbledon Dr Greenberg had given her. It turned out to be a solid and large brick building in a quiet, tree-lined street full of similar homes, not at all what she had expected. The woman who answered the door was well dressed and quietly spoken, her accent middle-class. 'Do come in. I'm Judith Murray-Brown. Dr Greenberg telephoned to say you were on your way.' She looked to be in her mid-forties. Calm brown eyes, brown hair, cut short and brushed back from her face which was devoid of make-up.

Claire entered the house. 'Thank you.'

'Tessa would be most welcome here,' Judith Murray-Brown said. 'I'll show you around in a moment.'

'She may choose not to come,' Claire said sharply, resentful that Tessa's future appeared to be in the hands of Dr Greenberg and this woman.

'Of course.' Judith Murray-Brown's voice was warm and full of understanding.

Claire got straight to the point. 'The men who come here, what are they like?'

Judith smiled. 'Men don't come here, Mrs King. Our girls are booked out and go to them. Sometimes our clients want a girl to accompany them on business trips or holidays. The girls travel a great deal.'

'So the neighbours don't know that the girls are . . .'

'Hostesses?' Judith sat on a settee and indicated that Claire should join her. 'I would expect they do. Does that bother you? Coffee?'

'Thank you.' Claire chose a chair opposite. 'Quite frankly, I don't know what bothers me any more.'

'We are very discreet you know. Still, I suppose it must be hard for you. Cream?' She passed Claire a cup. 'Help yourself to sugar and biscuits.' She waited while Claire stirred her coffee. 'May I speak frankly?' When Claire nodded, she went on. 'A companion agency is nothing more or less than the name implies. If it's straight sex my clients want I advise them to go elsewhere. Of course, nine times out of ten relationships develop into sexual ones but, after all, this is the swinging sixties. The girls here aren't doing anything that anyone else isn't. It's just that, to protect them, they're doing it under controlled circumstances.'

'You're very direct.'

'Claire. May I call you Claire? Good. I have spent a fair portion of my life summing people up. Now you, I'd say, are as innocent as the day is long. How many men have you known? No? Okay, none of my business. You're practical, intelligent and like to play fair. But life isn't all plain sailing and, as far as Tessa is concerned, you are, in my opinion, way out of your depth and desperate for answers. Yes, I'm direct. Isn't that why you're here?'

Claire could only nod.

'There is an up-front security deposit which must be paid in advance. It's not large but it covers me against breakages.'

Claire blinked.

'I take pride in my home and expect the girls to do the same. There are usually four or five of them here at any one time. They come and go as they please. They're free to have boyfriends, in fact, they lead perfectly ordinary lives. There is a fixed monthly deduction for board and lodging. Six monthly medical check-ups are mandatory.' She smiled briefly. 'There are no contracts, no ties. If a girl wants to leave she does so with my blessing.'

'But you send them off with men.'

'You make it sound like a death sentence.'

'It's . . . prostitution. You can dress it up any way you like, that's what it boils down to.'

'Technically, I suppose you are right.'

Claire's voice went hard. 'My daughter is only eighteen.'

Judith's tone matched Claire's. 'Which would you prefer? That Tessa ends up on the street or she comes here where she'll be happy and, more importantly, safe? I'm not running a brothel, Claire. I'm trying to *help* people like Tessa.'

Two hours later, heading back to the clinic in a taxi, Claire's usually concise mind was in turmoil. She was out of her depth and knew it. Peter had offered to accompany her and, right now, she could have used some of his unemotional pragmatism.

Judith Murray-Brown had impressed Claire with her forthright and completely unapologetic explanation of the business she ran. She was obviously committed to helping girls like Tessa and worked closely with the clinic.

'Tessa's not a bad girl,' she'd said to Claire. 'She just *thinks* she's bad. The first thing she's got to learn is to love herself. How far do you think we'd get with that process if we kept sending her off to group therapy or prayer meetings?'

'That's all very well, but what about the other side? The risk of disease, the danger of falling into the hands of a weirdo? I mean, what kind of a man *pays* for a companion?'

Judith had given an answer to that as well. 'Busy men. Newly divorced men. Shy men. Men from overseas on a business trip. All kinds of perfectly nice, ordinary men who, for whatever reason, do not get the chance to meet women.'

Claire was still lost in thought as the taxi came to a halt. She paid the driver and, straightening her shoulders, started up the steps of the clinic. Her mind was made up. Entering Tessa's private room, Claire steeled herself. The doctor had said to expect fireworks. Tessa was sitting up in bed wearing a shawl Claire had bought for her, eyes bright but wary. Claire smiled at her. 'Good morning, darling. That looks nice.'

'Thank you.' Tessa's voice was clipped, determined and rebellious all at once.

'How do you feel?'

'Better. Worse. Frightened. I don't know.'

Claire sat on a chair and crossed her legs. 'Has Dr Greenberg spoken to you?'

Tessa's eyes filled with tears.

'Come on, darling. Don't cry. There's no need.'

'No need,' Tessa spat. 'What do you know about it? It's all right for you to talk. You're not sick.'

'Neither are you,' Claire said gently. 'Just a little mixed up.'

'I can't help myself,' Tessa yelled. 'Pull your head out of the sand, Mother, just this once. I'm a nut case.'

Claire allowed a silence of nearly thirty seconds to go by. Then, as cool as a cucumber, she nearly blew her daughter away.

'You are addicted to sex, Tessa. It's no more or no less than being an alcoholic or a druggie. You need to . . . fuck. It's not lovemaking, it's fucking. In that beautiful little head of yours you equate having sex with affection. I know it isn't so. You know it isn't so. But that's what drives you. That's the problem. Question now is, how do we fix it?' Claire was flushed but her eyes held steady, looking directly at her daughter.

Tessa's mouth opened and shut but no words came. Finally she managed, 'Mummy?'

'What, darling?'

'Please don't use that word.'

Claire flicked an imaginary speck of dust from her lapel. 'Okay,' she said. 'Tell the truth, I don't very much like it. I only used it to get your attention.'

'It worked.'

'I must be learning. Now, can we talk sensibly. According to Dr Greenberg you have a number of options.'

Tessa looked down at her hands. 'Sure,' she said bitterly. 'Some options. A bloody nunnery, a walking zombie drugged to the eyeballs so she can't remember her own name or some pathetic little program where a bunch of nymphos sit around and swap stories.' Tessa folded her arms. 'They probably leave the meeting and race for the nearest motel.'

Claire grinned at the mental image. 'So what do you want to do?'

'None of them. They won't help.'

'I tend to agree.'

'It's hopeless. I'd be better off dead.'

'Don't be ridiculous.'

'I'm not. You have no idea . . .'

'Well actually, darling, I do. I've been talking to some very interesting people.' Claire leaned forward and, for the second time in as many minutes, took her daughter's breath away. When she had finished, she sat back in her chair. 'Judith is looking forward to meeting you.'

Tessa gaped at her. Her eyes filled with tears again. 'What?' she asked, in a strangled voice.

'I've been there, even seen what would be your room.' Claire fiddled with a flower arrangement beside the bed. 'I met some of the other girls too. They're nice.'

'Mother!'

Claire reached over and took one of Tessa's

hands. 'I understand, my darling. I know so much more now. I'm so sorry. I should have realised there was a reason. It's okay, Tessa. It really is okay.'

Tears poured down Tessa's face. 'You mean it? You really mean it?'

Claire squeezed her daughter's hand. 'Yes.'

Tessa took a shuddering breath. 'I would die in a convent.'

Claire smiled. 'So would I.'

'I want sex all the time.'

'I know.'

'You don't hate me for it? Doesn't it shock you?'

'No to the first question. Yes to the second.'

Tessa bit her lip. 'I've been quite a trial too.'

'Not at all,' Claire reassured her daughter airily. 'You've actually been hell on wheels.'

A small smile.

Claire looked at Tessa sympathetically. Here was a young woman on the threshold of life, so mixed-up and confused, about to tread a path few took by choice and yet, one so right for Tessa. Claire realised just how far she herself had come in the past few weeks in terms of broadening her own mind. And she could see that something like peace had entered Tessa's spirit, though whether that was from finally being able to talk about how she felt with her mother or from the anticipation of a life previously undreamed of, Claire had no idea. Tessa must have doubts, lots of them. For all her rebel-liousness, she was still a well brought up young lady with all of society's preconceived ideas about men who paid for women's company, sex or no sex. Claire decided it was time to give her daughter's self-esteem a little nudge, so she told her the truth about Gregor.

'You see, darling, I'm not as good as you think.'

'I love you, Mummy.' The bed sheets rustled as Tessa hurled herself into her mother's arms. And then, for the first time in her life, she apologised. 'I'm sorry I stole your jewellery.'

Two weeks later, with a completely changed Tessa installed at Judith Murray-Brown's boarding house, Claire indulged herself for two days with Peter Dawson before returning to UBejane and the wedding preparations. She still had reservations about the solution to Tessa's problems but, for the life of her, couldn't come up with a better one.

Peter, conventional and decent as any, put it well. 'She's happy, she's safe and she's in good hands. It may be a little unusual but, darling, the other options were not going to work. I admire you tremendously for this. You've gone completely outside your own natural instincts and put your daughter's welfare before your own moral standards. That's not easy.'

As they said goodbye at Heathrow, Peter put his hand in the pocket of his jacket and pulled out a small box. 'Open it on the plane.'

'Is it a bomb?' she teased.

'I don't know,' he admitted. 'That's up to you.'

She was wearing the diamond ring on the third

finger of her left hand when Michael met her at Durban airport. 'How is she?'

'Much, much better.'

'You were quite vague on the phone. When will she be back?'

'I don't know. For now Tessa's staying in England.'

'And doing what?'

Claire gave it to Michael, right between the eyes.

He listened in silence, driving much more slowly than his normal lead foot pace.

'It's all very controlled,' she finished. 'Tessa is, in reality, in a self-help program.'

'I'm finding this a little hard to deal with,' Michael admitted.

'I know. So am I.'

'What do we tell people?'

'I've discussed it with Tessa. We're going to say she's in a convent.'

'I wonder what the good Lord would think of that?' Michael grunted. 'Some convent! What about Sally and Gregor?'

'Sally will be told the truth. I'll wait until Gregor is a little older.'

'Mother.'

'Yes, my darling.'

'You're one hell of a woman.'

Claire held out her left hand, diamond flashing. 'Someone else thinks so too.'

Michael stopped the car and gathered his mother up for a seriously enormous hug.

*

The wedding of Michael King and Jennifer Bailey was a grand affair to which half the European population of Zululand had been invited. UBejane was up for sale and the house and gardens looked immaculate, making an ideal setting for both the wedding and reception.

Peter Dawson had flown over from England for the occasion and Claire, elegantly beautiful in soft moss green, was happier than Michael could ever remember seeing her. The sparkling diamond on her engagement finger made a not unexpected announcement to Claire's friends. That, and the fact that Peter did not leave Claire's side for so much as a moment.

Gregor, handsome and stylish, was carrying out his duties as best man with accomplished ease. At twelve, he was already tall, good-looking and confident. As he stood with Michael on the verandah, waiting for Jennifer to arrive, he nodded towards where Claire and Peter greeted guests. 'Mother had a long talk with me last night. Told me the truth about . . . you know.'

'Good,' Michael said a trifle absently. The bridal party had started to arrive and he felt a sudden wave of nerves.

'Yeah,' Gregor breathed happily. 'Bloody marvellous in fact.'

'Does Peter know that you know?' Jennifer's car had stopped in front of the house and she was just emerging from the back, a vision of silky white perfection. The nervousness left as quickly as it had come when she looked up and winked at him.

The lack of any response from his side suddenly alerted him that Gregor had only been fishing and that he, Michael, had jumped into the trap with both feet. 'You little shit!' he said quietly from the side of his mouth.

Gregor grinned triumphantly.

'Keep it to yourself,' Michael warned as he and Gregor left the verandah to take their places on the lawn where the priest waited. 'She'll tell you soon enough.'

'Sure,' Gregor agreed. He waited until they drew level to where his mother and Peter were seated. Then he leaned towards them and whispered, 'Hi, Mum, Dad.'

Michael heard him and could have throttled his brother. Claire gave a small gasp of surprise. Shock, and then joy swam in Peter Dawson's dark eyes. There was no time for much more. Jennifer, on her father's arm, was ready to walk down between the guests. Peter smiled and said softly, 'Hello, son.'

It was as natural as it should have been all those years ago.

Jennifer looked stunning in crisp white silk. Later, as the photographs were being taken, Michael bent his head and, in a whisper, told her so.

'Wait till you've seen my knickers,' she whispered back, smiling for the camera. 'They're electric blue.'

Wilson and Nandi were there, shyly keeping to themselves. Strictly speaking, alcohol was not supposed to be given to them, it was against the law. The other guests, robust and outgoing Zululanders mainly, couldn't have cared less about the law but they understood the Mpandes' reserve and went out of their way to exchange pleasantries with them, usually in Zulu. Although Nandi stuck to soft drinks, Wilson's glass was regularly topped up by anybody noticing it needed it. No-one thought their presence strange, though a few remarked that mixed gatherings were becoming rather risky.

Raj, Balram and their families were also at the wedding. Balram, the women and children, like Wilson and Nandi, kept to themselves. Raj was under no such constraint and strode around acting, for all the world, as though he were Michael's father. With his tall, thin frame resplendent in ceremonial satin and his hawklike features and bushy white beard emphasised under a matching turban, he was an imposing and dignified figure.

Sally had flown back from France for the event. Looking fresh-faced but chic, wearing a simple blue linen sheath with matching box-shaped jacket, one of her own designs, she moved easily through the crowd greeting friends and relatives. Her curly black hair had been cropped, Audrey Hepburn style, a look that was all the rage in Europe.

Questions about Tessa were fobbed off. 'She couldn't get away from the convent. She's not allowed to break her vows of silence but sends her love.'

Most of the guests believed that Tessa's sudden defection to religion was a passing thing. If she had turned out even half as good-looking as her twin, she was lamentably wasted in a convent. No-one guessed the truth.

UBejane was sold to a cynical individual from up north who had deserted the central African feder-ation colony of Northern Rhodesia soon after it gained independence from Britain and became Zambia. 'Africa's going to the dogs,' he complained to Michael and Claire. 'At least we're safe in South Africa.'

Claire felt guilty about the Zulus on UBejane, most of whom would probably lose their jobs. 'They're welcome to stay,' the one-time copper miner said. 'But I know enough to know that this isn't cattle country. I'm going to try bananas on those hills.'

'The Zulus won't work with bananas,' Michael warned. 'It's beneath them.'

The new owner shrugged indifferently. 'Then they'll have to leave.' He winked conspiratorially. 'Know what's the similarity between bananas and politicians?' He didn't wait for an answer. 'They're all yellow, all bent and they all hang around in bunches.' He laughed uproariously at his own joke.

Written into the deed of sale was a ninety-nine-year lease for the house and one-acre garden where Raj had retired. Michael was satisfied that at least the old Sikh, his children and grandchildren would have some security.

Wilson and Nandi planned to move their family to Kwa-Mashu, a sprawling African township close enough to Durban that the white inhabitants of that city had ready access to the deep well of largely unskilled labour for their homes and gardens while not having to put up with blacks living on their doorsteps.

The transfer deeds were lodged two weeks after Michael's wedding, the day he and Jennifer returned from their honeymoon. The house was a sad sight. Furniture had been put into storage, some sold, other pieces given to the servants. With the packing up well advanced, both Claire and Michael found themselves anxious to get the painful process over and done with. Farewells to employees and servants alike, some of whom had been on UBejane longer than Claire, were distressing for everyone. As he said goodbye to dear and familiar faces, Michael knew he'd probably never see most of them again. They were his past, to be held close in memory until they blurred, faded and finally were blown away, like dead and fallen leaves, by the winds of time.

One farewell was particularly painful. Michael visited Wilson in the Zulu compound. 'Any word from Dyson?'

'Not yet, *Nkosi*. Not since he arrived in London. His letters have to go through others.'

'I wish I knew he was all right. When you write to him, ask him to stay in touch.'

'Can Miss Tessa receive visitors in a convent? Perhaps Dyson could see her there but I had heard that in these places you are not allowed to speak.' Wilson frowned. 'Forgive me, *Nkosi*, but sometimes your ways seem strange. What God would forbid his children to speak?'

Michael leaned back against the tree under which they were sitting and shut his eyes. *Strange ways indeed! To hell with this.* 'She's not in a convent. That's just a story we tell people to hide the truth.' He told Wilson everything. 'Funny,' he mused with a half-smile when he'd finished, 'I trust you with the truth but I cannot tell my own cousins.'

'The *Nkosi* honours me with his words and the obligation they create shall not be treated lightly. None shall hear of it from me.'

'Thank you.'

'We cannot always choose those we would trust but an honest man will feel in his heart when it is right and a wise man will speak at such times. I, too, would share a secret.'

'It will go no further.'

'The day is near when Inkatha will rise from the ashes of the Zulu nation. Chief Buthelezi is to be our leader. I have been asked to make the people of Kwa-Mashu ready.'

'So that is why you go to the city. Be careful.'

Wilson grunted, amused. 'I wonder what the English woman, Pankhurst, would have said to such advice.'

Michael smiled. 'You make a good point. I confess my reasons are selfish. I respect your judgment in such matters but I repeat, take care.'

Wilson did not respond to the warning. He said, 'Some whites have indicated that they are ready to join us.'

Michael heard the invitation and responded immediately. 'If you are in trouble I will come at once. If you are arrested, Nandi and the children will be taken care of as if they were of my own family. If you, or someone dear to you, needs a safe haven you have no need to ask, it will be given with no questions. You know how I feel about the Zulus. I would dearly love to see an independent Zululand. But, Wilson, I will not join Inkatha.'

'*Nkosi*, I think you just did!'

Michael laughed, then grew serious. 'You are going away from here. I too am leaving. The farm's as good as sold. I feel as though I'm dancing with shadows. Sometimes I wish everything could stay the same.'

'Only the good things, *Nkosi*. There is much evil to be undone too. The shadows you dance with are your past.'

'You are right, of course. Pity though, isn't it?' He saw a question in Wilson's eyes. 'I mean, we cannot change without leaving a part of ourselves behind.'

'When we put the cattle into new pasture, they grow fat.'

Michael grinned. 'Okay, you win, but remember this. A famous American writer once said, "When you get there, there often isn't any there there".'

Wilson chuckled. 'Now that is something I have to find out for myself.'

'Somehow, Wilson, I find it hard to imagine you in a city.'

'It is my destiny. The *sangoma* predicted it a long time ago. Now it is time.'

Michael jumped to his feet, Wilson took a little longer.

'Something wrong with your back, Wilson?'

'Hau! It is nothing. I am too *madala*.'

'You are certainly not an old man. I'll give Nandi a note for the doctor.' Michael looked around the compound. It had changed a great deal since the days he spent time there as a boy. Gone were the beehive huts. In their place, neat rows of brick cottages with flat tin roofs. The Zulus preferred them. They were weatherproof and the corrugated iron made an ideal spot for ripening pumpkins.

Wilson followed his gaze. 'In progress there is always sadness for that which could not keep up.'

'The huts?' Michael gave a rueful laugh. 'I miss them.'

'You did not have to live in them.' Wilson shrugged. 'But I miss them too.'

'Listen to the two of us. We gossip like women. I have work to do. Have the cattle ready by ten tomorrow. The trucks will be here at lunchtime.'

'All the cattle, *Nkosi*?'

'Every last one. The new owner wants to grow bananas.'

Wilson shook his head derisively. 'Bananas! Can they give you milk? Can one banana feed a whole village? Can its skin keep you warm at night?'

'You said it yourself, father of my friend. Progress always means losing something.'

Michael and Jennifer drove Claire and Gregor to Johannesburg and saw them off at Jan Smuts airport. As his mother and brother disappeared into

413

the Passengers Only section of the airport Michael felt sympathetic fingers squeeze his arm. Taking a deep breath he looked into the warm eyes of his new bride. She was the now and the future. 'I love you,' he said, husky with emotion.

She leaned her head against his chest. 'I love you too.'

Hand in hand they left the airport and returned to the hotel where they'd all spent the night. Tomorrow they were driving to Bechuanaland and the start of a new life.

THIRTEEN

When Michael drove Tessa out of Bechuanaland, Dyson lost no time in making preparations to leave. Although technically a different country, the main centre of Gaberones was too close to the border with South Africa for his liking. The British government had never made any bones about its disapproval of apartheid and had steadfastly refused requests by Pretoria to allow the South Africans to administer the small British protectorate. But Dyson still felt vulnerable. Claiming refugee status, it wasn't difficult to convince the British to give him a passport and the right of temporary abode in the United Kingdom.

He made contact with a small cell of the African National Congress in Gaberones. They agreed with his decision to leave Africa. There had been recent kidnappings of ANC members in exile by the Security Police, raids made under cover of darkness where the unfortunate victim was either assassinated on the spot or smuggled back into South Africa to face interrogation, torture and life imprisonment. Dyson was a prime target for such an illegal strike. The South Africans would be desperate to get him back before he could reveal the truth of what was really going on in their country. Dyson was given the ANC's London office address and a letter of introduction.

Michael's cheque was generous. Just over twice the amount he needed for the airfare. Dyson bought himself a few more clothes and a suitcase and reimbursed his aunt for the money she'd spent on him. He wrote a long letter to his parents and, to keep them safe, had his aunt address the envelope to Michael. In it, Dyson poured out his despair at leaving Africa and promised that one day he would return. He asked Dorcas Sobona to post it after he had left.

Not taking any chances, Dyson flew Zambia Airlines from Gaberones to Lusaka, changed planes and went on to Blantyre in Nyasaland, then KLM to Nairobi and British Airways to London. Half expecting the heavy hand of authority to grab him each time he waited for the next leg of his journey, he nonetheless left the continent of Africa with a heavy heart.

When he landed at Heathrow, Dyson might have been on a different planet. He had never felt more alien or alone. In all his dreams and expectations, not once did he imagine life beyond Africa was his destiny. While whites like Michael had historical connections with Europe which made touching base with places like London easy, Dyson had no such bond. Everything, from the weather to the people, was different, strange, even frightening.

Standing at Heathrow, wondering what to do next, for one wild moment Dyson thought that the South African prison would be preferable to this.

'Get a grip,' he told himself, pushing away the self-pity that rushed him. Instinctively Dyson went directly to the Penton Street offices of the ANC in north London, needing to be in the company of fellow Africans. He expected to be welcomed with open arms. He thought they'd jump at the chance to talk to him. He longed to speak Zulu with someone.

The receptionist was a Nigerian who had lived in London from the age of four and who spoke English with an East End accent. She asked Dyson to wait until someone could spare the time to talk to him. So he sat for two hours, watching people. From what he could see, the ANC was staffed by everybody under the sun except Zulus. And, observing them, they all appeared to have the time to speak to each other, make jokes, tell stories, but no-one had time for him.

At first the bustle in the office intimidated him, he was acutely aware of his outsider's status. But as the minutes ticked into one hour, and then two, Dyson became angry. So when a door opened and he was beckoned into an office by someone who was almost Arab in appearance and dress, Dyson was in a fighting mood.

'Sit down, Mr Mpande. What can I do for you?' The man's accent confirmed Dyson's first impression. He was north African, Sudanese most probably, a place thousands of kilometres from the troubled south.

'So nice of you to see me.' Dyson's sarcasm was involuntary.

The man ignored it and pointed to Dyson's suitcase. 'Just arrived?'

'Yes. I came straight from the airport.'

'Not a good idea bringing a suitcase in here.'

'Why not?'

'This is the ANC, Mr Mpande. Your case could contain a bomb.'

'Check it out if you like.'

'No need. We checked you out instead. That's why you had to wait. Now, why are you here?'

'I need work.'

'Try British Rail.'

This was too much. How dare this . . . Arab . . . who had nothing whatsoever to do with the freedom struggle in South Africa, how dare he sit there, smugly secure in a job he had no right to, and advise Dyson to try the British railway system for work. Dyson was aware that a door connecting the office to another had opened but he was too furious to care who heard him.

'Who the hell do you think you are?' Before he could stop himself, he was relating all that had happened, from his arrest at the Umkhonto meeting, imprisonment, his escape and subsequent arrival in Bechuanaland. 'I've paid my dues, which is probably more than you can say. I've been locked up, tortured and hunted like an animal.' Dyson stood up. 'If this is the best the ANC can offer you can stick it up your arse. Jesus!' He bent to pick up his suitcase. Straightening, he said coldly, 'It would appear that

418

the brotherhood of Africans becomes weaker the moment it goes offshore. Do not bother to see me out, I'll find my own way.' He turned to leave.

'Wait, Zulu.'

Dyson stopped.

'Have you any idea how many come to us for work?'

'Us?' Dyson turned back. 'You are not us.'

'Do not be too sure,' a voice from the doorway said softly. 'You said it yourself, the brotherhood of Africans.'

Dyson turned to look at the speaker and realised with a shock that it was the Xhosa ex-lawyer, Oliver Tambo, who used to be a leading figure in the ANC in South Africa. When the State of Emergency had been called in 1960 after Sharpeville and Albert Lutuli and Nelson Mandela arrested, Tambo had managed to evade capture by escaping to Bechuanaland and from there to London. He now headed up the ANC's London office.

'Give him work,' Tambo said suddenly. 'God knows, he's earned it.' He disappeared, shutting the door behind him.

Dyson started at the bottom, stuffing envelopes in the mailroom. There was a continuous stream of correspondence, information leaflets and letters asking for donations mainly, that poured from the offices each week. The volume was incredible. But, as it was explained to him, ignorance about South Africa had to be overcome and since they couldn't afford large-scale advertising campaigns this was the next best way.

At home, Dyson had believed that the entire world knew what was going on in South Africa. He was surprised, therefore, to discover that in Britain those disposed towards protest generally concentrated on nuclear disarmament. Human rights issues received very little support, either from the public or the media. Some people had heard of apartheid. Most associated it with sport. He was also shocked to discover that racism was not confined to white South Africans. Although rules did not exist to keep black and white apart, attitudes did.

Because he learned quickly and was happy to put in the long hours required, and because his English was excellent, he was swiftly promoted to the department that lobbied for sanctions against South Africa. The work was diverse and interesting and became the focal point of his existence.

Hasan Yaak, who had initially interviewed Dyson, was indeed Sudanese. He had fled Sudan in 1961, five years after the British and Egyptians pulled out and a civil war erupted between the Arab-dominated north and the African south. Hasan was the result of a liaison between his rich Arab father and well-connected African mother. He was perceived as a man with a leg in two distinctly different camps and was therefore earmarked for assassination. He accepted his exiled status philosophically and remained adamant that one day Sudan would settle down and he could return home. Dyson didn't see much of Hasan except at the office but the earlier animosity he'd felt dissipated once the full extent of the horrors unfolding in Sudan became apparent. While Hasan was not affected by what was happening in South Africa his own experiences made him sympathetic towards the ANC, and he was using his considerable influence with wealthy Arab contacts for substantial donations.

Dyson had a social life of sorts, mixing mainly with colleagues, most of whom were Xhosa. There was a kind of camaraderie between them where tribal differences were secondary to the fact that all of them were out of their normal habitat. But Dyson was not particularly happy. He missed Africa. Above all, he missed Zululand.

He found a flat in Soho and, perhaps as a deliberate reflection of his feeling of not belonging, he kept it impersonal. What helped Dyson get through those first few months was the absolute certainty that one day he would return to Africa. He clung to that belief desperately. But, after several months, even that possibility seemed remote. The more he learned through his work with the ANC, the more he realised just how long and desperate the fight for equal rights would be.

Winter coincided with this bitter realisation. Dark, cold days matched his mood. Rain, the lifeblood of Zululand, obscured any chance he might have had of learning to appreciate the more subtle beauty of England. When it rained at home the heavens overflowed and sang to the parched earth to the dramatic accompaniment of lightning and thunder. Here, the incessant soft drizzle simply made life more miserable than ever. The language jarred his ears. Once he'd believed that English was English. The myriad of accents in London was so diverse that each dialect might as well have been a different language.

He had been in London for nearly five months when a letter arrived from his father giving him Tessa's address and telephone number in London. The fact that he hadn't liked her as a child, the shocking details of Tessa and Jackson's disastrous relationship, his knowledge of what she now did for a living, none of it mattered. Dyson was delighted to have the chance to spend time in the company of someone who not only knew his land but spoke his language. He called her and suggested they meet for coffee.

Tessa had been thrilled to hear from Dyson. Although she was happy in London she too missed Africa. True, her mother was now living just outside Hertford and she saw her often. Sally, who had settled just across the channel in France and was working for a fashion designer, was accessible. Gregor was in boarding school and she saw him occasionally. Still, she missed the open spaces, the colours, the smell and feel of her own land. Dyson represented home. He symbolised the cultural diversity that was unique to Africa. And while her childhood had not been a happy one, the chance to spend time with someone who had shared it, albeit indirectly, was a nostalgic journey she was eager to accept.

Tessa was a changed person. For the first time in

her life she did not feel out of step with everyone around her. The change did not occur overnight but, after five months, it was noticeable to all, including Tessa herself. At first she had found it difficult to accept that men paid money for her company, it was too close for comfort to her experience in the brothel in Gaberones. However, after a couple of weeks it became apparent that it was only her company men paid for, not sex. There was a subtle difference. Talking to the others she quickly realised that while Judith's clients might hope that the evening end up in bed, whether it did or not was up to her. And that, she reasoned, was no different from all the other girls out there in London accepting dates.

None of the girls realised that Judith kept in constant touch with Dr Greenberg and the clinic. This fact was kept secret for two reasons. First, Judith's girls had a history of being difficult, outrageously and unacceptably unconventional or having the capacity to self-destruct. There wasn't one of them in her establishment who hadn't previously refused a self-help program. The other reason was that while Judith's experiment was, in effect, self-help based, it was so radical that the clinic did not wish to be publicly identified with it. But, with Judith's input, case histories were showing remarkably similar results, all of which were encouraging.

The bottom line for Dr Greenberg was that the program seemed to be working. Girls were recovering and going on to lead normal lives. That in itself was enough for him. A bonus was the invaluable data he collected which might, one day, mean helping others through more conventional methods. That same bottom line for Judith was that the girls were safe. There were failures, of course, but these were far outweighed by the successful rehabilitation of many. As for the girls, they were happy and in the company of others who liked and approved of them. And, human nature being what it is, this encouraged them to like and approve of themselves. A simple philosophy, too simple for those who would devise complicated therapy; too radical for the do-gooders; too good to be true for the girls themselves.

On the day she was to meet Dyson, Tessa took great care with her appearance. She was embarrassed by their last encounter and anxious that he see her in a different light. It was important to her that Michael's friend be impressed. 'Why?' she asked herself, not knowing the answer. It would have surprised her. 'Because I want Michael to like me.'

She arrived at the coffee shop ten minutes early but he was there before her, sitting in the alcove of an exaggerated bay window. He jumped to his feet when he saw her. 'Tessa, you look wonderful.' She did too. Dressed entirely in black, trousers, roll-necked jersey, jacket and boots, beret and scarf.

She took off the jacket, smiling at the compliment, then sat opposite him. 'So do you. It's so good to see you.'

A waiter hovered and they ordered coffee and sandwiches. Outside, rain splashed down and the world was cold and grey. Inside, the delicious aromas of freshly brewed coffee and newly baked bread and cakes had a homely feel. Both relaxed immediately.

Their conversation slipped easily between Zulu and English. They were so engrossed that the waiter had to clear his throat three times before they noticed that he needed them to lean back so he could put their coffee and sandwiches on the table.

Once they were alone again, Tessa broached the subject they had both avoided. 'I never did thank you for, you know, rescuing me in Gaberones.'

'Forget it. You are my sister. What else could I do?'

'I'll never forget it, Dyson. You saved me from a living hell.'

'Michael too.'

Her eyes held steady with his. 'You both did. Up till then I didn't think . . .' She bit her lip.

'That you were worth saving?'

'Something like that. I knew I wasn't very nice back then, just couldn't seem to help myself.'

'And now?'

'Um . . . there's something you should know.'

'I already know.'

Tessa smiled wryly. 'The convent story didn't go down well with you?'

Dyson laughed. 'You forget. I have known you all your life.'

'Yes.' Her eyes sparkled suddenly. 'You have no idea how good that feels.'

'Besides, my father told me.'

She giggled.

Dyson grinned at her. 'You look just like Sally.'

He couldn't have known it but it was the best compliment she'd ever had.

That was three years ago. Tessa and Dyson saw each other regularly after that first meeting. Once a month at least. Tessa took him to Hertford to see Claire and Peter. They became almost like surrogate parents to him and Dyson's feeling of isolation and homesickness temporarily disappeared when he was in their company.

Tessa opened Dyson's eyes to the wonders of London and beyond. She insisted they visit museums and art galleries, suggested day trips into the country, bartered for bargains at markets, listened to the soap-box loonies in Hyde Park, stood for hours to catch a glimpse of the queen, went to rock concerts. She took control of his flat and, before long, the barren bricks and mortar had been transformed by rugs, wall-hangings and paintings, pot plants, softly glowing lights and all manner of knick-knacks, some of which she'd bring back from trips.

For his part, Dyson brought to the evergrowing friendship an understanding by Tessa that men and women did not necessarily need sexual combat for a relationship to flourish. It was okay to like a man for himself. Slowly, Tessa came to see that a platonic friend was every bit as good, if not better, than one with whom she ended up in bed.

With Dyson, Tessa could be uncomplicated. Something she had never achieved as a child.

Dyson glared at his reflection in the mirror and tried for the third time to get his tie properly knotted. How he hated dressing up, yet he had only himself to blame. It was he who suggested they see the show and have dinner afterwards.

Actually, he was looking forward to the evening. Being with Tessa was fun. She took delight in things, unlike the others he dated occasionally who appeared to consider it their moral duty to act unimpressed by just about everything.

Dyson had come to accept that London was his life from now, that the chances of him ever being able to return home were slim. It wasn't a bad life. His flat, thanks mainly to Tessa, had developed a homeliness which he found comforting. His workload had increased and he had been promoted several times. His circle of friends was small, diverse and interesting.

Two things were missing. His native Zululand whispered to him – shimmering heat, sweeping rivers, deep valleys, sparkling ocean, wide blue sky – challenging him to forget her. As if he ever could! Zululand was as much a part of him as the colour of his skin. It could never be wrenched from him, could never fade from memory. He would stare down from his lounge window to the Soho street below, at a sea of umbrellas, at crowds of people hurrying every which way, and ache for the wide open spaces. Huddled over his gas fire, he would yearn for the cooking fires and the enticing smell of roasting mealies. But Dyson held on to the fact that at least he had those memories. Others, all those grey faces of London, had never experienced the rich smell of rain on hot red dirt, never known the black velvet of a warm Zululand night, never heard the eagles call high and wild as they hovered against a perfect blue background. He might miss Zululand but at least he held her in his heart and mind.

More and more of late, Dyson had also become aware of something else missing from his life. A woman with whom he could share it. If he'd been at home he'd have flown the white flag years ago. The women he met in London were outrageously provocative, staring for long periods directly into his eyes, insisting they walk alongside him instead of behind, drinking beer and then burping, speaking before they were spoken to. At least Tessa was aware of Zulu etiquette and took pains to observe the most rigid of rules, although even she refused to comply with some of them, telling him he was in white man's land where people did things white man's way. But whenever she came to his flat, she always made certain she sat in the seat reserved for women, the one to the left of his door. She always greeted him properly: *sawubona*, I see you. If she passed him anything, it was always with her right hand with the left held under her right lower arm.

These small gestures she made unconsciously. She was the closest thing to a Zulu he had found and, although she didn't mean to, her observations of his customs increased his feelings that he needed to share his life with someone who understood his ways and every mood. Since he and Tessa were such close friends he'd mentioned it to her a little while ago. 'Oh dear,' she'd laughed. 'I do believe you are growing broody.'

'Could be,' he'd admitted.

'Make sure I like her too.'

'You won't have to live with her.'

'No,' she'd said seriously, 'but I'd have to share you with her.'

The comment both touched and stayed with him, especially since she went on to admit, 'You're lucky to want those things. I never could.' She looked so sad at the knowledge he'd wanted to hold her close and comfort her. But he'd never touched her that way and was uncertain how she'd react. For all her history with Jackson and the unconventional life she now led, Dyson was aware of how important it was to Tessa that she sustain at least one friendship with a man that didn't bring with it all the emotional baggage of her childhood. If he held her, irrespective of an intention to comfort her, those wires she was just learning to control could become crossed. He wouldn't do that to her, not for anything in the world.

The last time he'd seen her she had come to his flat for dinner. After their meal, they sat at the small table in his lounge, playing cards. Tessa had looked up at him, smiling. 'You know, Dyson. You're like an old pair of slippers.'

'Thanks,' he'd responded dryly.

'You know what I mean. Nothing pinches when I'm with you.'

For some reason, the comment had hurt. But it hadn't prevented him from inviting her to a show and now, here he was, trying to knot his bloody tie which seemed to have a mind of its own.

They'd arranged to meet at the theatre. Dyson arrived first, as usual, and scanned the crowds for her. She came up the steps and into the foyer a few minutes later. He watched her. Tall and graceful, dark hair left free to frame her face and cascade over bare shoulders. The black sheath gown she wore was simple and elegant. Sleeveless, high round neck, it fell to the floor, touching breasts and hips in such a way that was both modest and sexy. Her make-up discreet, but for a blaze of red on her lips. He knew, when she reached him, she would be wearing that musky perfume she loved so much. She turned slowly, searching for him. At that moment, something happened to Dyson's heart. It started thumping wildly. He could scarcely breathe. His legs turned to jelly. She saw him, smiled and made her way through the crowd towards him. Dyson could not believe what was happening to him. The very last thing he'd expected, or even wanted, was to fall in love with Tessa King.

'Hi. Don't you look handsome.' She slipped her hand through his arm.

'And you look beautiful.' His voice was steady,

thank God. 'I've bought us some chocolate. Shall we go in?'

The play took an agonisingly long time to finish. Dyson barely saw it. He was too aware that Tessa was beside him. He was confused by his feelings. *How could I love her? She's like my sister. She's a friend. She's a white South African. It's not possible. It's madness.* His thoughts went round and round. But while he questioned the how's and why's, the answers evaded him. He was left with only one certainty. He loved her.

After the show, as they waited for their late supper, Tessa chattered away as she normally did, not noticing that Dyson was unusually quiet. When he put her into a taxi and she leaned out and kissed him on the cheek goodnight, it was all he could do not to reach over and crush her to him. 'I'll call you,' he said, his voice strained.

'I'll be away for two weeks.'

'Fine.' He did not ask where or why. It would be work. In the past he had merely disapproved. Now it nearly broke his heart.

On his way home, he cursed himself for a fool. Tessa was not the kind of girl you fell in love with. They'd had many conversations on the subject of relationships and she'd made it plain enough more than once that she doubted her ability to remain faithful to one man. Dyson doubted it too. And children? To a Zulu, children were insurance against old age. For as long as you had children you had company, a roof over your head, food in your belly and money in your pocket. Tessa couldn't have any.

Then there was Michael. Dyson and Michael had a rock-steady friendship going back more than twenty years. A friendship that had weathered a political system determined to prevent such things. But how far did that extend? Was Michael, or even Dyson for that matter, completely impervious to the brainwashing that took place in schools, churches and the media? And even if racial prejudice was not a major factor, cultural differences were.

Whichever way he looked at it, the odds were against a successful and lifelong liaison between him and Tessa.

'She must never know,' he told himself. 'I must never let it show.'

PART FOUR

1969 onwards

FOURTEEN

The sun was going down, a huge red orb sinking behind the trees, leaving them as standing silhouettes, rooted to earth against the pastel-grey backdrop of a cloudless evening. It was a sight so timeless that Michael wished he could capture the moment and preserve it somehow, so it would stay that way forever. He had a camera with him but two dimensions could not record the sounds of bird call, or the smell of animal dung mingled with leaves. It would fail to reproduce the slight chill on his skin. A photograph might invoke a memory, but it could never truly capture the whole sensation. A moment in time as exquisite as this had to be experienced fully or not at all. Michael left his camera where it was hanging.

He was perched comfortably in the lower branches of a mopane tree supposedly watching a big male rhinoceros as it made its way through the tall dry grass to its waterhole. The setting sun coloured everything in shades of magenta and Michael's attention had been diverted by the deepening indigo shadows that touched every stem of golden grass, tingling them pink as they swayed gently in the little breeze that accompanied these last minutes of the day.

He never tired of the African bush. It never ceased to thrill, an element of danger combining with the tranquillity and depth of nature's finest artistry. Mentally shaking himself, Michael dragged his attention back to the task at hand, raising the binoculars and scanning the bush where he'd last seen the rhinoceros. The animal had disappeared. It didn't matter. He knew where it was going, what it would do when it got there, how long it would stay and where he could find it in the morning. Despite the unrestricted vastness of this natural habitat, individual animals were territorial, remaining in their own well-demarcated areas. Michael lowered the glasses and folded his notebook. The light was going fast. Time to head for camp. It was a drive of almost one hundred kilometres. He allowed one last glance at the spot where the rhinoceros had vanished, saddened to think that the project was coming to an end and that his and Jennifer's way of life, which they had come to love so much, would cease with it.

Over the past five years, the entire team had developed an understanding and affection for what was, unquestionably, the most bad-tempered, nastiest and predictably unpredictable creature God ever put on this earth. The almost prehistoric African black rhinoceros. Their research area was vast, stretching from the Chobe River to the east, through northern Botswana and extending into the Caprivi Strip – land which belonged to the

South-African administered territory of South West Africa.

At the beginning of the project their base camp had been set up on the south side of the Linyanti River in the territory known as the British Protectorate of Bechuanaland. Following independence the new Botswana government continued its support and moved quickly to establish the Chobe National Park, and invited the team to relocate. For a while the park became their headquarters, but the area was not known for its population of black rhinoceros and the few that had been introduced into the park refused to breed. So the team moved to a habitat more favoured by the animal. The Caprivi Strip. From there, the study ranged right up to the Zambezi River, where Botswana, Zambia and Rhodesia shared its banks as a common border. They had been granted ready access to the entire Okavango Delta as well, with its twisted waterways and complex network of channels, ox-bow lakes, floodplains and grassy islands.

Locating rhinoceros had, at first, been frustratingly time-consuming. Their numbers were alarmingly few and being solitary by nature didn't help. Once found, however, a couple of months of observation would establish an animal's selected patch and its territorial behaviour did the rest. They were creatures of habit with an almost monotonous daily routine, and the research team had come to know each beast so well that they could generally pinpoint, to the nearest kilometre, where a particular animal would be at any given time of day. The one Michael had been watching lived in an area that straddled the Linyanti River where it divided the Caprivi into east and west, and extended some ten kilometres on either side. The animal generally stayed on the eastern side, enjoying the lush vegetation but sometimes, as now, it wandered into the virgin bushland south of Angola.

Michael's work, and that of the other field staff, had initially involved locating, darting and recording details of as many black rhinoceros as possible. Tranquillising and eartagging had accounted for a large proportion of the first year. It was hot, dangerous and, sometimes, heart-breaking work. The animals did not respond well to some of the drug combinations and several had been lost, not regaining consciousness and slipping quietly into death. The lowest dosage they dared use was 20cc but this was still a lot of liquid, slowing the dart in flight and making its trajectory unreliable.

It could take twenty minutes before a darted rhino went down and, in that time, the animal would blunder through the bush in blind panic for anything up to eight kilometres. It quickly became evident that the stress this caused to the animal was a major factor in its inability to recover from the tranquilliser.

Michael was on the point of suggesting a halt in the darting program when a new drug, M99, became available. A potent derivative of morphine, and deadly to humans, it required only a 3cc dosage, cut in half the time it took for a rhino to succumb and reduced stress to a minimum.

Immediately an animal was down, even before being measured and tagged, an antidote was injected into its ear. The dazed rhino was then 'walked' until it recovered. Judging the right moment between this and a charge became an art form in itself.

Despite the fact that poaching was mainly responsible for the alarming reduction in populations, this was not the sole reason. The animal bred slowly and was incapable of coping with changing climatic conditions. Even in times of severe drought, a rhinoceros seldom ventured from its own territory and so, unlike many species which would migrate from depleted areas, it simply gave up, starving to death or dying of thirst. Poor eyesight meant that many would blunder into danger zones, falling from river banks, breaking a leg between rocks or in unseen antbear holes. In addition to this, its aggressive personality often meant injury through confrontation with other rhinoceros, or even an elephant. Fate appeared to be against it and the rhino was not cooperating. Attempts to breed the animal in captivity had been a virtual failure.

By providing the rhinoceros with familiar and acceptable territory, the intention was to try to change its decline. Anything that could be learned would be beneficial. Alleviating the poaching problem by removing their horns had been suggested, but for this study everything had to be as nature had designed it.

The project team was as diverse a group of people

as could be found. It was headed by Dr Emil Daguin from the University of Gascony in France's Bordeaux region. Emil had a passion for red wine, Africa in general and black rhinoceros in particular. He spoke his native tongue with a strong regional dialect and appeared astonished when the others, whose proficiency in French varied from Michael's schoolboy memories to Jennifer's near perfect mastery of the language, simply could not understand him. However, they all preferred it to his attempts at conversing in English. He was a genial man, large and round, with wild, wiry black eyebrows and a smile that spread from ear to ear, exposing square, crooked, and very white teeth. Emil didn't laugh, he chortled. A cross between a chuckle and a snort, in the finest Lewis Carroll tradition, which was so infectious that even failing to pick up on what amused him, you couldn't help but laugh with him.

Emil had been chased up more trees by charging rhinoceros than the rest of the team put together. This was mainly because, despite his enthusiasm and pleasure in seeing the animal, the object of his interest invariably resented the intrusion and, with no apology or hesitation, was inclined to vent its ill-temper. Totally unfazed by such antisocial exhibitionism, Emil continued to blunder through the thickest of bush, apparently convinced that his love of the great beasts would protect him from harm.

Thanks to Emil and his dedication to good food and fine wines, the team ate exceedingly well, with fresh food being flown in once a week from

South Africa. Beer was banned from the camp because Emil worried about what to do with the empties. Fortunately he was not afflicted by the same concern over empty wine bottles and the produce of Bordeaux flowed freely at dinner. Michael and the others presumed the cost of such luxuries was borne by the project grant, because, whenever one of them queried the expense, Emil would beam and say, 'C'est possible. Pas problem.' It was many months later they learned that Emil had been paying much of the expense himself. When the discovery was made Emil reluctantly admitted that his wife's family owned a fair slice of the Bordeaux region and that, on her death, he had become an extremely wealthy man.

Technically, Emil Daguin was too old for the physical rigours of fieldwork. His job of translating and interpreting everyone else's notes into some semblance of order, developing their combined conclusions and writing a comprehensive report, kept him in camp most days, much to the relief of those who had experienced his lack of caution in the field.

Jennifer had set up a veterinary laboratory of sorts. An army mess tent, it now housed work benches, filing cabinets, paraffin refrigerators and all the scientific paraphernalia she required. Large panels of mosquito netting allowed some movement of air but, in the hot weather, Jennifer still battled to keep her refrigeration units at a constant temperature. Consequently, the tent had been erected so that, at all times of the day, it was in the deep shade of mature wild figs.

She loved her work with a passion, often becoming so engrossed that she had to be forcibly removed from the laboratory to come and eat. No two days were ever the same. Twigs and leaves were examined, grouped together and either discarded or noted as being suitable black rhinoceros fodder. Water was studied to see if there were any individual properties peculiar to those sources favoured by the animal. Droppings proved a mine of information about diet and intestinal parasites. A stillborn baby rhinoceros removed, at great risk to all concerned, from its angry and very bewildered mother, not to mention an uninvited audience of scavenging hyena, provided valuable clues to the animal's biological make-up. Bits of the unfortunate creature floated in formalin-filled jars all over the laboratory. The one everyone said they hated most was an eye. It seemed to follow you everywhere, almost as though life hadn't fled at all, simply been suspended, asking just when it could get the hell out of this jar and back into the bush. Jennifer said they were all being fanciful, it was a lovely eye. But the day it disappeared there was not one member of the team who did not feel bereft, especially when she unemotionally informed them that it had been dissected.

Michael was in overall charge of the field research. He had expressed doubts when Emil had told him that even the most highly qualified scientists would be answering to him. 'Poof!' Emil had scoffed. 'Academics are often impractical and myopic. To pull this lot together I need somebody

442

who poses no threat to any fragile egos and will not lose sight of the big picture. That, my friend, appears to be you. Are you in or not?'

As it happened, Michael needn't have worried. The final selection were hardly hard-core academics and, with one exception, Emil's instincts for a group who could work together proved to be impeccable.

Jennifer and Michael had the only reasonably substantial accommodation at the camp – a prefabricated, portable oblong room to which they annexed their large sleeping tent. This had been a surprise gift from the others when, after nearly two years into the project, Jennifer and Michael became the proud parents of a son – Jeremy.

'A nursery,' Emil had told them. 'Somewhere the child will be safe.'

It was perfect, though became somewhat crowded when, eighteen months later, a second son – Andrew – came along.

Jennifer had no difficulty juggling her work with motherhood. Aside from having employed a young African nanny, the other members of the team found any excuse they could to spend time with the children. Their presence in a camp filled with dedicated and work-focused adults introduced a family atmosphere, appreciated by all.

There were four others involved in the field-work. Terry Silk, a recent graduate in wildlife management from the University of Natal, was an enthusiastic, though somewhat easily diverted, twenty-two year old from Zululand whom Michael knew slightly as the younger brother of an old school friend. He had a tendency to wander away from the main theme, often bringing back interesting, but entirely useless information on anything from elephants to dung beetles.

Each time Michael steered him back to the project he would say, 'But this could be relevant, man.' It became a catchphrase among them all and, for a year or so, was done to death until even Terry stopped using it.

Andre van der Merwe, an Afrikaner with a masters degree in animal genetics from Stellenbosch University, was a quietly spoken young man of twenty-five who, at first, far from being interested in or concerned about the fate of the black rhinoceros, applied for the job seeking a couple of years' bush experience. He soon became totally focused on the project even if some of his photographic observations were more concerned with composition rather than the subject matter itself. There was just one problem with Andre. He discovered, in his very first week, that he was terrified of snakes. Unfortunately, his aversion to that particular reptile guaranteed that close encounters would become a regular occurrence.

It was Andre's bed in which a black mamba chose to spend a night, coiled up and dozing happily until it was rudely awoken by his strangled scream of fear. Of all the trees Andre might have chosen to climb in order to watch a wallowing rhinoceros better, with almost fatalistic inevitability he chose one with a boomslang in residence.

Happily for Andre, the snake decided the tree wasn't big enough for both of them and left for more solitary surroundings. This was especially lucky since the antidote serum was so rare and had to be kept under such strict laboratory conditions in order to maintain its efficacy that it could only be procured by written request to Pretoria! If a puff adder was out sunning itself, it was inevitably Andre who nearly stepped on it. It was hardly surprising, therefore, that within a very short time he had developed such paranoia it took him twice as long as anyone else to go anywhere or do anything. The others made fun of his fear but it did occur to Michael that Andre seemed to cop more than his fair share of narrow escapes from some of the world's most deadly inhabitants.

Bruce Jenkins was Australian. A veterinary surgeon from Perth, he'd headed for Africa and whatever it offered when his marriage of seven years collapsed in divorce. He had literally been hanging around the bar at Riley's Hotel in Maun when the team arrived to spend a night en route to the Linyanti River. Emil, impressed by Bruce's qualifications and willingness to 'try anything once', liking the way he spoke of his ex-wife with affection and respect, cheerfully accepting fifty per cent of the blame for their break-up, decided to include him in the team. Bruce was as Australian as his name and, before long, everyone was saying, 'Gawd's struth.' Even Emil, though when he said it it came out as, 'Caw's strute.'

The last member of the team was Emil's godson,

a young American in search of adventure for a year before returning home and going to college. Bobby Peach had always intended to study and qualify as a medical practitioner. He was still with the team after five years, planned to stay in this part of Africa for the rest of his life and was talking about joining a safari company when the project was finished. Cheerful, easygoing and ruggedly good-looking, Bobby had the uncanny knack of finding girls where it was thought none existed.

There had been one other at the beginning. Professor Athol Rogers, another American, who called himself a Doctor of Animal Behaviour. He had turned out to be everything Emil said he didn't like about academics – self-opinionated, selfish, concerned only with his own theories, impossibly arrogant and, on top of that, convinced that all women lusted after him. Bruce, a man ahead of his time who detested Professor Rogers' predatory behaviour around members of the opposite sex, quickly dubbed him Rogering Athol. After three months of listening to the professor expound his views, a pastime he seemed to prefer over going out and actually doing anything, Emil allowed his Gascony temper the freedom of the afternoon, stunning everyone within earshot with his inventive creativity in about eight languages. Rogering Athol left the project.

It would have been natural enough working in such close proximity for differences of opinion to escalate into conflict. The fact that they didn't was down to the individuals themselves, Emil's insistence that grievances be aired in front of everyone and the fact that each of them took six weeks' leave a year. With the exception of Michael and Jennifer, no two people could be away at the same time. So, for more than half of each year, someone was always absent. It was amazing how the feeling in camp varied, depending on who it was. In addition to leave, they all had work which involved spending days or even weeks away from camp. So, while it may have seemed as if they were breathing down each other's necks, in reality, that rarely happened.

Variety of a different nature added interest to each day. Elephant, lion, leopard, cheetah, hippo, giraffe, warthog, monkey, and innumerable species of buck passed through the camp. Michael and Jennifer had been watching a family of warthog one day when suddenly, one of the youngsters, in a flurry of high spirits, ran headlong into a tree. He was knocked out cold and lay, flat on his back, legs splayed, for a full two minutes while his mother nipped at the soft skin of his belly trying to revive him.

A leopard tom lived close by and regularly hunted just outside camp. Lion they saw most days and heard every night. Two shy giraffe looked in on them from time to time, peering down through the treetops. A lone bull elephant became a regular visitor having found the wooden support poles of the ablution enclosure – upright poles and yards of hessian – very appealing for scratching his rump. They had lost count of the snapped uprights and torn material that needed replacing and of the times their showers had been rudely interrupted by an elephant with an itch.

Days were full of interest, nights of good conversation. Rarely were all seven of them in camp together. Last week, however, with the entire team present, Emil sadly touched on the thought that had been on all their minds. Within a couple of months, the project would be finished.

'My friends, it has been almost five years.' He searched their faces in the flickering firelight. They were as close as family. 'We have learned as much about ourselves as we have about the black rhino. We work well as a team. It saddens me to think that we will soon go our separate ways.'

'And we're still learning,' Andre added. 'There's so much more to find out.' Despite his initial reasons for joining the team, he had become so fanatically dedicated to saving the black rhinoceros that he was planning to publish a book on the subject. His photographs were still more artistic than scientific but they were unquestionably some of the best visual reference material ever assembled.

'Yer right there, mate.' Bruce slapped at a mosquito on his arm. 'We're still scratching the surface, wouldn't you say, Em?'

There was not one of them that Bruce called by their proper name. Michael was The King. Jennifer was Doc. Bobby and Terry had their last names tampered with becoming Peachie and Silko, and Andre was simply Van. That's when he wasn't calling them mate or sport.

'Five years. That's what we were given. Where

has it gone?' Emil sipped his wine reflectively. 'But we've learned a great deal.'

Jennifer nodded. 'The report will certainly change the way rhino are treated in captivity. There's been an unbelievable amount of interest in our work. No-one has collected so much data over such a long period. You're right of course, Andre, there is a great deal more to learn but Emil's report will be the most comprehensive ever published. We've had requests for sneak previews from all over the world.'

'But there are still so many unanswered questions,' Andre objected.

'Others will continue,' Emil reassured him. 'With your experience I can probably get you on to another team.'

Andre nodded, satisfied.

'Yer better make it in New Zealand, Em. No snakes there.' Bruce chuckled. 'What about you, Silko?'

Terry shrugged. 'I'm twenty-seven. Probably time I settled down.'

'Got anyone in mind?' Bobby asked. 'I know a few . . .'

'Thanks, pal. If you don't mind I'll do this on my own.'

'Have you heard from Umfolozi?' Emil asked Michael. They all knew that he and Jennifer had applied to join their white rhinoceros project.

'Not yet. Might be something in the box. Jen's going to Maun next week.' Once every month or so one of them drove down into Botswana to

Maun, the commercial hub of the Okavango Delta, to collect mail and pick up extra food supplies.

'Will you go back to Australia?' Michael asked Bruce who had been fairly quiet on the subject of his future.

'Yeah, reckon. Last time I was over it felt pretty good.'

'Not a patch on Africa though,' Bobby ventured. 'All kangaroos and koalas. Pretty tame stuff after this.'

'Maybe,' Bruce allowed. 'But I tell yer this for free, mate, give me the Aussie outback any day.'

'Why?' Terry asked the question.

'Because no bastard puts landmines in it. That's why.'

Heads nodded.

'You blokes are headed for trouble,' Bruce went on. 'You can't keep the blacks down forever. Look around you. Botswana got independence three years ago. Zambia's been on its own for what, five years? Africa's going back to the blacks and, one way or another, Rhodesia and South Africa will as well.'

'No chance!' Andre was appalled by the very idea. 'Anyway, what about Australia?'

'What about it?'

'You're always going on about how Africa is going back to the blacks. What about Australia? If you feel so strongly about it, shouldn't Australia go back to the Aborigines?'

'Don't be bloody stupid. That's different.'

'No it isn't.'

Michael cut in smoothly. 'I can't talk about your country, Bruce, but you've got a point about ours. What's happening here is just the tip of an iceberg.'

It was an old topic, regularly discussed around the campfire, especially since SWAPO, the Soviet and Cuban backed South West Africa People's Organisation, rebel groups had become active along the Caprivi.

'I hate to think of this place becoming a war zone,' Emil said. 'The poaching is bad enough as it is. What happens to the animals? It's always them that suffer. I hope it doesn't come to that.'

'It's already starting.' Terry Silk adjusted a stick in the fire. 'I saw a group of so-called freedom fighters only two days ago.'

'How do you know what they were?' Jennifer asked. 'They might have been local tribesmen.'

'The locals don't walk about the bush for the hell of it. They're going somewhere, fishing, hunting, visiting, whatever. They don't wear European clothes and they always carry traditional weapons. The lot I saw were lined up along the road trying to look innocent, waving and smiling. Not a spear among them. In fact, they carried nothing. Probably got rid of it in the bush when they heard the vehicle.'

'You reported them I take it?' Emil asked.

Terry looked wry. 'Yes. For what it was worth. By the time the police got there they would have been long gone. What a mixed bunch they were too. One of them was a Zulu, I swear it.'

Andre flicked his half-smoked cigarette into the

451

fire. 'We should carry guns. Shoot the bastards on sight.'

'That's a bit extreme,' Emil remarked mildly. He'd heard Andre say things like that many times.

'Why not?' Andre asked aggressively. He was growing progressively more impatient by what he perceived to be a lack of retaliatory action on the part of the South Africans. 'Any fool can see what they're up to. It's not Angola or Namibia they want to liberate. They're after South Africa and they've got the commies' backing.' He lit another cigarette. 'I'm telling you, man. Unless the army does something about them pretty soon they'll be laying their landmines inside our borders.'

Lying in bed later that night, Michael returned to the fireside conversation. 'There's no way around it, Jen. The government won't give an inch and the opposition, be they ANC affiliated or not, are too committed to give up. There's no turning back for them. Who knows where it's all going to end? You've got people like Dyson in exile in London beavering away for a peaceful solution. Then there's his brother Jackson, last heard of heading for Zambia and probably so brainwashed by now that he's forgotten what he's fighting for. Bombs are going off at home killing innocent people, black and white, and, half the time, no-one knows if it's a protest or if our bloody government is responsible in a macabre attempt to curry world sympathy. Mandela's been in prison seven years and the longer he stays there the more notice the rest of the world takes of us. It's a mess, Jen. A bloody mess.'

Jennifer rolled towards him and put an arm over his chest. 'If we miss out on the Umfolozi job why don't you think about becoming more involved at a political level?'

'It's been on my mind for a while,' Michael admitted. 'How would you feel about such a change of lifestyle?'

'I'd back you, of course. I love working out here but the boys can't stay in the bush forever. In a couple of years, Jeremy will have to start school. It's been on my mind too. I can always go into private practice.'

Michael placed a hand gently on his wife's stomach. 'How's our daughter this evening?'

'Coming along nicely.'

'What if it's another boy?'

She snuggled against him. 'Then we'll just have to try again.'

They were attuned to each other so finely that it was often possible for one of them to guess what the other was about to say. Michael discovered in himself a capacity for love so intense it sometimes frightened him. The past five years had flown. They had been on the project a little over a year when Jennifer fell pregnant. She worked right up until two weeks before the baby was due, then Michael had driven her south through hundreds of kilometres of mud and sand, crossing into South Africa at Tlokweng and arriving in Johannesburg four days after the trip began. Michael worried constantly about his wife going into labour on that long journey. He could not understand how she could be so calm. However, Jeremy Michael King, having consideration not normally associated with babies, arrived exactly on his due date, September 30, 1966, the same day that the British Protectorate of Bechuanaland became the independent Republic of Botswana.

Eighteen months later, Andrew Dyson King was born. And now, Jennifer found herself pregnant again and hoping for a daughter.

Michael knew it was time for change but, like the others, felt sorry that the project had to end. In spite of their differing backgrounds and personalities, they were all close. Sure, Terry sometimes needed to be steered back to the task in hand; Andre could be argumentative about politics and a downright pain in the arse over snakes; Emil had moments of deep depression over his wife's death which were so intense no-one could break through to help him; Bruce often angered the South Africans with withering sarcasm about their country; and Bobby kept allowing young backpackers to lure him away. However, by and large, considering they were seven people who had been thrown together to live under fairly basic conditions for five years, the team had fared well.

Michael shook himself out of his reverie. He was as bad as Terry sometimes, allowing thoughts to divert him. 'Rhino,' he told himself. 'The project may be nearly over but you're still on the job.'

He'd come a long way in his knowledge of the rhinoceros. It was a gloomy day indeed when he finally had to confront the truth about them, that the black rhinoceros was demonstrably the most stupid animal in the African bush. All things wild were unpredictable, he knew that, but none was so hard to read as the black rhino. Michael doubted that the animal itself knew whether it would charge or run away. He had witnessed mindless attacks on countless occasions, once on his own vehicle that he'd left in the shade of an umbrella-like acacia. The rhino had blundered out of the bush, spotted the Land Rover and, with no hesitation, charged, opening up the driver's side door as if it had been paper. Not satisfied, and in an awesome kind of blind rage, the animal pushed and shoved the vehicle until it lay on its side. Then, appearing to forget the incident altogether, the young female, no more than six years old, spent the next hour browsing peacefully on the nearby shrubbery.

Another time, one of the many narrow squeaks experienced by Emil, Michael had diverted what looked like impending disaster by throwing his leather jacket in front of a battle-scarred old bull as it gained, with deadly intent, on the fleeing Frenchman. The animal lost interest in Emil, could easily have veered towards Michael but didn't and proceeded to kill the jacket. The last Michael saw of his favourite piece of clothing was its tattered remnants as the rhinoceros galloped away trying to free itself of the offending thing that had become impaled on sixty centimetres of rock-hard matted hair.

Michael had learned that the beast was unapologetically bad-tempered. The black rhino would kill for the hell of it, thrusting low with its horn, often between a victim's legs, before tossing it high into the air. He'd seen the end result of one such attack, the pathetic remains of a little Barakwengo Bushman who had been efficiently emasculated and left to die. It was a twisting spiral of vultures that led him to the unfortunate man. Others of his clan were there already, keeping the scavengers at bay. Using sign language and the Bushman's gift for mimicry, the fallen man's companions explained that they had been hunting and that the rhino had boiled out of the bush, swung its great head and removed their friend's appendages before continuing on its way.

Michael was not surprised. It was the rainy season and, for some reason, at that time of year the black rhinoceros always rubbed its horns against rocks or bark, sometimes changing the shape of them considerably and, without doubt, sharpening the points into a formidable weapon. Nobody was certain why they did this. Jennifer favoured the theory that in the humid build-up of rain, parasites attached themselves to the horns and rubbing was simply a way of removing them. Terry thought it might be a prelude to the mating season. Whatever the reason, it was just another example of how little they actually knew.

There was nothing predictable about the animal, with the notable exception of its insatiable curiosity. At the first hint of a foreign presence, man or beast, up would come its head. Circling and wary, sniffing for scent, the rhinoceros would investigate further. Using smell rather than sight, *uBejane* was not satisfied until the interloper had been located. It was at this point, with little or no provocation, that 1000 kilograms of prehistoric monster would either come at you like an express train or run like hell in the opposite direction. There was no way of knowing which to expect: no telltale twitching ears, no little flick of the tail. The only unanimous conclusion reached by Michael and the others was that once committed to a charge, the rhinoceros rarely changed its mind. Irascible, ugly, unpredictable, aggressive and incredibly stupid, the black rhinoceros seemed like a bad joke of nature. But Michael loved them for all that.

It was nearly full dark when he gathered up his camera, water bottle and notebook. The vehicle was a couple of hundred metres away. With the big bull in the vicinity, Michael felt it would be prudent to reach it while there was still some light. Ready to drop from the tree, he strained his eyes for one last glimpse of the animal. In that instant, the silence was torn apart by the deafening roar of an explosion. In the gloomy light, Michael saw an object rise high in the air and, almost in slow motion, turn lazily over before giving in to the forces of gravity. It landed close to the tree from which he had so nearly fallen. The bloody stump was barely recognisable as part of the rhinoceros' leg.

His senses at full strength, Michael made it to the ground and froze, listening for anything out of the ordinary. The bush had gone quiet again but for the crackle of flames. A pall of smoke and dust billowed against the sun's last rays. Michael knew exactly what had happened. The rhinoceros had stepped on a landmine, releasing 3000 degrees centigrade of concentrated inferno and blasting a crater beneath it almost a metre deep.

Jackson Mpande grunted in the sultry heat under the combined weight of his backpack and an AK-47 assault rifle. The sun had set but there had been a shower and the air was heavy with humidity. Somebody in front stumbled but quickly righted himself. Jackson nodded in approval. The men with him were well-trained professionals, capable of disregarding their own personal discomfort in order to get a job done. Sweat ran freely down his face but he ignored it. They had seven or eight kilometres to go before reaching Katima Mulilo and slipping back across the border into Zambia. Jackson knew the safe route like the back of his hand. The group had been laying mines along the Caprivi Strip for some months, in recent weeks making five trips deep into the western end.

Jackson had been a member of SWAPO for nearly five years. Based in Zambia, the aim of SWAPO was to create disruption in the only buffer between Angola and South Africa. The Marxists wanted South West but, more than that, they wanted its mineral-rich administrator. Laying mines in the Caprivi Strip was a way of spreading the already stretched defence resources of Pretoria. It was a niggle, nothing more.

After Jackson left Tessa in Gaberones, he had made his way north towards Zambia. He picked up occasional work but lived mainly on his wits. The people of Bechuanaland, the Batswana, seemed disinterested, even hostile, towards him. They were not impressed by his quest to join the freedom fighters. Their own country was on the brink of independence, a peaceful and bloodless achievement won by a handful of far-seeing and committed men. As far as most of the population were concerned, the problems afflicting neighbouring South Africa might just as well belong to another continent. Jackson grew frustrated by their apparent lack of understanding and this made him even more determined to play an active part in the liberation of all still held down by colonial oppression.

Somehow, in his mind, freedom throughout Africa was synonymous with the Zulu dream of their own independent country. Jackson believed one would follow the other. And achievement of both was reliant on the fall of white supremacy in South Africa.

He left Bechuanaland, crossing the remote Caprivi Strip and entering Zambia at Katima Mulilo. At some stage in history an international boundary had been drawn through this isolated village leaving most of it on the South West African side. Both Zambia and its southern neighbour were content to continue using the name and so, within five kilometres of each other, in two different countries, were two places called Katima Mulilo. Once into Zambia, Jackson felt more relaxed, making no secret of his intentions and openly asking directions to SWAPO training camps. Much to his astonishment no-one seemed to know of any. They were not hiding the truth from him, and it was clear they thought this young Zulu a little touched in the head if he believed that such places existed in Zambia. More often than not, he was advised to try Angola.

At Sesheke, just over the Zambezi River, Jackson asked one question too many and found himself in the back of a truck with five other men. The only difference was, they were free and armed while he sat handcuffed to a grille behind the driver's cab. Demands about where they were taking him and why he was trussed like a chicken brought no response. It was as if they could not hear him. On the few occasions they conversed with each other their words were foreign, a different African tongue that Jackson could not understand.

After five hot, dusty and bumpy hours, the truck left the road to crash and groan its way through the bush for another forty-five minutes, finally stopping in what appeared to be the middle of nowhere.

'Out,' one man said in English, unlocking the handcuffs.

Rubbing circulation into his wrists, Jackson clambered off the back.

'Walk.'

He was placed third in line and they moved forward in single file, following no path that he could see. Twenty minutes later, three heavily armed men materialised from seemingly nowhere and a heated exchange of words took place. Although Jackson could not follow the conversation, it was clear they were discussing him, their voices loud with aggression. Finally, and with some reluctance, Jackson and his escorts were allowed to pass.

They reached the camp a few minutes later. It was not visible until they were almost on top of it. For such a large place it was very well camouflaged and, from the air, would have been almost impossible to see.

'Wait.'

Three men stayed with him, the other two walked away. Jackson looked around with interest. Camouflaged tents had been erected under substantial stands of trees. While this screened the camp from above, on the ground it sprawled, with no apparent sense of order, in a rough semi-circle. Not one person could be seen on the open ground within the arc. No smoke rose from cooking fires. He heard no murmur of voices. Either the camp was deserted or discipline so tight that the men were trained to live in virtual silence.

Five minutes passed before he heard the sound of someone approaching. The three with him visibly stiffened their stances. Jackson too squared his shoulders and stood taller, anxious to make a good first impression. He was completely unprepared for the man who strode towards them. Tall and clearly very fit, broad shoulders, face lean from living rough, eyes hard and mouth set firm; all things Jackson expected. Except for one thing. Well, two things really. The man was white. And, as he got closer, Jackson could see something more startling. He wasn't a man at all. Try as he might to prevent it, Jackson's jaw dropped.

Cold blue eyes flicked over him briefly. 'Come.' Without acknowledging the others, she turned on her heel and strode away. Jackson followed.

She led him to an open tent slightly larger than the others. 'Close the flap.'

Jackson undid two ties, releasing the canvas triangle. When he turned back she was leaning against a desk. 'You are?'

'Jackson Mpande.'

She made him nervous. He felt as though his tongue was glued to the roof of his mouth. She was wearing a faded green uniform and, when she removed her hat, he could not help but stare. Her hair had been cropped into a crewcut and, what was left of it – white or grey, he couldn't tell – did little to hide the fact that her head was shaped like a bullet. She scratched to relieve the itch of dried sweat. 'You ask too many questions.' Her voice was hard, the accent difficult to understand.

Jackson found her repulsive. 'I want to join you.'

'Why?' It came out flat, as though she couldn't care less.

'To free Africans from . . .' He hesitated, wincing inwardly when she made no effort to hide cynical amusement.

'Ha!' she spat at him.

Stung, Jackson added, 'In South Africa.'

'So! It is not Angola that interests you?' She smiled for the first time, revealing several gold teeth. 'You are honest at least.'

Russian. She must be Russian. 'My interests are no different from yours.'

She stared at him coldly. 'Do not flatter yourself, Zulu. Our interests are worlds apart.'

Her eyes warned him. She was testing him somehow. 'That may be so,' he said sharply, hoping it was the correct response. 'But in order to gain what we seek our methods are the same.'

Approval flared briefly in her pale blue eyes. 'Good. Very good.' She poured water from a jug on her desk and drank thirstily. She did not offer him any.

Jackson said nothing, sensing she was coming to a decision about him. Silence stretched between them, so deep that Jackson could hear it.

'Go home, Zulu,' she said suddenly. 'You have your own quarrel.'

Jackson stood his ground. 'My quarrel is linked to yours.'

She shook her head. 'I've had your people here before. They're trouble.'

'I won't be,' Jackson said quietly. 'I can never go back.'

The woman moved behind her desk and sat down, indicating impatiently with a hand that he should do likewise. 'I am Comrade Yelena. This is Base 37. Already you know enough to die. Answer my questions truthfully. Why do you come here?'

'To join.'

'Why?'

'To free my people,' he repeated.

'Ha!' she mocked him. 'One Zulu. You have the dreams of a child.'

'No,' he disagreed. 'I have the dreams of every Zulu. It is in my blood. I will die like the ancient warriors if I must. And like my ancestors, when this blood runs hot I must act. I am not a coward. I am not a troublemaker. I will do as I am ordered and do it as well as the next man. Even better than the next man.'

'Or woman?'

He inclined his head. 'If women are soldiers I will treat them as such.'

She ignored that. 'You have old tribal enemies here.'

Jackson met her stare calmly. 'Zulus do not harbour grudges. Yesterday's enemies can be the friends of today. That is our way.'

'Do your enemies feel the same?'

Jackson shrugged. 'If they do not I will kill them.'

Her eyes narrowed.

Realising his mistake he went on quickly. 'If a man runs from a snake and the snake runs from the man then the killing ground remains empty.'

Comrade Yelena permitted a small smile to escape, but only for a fleeting moment. 'You say you cannot go back. What do you run from?'

'The police.'

'You killed someone?'

'No.'

She stared him down and Jackson relented. 'I got a white girl pregnant. We ran away.'

For the first time he felt he had impressed her.

'So,' she said softly. 'You have balls. I like that.'

He was not sure if she was referring to his sexuality or his courage.

Abruptly, she threw her head back and laughed, gold teeth glinting. Then, standing, she put two fingers in her mouth and blew a piercing whistle. Immediately, the tent flap was flung back and a massive shape appeared in silhouette, an AK-47 held in one hand pointed unwaveringly at Jackson's stomach.

Comrade Yelena shook her head impatiently. 'This Zulu is Comrade Jackson. He is joining us. Find him somewhere to sleep. His training starts tomorrow. And watch your shoes, comrade, he could be standing in them tomorrow.'

The man was no Zulu. His features were vaguely European, yet the skin over them was jet black. Comrade Yelena had effectively and deliberately created a potential enemy. His second test. Jackson wondered why. However, he was more than a match for this scrawny white woman. Smiling at the tall African he commented quietly in English, 'The shoes of the father is no place for the child until he has worn out as many pairs.'

Comrade Yelena's eyes gleamed with mocking approval as Jackson followed the other man from her office.

Once out of earshot, the man turned and raised an open palm to Jackson. 'You speak well, Zulu. I am Comrade Selveira. My home is Angola. Do not let that bitch get to you.'

Jackson shook his hand. 'Is she really in charge here?'

Selveira cast a quick look towards the tent and lowered his voice. 'A temporary arrangement. She's an experiment. The Russians use us as a dumping ground for their rejects. You will find out soon enough that they are no better than the British, the Portuguese or any of the others.' He shrugged. 'No matter, Comrade Jackson, no matter. It is but a small price to pay for the supply of arms, hey?' A short bark of laughter. 'We use them, they use us. At least we fight a common enemy, if not for a common goal. They will find sooner or later that we can bite their hands just as easily as we bite others. Do not concern yourself with Comrade Yelena and her games. She will be recalled to Moscow soon, if one of us does not kill her first. They do not last long in Africa, these Russians.'

'I felt she was testing me somehow. Does she always . . .?'

'With everyone,' Selveira said emphatically. 'You did well. Many fail her stupid tests.'

They started walking again. 'You would be dead by now if you had. I, myself, would have killed you.' Another short laugh. 'Unless of course she had felt like killing you herself.'

Jackson shuddered.

'She hates men, that one. It's women she prefers.'

Jackson was scandalised and it showed.

'Heh!' Selveira was amused by his innocence. 'You'll find out soon enough.'

'White women have no shame,' Jackson burst out. 'None at all.'

Selveira laughed long and hearty. 'And how would such a puppy know?' he managed at last. 'One so young as you should not have got it wet yet.'

'Well I did,' Jackson said, stung. 'Well and truly wet.'

'So!' Selveira was still amused. 'I thought Zulu girls kept their legs together.'

'She was not Zulu,' Jackson boasted. 'She was white.' This was the first time Jackson had discussed sex in such detail with anyone. It made him feel worldly.

But Selveira changed the subject suddenly. 'Why do you want to join us?'

'For the same reason as you.'

'I think not, my young friend.'

'I want freedom. Isn't that what we're fighting for?'

'No.' Selveira's voice suddenly went hard. 'You'll learn soon enough. Freedom is not why we fight. It's something more than that.'

'What then?' Jackson was truly puzzled.

Selveira gave him a pitying look. 'Power, of course. The old order has been destroyed. Power and leadership is up for grabs. I plan to be calling the shots when the time comes. No more taking orders, I'll be one of those giving them. Call it freedom if it makes you feel any better but you'll learn, as we all have, that the child we once called Idealism soon grows into the man known as Ambition.'

Jackson was not convinced. 'But without freedom there can never be power.'

Selveira grinned mirthlessly. 'There is no such thing as freedom. You will learn soon enough.'

Jackson thought it would be unwise to continue the conversation. He sought safer ground. 'At least you're doing something. My people still talk of the past, even about bringing back Inkatha. Where will that get them?'

'You make a good point, comrade. Bullets kill. Words can only wound.'

'But the South Africans are worried. Their faith in themselves has been badly shaken. You have already achieved much. More and more join your cause. Success . . .'

'What makes you think we are successful? We lose more men than we kill. The South Africans are very good.'

'We can be just as good.'

Selveira sighed and stopped. 'This is your tent. Make yourself at home. Tomorrow you may wish to be dead.'

That was nearly five years ago. Comrade Yelena had, as Selveira predicted, not lasted long. Recurring intestinal malaria left her weak and unable to carry on. The camp breathed a collective sigh of relief at her departure. She had been replaced by a drunken oaf of a man who spent all day in his tent drinking vodka, content to leave the training program to his minions. After him came the youthful and extremely inexperienced son of a high-ranking Soviet official who arrived with a loud voice and high hopes and left, two weeks later, in a body bag, having blown himself into tiny little pieces with one of the Russians' own, and extremely unreliable, TM-46 landmines.

Much to everyone's relief, the Russians then decided that a handful of African recruits who had been specially trained in the Soviet Union were capable of running their own show. For the past three years, Base 37 had been under the command of Comrade Selveira. He was a popular choice and, most of the time, the camp operated like a well-oiled machine, only developing engine trouble when the Soviet hierarchy paid an unannounced visit to check on their investment in Africa.

Jackson was now a junior officer. He had trained hard and learned quickly, believing every word of the instructor's rhetoric. After two years at Base 37 he had been singled out and sent to Russia for specialist training in explosives. Now, at the age of twenty-three, he was the leader of a small group who made frequent incursions into the Caprivi Strip, laying landmines. Their first targets were the South African police in Katima Mulilo who, in an effort to discourage the escalating incidence of SWAPO insurgent activity in the area had increased the intensity of their patrols along Caprivi's northern borders with Angola and Zambia.

The regime in Pretoria quickly became so concerned at the number of men and machines suddenly being blown to bits that they sent in a special army unit to devise a vehicle which could withstand the withering blast from landmines. With the army in place, it became obvious to Jackson that a better option would be to start hitting civilian targets. This would focus world attention on the region. Besides, civilians tended to crumble with shock in the face of a violent explosion, which meant Jackson and his men stood an infinitely better chance of getting safely back into Zambia. The South African Defence Forces on the other hand were highly trained and, in an adrenalin-filled confrontation, inevitably came out on top.

Jackson had put his suggestion to Selveira who agreed with him but delayed issuing an order until it had been cleared by Moscow. While they were waiting, news came in that a partly South African wildlife project operating in the Caprivi Strip was being wrapped up. 'This is our chance,' Jackson urged Selveira. 'The whites are pulling out.'

'There'll be others,' Selveira told him, still reluctant to take responsibility himself.

'Not like these, not right under our nose. We know where their base camp is set up. We know the routes they travel. We can hit them hard.'

What turned the tide in Jackson's favour was that many of the men agreed with him. They were now returning from laying mines on selected tracks west of the Linyanti River. Tracks used all the time by members of the research team. The unfortunate rhinoceros, blown to smithereens as Michael King watched, was a victim of work done weeks before. The animal had detonated a mine meant for the South African border police.

FIFTEEN

As he drove back to camp, Michael's mind kept returning to the landmine. 'How many more are out there?' he wondered. It was not the first time an animal had stepped on one, nor would it be the last, but it was the first time Michael had witnessed both the explosion and the result. The rhino, instead of cutting through the bush, had chosen a track made by the border patrol, which passed that way once or twice a month. Michael was devastated by the loss of this particular beast. In just two weeks' time, Natal Parks Board rangers were due to arrive and dart that rhino. It had all been so carefully planned. They were to transport it to Mkuzi Game Reserve, north of Umfolozi, where Emil Daguin had identified a habitat as close as possible to the one where the animal had lived. Waiting for the bull were others, both male and female, part of a breeding program that had already recorded a more than promising level of success. While the loss of this bull did not jeopardise the project at Mkuzi, it was one more senseless death in a population already suffering more losses than gains.

Michael swung off the border track and on to the section that connected their base camp to the road leading into Botswana. Under a tarpaulin in the back were the only parts of the rhino that he'd managed to find. Jennifer might be able to use them, though for what he didn't quite know. He wondered if she had returned from Maun.

Although they were supposed to take it in turns to make the monthly trip for mail and supplies, lately, and at her suggestion, the job had fallen to Jennifer. She always took the boys and stayed with friends for a couple of days. Several families living beside the Thamalakane River just outside town had children of similar ages to Jeremy and Andrew, so it was a welcome opportunity to let the boys mingle with others.

In the headlights, Michael tried to see if any other vehicle had recently passed this way but, though there were many tracks, the newest were his own from this morning. He was surprised but not unduly alarmed. Although Jennifer hated driving at night she was sometimes delayed in leaving Maun. She was probably no more than a few kilometres behind him.

Michael missed his family when they made these monthly trips away. Jeremy was now a sturdy little fellow of three. He had a bright, inquiring mind and would dismantle almost anything just 'to see how it works'. Michael spent a great deal of his time putting his elder son's handiwork back together again. In a way, Michael was pleased that the project was nearly finished. Jeremy needed the stimulation of others his own age, something he would have for the first time if they got the Umfolozi job.

Jeremy looked a lot like Michael. Blonde hair, blue eyes, wide mouth and a sprinkling of freckles over his nose. He could amuse himself for hours on end and called all forms of life 'God's creatures'. Those he accidentally stood on or deliberately squashed became 'poor God's creatures'. His open and friendly disposition made him immensely popular with everyone.

Andrew, at eighteen months, was tall for his age. He was also fair, with his mother's angelic face. Shy with others, he followed his older brother around incessantly and tried to imitate everything Jeremy did.

Being constantly in the company of adults, both boys had vocabularies well beyond their years. They also conversed with Emil in simple French, spoke Setswana to the young African girl who had been hired as a nanny and, to the delight of Bruce who had spent many hours working on it, said 'Gawd's struth' in pure Australian.

Jeremy was, in Jennifer's opinion, shaping up as a man's man. 'He's the doer,' she insisted. Andrew, on the other hand, was sensitive and affectionate. 'A lover, not a fighter,' Jennifer claimed.

Michael was less inclined to slot his boys into niches. All he knew was that these little beings had quickly found places in his heart. He was absurdly smitten and proud of them and, both boys, he knew with absolute certainty, would make their marks on the world.

Michael frowned when he saw a straggle of African men in his headlights. 'What are they doing out here?' There was something about the way they lined up along the road, smiling and waving, that wasn't quite normal. The few inhabitants of the Caprivi were primitive, mistrustful people who tried to avoid contact with others. Batswana tribesmen rarely ventured into the area. Terry had come across men like this a few days ago. Michael could see why he'd been suspicious enough to report their presence, they looked out of place somehow. He decided to radio the border police as soon as he got to camp. With SWAPO becoming more active along the Caprivi it didn't do to take chances. These men could well be innocent but, then again, they might be terrorists. They could even be the ones who laid the mine that blew up the rhinoceros. As he lurched past them on the bumpy road, one of the men raised his head and stared directly at Michael. There was something about him, something familiar. But the road quickly reclaimed his concentration and he dismissed the man from his mind.

His headlights picked up a sandy spot ahead and he turned slightly to avoid it. The tracks were a treacherous combination of ruts, potholes, corrugations, hard calcrete outcrops and stretches of deep, soft sand. Michael now knew this section like the back of his hand but, in the early days, it had been a different matter. The sand cover was ever-changing and deep potholes could inexplicably develop to catch the unwary. Hitting one at speed could severely damage a vehicle.

His wheels missed the rim of the landmine by a fraction.

Jackson had heard the vehicle travelling quickly in third gear way before he saw its headlights. They had no more than two minutes. 'Quick,' he snapped. 'Get that mine buried.' It took only seconds in the soft sand before the men were moving forward again towards the approaching vehicle, weapons, rucksacks and clothing discarded into the bush. They made no attempt to hide. Very often, vehicles out after dark were driven by hunters who carried powerful spotlights. Men seen crouching in the bush would raise more suspicions than those walking openly along a road.

They moved swiftly, wanting as much space between them and the mine as possible. When a vehicle detonated a mine, the combination of its momentum and the resultant explosion very often flung it up and forwards. This was why they walked towards the approaching vehicle rather than away from it.

The headlights on full beam nearly blinded them. One of his men laughed and slapped another on the arm as if sharing a joke. Although striving to look natural all were strung tight with tension. Border patrols rarely used this track but occasionally they'd seen one and knew that the South Africans would shoot first and ask questions later at the slightest suspicion of SWAPO. But the vehicle did not stop, or even slow down. Jackson barely had time to register that it was driven by a white man. He smiled foolishly as the vehicle passed and waved with the others, holding his breath as it went over the landmine. Then it was gone.

'We must hurry,' he said to his men. 'He'll report seeing us.'

'How much longer, Mummy?' Jeremy quizzed.

'Not long, darling. Another fifteen minutes.'

She was tired. It was a long drive up from Maun and, although Jennifer enjoyed being there, the trip home seemed to take forever. A puncture hadn't helped either. Not being strong enough to undo the wheel nuts, they'd been forced to wait nearly two hours before another vehicle came along. She glanced back to where Andrew was now asleep on the back seat. 'Why don't you lie down too?' she suggested.

'No thanks Mummy,' Jeremy replied politely. 'I'll stay awake and keep you company.'

Too late, Jennifer saw the same soft spot in the road that her husband had driven past some thirty minutes before. Praying it did not hide a pothole, Jennifer gripped the steering wheel tighter and drove straight over it. The front slid out slightly in the sand but one back wheel passed directly over the metal pressure plate. Instant detonation blew the vehicle forwards and upwards, turning it sideways in midair before it crashed, nose down, and flipped crazily end over end three times, finally coming to rest off the road and upside-down. The back of the vehicle had been literally blown apart, an unrecognisable mess of twisted metal.

Andrew was spontaneously ejected by the blast, straight up through where the two-layer tropical roof had, split seconds earlier, parted company with the other bodywork. Jeremy, not restrained in any way, had been catapulted through the front windscreen as it disintegrated, his body skinned alive before being crushed beneath the front bumper as the vehicle crashed back to earth for the first time. Jennifer was killed instantly, flying shrapnel tearing through the back of her head and the rigid steering wheel smashing every bone in her young ribcage.

In the pitch dark of the African night, the silence that followed was the silence of death.

The blast was heard by two members of a South African police patrol who were on a converging track about a kilometre away. They knew immediately what it was. Approaching cautiously, taking care to drive over the same tracks as other vehicles, weapons cocked and at the ready, they found what was left of Jeremy first, on the road where the vehicle had crushed him. His little body, so full of life a few minutes earlier, lay flattened and lifeless, bloody and covered with sand. Neither man could bring themselves to touch or even look at him for very long. His skull had been shattered but the freckled face was untouched and serene, asleep and at peace, while the rest of him had been so cruelly disfigured.

'Oh Jesus, oh Jesus! The bastards!' one of the policemen gasped as rising nausea hit him.

Moving carefully forward, powerful torches

probing the night, checking the ground ahead for signs of any more mines, they made their way towards the smoking, twisted wreck. Jennifer was inside, arched strangely forward over the steering wheel, arms hanging limp on either side, what was left of her head thrown back, blonde hair red with blood. The stench of burning flesh was overpowering.

'Anyone else?'

The policeman closest shone his torch around. 'No.'

'It's Dr King from the research camp,' the other, older and more experienced officer said. 'At least, I think it is. It's one of their Land Rovers.'

The younger man bent double and retched. 'That'll be one of her boys then,' he said, straightening and pointing back towards their vehicle. 'Hard to say which.' He turned and vomited again. 'Jesus Christ! The bastards! Jesus Christ!'

'Come on,' his partner sensed the onset of shock. 'We've got to report this.'

They walked cautiously back to their own vehicle, carefully avoiding the body that had once been Jeremy King. The younger man reached inside and grabbed the radio.

But his mind had gone blank and it was the other policeman who took over the handset and reported the incident to headquarters. 'You'll have to let them know at Linyanti too.'

'Roger that.' The tinny voice of the radio operator sounded shockingly loud. 'We'll get help to you immediately. Don't leave until it shows up. And watch out for predators.'

The two officers waited in their vehicle, lights off, smoking, not talking, each busy with his own thoughts, coming to terms with the terrible carnage only metres away. They both heard it at the same time, a thin wailing sound. It appeared to be coming from somewhere off to their left.

'Pass me a torch and hit the headlights,' one whispered. Older and more experienced he might have been but the noise had made his scalp creep. He shone the powerful beam into the bush while lights flooded the track in front of them. The wailing stopped. 'What the hell was that?'

'Bushbaby?' the other suggested, referring to the tiny squirrel-like creature who had fooled more than one into thinking there was a baby out there somewhere.

'No way, man. Bushbabies don't sound like that.'

'Wild cat?'

The wailing started up again.

'That's human. Jesus Christ! It's the other kid.'

Andrew toddled out of the bush and onto the road. He stood blinking in the headlights. There was a cut on his forehead and blood trickled down one cheek. Otherwise, he appeared to be unhurt.

'I'll go,' the younger policeman said, dipping the lights and opening the driver's door. He moved away from the car, talking quietly and carefully avoiding the headlights which would make him appear as a frightening silhouette. 'Hello son, are you all right?' he said softly, cursing to himself that he couldn't recall the boy's name. 'I'm a friend of your daddy.'

Andrew didn't react.

The policeman advanced slowly. As anxious as he was to reach the boy before he turned and saw the wreck or the body of his brother, he knew any sudden movement might panic the child. 'I'm a policeman. I won't hurt you. Come here, son, it's okay.'

Andrew stayed where he was.

He reached the boy and dropped to one knee. 'Would you like to ride in a police car?'

No reaction. The silence was unnerving.

'We'll take you home if you like.'

Nothing.

Reaching out he gently touched the child's shoulder. Andrew went rigid. The policeman wondered if he was old enough to have learned never to speak to strangers. He dropped his hand. 'It's all right, son. You're safe. It's all right.'

Still nothing.

He heard his partner get out of the car.

'Stop buggerising around, man. The lad's in shock. He needs to be *told* what to do, not asked.' He walked straight up to Andrew and held out a hand. After a moment's hesitation, the boy took it trustingly and walked with him back to the police vehicle.

Andrew was gently placed onto the back seat where he sat, staring at the two officers with large, solemn eyes.

'How old would you say he was?' the younger man asked.

'Dunno. He's still a baby. Maybe two.'

'Poor little bugger.'

Andrew yawned, then lay down on the seat and put a thumb in his mouth. Within a minute, he was sound asleep. Although it was a hot night, they covered him with a jacket.

'Do you think he's all right?'

'Looks okay but he doesn't seem to hear anything.'

'Jesus Christ! I wish those okes would hurry up.'

Michael was getting worried. Jennifer was never this late. 'Probably car trouble,' Emil said soothingly, although he too was concerned.

'Listen,' Michael turned his head slightly. 'It's the Land Rover. Here she comes.'

Relief gave way to an ice-cold premonition when he saw it was the South African police. 'Mr King,' one of the officers spoke to him. 'I'm afraid I have some bad news for you.'

There was no mistake and no escape. Reality held him in a vice and would not let go. Michael did not want to open his eyes. Out there, in the world of tomorrow, a terrible hurt waited for him. He lay on his back in the dim light of dawn, still sluggish and confused from the hefty dose of Valium prescribed by Emil, vainly hoping that if he went back to sleep the truth might go away. But, oh God, here it came again. It started in the pit of his stomach, rising in choking waves of memory until salt-laden tears erupted from tightly shut eyes, their trails drying like chalk against his sun-bronzed skin. Shuddering sobs racked his body and, in trying to keep them quiet, Michael snuffled and gasped, rolling over into the pillow, keening in utter anguish and despair.

Emil heard his grief. It was hard enough for the rest of them to accept. Jennifer, lovely and vibrant, intelligent and funny, warm and kind, pregnant. And suddenly, gone. Jeremy, inquiring and serious, outspoken and intelligent, his life only just begun. Gone. Andrew, eighteen months old and probably deafened by the blast. 'Dear God,' Emil thought, struggling out of his chair by the smouldering campfire, 'What a terrible world this is.' He turned back the flap to Michael's tent and went in. Standing helplessly beside the bed, he looked down at his friend's shuddering, aching pain. Tears filled Emil's eyes. In an instinctive gesture of comfort, he sat on the side of the bed and put a hand on his friend's shoulder.

Michael stirred, turned on his side, wrapped both arms around Emil's waist and clung to him for dear life. Very quickly, his tears soaked through Emil's trousers as Michael cried out his terrible heartbreak.

They had to get Andrew to a hospital quickly.

The combined police and army had taken over. They did not consult anyone, simply informed

Emil of what was expected. They were good at this. This work was not new to them. On the surface, they kept a tight lid on any emotion, moved quickly, spoke normally, even joked about other things. But somehow this incident was different. Their own dead were an occupational hazard. This woman, this child, got to them, crept through the barriers that went up. It showed in little ways. Small huddles of men, suddenly pensive and silent, chain-smoking till their throats ached. Forced laughter. Tempers flaring at nothing. No-one voiced it, no-one. But the thought was in all their minds. *This is the beginning of the end*. It made them afraid but, much more than fear, in each and every man's heart and soul burned a terrible rage for revenge. And even beyond their instinctive craving to hit back lay a deeper and more consuming emotion. Sorrow. Not so much for the woman and child but for something that was changing forever, the white man's paradise of South Africa. *The beginning of the end*.

Yet they did what they had to. The bodies of Jennifer and Jeremy were wrapped in bags and driven to the airfield at Katima Mulilo. From there they were flown to South Africa. The wrecked Land Rover could not be towed away so a hole was dug and they buried it. There was no need to examine the damage, it was typical of what could happen to an unprotected vehicle.

Long before it was light the army had swept all routes leading to and from the camp. They found four more mines, one on each track, and all within ten kilometres. Even before Michael awoke to his pain, the army was aware that the name of the game had changed. SWAPO was targeting civilians.

At eight-thirty an army helicopter, at some risk to the pilot, landed in the dry river bed. Michael barely paid it any mind. He was sitting on a chair outside Jennifer's laboratory tent, unable to bring himself to face the memories within. Andrew was in his arms.

A policeman found Emil to let him know what arrangements had been made.

'You'll land at Lanceria,' he said, naming the small airport just outside Johannesburg. 'There's an ambulance waiting and an ear, nose and throat man on standby at Sandton Clinic. We've also asked for a psychiatrist.'

Michael, pale and withdrawn, holding Andrew as though he could not bear to let him out of his sight, made no comment when Emil said he would go with them. It was Emil who packed a bag for Michael and his son. 'Come on,' he urged his friend who appeared distant and strangely reluctant to board the helicopter.

Michael frowned. 'There's something . . . I keep trying to remember. Something significant.'

'What sort of something?' Emil asked gently.

'About yesterday.' Michael's face was screwed up with concentration. 'It's important.'

'Try to work it out on the way,' Emil suggested, anxious to get going. Although he kept his concern to himself, he was desperately worried about Andrew. Apart from the loss of hearing, he seemed fine. But Emil would not rest until a thorough medical examination had been undertaken. The cut on his head was superficial but a child's skull is soft. He could have concussion, could be haemorrhaging – anything.

'Jennifer . . . Jeremy . . .' Michael's voice broke and he could not bring himself to ask.

Emil understood. 'They were flown to Johannesburg earlier this morning.'

It seemed to give him the impetus he needed. Michael handed Andrew to Emil, climbed into the helicopter, then reached out to take his son.

'Let him sit up front,' Emil said. 'He might enjoy it.'

But Michael shook his head. 'He'll sit on my lap.'

Emil left it. Michael didn't have much to cling to but, if by holding his son he found some comfort, it was a small beginning.

The pilot wasted no time. They were airborne within minutes. Half-an-hour later, Emil heard a small gasp of shock. He turned in his seat and saw that Michael's face had gone white under a mask of perspiration.

'I've remembered what it was. Last night. There were men on the road.'

The army helicopter pilot had his earphones off and heard. 'We know that, sir. They were tracked into Zambia. Don't you worry about it. We'll get them. There's nowhere they can hide.'

Michael went to say more, then stopped. His mind replayed the face he'd seen briefly in the headlights, one vaguely familiar, a face he could now see with startling clarity. Jackson Mpande. Matured but unmistakeable. A face he already hated. But now! *Oh sweet Jesus!* Now!

Realisation hit him hard. His mind suddenly clear and focused.

For as long as it takes, you bastard. You're mine.

Something cold closed around his heart. Vulnerability over Jennifer and Jeremy retreated to be dealt with later. If it took him the rest of his life, if he had to die in the attempt, there was now only one thought in Michael's head.

Jackson Mpande was a dead man.

SIXTEEN

I f it had been left up to Michael he'd have taken his son straight to England for medical treatment. Not because he didn't trust the facilities in South Africa, he did. Some of the finest practitioners in the world were there. It was just that all Michael's instincts told him to get away from Africa for a while.

The decision was made easier by the fact that Jennifer's mother in Zululand, who might have reasonably been expected to want a hand in helping, had herself died of cancer the previous year. Jennifer's father, while mourning the loss of his wife and then his daughter and grandson, was in no shape to take on Michael and Andrew.

Besides, Michael wanted Andrew in England, removed from the increasing unrest that surrounded them. He yearned to be in the calm and loving company of Claire, to give his jarred and twitching nerves a break. Above all, Michael needed time to think.

The cold rage that had closed around his heart was not only a welcome diversion, it was essential to his sanity. He knew he wasn't thinking clearly so, while allowing it to prop him up, he was honest enough with himself to put his desire for revenge into some kind of perspective. Jackson Mpande would die, that issue wasn't in question. Michael had to be patient, to control his blinding rage. When Jackson died it would be the single most satisfying thing that Michael had ever done.

Only time would enable him to reach that stage. Getting away from Africa might help too. But when the helicopter landed at Lanceria an ambulance was waiting, competent people were on stand-by to assist and so, at Emil's urging, Michael accepted that his son's welfare had to come first.

Two months, and exhaustive tests later, the specialist informed Michael that, as far as he could tell, no permanent damage had been done to Andrew's hearing. 'It's shock. Give him time.'

'Don't be stupid,' Michael had snapped at the doctor. 'Try making a noise behind him or offering him some chocolate. He simply cannot hear it.'

As well as the ENT specialist, and once again at Emil's insistence, Michael, and to a lesser extent Andrew, had been seeing a psychiatrist. At first Michael had been convinced he could handle his grief without the interference of a stranger. The thought of lying on a couch and pouring out his heart to someone who would listen with clinical detachment was totally alien to his nature. What he didn't realise was that Emil, sensitive to Michael's intentions, worried about Andrew. While he sympathised with Michael's need for revenge he wanted to be certain that Andrew wasn't neglected because of it. In fact, Emil secretly hoped that the psychiatrist would remove Michael's rage and ease away his dreadful plans.

It was Emil who made the appointment and insisted Michael keep it. Michael went reluctantly, hoping that this Dr Devilliers was nothing like the psychiatrist they took Tessa to all those years ago. 'One visit,' he agreed.

Emil nodded, relieved. He'd had some grief counselling himself when his wife died and hoped, if Dr Devilliers was any good, that Michael would not stop at one visit. Once the ice was broken, in Emil's case anyway, each subsequent visit led him further along the road to confronting reality. Although this inevitably caused terrible anguish, it was a journey he took with increasing urgency, anxious to reach the end.

Michael arrived three minutes early for his appointment. The waiting room offered the usual out-of-date magazines and several pamphlets on mental health. The receptionist was African, something of a novelty in a white-dominated workplace except for the most menial of positions. Two other patients flicked disinterestedly through the reading material. Michael sat down, anticipating the usual long wait associated with the medical profession. A buzzer sounded. The receptionist spoke into the telephone then looked across at Michael. 'Dr Devilliers will see you now.' She led him down a passage, knocked on a door at the end, opened it and indicated he should enter. Michael went in and the receptionist shut the door.

He didn't see the doctor immediately, there was no-one behind the large mahogany desk.

'Over here.'

He turned. She was seated in an easy chair behind a coffee table. 'You!'

A chuckle. 'I wondered if it was the same Michael King.' She patted the empty chair next to her. 'Come and sit down.'

Michael stayed where he was. 'Is this such a good idea? You weren't much help last time.'

'I didn't get a bloody chance. How is your sister anyway?'

'Fine,' he said shortly.

'I know why you're here, Michael.' Her voice was soft but businesslike. 'Take your time. We can talk about Tessa if you like.'

Her wildly curly blonde hair was scraped straight back into a knot but stray strands had sprung back, framing her face. Jennifer's features swam before him and he found he was incredibly angry. *How dare she! This calm and clinically detached woman, how dare she think I will discuss my love, my grief, my rage. Who the hell does she think she is?* He was unaware of it but, as he stood indecisively, his fists were clenching and unclenching.

'I see your anger, Michael. Most of it should be directed outside this room. I'm sorry we fell out over Tessa but you didn't exactly give me a chance. I hope you're not going to make the same mistake this time. You do need help whether you like it or not. If it makes you more comfortable I can refer you to one of my partners.'

'I didn't know it was you. Last time you were Dr Lewis. You've changed your name.'

'Women do that when they get married.'

'What makes you think you can help me? I don't even like you.'

She smiled slightly at his bluntness. 'I hope you don't mean that. It was what I was saying about your sister you didn't like, I suspect.'

'Perhaps,' Michael conceded.

'Would you prefer to see someone else?'

'To hell with it,' Michael said suddenly. 'Let's get this over with.' He folded his arms and stared at her. 'Where do I lie down?'

She laughed outright at that. 'If you insist I suppose I could clear my desk.' She leaned forward and picked up cigarettes and a lighter from the coffee table, lit one and blew smoke towards the ceiling. 'I think I'd prefer it if you came over here and joined me.'

Michael crossed the room. 'You shouldn't smoke.'

'I know. Does the smell bother you?'

Before he knew it he was telling her how he'd once tried smoking while still at school but it made him dizzy and sick, and then somehow that led him to talk about UBejane and random boyhood memories and, because she questioned the name of the farm, he jumped to the problems of rhino in captivity and then somehow went back to sugar farming. He was surprised when she glanced at her watch and announced that the session was over.

'Next week. Same time.'

He heard himself agree. 'I was only going to see you once but, seeing as we didn't discuss anything . . . my so-called problems, I suppose one more visit . . .'

'Fine.' She smiled.

The following week he told her about Claire, the difficulties she'd faced most of her life and how glad he was that she'd finally found peace and happiness with Peter Dawson.

'Next week. Same time.'

'Okay.'

It took seven weeks for him to touch on Jennifer and Jeremy. As soon as he did the floodgates opened and he found it terribly easy to pour out his rage. To his absolute surprise, when he dried up and had no more to say, Annie Devilliers had tears coursing down her cheeks.

'Hey, I'm sorry. I didn't mean . . .'

She dabbed at her eyes. 'Do my tears make you uncomfortable?'

'No.' It was true enough, they didn't. 'It's just that . . .' Dammit! It was happening to him too. He'd been able to tell it with anger, holding his sorrow together, but now his own tears blinded him and a great sob welled up and, before he could stop himself, he was telling it again. This time nothing held him together and when at last his grief subsided and he was able to think straight, he found an inner peace that hadn't been there since . . . But no. He'd come a long way but not that far.

He felt her hand on his arm. She said nothing,

just gripped his arm with long, strong fingers. Michael was powerless to prevent what happened next. Looking back he supposed he'd been desperate for human contact. He had unloaded everything on to Annie Devilliers and he needed, no matter how fleeting, to be physically close to someone. He rose and pulled her up with him and drew her into his arms. She offered no resistance. Michael wrapped his arms around her and buried his face in her neck. He felt her arms slide up his back and she hugged him tightly. How long they stood together like that he had no idea. He was the one to break away. 'Sorry.'

She grinned. 'Bullshit! You loved it.'

Michael blinked. Her language had a habit of taking him unawares. 'Er . . . yes . . . well . . .' He was actually blushing.

'You needed a hug,' she said lightly. 'Simple as that.'

Michael paced in front of her.

'You weren't being disloyal to Jennifer, if that's what you're thinking. Do sit down, Michael, you're making me dizzy.'

'It's not that. It's, damn it, Annie, I owe you an apology.'

'You can be pretty rude sometimes.'

He shook his head impatiently. 'For Tessa. I can see now that . . . that the things you do take time. I was wrong back then and I apologise.'

'Sit down,' she said gently. When he did she went on. 'There are times, many of them, when my work makes it necessary to bludgeon my way beyond acceptable levels of other people's privacy. I could see how troubled Tessa was and, from what she was saying about you, it was pretty evident that most of her anger was directed your way. I see some fairly base things in my line of work, Michael. Before I went any further with Tessa I had to rule you out as . . . as the root cause of her problems.'

'Are you saying what I think you are? That you actually thought I might be abusing my own sister?'

'It happens. More often than anyone realises. I had to be sure.' She shrugged. 'I don't blame you for being angry. I could have handled it better. I was reasonably inexperienced back then.'

'Could you have helped her?'

'Probably not.'

'Why?'

'She didn't want to be helped.' She looked at her watch. 'Okay, that's it. Next week. Same time.'

'One last visit. After that I'm on my own.'

She lit a cigarette. 'You're never on your own,' she said around the smoke. 'Don't ever forget that.'

And now, on this his final visit, he was telling her how the stupid specialist said there was nothing wrong with Andrew's hearing.

'Shock works in many different ways,' she said gently. 'Andrew's body and mind underwent a massive upheaval.' For once they were either side of her desk and she was scribbling on a pad as she spoke. Ripping the page off, she handed it to Michael. 'This is the name and address of one of the finest specialists in Europe. If you want to put your mind at rest, take your son to him. He's done brilliant work with shock victims.'

Michael glanced at the paper, distracted, running a hand through his hair. 'Europe!'

She smiled slightly. 'That's where you're going isn't it?'

'I don't know.'

She leaned back in her chair, folding her arms. 'Michael, I've been listening to you for nine weeks. I know what you're planning.'

'Oh yes. And what might that be?' Michael asked belligerently. All week something had been building up inside him. Impatience, yes. Perhaps a need to move on. But there was no rage, that had subsided.

She ignored his tone. 'Unfinished business.'

Michael stuffed the piece of paper into his shirt pocket.

'Am I right?' she pressed.

He stared her straight in the eyes, saying nothing. 'Yessss! I believe I am.'

'And it's none of your business,' he said bluntly.

She blinked and shook back her hair. Today it flowed free, a waterfall of tumbling blonde curls, a frame for the violet colour of her eyes.

'I really haven't made up my mind,' he lied, though in a gentler tone. His emotions were on a seesaw and he never knew, from one moment to the next, whether he'd be angry or calm. It was unsettling to say the least but he was powerless to prevent his mood swings.

'Tessa. Jennifer. Jeremy.' She ticked them off on

long, tapering fingers. 'Three powerful reasons for not turning the other cheek.'

Anger surfaced. 'Not to mention South Africa. People like him don't deserve to live.' His voice hardened again. 'He's got to pay.'

She nodded. 'And you feel it's your responsibility to collect the debt?'

'Isn't it? I seem to be the one selling the goods.'

She ignored that too. 'And you can't do anything with Andrew in tow, which brings us back to Europe. You're taking him to your mother aren't you?'

'Best place for him, I reckon.'

'Stay with him. If only for a little while.'

Suddenly he knew what it was, this build-up. True, he was impatient but he was also thinking clearly. He was ready and itching to go. And she was asking him to wait. 'I love my son very much,' he said, more harshly than intended. 'I owe it to him as much as to myself.'

'I don't blame you,' she replied, surprising him. 'Only I'd like to see you spend a bit of time with Andrew first. You're all he's got. He needs that contact, Michael.'

'He's a baby. What can he remember?'

Anger passed over her face briefly. 'I'd like to see you ask that question in twenty years. The human mind is a miraculous thing, Michael. What happened to Andrew will surface one day, believe me. What you do now is critical to his future well-being. Give the little chap your time, for heaven's sake. It's not asking a lot. Unlike you, he can't analyse his experience. He has no outlet. Comfort him. Be there for him.'

'Sure,' Michael said bitterly. 'And while I'm doing that, the man who killed my wife, my other son and our unborn child melts away. How much time do you suggest?'

She looked at him, pity in her eyes. 'The rest of your life would be good. If you can't manage that, at least allow your son the security of transferring his affections to someone else.' She was trying not to be cross with him but not making a very good job of it. 'If you leave him now you'll regret it. You can't waltz in and out of his life at will. Make up your bloody mind. You have obligations to your living son. I can't put it plainer than that.'

'Fine.' He was anxious to get out of her office, away from her words. He knew she was right. 'Don't worry. Andrew will be well looked after. My mother . . .'

She stood up suddenly, very angry. 'Don't fuck with him, Michael King. He needs you now more than ever. You don't have to screw that up. Is that clear enough?'

Michael dropped his head, mainly to hide the beginnings of a grin. She looked so ridiculous, leaning over her desk, hands on hips, swearing at him. He realised suddenly that it was the first time he'd found anything amusing since . . . *Steady. Can't think of that.* He glanced up at her. 'That's perfectly clear.' He rose as well. 'I hear you. I'll give Andrew time. I promise. May I be excused now, ma'am?' He turned to go.

'Michael.'

He turned back. 'Yes.'

She was grinning at him. 'I just wanted you to know I don't usually speak to my patients like that.'

Michael managed half a smile.

She was nodding. 'Good, the next smile will be easier.'

He inclined his head, doubting it.

Annie Devilliers was writing something else on the notepad and did not look up. 'When you get back, go and see this man. If anyone can assist, he can.' She passed the sheet of paper to him.

Michael glanced at it. It was a name and a telephone number. 'I take it Sacha Devilliers is your husband?'

She nodded.

'No address?'

'He moves around. Phone that number and leave a message.'

'What's his story?' Michael had some misgivings. Her answer had been evasive. Was he some kind of mercenary? Or somehow connected with the Bureau of State Security? Either way, how would he feel about his wife handing out his telephone number to a total stranger? 'I mean, exactly what does he do?'

'I can't tell you that.'

'Can't or won't?'

'Bit of both really.'

'Then tell me this. Is he army, government or private?'

She seemed to be considering the question but,

in the end, all she said was, 'All I can tell you is that he will, most likely, know where your man is.'

Michael folded the paper. 'Thank you.'

'Tell him I gave you the number.' Her mouth twisted slightly. 'Not that it'll make a difference,' she added in a strangely wistful tone.

They said goodbye, shaking hands. Michael was sorry in a way. He had developed a great respect for this young woman. In her quiet, non-pushy way, she had prompted him to talk about everything under the sun, feeling his way towards the moment when he could speak about Jennifer and Jeremy. She had made no judgments until this last visit and even now her words were more to do with Andrew than his intentions regarding Jackson. She had developed a complete package for listening, from the expression in her eyes, to a breeziness and sometimes earthiness. Even her body language invited confidences. Michael felt he could tell her anything and everything. 'Face it,' he thought wryly, stepping into the lift. 'You bloody-well *did*.'

Returning to the hotel where Emil was caring for Andrew, Michael's impatience returned. On impulse, he found a travel agency and bought tickets for himself and Andrew to London. Andrew's was one way. Just in case.

Emil was sad they were going. Being there for Michael and Andrew had gone some way towards relieving an unspoken sense of responsibility that had never quite left him. 'Perhaps we meet again one day.'

Michael thought it unlikely but agreed, 'Perhaps.'

To see Emil again would bring everything back. He had to look ahead, not behind. There was just one task to be completed first.

On the flight to England, the quiet, solemn little boy with large dark eyes captivated one air hostess to such an extent that she asked if she could take him up to see the cockpit. When he was returned, half-an-hour later, Michael sensed a change in his son. His eyes were bright with interest as he wriggled out of the hostess's arms and clambered over Michael's lap to reach the window seat. 'Steady on, old chap.'

Andrew immediately picked up the drawing pad and pencil that the air hostess had given him earlier in the flight. Frowning with concentration he began to draw a picture of the flight deck. It was a typical child's scrawl, uncoordinated and simplistic. Satisfied with his efforts, he tugged at Michael's sleeve and pointed at the drawing.

'Very good.' Michael leaned over to give the picture his full attention. 'It's the cockpit where the pilot sits,' he added.

'Yes,' lisped Michael's son absently, adding a few more touches to the page.

Totally absorbed Andrew did not see the sudden wetness in his father's eyes, or hear the whispered, 'Thank you, God.'

Although he spoke not another word during the flight, Michael was elated. Annie had tried to explain that Andrew's brain, protected by some kind of defence mechanism of its own, was entirely capable of shutting down the boy's hearing or blocking his speech. 'It will come back when it's ready,' she'd said. 'The more secure he is, the sooner that will be.'

'But he knew nothing,' Michael had protested. 'He falls asleep as soon as the car starts, always has.'

'Even if Andrew had dozed off,' she said, 'subconsciously he knows something has changed. The poor little bugger wakes up in the pitch dark in the bush, not knowing how he got there, and hasn't seen his mother or brother since.'

'Are you telling me he's grieving?'

She had thought that one over for a few seconds. 'Not in the accepted sense, no. It's more like a refusal to focus. But because he's so young it's hard to tell. Does he seem different to you?'

'Yes, but only because he's so quiet. He plays with toys, looks at picture books, draws. He's always been pretty creative. Of course, he spent most of his time with Jeremy . . .' Michael's voice became strained, 'so it's difficult to judge.'

She had nodded sympathetically and dropped the subject.

Well, the medical profession appeared to have got it right. Andrew could hear. He was just unable or unwilling to talk. Now that he knew that, Michael was content to allow his son all the time it needed. Watching Andrew draw another cockpit, Michael suddenly realised that not once in over two months had he drawn one of his many pictures of Jennifer or Jeremy. The refrigerators and shelves in the laboratory, the kitchen walls and even the sides of their tent had been literally papered with them, mostly of Jennifer. Annie Devilliers had helped him to think clearly but, for Andrew, it was as if the past did not exist. His heart went out to the boy.

Claire met them at Heathrow. Michael had refused her earlier offer to fly out but he could see how much the tragedy had aged his mother. She hugged Michael, then bent and picked up Andrew. 'Hi, big boy,' she said huskily. 'We're going to be special friends.'

Andrew stared at her, his eyes unreadable and serious. Michael explained. 'He can hear you. He just doesn't talk.'

'Then we'll get some help,' Claire said firmly.

'I've got one name in London. A chap who specialises in shock victims.'

Claire eyed their luggage. 'Is that all?'

'It's mainly Andrew's. The rest is in storage.'

'Because you're going back?'

'Yes.'

She regarded him closely. He'd lost weight, fine lines of pain and determination etched his drawn skin. Six months earlier, when she and Peter made one of their regular visits to South Africa, Michael's face had been smooth, healthily tanned and happy. She could only imagine what he'd been through. 'What good will going back do?'

'It won't do Jackson Mpande a hell of a lot of good,' Michael said grimly.

'Jackson? Dyson's brother?' Claire was shocked. 'Why?'

'Because he was responsible. I saw him that night, Mother. Jackson Mpande laid that bloody mine.'

'But why?' she whispered with an anxious glance towards Andrew. 'It must have been a mistake.'

Michael seemed unaware of a need for caution in front of his son. 'This was no mistake. The army found four more mines around our camp.' He took a deep breath and went on. 'Things have changed. Civilians have become targets. We knew it would come to this, but not so quickly. There's no stopping it, Mother.' He shook his head in disgust. 'When is Pretoria going to wake up? If only they would *listen*. But no. The Nats still believe that God is on their side. I tell you, Mother, it's going to be a bloodbath.' He was unaware of it but tears glistened in his eyes and his voice rose.

'As for the cowards who laid the mine, all they care about is world attention. They probably regard Jen and Jeremy . . . as . . . as a triumph.'

He could not go on. Claire, aware that people were staring, realised how close to the edge Michael still was. 'Come on, darling. Let's go home.'

Michael ran a hand through his hair. 'Sorry.' He held out his arms for Andrew. 'Here. Give him to me. He weighs a ton.'

On the way to the car, Claire mentioned Dyson. 'How do you feel about seeing him? I know he'd love it if you made contact.'

'I don't know,' Michael admitted. 'It might not be a good idea if he knows I'm going back to find his brother.'

Claire stopped. 'Michael, what exactly *will* you do if you find Jackson?'

'Oh, I'll find him all right, Mother. You can be sure of that.'

The soft flatness in his voice answered the question. Claire shivered with fear for this son of hers who had come to hate so very, very much.

Claire and Peter Dawson lived on the outskirts of the quaint old farming town of Hertford. Claire loved the cobbled streets and ramshackle meander of the town. To Michael, after a couple of weeks, and in spite of its soft beauty, Hertford and its surrounds became claustrophobic. 'You can't get away from people,' he complained more than once to his mother.

'But they are very nice people,' she would reply calmly.

That was true enough. Friendly, neighbourly people, always ready for a chat about the weather. Not a Zulu in sight. No lingering smell of wood smoke or roasting mealies. Here, they didn't even call them mealies, they were corn on the cob. Here, they used medicine, not *muthi*. Here, they spoke of villages, not *kraals*. England was lovely, no doubt about it, but it was so bland. Walk in the woods and all you had to worry about was stepping in a rabbit burrow and breaking an ankle, not the possibility of running into a protective lioness with cubs. Telephones worked all the time, potholes in the road were repaired immediately, water did not need to be boiled or conserved, ill health generally meant influenza, not malaria, tick fever or bilharzia, shops sold everything under the sun, life was cocooned by safety, comfort and predictability.

'So what's wrong with that?' Michael asked himself. The answer, whether it made sense or not, was always, 'It's boring, and it's so bloody cold.'

Still, he made no move towards leaving.

His mother and Peter's house was large, set on nearly two acres of landscaped garden overlooking a much frequented duck pond that separated their property from the open common beyond. Peter had a thing about geese and collected original Peter Scott paintings. He would spend hours with his binoculars, becoming quite excited when some new or migrant bird appeared beside the ice-covered water.

Michael and Andrew shared a two-bedroomed granny flat on the ground floor that had access to the rest of the house through a conservatory. They ate their meals in the warm, country-style kitchen beside a large Aga stove that never went out, a kettle always on the hob, family washing drying on pulleys suspended from the ceiling. Andrew spent most of his time in the company of Claire who chattered away constantly, never expecting a response, content to bond with her silent grandson at his own speed.

Michael made an appointment with the trauma

therapist Annie Devilliers had recommended and took his son to see him. The man seemed more interested in discussing South Africa's problems than addressing Andrew's symptoms. When Michael did manage to steer the conversation back to the reason for their visit, all the specialist said was, 'Company his own age would be good. Otherwise keep on with what you're doing. Love, affection, routine, healthy food and a warm comfortable bed. Love him to pieces and be there for him. Now tell me, Mr King, do you think all this unrest would stop if Mandela were released?'

'Shock therapist!' Michael thought sourly on the way back to Hertford. 'The only bloody shock was the size of his bill.'

But he followed the man's advice about a companion and contacted Sally in France who readily agreed to bring her daughter, Dominique, to England for a couple of weeks. 'We were coming over anyway,' she told Michael over the telephone. 'Just thought you'd like to settle in a bit first. How's the weather over there?' Just talking to his sister helped Michael to feel normal again.

Sally, her husband, Marcel, and Dominique arrived a few days later. Marcel, who ran his own clothing factory, could only spare a weekend but Sally stayed on with their daughter. Dominique, only two months older than Andrew, was a hyperactive little girl who managed to find something funny in everything. The two children immediately hit it off. Within a few days Andrew was responding verbally, just a yes or no at first but, by the end of his cousin's visit, he was chattering away as clearly as ever.

Then the nightmares started. Without any warning, his terror burst forth from another world. It was a rough time for everyone. Nights were shattered by piercing screams. All he would ever say was, 'Monsters.' So Andrew would be held and soothed back to sleep and Michael, watching his son's once again peaceful face would wonder if their lives could ever get back to normal.

The nightmare problem was solved by Gregor. At seventeen, and in his last year of school, he'd come home for the Easter holidays. Intelligent, sensitive and extremely talented artistically, he was supposed to use the break to study for his forthcoming A Levels. But a special rapport quickly developed between Andrew and Gregor. Andrew followed his uncle everywhere, giggling helplessly at his play-acting and stories.

Gregor dug out an old Punch and Judy set from the attic. Taking advantage of the fine spring weather, he assembled it, much to Andrew's intrigued pleasure, in the garden. Chairs were brought out and Andrew, full of self-importance, told everyone where to sit. Gregor put on the show.

Andrew was rapt. He laughed, clapped his hands, booed with everyone else and became completely involved. Then came the loud bang. Andrew jumped with fright, his face drained of colour and he began to tremble. Claire reacted first, hissing and booing loudly. Peter and Michael joined in, desperately trying to convince the child it was all part of the show. Andrew sat frozen. Michael was about to tell Gregor to stop but his younger brother, realising what was wrong, acted instinctively, putting on the show of his life. Improvising frantically, the traditional Punch and Judy script was modified. Punch became more of a bumbling fool, tripping over things, making sillier than ever jokes. Gregor changed his voice, made it softer. Andrew, still watching, remained wary and unresponsive.

Then the masterpiece. The loud noise explained as Judy breaking wind, Punch fainting from the smell. Andrew shrieked with laughter. Poor old Judy nearly turned herself inside-out, the noises becoming more and more outrageous. Punch ran around the set swiping at the air, covering his nose, sitting with head in hands. Andrew begged for more.

That night Michael dealt with the nightmare by using the same level of toilet humour. It worked. After a week of the new, though not necessarily improved, Punch and Judy and, at night, hunting under the bed and in wardrobes for the naughty, flatulence-suffering Judy, the nightmares stopped.

'You're a genius,' Michael told Gregor.

'I know.' Gregor grinned. 'I can't wait to tell the maths master that I was too busy farting to study.'

Michael laughed. 'You might not get the marks you want but I'll tell you this, little brother, you'll never go short of work. You're good. You could fart for England.'

After Gregor returned to school, Andrew appeared lost for a couple of days. It was only when

509

Michael realised what was bothering his son and assured him that Uncle Gregor would be back soon, that his face lit up. 'Thank God,' Claire said that evening. 'I thought he might, you know, think that Gregor would go away and never come back like . . .' She left it hanging, uncertain how Michael would react.

He had put an arm around her shoulders. 'Like his mother and brother,' he finished quietly for her.

Claire looked into her son's face. 'Are you healing, darling?'

'Yes I am.'

'But you're still determined . . .'

'Yes I am.'

'When?' she whispered, afraid for him, afraid for his son.

'Not yet.' He sighed, closing his eyes. 'I'm still too close to it. When I kill Jackson Mpande it will be in cold blood.'

She'd known his intention, of course. But hearing him voice it for the first time filled her with dread.

With Sally, Dominique and Gregor gone, Michael found himself thinking about Dyson. Claire had a number where he could be contacted. Michael had deliberately put off seeing his old friend, concerned that Jackson would come between them. In the end, however, he made the call and arranged to meet Dyson at a pub near York Gate in London, just off the Marylebone Road.

Dyson put down the telephone, elated to have

heard from Michael. Claire had called to tell him about Jennifer and Jeremy. She gave no details, only mentioning that Michael would probably spend some time in England. But that was months ago. 'Old friend,' he responded to a colleague's raised eyebrows. 'We grew up together.'

'He sounded white and South African,' said the man who had answered the telephone.

'He is.'

'You know the rules.'

Dyson nodded, irritated by the comment. He needed no reminding. Caution was the name of the game. God knows how many times infiltration attempts had been made. The South Africans were clever, recruiting friends or even relations of known ANC members. Dyson knew he had to be careful, even with Michael. At the time of Claire's telephone call he had already known that Michael's wife and child had been killed as a result of SWAPO activity in the eastern Caprivi. There was every chance that it was Jackson's group who had laid the very mine responsible. Not much got past the eyes and ears of the ANC. Dyson was fully aware of Jackson's specialist training in Russia.

This aside, it would be good to see Michael again.

They'd arranged to meet at five-thirty. Michael caught the train into Kings Cross and walked from there. The pub was jammed with thank-God-it's-Friday drinkers. He squeezed into a space at the bar and ordered a pint. A girl bumped him, apologised, had a second look, liked what she saw and smiled. 'Haven't seen you here before.'

'New in town.' He had to shout to be heard. 'Is it always this crowded?'

She leaned towards him so he could hear. 'By six-thirty most of them will be gone. Friday night is club night.'

He caught a whiff of her scent. It caught him completely off balance. Madame Roche. Jennifer's favourite. He jerked back, looking frantically around and, spotting a space by the back wall, excused himself and made his way towards it. The girl watched him go, regret in her eyes. Married. You could always tell.

Dyson arrived ten minutes later. He spotted Michael immediately, waved, indicated he'd get two beers and went to the bar. Michael watched him weave his way through the crowd, noticing how much at home he looked, how comfortable he obviously felt in such a seething mass of bodies. He chatted to the same girl for a couple of minutes before threading his way towards Michael.

'I see you, *Nkawu*,' he said in Zulu, grinning. Then adding in English, 'There's a lady at the bar asked me to tell you she's unattached. You made a big impression.'

Michael looked him up and down. 'I can tell we'll have to get you out of England. You are becoming positively British, pinstripe suit, over-weight, the lot.'

Dyson laughed. 'Is that bad?' He handed Michael a beer.

'For a Zulu? You must be kidding.' He extended an open hand and they shook in the palm press, thumb clasp, palm press African way. 'Hell it's good to see you. Can we go somewhere quieter?'

'Around here? It's Friday night. Everywhere's crowded. It'll clear soon.'

Michael wanted to pound his arm, to speak with him in Zulu. Looking at his old friend made him feel like a boy again, brought back the total freedom of space, memories of rough-and-tumbles in the baking heat of a Zululand afternoon, the smell of the African bush after summer rain. Instead, they were crammed into a stuffy, noisy pub with smoke stinging their eyes and conversation impossible.

Dyson and the girl at the bar were right though, come six-thirty out they all rushed, like lemmings. 'God help the last one through the door,' Michael observed dryly. 'He must feel like one of life's failures. What is this? Mandatory exodus?'

They moved to a vacated table and sat down. 'Now we can talk,' Dyson said. 'Before anything else, my heart is heavy over your loss. I was shocked and angered by the news.'

'Thank you.' Michael took a deep breath. 'It's still too hard to talk about.'

'I understand.'

'But what about you?'

'Nothing new. I'm fine, as you can see.'

'The last time I spoke with your father he said you were working for the ANC. How's it going?'

It was a perfectly ordinary question but Dyson became wary. 'I can't discuss that, not even with you.' A strange look came into Michael's eyes and

Dyson added quickly, 'That mine was SWAPO, not the ANC. But you didn't hear that from me.'

Michael closed his eyes briefly. When he opened them all he said was, 'I know.'

Dyson changed the subject and they spoke of Wilson and Nandi and the two younger children, of Sally and her life, of Gregor and of old times in Zululand. Michael was aware that a friendship had developed between Dyson and Tessa but, when he asked about his sister, Dyson became vague and non-committal. When pushed, Dyson admitted that he and Tessa had seen a movie together a couple of weeks ago. Michael wondered what his old friend wasn't telling him. Jackson's name was carefully avoided by both men. There was constraint in their conversation. The old easiness had gone. Finally, as they were leaving, Dyson asked, 'What will you do now?'

Michael glanced at him briefly as he shrugged into a coat. 'Go back.'

'Why?'

'It's where I belong,' Michael answered evasively.

Dyson looked wry but added, 'You're lucky you can.'

They went out into the cold night. 'Will I see you before you go back?' Dyson wasn't even sure he wanted to.

'Sure. I'll be in touch.' Michael didn't think he would be.

They parted company and walked hastily away from each other. Dyson was thinking how much his friend had changed. Okay, he'd had a tough time but so had many others. At least he wasn't a fugitive from the Pretoria regime. Millions of black South Africans were suffering just as much. His friend seemed harder somehow.

As Michael walked towards the station he was reflecting that the reunion had not been anywhere near as enjoyable as he had hoped. Dyson didn't trust him and that hurt. He'd become a city man. That was weird. He just wasn't the old Dyson Mpande.

Neither man put their finger on the real reason: that they knew each other so well that both were aware the other was hiding something.

He hadn't seen Tessa yet, in fact, not even spoken to her on the telephone. It was simply coincidence but each time she called Michael was out and each time he returned the call Tessa had just popped out a few minutes earlier.

'Is she avoiding me?' Michael eventually asked his mother. They had never been close and his memories of her were not pleasant, but he'd been in England for two months and felt they should have met by now.

'She's nervous I suppose. Unsure how you feel about her. You *must* see her though, Michael, she's a changed person.'

'So ask her down for a visit. I won't bite.'

But Tessa stayed away, making lame excuses. Finally they managed to speak on the telephone, a difficult conversation that went in fits and starts and was impossibly polite. It was another three months before Michael took Andrew up to London to pay her a surprise visit. 'She's home for a few days. Don't phone, just arrive. And Michael, keep an open mind, I beg you,' Claire had urged.

On the way to Wimbledon he reflected that although his mind was wide open, never had he imagined taking his young son to visit his aunt, the prostitute. Dressed up as 'companion' or whatever else it was called, it still boiled down to the fact that men bought Tessa's company. Michael had looked at it every way he could but never seemed to come close to the level of acceptance of Tessa's occupation that his mother had reached.

Jennifer had once said, 'It's the old sister syndrome. It's okay to lust after everybody else's sister but God help the man who lusts after your own.'

Annie Devilliers had smiled when he told her. 'It's a delightfully eccentric solution to a very real problem. It's probably the only sensible answer for someone like Tessa.'

All of which left Michael feeling uncomfortably suspicious that women were more broad-minded and better able to deal with the bizarre than men.

The house was old, solid and respectable-looking, a replica of all the others in the quiet, tree-lined street. Ordinary and, yes, boring. As he paid off the taxi he half thought the driver would throw him a lewd wink, but the man simply nodded and drove away. Holding Andrew's hand, he went through a low picket gate. The tiny front garden was well kept and had a cottage garden appearance. From behind the front door came strains of Beethoven's Pastoral Symphony. Michael rang the bell.

It was answered by Tessa herself. 'Michael!' Her surprise was total.

'Hi, sis,' he said, emotions welling unexpectedly in him. She looked wonderful. Flawless skin, devoid of any make-up. Jeans, a white T-shirt and barefooted. Of the old Tessa there was no trace.

She smiled at him uncertainly. 'How lovely to see you.' She went to hug him, thought better of it and abruptly dropped to her haunches in front of Andrew. 'Hello, I'm your aunt Tessa.' She looked up at Michael. 'He's just like . . . just as I expected. And so big.' She rose. 'Please come in. We'll go through to the back garden. It's lovely out there at this time of year.' She was chattering to hide her nervousness. 'I've been meaning to come and see you but, well, with one thing and another, you know how it is. Through here. Would you like a drink? Can I get Andrew anything?'

She led them through the house. It was surprisingly large inside. Beyond the lounge and sunroom lay a courtyard. They went out through double glass doors. Wisteria covered a pergola. Two narrow flower beds separated the cobbled area from a small lawn beyond. 'Here we are.' Tessa waved towards a garden table with bench seats on either side. 'Please sit down. It's so warm today.'

Michael sat and Andrew climbed up beside him. The house rose three floors above them, bulky and imposing. 'Big place,' he commented, not knowing how to break through her nervous chatter.

'That's my room.' She pointed to a window on the first floor.

'How many of you live here?' He hadn't meant to but the way the question came out made it sound like some kind of interrogation.

Tessa pulled a slight face but otherwise didn't react. She calmly answered his question. 'Judith owns the house. She has a room on the ground floor. There are five rooms on my floor and three above that. The cellar has been converted into a bed-sit. Two girls share that. There are two tiny rooms in the attic. They're empty at the moment.'

'Where are the others?'

Again, she patiently answered. 'Judith is in her room writing letters. Two others are around somewhere. The rest are out.' She hesitated slightly, then continued. 'We live here, Michael, nothing more. I know what you must be thinking but we only live here.'

'No, no. I just wondered.' *Christ! This is going badly. Lighten up for God's sake.* 'Sorry, sis.'

'I understand, Michael, I really do.'

Andrew cut in. 'Where are the little people?'

'Little people!' Tessa glanced at her brother.

'Children,' Michael explained. 'That's what he calls them.'

'Oh! I see.' She laughed. 'There are no little people here, Andrew. Only big people.'

Michael liked the way she spoke directly to him. Andrew nodded and remained silent. The expression on his face was one of resignation.

Tessa smiled. 'I happen to know there are

cartoons on the telly at the moment. If you like I'll put it on for you. How about a glass of milk and some chocolate biscuits as well?' She'd won him. They went off together, hand in hand, Tessa telling him that if Judith heard the cartoons she'd probably come and sit with him because she loved them too.

Returning ten minutes later with coffee on a tray, Tessa sat opposite him and got straight to the point, her earlier nervousness gone, as though she'd had a stern talk with herself inside. 'I was shocked about what happened, Michael. You're a good person. It was so unfair.'

'Thanks.' His voice was steady. 'It's still hard but I'm learning to cope. Some days are worse than others.'

She nodded towards the house. 'He's a sweetie. Mum told me about his reaction. He seems fine now, talking nineteen to the dozen.'

'Largely thanks to Gregor and Dominique.'

At the mention of Sally's daughter, Tessa's eyes went soft. 'I'm her godmother you know.'

'Sally told me.'

'I see them often. Whenever I'm in Paris.'

She made it sound like a business trip. In a way, Michael realised, that is exactly what it was. At least the conversation was beginning to flow. 'And Gregor?'

She pulled a wry face. 'Don't see him much. He's young. Finds my life difficult to accept I suppose . . .' A slightly self-conscious laugh. 'Besides, I was always such a bitch to him.'

'You were always such a bitch to everyone.'

The old Tessa would have become defensive. To his surprise, she threw back her head and laughed. 'I know,' she said finally. 'Sorry for that. I didn't like myself much back then.'

'And now?'

She leaned forward, elbows on the table, chin in hands, sparkle in her eyes. 'Choc full of self-love, self-respect, self-worth. Get the picture?' She was making fun of herself. 'Seriously, though, it's all about self.' She leaned back. 'The shrink said I had to think of *me* for a change. Hell! Wasn't that what I'd always done?' She laughed again in genuine amusement. 'I always envied you, Michael. You never questioned who or what you were.'

'Neither did Sally.'

'I know. But I didn't envy Sally, I hated her guts.'

Michael grinned at Tessa's frankness.

'If I had the chance to start again, know what I'd do?' She was still laughing. Michael had never seen her so happy. 'I'd be the same selfish, lying, conniving, bloody little monster.' She shrugged, spreading her hands. 'I am what I am and I've learned to live with it. You might find that a bit hard to understand but it's true.'

Michael leaned towards his sister and took her hands in his. 'I understand this much, sis. Your demons have gone. You're calm, happy and, incidentally, you look lovely.' He squeezed gently. 'It's a little startling to think of what you do for a living but it could be worse.'

'Worse!'

'Yeah!' He grinned. 'Give me a minute. I'll think of something.'

They both laughed and the last of the restraint faded away.

'I saw Dyson last week. He says he's seen you a couple of times.'

'Yes. We've become friends.' She hesitated, then went on in a rush. 'I think Dyson's feelings for me are a little more than that. He's never said anything but . . . well, a woman can always tell.'

Michael was surprised but it would explain Dyson's reluctance to discuss Tessa the other night. 'How do you feel about that?'

She looked pensive. 'As you know, the question of colour doesn't bother me.' She was struggling for the right words. 'I like Dyson, but love? Love is too hard, too many restraints, too much commitment.'

'Too much control?' he suggested.

She nodded. 'That too. I'd be scared of hurting him.'

'Perhaps you're doing that already?'

'I know.' She sighed, bit her lip and looked away.

Michael could see that her fear of commitment saddened her. He realised suddenly what a compli-cated person she was. No wonder she'd been so difficult all her life. 'Sis, this life you've chosen for yourself, are you quite sure it's the one you want?'

'It's the first time I've been happy.'

'So what's troubling you?'

She thought about that for a long moment. 'Last

chance,' she said finally. 'Dyson seems like my last chance at everything that is decent, everything the rest of my family does instinctively.'

'Wrong reason for getting married.'

'I know. It's just that . . . Oh, I don't know, Michael. I don't think I could love someone for the rest of my life but it doesn't stop me wishing I could. It's so very tempting to try, especially with Dyson. Sometimes I think I could . . . I do love him.'

It came to Michael then that in her own strange way Tessa was about as honourable as a person could get. She was flawed and she knew it. She had learned to live with herself. She avoided commitment however much she might have wished for it because she knew she was incapable of sustaining a lasting relationship. Honourable was not a word he would have attributed to Tessa before now. Her eyes, held steady on his, revealed fear he would reject her and an aching need to be accepted but that didn't stop her from being brutally honest about herself. 'I love you, sis,' he said suddenly.

Unshed tears filled her eyes. 'I love you too,' she said huskily. She brushed at the tears. 'I'm sorry I was such a trial.'

'Trial!' Michael smiled to take the sting out of his words. 'You were bloody horrible.'

Tessa jumped up suddenly, came around behind him and flung her arms around his neck. 'I'm so pleased you came. I was dreading this meeting.'

He patted her arm. 'You always were a bit thick.'

It was a strange feeling. Two adults with so many bad memories between them striving hard to achieve an easy camaraderie which, all things being equal, should have come naturally. Even though neither one of them were acting normally, the easiness was happening. That was what was so strange.

When Michael left a few hours later with a chocolate-smeared son whom Tessa and Judith had done their best to clean up he asked, 'When are you coming to Hertford?'

'Soon,' Tessa promised warmly. 'And this time I mean it.'

As the taxi drove away, Tessa stood on the pavement waving. There was only one topic the two of them had avoided. Jackson.

Jackson Mpande was, at that precise moment, on a flight from the Zambian capital, Lusaka, bound for Nairobi in Kenya. From there he would pick up the connecting South African Airways flight to London. The white South African businessman sitting next to him wrinkled his nose in distaste at the body odour that wafted around him every time Jackson shifted position. 'Hasn't the bloody man heard of soap and water?' he wondered, the smell reaffirming his belief that while you can take the kaffir out of the bush you can't take the bush out of the kaffir.

In fact, Jackson was as clean as a whistle and wearing brand new clothes. He did not, however, use deodorant. He found the cloying sweetness of deodorant and aftershave sickening. As far as Jackson was concerned there was nothing wrong with a man smelling like a man.

It was almost impossible to find a comfortable position in the narrow, economy class seat. Although he was hardly a seasoned traveller, Jackson hated flying. He hated being cooped up in an aeroplane wearing constricting white man's clothing. If he'd had his way, he would not be making this trip at all. One of the Russians, thinking he was doing Jackson a favour and intending nothing more than rewarding him for work well done in the Caprivi Strip, had made a big fuss about selecting him as a courier to carry important documents that were needed urgently in London and had, for some reason, to be personally delivered. 'Take a couple of weeks,' he told Jackson expansively. 'You've earned it.'

Jackson had never been to England but one of the others had told him, 'The seasons are back-to-front and the skies, if you can see them, do not carry the stars as we know them.' Jackson had made the same observations on his yearlong training trip in Russia and would have much rather stayed in Africa and let someone else deliver the documents. However, when the Russian masters spoke, he had long since learned that it was best to obey. And quickly. So he feigned pleasure, approaching the so-called honour with an unspoken feeling of dread.

More and more of late Jackson had been experiencing pangs of homesickness. He longed for the lush tropical heat of Zululand, to watch an African sunrise from the mighty Indian Ocean, to smell the smoke of burning sugar cane, to walk the secret hills and valleys of the Umfolozi River. He'd give anything to go back there, to see his mother and father, his sister and brother. But would they welcome him? Could he ever go home?

The Zambian bush was hot, dust laden and sparsely vegetated. Day-to-day life had become monotonously boring with too few opportunities to go into a town, get drunk or pick up a woman. Sure, there were camp followers, but who wanted to lie with some whore who had been with every other man in camp? Who wanted to get drunk with men you knew so well that each time they opened their mouths you knew exactly what would come out? Even trips into the Caprivi had lost their lustre.

The Caprivi Strip was sandy country with stunted vegetation, malaria-carrying mosquitoes and scurrying, deadly scorpions. Jackson and his men had become so good at crossing the border undetected, laying their mines and getting back into Zambia that the danger of being caught was remote. Although satisfying to receive word of a hit, like that white woman and her child which had made world headlines, confirmed kills were few and far between. That one big success had been the highlight of more than five years with SWAPO. He would never forget the feeling of elation when the Russians showed him a South African newspaper which carried the report. The names Jennifer and Jeremy King meant nothing to Jackson, he made no connection with the King family in Zululand.

Jackson was becoming increasingly disenchanted with SWAPO. Their raids into South West Africa had achieved so little. The South Africans were worried, that was true, but this only made Pretoria more determined than ever to maintain their occupation of the Caprivi Strip. Jackson's youthful aim to help free the Zulu nation was nothing more than a pipedream, he could see that now. Maybe someone knew where SWAPO activities were leading, Jackson certainly didn't.

And now this. Constrained in a suit a little too tight for his liking, stuck for hours on aeroplanes which he hated, all so he could deliver an envelope to some address in South Kensington, wherever that was. Mission accomplished, he was then obliged to kick his heels for two weeks and supposed to be grateful. They had given him hardly any money. He couldn't afford two weeks in London.

There was only one positive aspect to this trip and even that wasn't a foregone conclusion. Dyson lived in London. Jackson had both his work and private addresses. He was ambivalent about the possibility of seeing his brother again but at least there was one person in London he knew. He wondered if Dyson would be happy to see him. There had been no contact between them since that evening, so very long ago, when his brother had been arrested by the South African police.

Much as the ANC kept a watch on SWAPO, so too did SWAPO know most things about ANC activities. It had been easy enough for Jackson, once he knew he had to make this trip, to find out where Dyson lived and worked. He had been aware for some years that his older brother had escaped and fled to the United Kingdom. But he also realised that Dyson would be in touch with their parents, which meant he must know about Tessa. Would he be welcome? There was only one way to find out.

The aeroplane was starting its descent into Nairobi. Jackson did up his seat belt. The white man next to him, who had studiously ignored Jackson throughout the flight, spoke to him suddenly. 'Thank God that's nearly over. I hate these mickey mouse airlines.' He stretched and, as he had done earlier over Jackson's body odour, Jackson wrinkled his nose as he caught the sickly, sweet whiff of deodorant mixed with perspiration coming from his body. 'Are you getting off in Nairobi?'

'No. I'm going on to London.'

The white man raised his eyebrows. 'You live in Lusaka?'

'Yes.'

'Forgive me for saying so but I'm from Durban. You look Zulu to me.'

Jackson shrugged. 'Sorry to disappoint you.'

'Oh well,' the man smiled vaguely then shut his eyes tightly as the aeroplane landed. On the ground, and barely waiting for the aircraft to slow down, he rose and rummaged in the overhead locker for his hand luggage. 'This yours?' He handed Jackson his shoulder bag, a free gift from the Lusaka office of Zambia Airways and emblazoned as such on both sides.

Jackson took the bag, saying nothing.

The man grunted as he sat down again. He eyed the colourful green and orange bag but made no comment. Jackson wondered what was going through his head. A Zulu-looking man from Zambia, flying to London via Nairobi had to raise suspicions given the paranoia of today's white South Africans.

His thoughts drifted back to Zululand. The home he loved with every fibre of his body. The brilliant green of sugar cane. The rich mahogany of cattle. The full-blown voluptuousness of a butter-yellow moon as it rises from the sea, so huge, so unashamedly piss-elegant that your heart creeps into your mouth in wonder. The blood-red sunsets diffused by drifting dust, the sun's ghostly outline filling the western horizon. The warm, rolling, restless Indian Ocean caressing countless beaches, marked perhaps by the footsteps of a single traveller. The chocolate brown of waters in full flood, roaring rivers rushing headlong to the ocean, staining the brilliant blue with rich soil for kilometres out to sea. The soft sea breezes that carry with them a hint of seaweed and the promise of relief from the day's humid heat.

Jackson sighed. He could never go back.

Passengers were moving slowly forward. The white man next to him rose stiffly. 'Enjoy your trip,' he said politely, squeezing himself into the line of passengers, his hand luggage gripped tightly in the crook of his arm as though it might develop legs and run away.

Jackson joined the queue without enthusiasm. He had hours to wait in the transit lounge and then a ten-hour flight to London. For some reason, although Kenya had added its voice to those African countries that had severed diplomatic and economic connections with South Africa, their stand did not seem to include its airline, although the Boeing 707's take-off time from Nairobi was midnight, thereby ensuring that as few observers as possible would witness the offensive flying springbok on its tail.

SEVENTEEN

Jackson breathed a sigh of relief when the aeroplane touched down into the dull grey wetness of London. 'No wonder the white man wants my land,' he thought. London was worse than Russia. At least in Moscow the buildings were interesting and, although it rained often, Jackson remembered days when weak sunshine twinkled with colour on crisp white snow under a canopy of the palest blue sky he had ever seen. First impressions being what they are, grey would remain Jackson's mental image of London for as long as he lived.

He emerged into the milling throng of people waiting to greet arriving passengers and was faced with a bewildering number of choices. Shuttle buses, courtesy buses, express buses to connect with the Underground at a place called Hounslow, ordinary buses, tour coaches, London taxis. If he knew where South Kensington was he might be able to work out how to get there. A taxi would be easiest but he couldn't afford one. Finally he stopped two airport policemen and asked.

'And where would you be from?'

'Zambia.'

'Long way from home.'

'Too far,' Jackson said with feeling.

The policemen, part of an extra presence on duty at Heathrow to discourage a recent increase in baggage theft but whose brief also included assisting visitors, took pity on this obviously bemused tourist. They went with him to cash some traveller's cheques, then on to a newsagency where he purchased a pocket-size A to Z of London. They even showed him how to read the symbols and work out a route.

Slightly more enlightened, Jackson first found himself on a bus headed for Hounslow and something called the Piccadilly line, and then on an underground train to South Kensington with the words, 'Piccadilly mate, don't even have to change tubes,' ringing in his ears. Jackson assumed the policeman had been speaking English but managed to understand that all he had to do was watch the route map in the carriage, keep an eye on the stations they passed and get off at South Kensington.

It was easier than he expected.

Tessa, who was on a train coming from the other direction, heading for an appointment, also alighted at South Kensington. She and Jackson missed each other by two minutes. By the time Tessa emerged from the tube station, Jackson was walking down the Old Brompton Road looking for Cranley Place.

Tessa drew admiring looks as she strode along South Kensington's Thurloe Square. Dressed in slacks the colour of cream with knee-length suede boots and a caramel silk blouse, she was the picture of elegance. Cascading from beneath a black beret, dark curly hair bounced off her shoulders as she walked and a black scarf, worn loose and trailing behind, added a further touch of chic. She was making her way from the South Kensington tube station to the Rembrandt Hotel where she had arranged to have lunch with a regular client. From there, they would go on to a flat he kept for his use whenever he was in London.

Kerry Glasshouse was typical of the kind of client favoured by Judith Murray-Brown. Well-spoken, discreet and considerate, he treated her girls with utmost respect. That he was rich, in his thirties, rather handsome and in good physical condition might have helped too. Tessa liked him. They had fun just being together, often no more than seeing a show and going on to dinner. He'd been a regular client of Judith's for nearly four years. At first he'd been happy to take out any of the girls, but over the past couple of years he specifically requested Tessa. She saw him about once a month. If she were unavailable, he would thank Judith politely and, just as politely, refuse her offer of another girl. Tessa was often teased about him.

'He'll ask you to marry him one day, wait and see.'

'You've bewitched him.'

'He's in love with you, he must be.'

To all of this, Tessa would smile and shake her head. She didn't want anybody to be in love with her or to ask her to marry him. It was like she'd told Michael. If there was one thing she'd learned about herself it was that any attempt to slot herself into what was generally regarded as a normal lifestyle would possibly lead to unhappiness. And she knew well enough that an unhappy Tessa was a bitch for all concerned. Or was it? Lately, and with increasing urgency, she had been considering leaving Judith and trying to make a life of her own with a regular job. If necessary, she was prepared to enrol in a college to learn typing and shorthand.

She glanced at her gold Cartier watch, one of many presents given to her by clients. Still a few minutes early. Slowing her pace, she picked her way around something recently deposited by a dog, left the square and began to walk along Thurloe Place. As she walked she turned over in her mind the options. Try for a normal life? Give it a chance to work? She could always go back to Judith if it didn't. What held her back? It always came down to the same answer. Dyson. If she went into the world, Dyson was there waiting. *Is that so terrible?* She conceded that it wasn't. *Then what is?* The prospect of commitment or the chance she'd hurt him? If she could reach a decision on that then her direction was a foregone conclusion.

Dyson's face swam before her. Such a dear, familiar face. Could she leave Judith and Dyson at the same time, start again somewhere else? No!

A life without Dyson was unthinkable. He was her closest friend. *Do I love him? Yes . . . yes of course I do. But do I love him that way? Think about it. He's never laid so much as a finger on you.* Tessa began to tremble. Her steps faltered. It came to her in such a rush that she could scarcely think straight. How she loved his smile. The feel of his hand under her elbow. The deep rumble of his voice. In her mind and heart it was as though a star had burst, radiating warmth and light throughout her body.

Tessa turned and walked quickly back the way she'd come. Meeting Kerry Glasshouse was out of the question. She would move out of Judith's house, get a flat and a job. As for Dyson? Finally, she believed she was ready to try.

Jackson had no idea who the documents were destined for, or why, or even what was in the envelope. Nor did he care. Right now he was more interested in making the delivery and finding somewhere cheap to stay. A hotel or his brother, either would do. South Kensington was obviously way out of his price range. His suitcase grew heavier by the minute. London. Since he was here, it would be a waste not to see something of it. Being careful, his money should just about see him through, especially if he could stay with Dyson. In the event that his brother couldn't, or wouldn't, put him up, he'd have to think again. Dyson lived in Soho but maybe he should call him at work? No point in trekking to Soho if he couldn't stay there.

As far as his brother was concerned, if Jackson hadn't been in such dire financial straits he probably wouldn't even have tried to contact him. When they were growing up, Dyson always appeared to be the favourite son and Jackson had come to resent him. Frankly, if he never saw Dyson again it wouldn't bother him. So what if they were blood brothers? The bottom line was he had hardly given Dyson a moment's consideration in all these years.

Jackson was so busy with his thoughts that he nearly walked past the house. Maybe they'd offer to put him up. After all, he'd come a very long way on their behalf. Jackson rang the doorbell. There was movement inside but it seemed to take ages for the door to be opened. He hadn't known what to expect but he certainly hadn't anticipated Comrade Yelena.

She recognised him immediately, or perhaps she had known in advance who was delivering the documents. 'So, Comrade Jackson, we meet again.' Gold teeth flashed as she smiled with no warmth. 'You have something for me I believe.'

Opening his shoulder bag to remove the envelope, Jackson reflected that the recurring intestinal malaria which caused her to leave Zambia had taken its toll. She had aged considerably. 'I have to find somewhere to stay. My brother is in London. Would you mind if I used your phone to call him?'

She led him through to the kitchen, making no offer to put him up. Jackson would have said no, having no desire to spend two weeks in her company, but some show of hospitality or gratitude on her part would have been appreciated. He waited until she'd left the kitchen before dialling his brother's work number.

Dyson put down the receiver with mixed emotions. He had not seen any member of his family for nearly nine years. Jackson's treatment of Tessa King had been brutally callous. But she had survived and was now fully recovered. Suspicions aside, Dyson had no actual proof that it had been Jackson who laid the mine that killed Michael's wife, son and unborn child. He was making excuses, he knew that. The bare truth of it was he was aching to connect, no matter how briefly, with his own kin.

The ANC and SWAPO were barely on speaking terms, and if it came out that his brother was with SWAPO there'd be hell to pay. Dyson didn't care. When Jackson asked if he could stay with him for a couple of weeks, as much as he knew he should probably say no, Dyson said yes.

'Who was that?'

'One of my brothers.'

'What's his name?'

'Mapitha.'

'You're getting a lot of personal calls these days.'

It would be reported. Dyson accepted that. If their roles were reversed, he would do the same thing. They had to be careful. By giving Jackson's birth name he hoped that inquiries would not uncover his SWAPO connections.

He left the office just after five and caught a bus to Soho. He called at a supermarket to pick up some extra supplies: milk, a loaf of bread, and, because it was a special occasion, a couple of T-bone steaks. On impulse, he also stopped at an off licence to buy two bottles of cheap red wine and six quart bottles of beer. Luckily, he didn't have far to carry them.

Jackson was already there, hanging around in front of the building. They greeted each other with much hearty laughter, banging of each other's arms and shouting insults in Zulu, supposedly demonstrating how delighted they were to see each other. To both men's ears, it rang a little hollow.

Jackson followed his brother up two flights of stairs and into the tiny flat. 'Home sweet home,' Dyson said. 'You'll have to sleep on the couch.'

'That's fine.' A couch, after the tent in Zambia, would be luxury.

Dyson dumped his purchases on the sink. 'Like a beer?'

'Love one. What have you got to go with it?'

'Spirits you mean? Brandy or gin?'

'Both.' Back in Zambia, because no-one got the chance very often, when they drank the objective was to get as drunk as possible as quickly as possible.

Dyson raised his eyebrows but poured two small glasses of gin. Jackson tossed his back and then pulled long on his bottle of warm beer.

Grinning, Dyson asked, 'Where did you learn to drink like that?'

'It's how everyone drinks.'

'Not over here.' But Dyson followed his brother's example and swallowed the neat gin, pulling a face as it burnt his throat.

They talked in fits and starts, both hesitant, both holding back. It became easier as the alcohol slipped down. By his third bottle of beer Dyson was a little unsteady on his feet and attempting to cook their dinner. 'No more beer,' he mumbled. 'I've got some red wine if you like.'

Jackson didn't much like the sourness of wine but, since there was nothing else, said that would be fine.

Dyson opened a bottle and poured two tumblers full to the brim, handing one to his brother. 'So what brings you to London?'

'You know what I do,' he stated flatly. 'It's business.'

Dyson shrugged, indicating that it didn't matter to him one way or the other.

But Jackson could see he was insulted. 'Tell me about our parents.'

'Why do you never contact them?' Dyson's voice was sharp. Jackson's refusal to explain his visit to London had hurt. It meant that his brother didn't trust him.

'It is safer this way. I didn't want them to know where I was.' It was Jackson's turn to shrug. 'Anyway, I've left it too long. It's probably for the best that I stay out of touch.'

'Our mother longs to hear from you. She fears for your safety. The least you could do is reassure her.'

'Then tell her you've seen me. Say that I am

well. Send her my love and send our father my respectful best wishes.'

'I will,' Dyson responded severely. 'But I think they would prefer to hear it from you.'

Don't get him angry, or he may not let me stay. Jackson smiled wolfishly at his brother. 'I hear you. I will write when I get back.'

Dyson was relentless. 'Why don't you do it from here? That would be safer for them.'

'You have a point, big brother. Perhaps tomorrow.'

It seemed to appease him. Dyson half opened then closed a drawer in the table. 'You'll find everything you need in here. My address book's there too. Our parents no longer live at UBejane. Their new address is in the book.'

'Thanks.' Jackson was genuinely surprised by the news. 'Where are they now?'

Both wanted to turn the conversation away from contentious issues. Dyson told Jackson about the sale of UBejane, and how their parents had moved to Kwa-Mashu, just outside Durban. 'I know you think it's a waste of time but there is a strong feeling at home that Inkatha should be revived. There is much speculation that Buthelezi is the man to do it.'

'And how is our father involved?'

'There is much to be done. Too many people have turned away from Inkatha. They say that if the ANC is supposed to represent all tribes why revive something which is for the Zulus alone. But they are wrong. Our father and others like him know that for as long as the ANC is a banned organisation, the people will not be heard. Something is needed *inside* the country. They believe this is our chance to become the black voice of South Africa.'

'I do not understand. You speak as though you agree and yet work for the ANC.'

'Given a choice, I would rather be at home working alongside our father.'

As the night wore on, the red wine loosened the tongues of both brothers. Jackson opened up a little when he discovered that Dyson was well aware of SWAPO activity in the Caprivi Strip and, in the early hours of the next day, even boasted to Dyson that he was the one who laid the mine which killed a white woman and her child. 'Perhaps you read about it. There was much publicity in newspapers all around the world.'

Dyson felt a sudden surge of drunken anger which he was helpless to hold back. Before he could stop himself he'd blurted, 'That white woman was Michael King's wife.'

'Michael King! From UBejane?'

'True. That Michael King. The one who was always so good to our family. My friend.'

Jackson was genuinely shaken. 'Honest to God, I didn't know.'

'Would it have made any difference if you had?' Dyson's voice was hard.

Jackson shook his head slowly. The alcohol had fuddled his brain but he knew instinctively that lying would only anger Dyson further. 'No. I had my orders. It's war. I had to follow orders.' *Jesus! If Michael King ever finds out he'll kill me.*

Dyson's voice dropped and, when he spoke again, it was with resigned sadness. 'First Tessa, now this. I understand the rules of war as much as you but don't tell me that the unforgivable way you treated Michael's sister was following orders. Leave that family alone, Jackson.'

Jackson rose from the couch unsteadily. 'Got to piss.' In the bathroom, he tried to regulate his breathing. Dyson's revelation had unnerved him. A white woman and her child had been nicely impersonal. Michael King's wife and son were not. He had never liked Michael, especially after being caught in Tessa's bed, but he would not have deliberately singled out the man's wife and child. Jackson doubted, however, that he would ever convince Michael otherwise. He squared up to himself in the mirror. 'Keep cool. Nobody knows it was you.' *Dyson! Is he in touch with Michael? What if he tells him? So what if he does? King can't get me in Zambia.*

Calmer now, he returned to the lounge. Dyson's head was nodding. Jackson shook him awake. 'Go to bed. I'll see you in the morning.'

Still half-asleep, Dyson stumbled to his room. Jackson remembered that his brother had never been able to hold his liquor. It was just possible that, when he woke, Dyson would not remember their conversation.

By the time Jackson stirred, Dyson had already left for work. A note was propped up on the sink, saying to make himself at home. *Anything you can't find just hunt for it. See you this evening.* Jackson showered, dressed in clean if somewhat crumpled clothes from his suitcase, made himself coffee and toast for breakfast, watched television for a while and then, restless, decided to take Dyson's advice and write to his parents. A quick rummage in the drawer yielded a writing pad, biro and the address book. He sat at the table and began to write.

Half-an-hour later, Jackson was still staring at *Dear Mother and Father.* Sighing, he picked up the address book and flipped idly through it. He wondered if Michael King's contact details might be in it. No harm in finding out where the man lived. A name jumped off the page at him. King, Tessa. The address was here in London. He couldn't believe it. Tessa here!

Jackson stared unseeing through the small window, thinking. The past seemed to be crowding in on him. It was all because of Dyson. His brother was the linchpin, around which a number of dangers suddenly circled. How had Dyson known that the woman and child were Michael King's family? From Tessa? He looked back at the address book but found no other King. Tessa must have told Dyson. Could he trust Dyson with his indiscretion of the night before? What if Dyson tells Tessa? Would she . . .

Think!

What exactly does Dyson know? He knows I'm with SWAPO; he knows I killed Michael's wife and son; he knows Tessa and he knows where I am right now.

542

That's four things too many. What about Tessa? If Dyson does tell her she hates me enough to let her brother know. So where is Michael King? He must have been with the rhino research team but they packed up and left the Caprivi months ago. UBejane has been sold so he can't have gone there. What if he's come to England?

Jackson rechecked the page but there was no Michael King. To be sure, he looked under M. Again, nothing. Surely Dyson would know if he were in England. Closing the address book he noticed a loose piece of paper tucked under the front cover. He pulled it out. Michael King. There was a telephone number, no address. Was it a UK number? Only one way to find out. Jackson dialled the number. It rang half-a-dozen times before a woman answered. 'Claire Dawson, hello.'

He hung up. The voice was unmistakeably Michael's mother. What did she say her name was? Dawson, that was it. Jackson flicked feverishly through the address book. Dawson, Claire and Peter. Got it. In Hertford. He went to his A to Z but that didn't help. Searching through Dyson's books, he found a *New Motorists Atlas of Britain*. There it was. His skin had gone suddenly cold. Dyson could have phoned Michael who might already be on his way.

The phone rang, startling him. Should he pick it up? What if it's Dyson? Reaching a decision, he snatched the receiver up. 'Hello.'

'Just seeing if you're awake yet.'

'I've been up for a couple of hours.'

'What are you doing?'

'Trying to write that letter.'

'What letter?'

Jackson relaxed. If Dyson had forgotten their conversation about writing home there was a chance he might not remember that stupid boasting about the landmine. He decided to find out. 'Look, we got a little drunk last night. I said some things I probably shouldn't have. It was just the booze talking.'

There was the barest hesitation at the other end of the line before Dyson laughed. 'I don't remember anything after the second drink. Sorry, got to go. See you tonight.'

Jackson hung up, frowning. Alcohol could do funny things to one's memory but there was something in Dyson's voice which warned him that his brother was not being completely honest. *Jesus! Now what do I do?*

In fact, Dyson remembered their conversation in every minute detail. It was as he suspected. Jackson had indeed been responsible for Michael's tragic loss. To have it confirmed did not change anything. The question now was what to do with the information? Whichever way he acted, whether he spoke out or not, he would be disloyal to someone. Who was more important? His oldest friend or his brother? Reluctantly, he reached a decision, acknowledging as he did that he really had no option. In Dyson's mind, despite his long friendship with Michael, Jackson was blood. That's where his loyalty had to be even if the truth shocked and disgusted him.

Jackson was working himself up into a panic, convinced that Michael King was in England and, by now, looking for him. Tessa was the link. Obviously Dyson had contact with her otherwise she would not have been in his address book. He reached a decision. She had to be silenced.

It was easy enough to work out how to reach the address in Dyson's book. He caught the underground to Notting Hill Gate, then changed to the district line for Wimbledon with no difficulty. The A to Z showed him how to get to her house from there. It started to rain and he pulled the hood of his cheap plastic waterproof over his head. Arriving at the address, he then tried to decide what to do next. He'd expected a flat, not a three-storeyed house. She couldn't possibly live there alone.

Standing across the street trying to make up his mind whether he should ring the doorbell or not, Jackson caught his breath when Tessa unexpectedly emerged. She really was beautiful. There was no place for him to hide but he needn't have worried. She opened her umbrella and without even glancing across the street set off at a leisurely pace. He followed.

Tessa, on the spur of the moment, had decided to go away for a few days. She had her own key to

Kerry Glasshouse's flat and, when he telephoned to find out why she had not kept their appointment and she'd told him she would not be seeing him again, he'd begged her to take a few days to think it over. 'Use the flat. I'll be in the States on business. And, Tessa, whatever you decide, I wish you well.'

She wanted time on her own. She wanted to be absolutely certain that she was doing the right thing. More than anything, her resolve had to be rock solid before she said anything to Dyson. Judith too had encouraged her to be very sure in her own mind. So when Tessa mentioned going to Kerry's flat for a few days, Judith thought it a good idea.

It was raining heavily outside. She shook out her umbrella, debating whether or not to catch a cab. She decided against it. The tube station was just down the road and the underground would take her to within two blocks of Kerry's flat. It would be quicker than going there by road.

At the tube station Jackson had no idea of her destination so bought a Go-As-You-Please ticket that allowed him unrestricted travel on the underground for four days. He boarded the adjoining carriage to hers and sat where he could see through to where she was sitting. Tessa pulled a magazine from her bag and began to read.

Jackson was surprised when they reached South Kensington Station and Tessa rose to leave the train. He kept her in sight, staying behind half-a-dozen other passengers. She walked out of the tube station and turned left. It was still raining. Five minutes later, outside a terraced house that had been converted into flats, Tessa stopped. She rummaged in her bag, produced a key and disappeared inside.

Jackson waited for a couple of minutes then followed. There were six letterboxes outside, the same number of doorbells and a single loudspeaker panel. The names over individual buttons meant nothing to him. Then he noticed that the outer door had not shut properly. But which flat did Tessa enter? He felt in his pocket and found the piece of paper on which he'd written Tessa's address. He folded it several times and wedged it over the latch. Then he crossed the street and, taking cover in a bus shelter, stared upwards. There! Movement at a window on the first floor. The curtains opened and Tessa stood, stretching. As far as he could tell, she was not speaking to anyone inside. Was she alone?

He ducked back out of sight as her gaze travelled slowly along the street. When next he looked, she was gone.

Now what? He could knock on the door of the flat and, when she opened it, force his way inside. But what if she had company? He could brazen it out, try charm, get inside and then, if they were alone, kill her. What if she wouldn't let him in? Why should she? If he barged in against her will and there was a man in the flat, what then? Leave, pretend to be an outraged ex-lover. It was flimsy but it was the best Jackson could come up with. A bus came along, slowed when it saw him but picked up speed as he waved it by. He was thinking too much. Tessa was not Tessa, she was the hit. That's what he'd been taught. 'Don't think of civilians, women or innocent children. They're just a means to an end. Think of the cause.'

Committed, Jackson left the bus shelter, entered the building and almost ran up the stairs to the first floor. There were only two flats on that level, the one to the left obviously at the front of the building. He knocked. His breathing was steady, his mind focused. The door opened. Before she had time to recognise him and react, he had pushed her back, stepped inside and shut the door with his foot.

'Jackson! What on earth . . .'

His eyes darted around. Two doors he could see. The lounge was empty. 'Are you alone?'

'Yes . . . no . . . no, Kerry, quick.'

No-one came. Jackson looked at her and smiled. 'There's no-one else is there?'

Tessa was overcoming her shock. 'What the hell are you doing here?'

She would fight back. He had to act now. Jackson stepped towards her, hands reaching out.

Tessa had, at Judith's insistence, learned a bit of self-defence. Nothing special, just a few moves in case she ever found herself in trouble. She stepped back, crouching slightly. 'What do you want?'

Jackson lunged and she sidestepped, grabbing an arm and twisting.

'Bitch!' He'd shown his hand too soon. He flung her off with ease. She backed away, face white, fear in her eyes. Reaching into his pocket, Jackson drew out the knife he'd taken from Dyson's kitchen.

'Jackson, don't.' She had backed against the far wall. 'Please. We can talk.'

He had to act fast, before she screamed. His move was quick but she sidestepped again. Concentrating on the knife, she tripped on a leather pouf and nearly lost her balance. Jackson swung, but she threw up an arm and the blade sliced it to the bone. Tessa opened her mouth to scream and he was on her, throwing aside the knife, his hands grasping for her throat. She fought like a wildcat. They crashed to the floor, knocking over a lampstand. Blood flowed freely from her arm. There was so much of it. It was everywhere. His hands were slippery from it. He squeezed and squeezed. Would she ever be still? By the time it was over his hands and arms had cramped.

Wheezing for air, he staggered to his feet. *Jesus! Look at it!* Blood up the wall, on the floor, staining the sofa. His stomach heaved and, bent double, he sought the bathroom, not making it and vomiting on the bedroom carpet. A full-length mirror showed that he too was covered in Tessa's blood. The cupboard revealed a man's wardrobe. That would do. He found the bathroom, stripped and showered. Helping himself to the unknown benefactor's clothing, he dressed in corduroy trousers, a shirt and jersey. There were shoes, but too small a size, so he wiped the blood off his own and put them back on. An oilskin jacket was hanging behind the door, which he grabbed before going back into the lounge. Tessa hadn't moved. Cautiously, he approached, watching for any sign of breathing. Nothing. He did not want to touch her.

In the small kitchen, Jackson found her handbag. There was nearly £350 in it. A fortune. He went to put it in his wallet then realised it was not there. *Get hold of yourself.* The wallet and a key to Dyson's flat. There was nothing else in his pockets, but he went through them three times to be sure before stuffing them into a plastic bag which he rolled up and placed inside a larger, sturdier bag. He'd get rid of them somewhere. He'd been carrying a knife. *The knife!* Where the hell did it go? He spent five minutes frantically searching before he found it. It had skittered under a chair when he flung it away. He picked it up using a paper kitchen towel. He'd have to get rid of it. No. Clean it and take it back, otherwise Dyson would miss it.

Before leaving Jackson had one last, long look at Tessa. Even dead and covered with blood she was beautiful.

Jackson was back in Dyson's flat by a-quarter-past-five. By the time his brother arrived home, he had their dinner cooking and the knife, thoroughly scrubbed, was back in the drawer where it belonged. Conversation between them soon lapsed. They had nothing in common. Television spared them the effort of talking to each other. Jackson had already decided to try to change his flights back to Zambia. He'd much rather spend time in Lusaka than London. Anyway, just to be safe, it would be best to leave England as quickly as possible.

In the morning, having feigned sleep until Dyson left, Jackson dressed and went out to find some breakfast before calling at a travel agency. They were most helpful but could not get him on to a flight until the following Tuesday. Today was Wednesday. Nearly a whole week to wait.

Tessa's body was discovered the following day by the woman who cleaned the flat. Inspector John Dyer of New Scotland Yard pulled the case and arrived around 10 a.m. with his assistant Detective Sergeant Brian O'Callaghan. 'Good-looking bird,' Dyer commented.

The char, a Mrs Webb, was in the kitchen drinking tea and talking excitedly to anyone on the forensics team who would listen. Dyer wouldn't listen. O'Callaghan was not surprised when his boss, with customary disregard for good manners, overrode her monologue.

'What's the young lady's name?'

''Ow should I know?' The woman was miffed at the policeman's lack of interest in the fact that she just knew something was wrong the moment she'd put her key in the door.

'Who owns the flat?'

'Dunno, luv. You'll have to ask the agency.'

'Which agency?' Dyer asked heavily.

'Sir.' O'Callaghan had Tessa's handbag. 'There's a card in her purse.' He was peering inside and read it with difficulty, not wanting to interfere with possible evidence. 'Tessa King.'

'Address?'

'Yes, sir.'

'What *is* it?'

'I can't read it, sir.'

Dyer sighed. 'Okay, get down to the cleaning agency and find out what you can. I'll poke around here and do the neighbours. Someone must have seen or heard something.' He glared at the suddenly silent Mrs Webb. 'You won't be working here today. Might as well give the constable a statement and hop it.'

She rose stiffly and he added, 'Oh, and don't go disappearing to Majorca or anything like that, will you, love. We'll want to talk to you again.'

Her only response was a loud sniff of disapproval.

John Dyer went to check on progress in the lounge. The pathologist had arrived. Christ! The girl had been stunning. Still was. 'Jesus! What a fucking waste. Hello Doc, when can you give me something?'

Later the same day, Dyer and O'Callaghan drove to Hertford. They had obtained the address from Judith Murray-Brown. From years of practice, they were professional, sympathetic and impatient to get on with the case. Claire Dawson broke down and had to be given a sedative. The two detectives were left with a white-faced but calm Michael King, apparently the dead girl's brother.

'The occupant of the flat above says she saw a

black man hanging around the bus shelter outside. She thought it was strange because he didn't seem interested in catching a bus. Did your sister know any black men?'

'My sister knew a lot of men, Inspector. She was a professional companion,' Michael said flatly.

Dyer blinked. He had known that, just hadn't expected to hear it put so bluntly by her brother.

'The flat belongs to a man called Kerry Glasshouse from York. He can account for his movements. Right now, he's probably trying to account for his reasons. His wife had no knowledge of the place.' Dyer grinned, then coughed and covered his mouth, remembering who Michael was. 'Is there anything you know about your sister that might assist with our inquiries?'

'Sorry, nothing.'

'Are you sure, sir? If you need a moment to think . . .'

'Inspector Dyer, I've only been in England for a few months. In that time, I've seen my sister once. Why don't you speak with Judith Murray-Brown? She might be of more help.'

'We'll be doing that, sir.' Dyer rubbed his thumbs against his temple, a habit that had virtually removed the hair from either side of his head. 'Mr King, if, as you say, your sister was a . . . hostess, and if Mr Glasshouse let her use his flat in London, it would appear that they had some kind of special arrangement. What I'm trying to say, sir, is that I don't believe she would take another client to that particular flat. So where does that leave us?'

'Somebody she didn't know,' Michael suggested.

'Want to know what I think?' Dyer said to O'Callaghan as they drove back to London.

O'Callaghan made no response. Dyer would tell him anyway.

'I think Michael King is hiding something.'

'You think he did it?'

'No. But I think he knows more than he's telling us.'

Black man. Black man. Michael could not get it out of his mind. There were millions of black men in London. Why then did the name Jackson keep coming into his head?

It was on the nine o'clock news that night. Not a major story, simply that a woman had been found dead in South Kensington, that she had been ident-ified as Tessa King and that the circumstances surrounding her death were suspicious. Both Dyson and Jackson were watching the bulletin.

'No!' It burst from Dyson, a cry of horror.

Jackson was startled at the raw pain in his brother's voice. 'Tessa! Well, well. I guess she got what she deserved.'

Dyson had a sharp retort ready but the look on Jackson's face stopped it. Dyson had seen that look before, many times before, when Jackson was growing up. It was secretive, gloating. In a blinding flash of realisation, Dyson knew that it was Jackson who had murdered Tessa. Without a word, he rose and went to the drawer where he kept the address book. He flipped it open under Jackson's nose. 'You found this.' Dyson could barely speak. 'You found this and you couldn't leave things alone. Why, Jackson? What in God's name made you do it?'

'Do what?' Jackson's eyes were wide. 'What are you talking about?'

Dyson flung the address book down. 'You know very well what I'm talking about.'

'I swear to God, I don't. What's got into you? So Tessa's dead. What makes you think I had anything to do with it?'

Dyson paced the small room, rubbing a hand abstractedly over his hair. 'I should have known. You bastard! What were you afraid of? That I'd tell Tessa about you blowing up Michael's family?' He broke off and stared at Jackson. 'That's it, isn't it?'

Jackson rose. 'So,' he said slowly, 'you do remember.'

'Of course I remember. You don't think I'd forget something like that.'

'And?'

Dyson frowned at him. 'And what? You're my brother.'

Jackson forced himself to look grateful.

'You'll have to go. I won't have you staying here knowing . . .' He choked, and tears ran down his face. 'I was in love with her,' he said hoarsely.

Jackson actually laughed. 'With Tessa! You must be joking. She was a whore.'

A deadly cold rage ran through Dyson. His brother was evil. 'I know what she was. I loved her anyway.' His voice was soft. 'I loved you enough to forget who turned her into one, enough to hide the fact that you were in London.' He took a shuddering breath. 'I loved you enough to betray my best friend.'

They were facing each other, eye-to-eye, no more than two metres apart. A message communicated itself. The other had to die. Both men reacted instantly, stepping up and trading blows. This was no scuffle in the heat of the moment. This was kill or be killed, a desperate hate-filled fight to the death. Punches found their mark and went unfelt. Furniture smashed and went unheard. Their eyes were locked tightly, while that which bound their hearts sprang open.

Dyson was losing. The rage that gave him strength was not enough to combat his brother's five years of bush-hardened stamina. Jackson had a grip on his throat and Dyson saw the murderous punch coming, saw the intent in his brother's eyes, and was helpless to avoid it. The blow caught him squarely on the jaw, knocking him off his feet. He went over backwards and his head made contact with the hard marble hearth of the small fireplace. A sickening crunch of bone and flesh, and Dyson knew no more.

Reality returned slowly to Jackson. He became aware of someone banging on the wall and shouts of, 'Shut up in there or we'll call the police.' He looked at the trashed room. How long had they been fighting? The adrenalin rush left and he felt weak. Dyson lay unmoving, blood spreading out from under his head. The banging stopped and he heard voices in the hall.

'What's going on?'

'Haven't a clue. A fight of some kind.'

'Bloody wogs. Bunch of savages if you ask me.'
Doors closed. Silence descended.

I have to get away.

Jackson went into the bathroom and looked in
the mirror. Swollen top lip, cut eyebrow, left eye
beginning to close. He splashed water on his face,
wincing at the sting. A small tin of Zam-Buk, an
ointment used extensively in Africa for anything
from mosquito bites to sore muscles or burns, was
on the side of the sink. Wondering how Dyson
managed to find it in London, Jackson smeared the
soothing cream on his lips and eyes.

Returning to the lounge, he searched carefully
for anything that might give away his presence.
Then, picking up his suitcase, he went to the door.
Dyson still hadn't moved and Jackson, eyes flicking
over the body of his brother in one last search of
the room, wasted no time on pity or sorrow.

He encountered no-one on the stairs. He
walked three blocks before splurging on a cab, asking the driver to recommend somewhere cheap
but clean to stay. He was taken to a bed and breakfast establishment in Earls Court. There he booked
a room, paying for four days in advance. Feeling
anonymous and safe, he decided that London
wasn't as bad as he first thought.

Dyson was not dead, though he was perilously
close to death. An elderly Nigerian man in the flat

below had been roused by the fight from where he was dozing in front of his television. He listened for several minutes before picking up the telephone and reporting a serious disturbance. The police arrived thirty minutes later. Two police constables broke down Dyson's door and found him. He was rushed to hospital where an emergency operation was carried out to remove pressure from his brain. He was then put into intensive care.

Detective Inspector John Dyer had not been assigned to the Dyson Mpande attack but a colleague who worked out of the same office was. Going through Dyson's address book, the name Tessa King rang a bell. It was a couple of hours before he remembered that John Dyer was working on the murder of a hooker by that name. When Dyer asked to see the book, a piece of paper fell out bearing Michael's name and telephone number.

Dyer and O'Callaghan went back to see Michael. 'Do you know a Dyson Mpande?' Dyer got straight to the point.

'Yes.'

'Are you aware that he was viciously attacked last night in his flat?'

'No.' Michael went cold. First Tessa, now this. 'Is he all right?'

'He's in intensive care in Shaftesbury Hospital.'

'God! I've got to see him.'

'He won't be taking visitors for a few days. He may not pull through at all.' Dyer gave Michael a couple of seconds to absorb the information. 'I'm not involved in this case but for one thing. Your sister's name was in his address book. Come to that, so was yours.'

'They would be,' Michael said absently, still trying to take it in.

'Mind telling me why?'

Michael took a deep breath and tried to concentrate. 'Dyson and I grew up together. His parents used to work for us in South Africa. They probably gave him this address when my mother remarried and moved here and I know they gave him Tessa's. They saw each other occasionally.'

'Perhaps it was this Mpande who murdered your sister?'

'No.' *Not that Mpande.*

'Bit of a coincidence, though, wouldn't you say? Someone trying to kill him too.'

'Are you suggesting that I had something to do with it?'

Dyer looked squarely at Michael. He was pale. Fine lines etched his face. Early thirties. A bit young to look so drawn. His eyes held steady though. 'No, sir. I'm just trying to make sense of a few things. I don't think you are involved but I'd bet my left testicle you have a pretty good idea who is.'

Michael didn't flinch. ''Fraid not, Inspector.'

Dyer didn't flinch either. 'Oh yes you do. I don't know what you've got planned, son, but whatever it is, do it on your own turf, not mine.'

'My sister's being buried on Tuesday. After that I'm going home, unless you have any objections.'

Dyer nodded. 'That should be fine, Mr King. Just keep us informed.'

'Know what I think?' Dyer said to O'Callaghan as they drove back to London.

O'Callaghan grunted non-committally.

'I think that whoever killed his sister and beat up his friend has good reason to be scared. I wouldn't like to be in his shoes right now, no sireee. Know what else I think?'

O'Callaghan sighed.

'I think our murder case is as good as closed. Well, near as, dammit. Or it will be just as soon as King gets back to South Africa. That's what I think.'

Michael was unable to see Dyson until Monday. The nurse warned, 'Only a few minutes, Mr King. He's still disoriented and gets upset easily.'

Michael tiptoed into the room. Dyson lay, eyes closed, bandage around his head. He heard Michael's approach and opened his eyes. '*Sawubona*,' he whispered.

'*Yebo, sawubona*.' Michael sat on a chair next to the bed. Dyson's eyes were closed again. 'For a Zulu, you look pretty damned white right now.'

The slightest stretching of Dyson's lips showed he appreciated the remark. 'Jackson,' he croaked.

A nurse came in and helped Dyson drink a little water, then left.

'Jackson,' he repeated in a stronger voice. 'He killed Tessa.'

'I know.'

'And your family.'

'I know that too.'

'He'll go back to Zambia.'

'I'll find him.'

'I'm sorry.' Dyson was apologising for his brother's actions.

'I'm sorry too.' Michael was apologising for his intentions.

Both men knew it.

'Kill him the old way.'

'I intend to.'

The nurse came back. 'I'm sorry, Mr King. We've been monitoring our patient and he's getting tired. You'll have to leave.'

Michael rose and reached over and picked up Dyson's hand. Gently, he clasped the limp fingers the Zulu way. 'Stay well.'

'Go well.'

As he left the hospital Michael was thinking, 'Yesssss, Mr Mpande. You can run but I'm coming for you, you bastard. And when I find you, you're going to die. Impaled on a fucking stake straight up through your bloody arse in the finest Zulu tradition.'

EIGHTEEN

Tessa King was laid to rest on a soft summer afternoon. Rain, which had threatened for most of the day, finally fulfilled its promise as the coffin was lowered into the ground.

Claire, composed but pale, stood leaning into her husband under a large black umbrella. The warmth and strength of his body was comforting. Her mind remained numb but she knew he was there.

Sally, Marcel and little Dominique formed a tight knot. Marcel had one arm around Sally, the other hand resting lightly on his daughter's shoulder. Sally's eyes were red from recent tears. It was as if a part of herself was being buried. The gentle rain went unnoticed by the three of them.

Michael and Gregor stood side-by-side with Andrew between them. Not fully understanding the significance of the event, Andrew and Dominique played peekaboo around their parents' legs.

Standing apart from the family were Judith Murray-Brown and five of Tessa's closest friends.

From the trees, a discreet distance behind the

mourners, Dyer and O'Callaghan scanned the cemetery hoping that, as sometimes happened, the murderer felt compelled to attend the funeral. They needn't have bothered. At the precise moment Tessa was being gently lowered to her final resting place, Jackson Mpande, in the departure lounge at Heathrow, heard the first boarding call for his flight.

A few days after the funeral, with Sally and her family back in Paris and Gregor once more at boarding school, Michael decided that no matter how much grief it invoked his mother had to talk about what had happened. So far she had refused to speak about Tessa and Dyson, or the possible link between them and Jackson. Why should she? She probably hadn't even made the connection. Claire did not hate Jackson so intensely that she could almost sense his presence. Even without the murder, Michael had reason enough for vengeance. But now it was as if he could see inside Jackson's mind.

He needed to choose his words carefully. Claire was already aware of his intentions. If she realised that he too could be in danger, she'd be frantic. Michael found her in the kitchen with Andrew. His son was sitting on the floor, scraping off a glass mixing bowl, licking up the last of a delicious chocolatey cake mix, face and hands smeared with it. A picture of pure happiness. Claire was singing him a nursery rhyme.

'Mother, can we talk?'

She was rinsing things in the sink. The singing

stopped, she turned off the tap, her body very still. She kept her back to him. 'I've always tried to live the way God intended.' Her voice was soft, almost abstracted. 'I have never believed that anybody could be all evil, I always thought there had to be a reason . . . a sickness of some kind. Even Jennifer and Jeremy were . . . I'm sorry, Michael, but they were random victims of politically motivated violence. There was a reason you see, something to get hold of and, even if you didn't agree, at least it was a starting point. Do you understand?'

Standing at the sink silhouetted against the window she looked ethereal, like gossamer.

'We all need it. When events are beyond our normal daily lives, we seek that one thing, no matter how small, to hold on to, to help us through. It's the only way we cope.' Her voice strengthened. 'I've found that small thing for Jennifer and Jeremy and I'm hanging on for dear life. But, Michael, what have I got for Tessa, for Dyson? His own brother, Michael, his own flesh and blood?'

She turned to face him, wiping her hands on a cloth. Tears were streaming down her face. 'There has to be something?'

He might have known she would have guessed. 'Will revenge do?'

She brushed at her cheeks. 'Andrew will be fine with us. When do you leave?'

The next day John Dyer paid Michael a surprise visit. 'I happened to be passing.'

'Come in.'

'If you don't mind, I'd rather you came out.'

'It's raining,' Michael pointed out, pulling on a coat.

'So it is.' Dyer looked surprised, as though he'd only just noticed.

They walked the length of the garden, down to the edge of the pond. 'Great place for ducks,' Dyer observed.

'We've got the happiest ducks in Hertfordshire,' Michael said dryly.

'I didn't say this.'

'About the ducks?'

Dyer shrugged. 'You want to hear it or don't you?'

'I'm not sure.'

'Take it from me, you do.'

'Okay.'

The detective faced Michael. 'I did some digging. Sorry about your wife and son.'

'Thanks.'

'Then I flashed my badge at a few people. Fellow by the name of Jackson Mpande caught a flight to Africa on Tuesday. Nairobi. Been over here just under two weeks.'

Michael let out a lot of breath.

'According to Dyson Mpande, his brother had been staying with him.' Dyer scowled. 'Nice of him to take so long to tell us. I don't suppose you can shed any light on this? I know you've been to see Dyson.'

Michael remained silent.

Dyer sighed. 'Thought not. So I've got two choices. Try for extradition or drop it. See, my problem is this: the legal process to prise a suspect out of Africa is so bloody long I'd probably be retired before he gets here, if indeed he gets here at all. On the other hand, letting a suspect off the hook gets right up my nose, know what I mean?'

Michael just looked at him.

'Justice is a funny thing,' Dyer mused. 'It catches up with most, one way or another.'

'One way or another,' Michael agreed.

'Like I said, you didn't hear it from me.'

Ten days later, as the South African Airways Boeing 707 touched down at Jan Smuts, Michael King had the welcome feeling of coming home. Africa was in his blood. With luck, it wouldn't be his blood in Africa.

He needed a base. Johannesburg was as good a place as any.

He bought a two-bedroom townhouse in a high-walled complex near Craighall Park, had his belongings taken out of storage and delivered and, not wishing to waste time, hired an interior decorator to worry about fixtures and fittings.

For the next four weeks Michael hardly stopped. The nest egg he and Jennifer had put aside disappeared, money spent as though there were no tomorrow. Maybe there wasn't. That thought, if it came into his head at all, was quickly swept aside by a renewed sense of purpose. A six cylinder, Series a Land Rover came out of the box. The agents fitted long-range fuel tanks and a canvas back. Camping equipment, most of which he didn't even bother to unpack, was dumped in the garage. From a sporting goods shop he picked up an ex-army Browning 9mm self-loading pistol, a second-hand 12-gauge Remington pump action shotgun and four boxes of buckshot, and a brand new Winchester 70 .375 H & H magnum with two packets of 300 grain silvertip bullets.

'You starting a war?' the owner asked.

'Something like that.'

The man shrugged. It was none of his business.

At last he was ready. Feeling cool-headed and focused, Michael unfolded the sheet of paper Annie Devilliers had given him and dialled the number. It was answered on the second ring. 'Ace Exports,' a voice growled.

Michael grinned. Sacha Devilliers might be with the Bureau of State Security or he might be a freelance mercenary, but he sure as hell had nothing to do with anything commercial, not with a receptionist who sounded like *that*. 'Good afternoon. Sacha Devilliers please.'

There was a pause. 'Who's speaking?' demanded the voice.

'He doesn't know me.'

'Who's speaking?' A steely ring had entered the growl.

'Michael King.'

'How did you get this number?'

'His wife gave it to me.'

There was silence on the other end. Finally, 'Where can we contact you?'

Michael gave him the number and the connection was immediately broken. 'And goodbye to you too,' Michael said to the dead receiver.

He didn't have long to wait. In less than twenty minutes the telephone rang. Before he could even give his name a voice asked, 'What do you want?'

'Are you Sacha Devilliers?'

'Of course, man. Why did you contact my office?'

Swiftly Michael told him. There was no point in holding anything back. For all he knew, Annie had already explained the situation, or at least some of it.

'So what makes you think I can help?'

'Annie suggested . . .'

Something like a grunt came down the line. 'I'll call you back day after tomorrow. Same time.' He hung up.

Two days later, precisely on cue, Sacha Devilliers called him back. 'Your man went back to Zambia.'

'Do you know where in Zambia?'

'Base 37. Mean anything to you?'

'Not yet.'

'Forget it. You won't get to him there.'

'I can try.'

'Are you sure you want to do this?'

'Yes.'

Devilliers sounded weary. 'Be very sure.'

'I am.'

'What makes you think you can take him?'

'I hate his guts.'

'You must have impressed my wife. She knows not to contact me when I'm working.'

Michael made no comment.

'Are you there, King? I said . . .'

'I heard what you said.'

'Well?'

'Well what? I'm not interested in your wife if that's what you're thinking.'

'You have no idea what I'm thinking, King. None at all.' There was a slight hesitation. 'I'm expensive.'

'All I need is a bit more information. I'm not using you.'

'You may not have a choice. Anyway, what makes you think I'll give it to you just like that?'

Michael's patience snapped. 'Look, what is this? Can you help or not? I'm not here to fuck about. You've told me where he is. I'll take it from there if I have to.'

Devilliers gave a short laugh. 'Bear with me, King. The information I have is, shall we say, sensitive. It doesn't get handed to any old oke just because his wife copped it.'

Michael swallowed anger.

'I'll level with you, man. We might just be able to help each other. If you can take Mpande out you'll be doing us all a favour. The man is very definitely up to something.'

'This information you have, how reliable is it?'

Again, the short laugh. 'Clever, King. Very clever.'

Michael was starting to dislike Sacha Devilliers. 'I'm not asking where it comes from. All I'm asking is if you can trust it.'

'That I can, King. That I can.'

'Fine. That's good enough for me.'

Devilliers cleared his throat. 'Okay. Listen and don't interrupt. You don't need to know what I am. That's the first thing. I'm legit and that will have to be good enough. I'm actually working on something else right now. Doesn't matter what but there's a lot at stake. We're so close to cracking it, it's not funny.' His voice hardened to emphasise his next words. '*I would hate to be called off now.*'

Michael wondered what Devilliers was getting at but said nothing.

'Last week,' Devilliers continued in his normal voice, 'I get a call from an acquaintance, someone I freelance for now and then. Wants to know if I'm available. SWAPO's apparently cooking up something huge. I tell him I should be free in a couple of weeks and he says he'll get back to me. My guess is that was no good. I haven't heard any more. Then you come along. So I do some digging and, guess what? Coincidence. Seems that your boy could be very much involved. Problem is, I just can't spare the time, King, not yet. This is where you get lucky. Believe me, I have a problem with civilians stepping into my arena. They usually get killed. So I'm giving you your boy. But let me tell you this, King, if you fuck up, if I have to come and save your arse, you'll wish you'd never heard of me. Okay?'

Michael couldn't help thinking that Sacha

Devilliers was given to the melodramatic. But all he said was, 'Okay.'

'Deluxe,' Devilliers said, appearing satisfied.

'So how do I find Mpande?'

'Don't bother rushing up to Zambia. Your friend is here, in Zululand.'

Oh Jesus! I can taste you, you bastard.

'Want to know why?'

'Only if it will help me find the bastard.'

'He's to infiltrate Inkatha.'

'So much for traditional Zulu loyalty.'

'We live in strange times, King.'

'What about your acquaintance? If Mpande is the reason he called you, how come he's not made contact again?'

'He'll be going through different channels. Official ones. Before the powers that be tell me to drop everything else and help out I'll give him a call, tell him it's under control. I'm sticking my neck out here, I hope you realise just how much.'

'Thanks.'

'Don't thank me, thank Annie. She's the one who said you can be trusted.'

There it was again, a kind of mocking challenge at the mention of his wife. Michael wondered about it but didn't react. 'Do you know where in Zululand?'

'Ulundi.'

'The Royal kraal. Why? It's in the middle of nowhere.'

'Think, man. What's his speciality?'

'Landmines.'

'And what tourist attraction is only twenty miles away? You know it well I believe.'

Michael went cold. *Umfolozi Game Reserve.* 'I thought you said he was to infiltrate . . .'

Devilliers didn't let him finish. 'Look, the Commies trained your friend in Russia. Word is they think his talents are wasted in the Caprivi. Sure, Mpande's mission may be to infiltrate Inkatha but they also want him to create a little chaos on the way. Destabilise the country's hospitality industry by blowing up a few innocent tourists. He's got to be stopped. Mpande's been at Ulundi for two days. We know he has a contact there. It's likely he'll move at night, plant the mines and keep going. If he does that, you've lost him. He'll go to ground in Kwa-Mashu. Right now Mpande seems to be in no hurry, as if he's waiting for something.'

'Jesus!' Michael swore. 'I think I know what it might be. The Natal Parks Board is hosting a two-day tourism conference at Umfolozi. The Minister and a whole bunch of politicians will be there, not to mention invited overseas guests, travel agents, airline representatives and the media. It starts tomorrow.'

'Shit! Are you sure of this?'

'Jennifer and I were invited. In fact, I was supposed to give a talk about our rhino program. The theme of this conference is how to tie tourism in with conservation projects. Get the tourists involved, that sort of thing.' Michael was thinking quickly as he spoke. 'Tomorrow. He won't move until tomorrow.'

'How the hell do you know that?'

'I know him. I can think like him.'

'And?' Devilliers pressed. 'You must have some-thing more than that.'

'The conference has booked all the accommo-dation. In fact, they're closing the reserve to day visitors for twenty-four hours. After lunch on the second day all the delegates will be taken for a game drive. Mpande will lay his mines tomorrow night. But the following afternoon he'll be in Kwa-Mashu.'

'How quickly can you get moving?'

Michael looked at his watch. A little after two. He could be on the road in half-an-hour, Durban around midnight and Ulundi three hours after that. 'I'm on my way.'

'Deluxe. Oh, one more thing. I have a contact in Ulundi. Edward . . . forget his last name. He's retired but used to work as a tracker for a safari company in Botswana. Zulu through and through and he's straight from the last century. Hates progress, hates fences and has absolutely no regard for the law. He's expecting you.'

'Expecting me. You mean we went through all of this . . .'

'Just checking you out.' Devilliers chuckled. 'Annie was right. I can trust you. Good luck.'

'Fuck you!'

'Deluxe.'

Despite the hour a paraffin lamp glowed through the window at the address Devilliers had given him. The door opened before Michael turned off the engine. 'I see you, *Nkosi*. Come,' he beckoned.

Michael followed. The house was an oblong, concrete block building, basic, untidy and not very clean. Inside, the Zulu's bloodshot eyes sized Michael up. 'This white man with the task of a lion is no more than a spotted cub himself,' he muttered in Zulu.

Michael replied in the same tongue. 'It is for this reason that the old lion comes with him.'

Edward cackled. The few teeth left in his head were brown with age. But despite his obvious years, he was sinewy, with well-muscled arms and legs. A veil of grey, like a sprinkling of castor sugar, covered his hair. He was wearing old khaki shorts and nothing else. 'So, cub. You speak my language as one of us. Tell me. This man you seek, is he a clever one?'

'Like a leopard.'

'Aahhh!' Edward breathed, strangely satisfied. 'Tell me of him. Then you must sleep.'

Although tired, Michael sensed how important it was for Edward to understand Jackson. He told him everything, leaving nothing out. Edward listened in silence, not interrupting once.

'A leopard, you say,' he commented when Michael stopped. 'I think he is more dangerous than a leopard.'

'Is anything more dangerous than a leopard?'

'Two leopards.' Edward pointed to a corner where a mattress lay. 'Sleep. There will be no rest after this night.'

Michael hadn't realised how tired he was. When Edward shook him awake it was almost ten in the morning. The Zulu had brought in all his equipment from the vehicle. 'You carry a lot of useless baggage.'

'If all goes well tonight you can have most of it.'

Edward bent and examined a price tag still attached to the tent. 'It costs a lot of money, this peace you seek.'

'If that is all it costs, it will be worth it.'

Edward grunted non-committally as he searched through Michael's tool kit. 'Wire cutters. Good.' He removed them along with a roll of soft wire.

'Done this sort of thing before, have you?' Michael grinned.

'Many times,' Edward admitted blandly. 'A man has to eat.'

Michael took the shotgun from its canvas case. 'Do you know how to use this?'

'You trust an old man with it?'

'Old lion, I am trusting you with more than a shotgun.'

'Have no second thoughts, cub. I am your man.'

'You are Sacha Devilliers' man too. Remind me to ask you about that.'

'Ah!' Edward said. 'That is a different thing entirely.' Then he changed the subject. 'Your leopard keeps out of sight this morning but he has had two visitors. Both carried something heavy. Both left with nothing.'

Michael nodded. 'Mines.'

'And you think he will move tonight?'

'Before then. It's twenty miles to the western side of the reserve and there are no roads in from this side. It's rough and remote country out there. He'll stick to the railway line until it crosses the river, pick up the boundary fence and follow it north. The tourist loop roads are maybe another six or seven miles from there. He'll want to be inside the reserve by nightfall. It's just about a full moon. He can lay the mines and be gone by dawn.'

'But what if an animal steps on one? Won't he wait until tomorrow?'

'I don't think so. Too risky. He's probably aware of the routes they will take, it's the usual VIP game-viewing tour. Guaranteed good sightings right up in the top corner, well away from the main camp. If an animal accidentally sets off a mine the explosion is unlikely to be heard.'

An urgent knocking at the door interrupted them. Edward opened it and a young man, maybe twenty years old, stepped inside, glanced at Michael, then spoke rapidly to the older man. 'He goes now.'

Edward looked over at Michael. 'You were right. The leopard does not wait for darkness.' He turned back to the younger man. 'Which way? How does he travel?'

'By the railway, *Babu*. Walking alone towards the morning sun.'

'Is he carrying anything?' Michael cut in.

'Yes *Nkosi*, on his back. It is heavy.'

'What do you want to do, young cub?' Edward asked Michael before speaking to the younger man. 'You have done well. Go now.'

'We must follow. Can you track him if he leaves the railway line?'

'Am I a tracker or a blind man?' Edward asked, outraged.

'We're about to find out,' Michael replied soberly. 'Damn it! I haven't sighted the rifle.'

'You are hunting a leopard, not a buffalo.'

He had a point. Better to travel light. Besides, a single bullet was not the vengeance he sought.

NINETEEN

They were probably an hour behind Jackson. Ulundi had been relatively cool but it quickly became hot and still as they dropped towards the White Umfolozi River. Much to Michael's relief the threatening cumulus clouds had come to nothing.

Tracking Jackson was child's play for Edward. At one point their quarry left the railway, but it was only to relieve his bowels. The discovery caused Michael to wish that Edward was not quite that good. They were about to move on again when Edward gave a sudden exclamation of surprise. 'The leopard is armed. See where he put his pack down.'

The indentation in the sandy soil would have gone unnoticed by Michael. His eyes followed Edward's finger. Next to a slight hollow left by something bulky and heavy was the faint outline of a gun stock. 'Not taking any chances,' Michael observed.

'This one is too sure of himself,' Edward remarked as they returned to the railway tracks. 'He does not stop to check behind.'

'How far ahead is he now?'

'Perhaps thirty minutes. No more.'

Thirty minutes! So close. With a conscious effort Michael pushed all thoughts other than Jackson Mpande from his mind. It was better that way. However he looked at his intention it still amounted to premeditated, first-degree murder. Michael had done with soul-searching. He'd run the emotional gauntlet – Jennifer, Jeremy, Tessa, Dyson – tried the justification route – South Africa, with her history of blood and betrayal, of tribes and races with impossible differences, of traditional foes struggling to develop, to live side-by-side in relative peace.

It was all bullshit.

What it boiled down to was there was not enough space on this earth for Michael King and Jackson Mpande to share. The reasons were no longer clear-cut, they'd been blurred by rage, revenge, by that one single thought that Jackson had to die.

At the river they found where Jackson had left the railway line. He had followed the river for perhaps three miles before turning north along the high game fence which formed the western boundary of the game reserve.

'Why didn't he stay with the river?' Edward wondered. It would have made more sense. The White Umfolozi ran straight into the reserve.

'You forget. He is used to doing the unexpected. There will be a hell of a fuss if he's successful so he's blurring the edges a little. That's how he's been trained.'

It was a little after four in the afternoon. Jackson was making no effort to hide his footprints.

'He does not yet know we follow,' Edward observed when they found where Jackson had slipped under the fence at a point dug and regularly used by warthog.

'Why would he?' Michael commented, crawling through the small gap.

'He is a leopard. He will know soon enough.' He joined Michael inside the reserve. 'This is clever to use such a place. His tracks will soon be hidden. We must think ahead of him.'

'I'm already ahead of the bastard. What is Umfolozi known for?' Michael didn't wait for a reply. 'Rhino. And where do the rhino hang out? All over. Sometimes you see them, sometimes you don't. No good. You've got buses full of VIPs who can't be disappointed. So where do you take them? Somewhere sightings are virtually guaranteed. Top corner. The northern loop roads.'

'You said all that before,' Edward pointed out. 'What makes you so sure?'

'Mpande operates on a law of averages but he's got to take some chances. I doubt he could carry any more than four mines. So he'll maximise the opportunities by minimising the chances.'

'Speak Zulu, young cub. You make no sense in English.'

Michael switched. 'He doesn't know which loops the buses will take. But there is only one road there and back. That's where he'll start. When we reach the road I'll do the bush, you watch the road.

And no talking. Laying the mines will slow him up and we must keep the element of surprise. Let's go.'

They walked in silence, reaching the road in less than fifteen minutes. It was crisscrossed with animal spoor over even the most recent vehicle tracks. They turned north again. The dull heat of the day had abated and game was starting to stir. Through years of experience detecting the whereabouts of rhinoceros, Michael was looking through the bush, not at it. He was relying on Edward for their direction. Even when the Zulu stopped suddenly, Michael's concentration was one hundred per cent focused on picking up the slightest shape or movement that was out of keeping with the surrounding country. 'What is it?' he whispered.

They were at a fork in the road and Edward was staring at Jackson's tracks. 'What does a man do when he lays a mine?'

'Digs a hole.' Michael tensed, then relaxed. The movement he'd seen off to the left was the twitching of a kudu's ear.

Edward pointed. 'He laid his pack down there.' A bit of flattened grass at the edge of the road. But for the lack of shade it might have been caused by an animal lying down. 'Do not move,' Edward hissed. He was half-crouched, his eyes slits as he scanned the ground. The shadows already fell long. Soon they would disappear in the dark of dusk.

'Potholes,' Michael said hoarsely. 'A vehicle would go around them.' He felt suddenly cold. There was one just beside his right foot. Between it and the flattened grass was a space of no more than a metre and he was slap in the fucking middle of it. He felt Edward's hand on his arm.

'Step back.'

'You sure?'

'No.'

Fucking great! 'Where is it?'

'The toe of your left boot.'

Michael looked down. The ground looked normal enough but then he saw what Edward meant. A swept area, devoid even of ant tracks. The toe of his left boot jutted on to it.

'Jesus!'

Gingerly, he crouched and brushed at the sand around his boot. His fingers encountered something solid and he froze. 'Jesus!' he whispered again.

Another centimetre and he'd have been on the rim. Standing, he went to move away, then stopped. What if there was another one? But Edward shook his head. 'Only one. You are safe.'

With legs like jelly, Michael stepped back.

Edward would not look at him. 'I apologise. I did not see it.' He was deeply guilt-stricken. His professionalism had let him down and the embarrassment he felt was total.

Michael knew the Zulu did not expect forgiveness and would despise any attempt at pity. 'If the eyes of the lion are too old to see, now would be a good time to say so.'

Edward looked at his feet. 'They are not too old.' He made no excuse.

'Very well.'

It was all that could be said. If Michael had been

black he would not have dared to censure the older man. If Edward had been white Michael would probably have throttled him. Both knew it. Each respected the other's culture sufficiently to accept the less than satisfactory compromise.

Edward looked fearfully at where the mine was hidden. 'I know nothing of these things.'

Michael didn't know very much about them either. He vaguely remembered being told that the Soviet-made TM-46 mines used in the Caprivi needed a weight of at least 300 kilograms on the pressure plate to cause detonation. So what? They were invariably unreliable and anyway, what if the device at his feet were something else? He advanced on the landmine, half expecting it to be booby-trapped. Lowering himself gingerly to the ground, flat on his stomach, he carefully dug around the sides of the mine. It was an evil-looking thing, like a round ham tin but for the fact that it was packed with TNT. Having cleared the way, Michael lifted it from the hole. He assumed it would need to be disarmed but had no idea how that was done. They could not carry it with them but neither man wanted to leave it lying off the road for some unsuspecting animal to tread on. In the end, Michael wedged it into the fork of a tree. It was the best he could do.

Edward, anxious to make amends, had moved on up the road, taking more notice than ever of its surface. As Michael set off after him Edward disappeared around a bend about a hundred metres ahead. Seconds later Michael heard a shot, followed immediately by the distinctive 'thunk' of a bullet finding its mark. Instinctively, he dived off the road, rolled over and slid backwards into the shrubbery, reaching frantically for the pistol at his belt. One shot. There was no follow-up but the shotgun carried by Edward also remained silent. From where Michael lay, he could not see the road. He had little doubt it was Jackson. And, with each passing minute, his hopes for Edward were fading. Michael's only option was to stay put and wait.

Jackson Mpande had lived too long in the bush to ignore the ever-increasing feeling that someone was behind him. It was instinct, nothing tangible, but he knew better than to carry on without checking. Having laid the first mine, he moved quickly along the road, finding somewhere close to hide. Screened behind bushes, he eased out of his pack and set the AK-47 to semi-automatic fire. Then he waited.

There was no reason to assume that he was being followed but then, the South Africans had got wind of other SWAPO operations in advance so the possibility of informers at Base 37 could not be ruled out. It would be dark in just under two hours. That was fine. The moon was nearly full and the clouds of earlier in the afternoon had rolled away. He had three more mines to lay before turning back to the fence. By morning, he would be long gone, heading south for Kwa-Mashu.

Hunkered down, Kalashnikov assault rifle at the ready, Jackson's mind was on only one thing. The job at hand. Half-an-hour later, his caution was rewarded when an African appeared around the bend in the road. The shotgun, slung over one shoulder, showed he was not trained for this sort of thing but Jackson knew immediately that the man was following his tracks. With no hesitation, he fired, grunting with satisfaction as his target crumpled and fell, like a floppy ragdoll, the solid 7.62mm bullet striking home, just below the heart.

Jackson waited. There could be more than one. No-one came. The man on the road had not moved. Jackson studied him. Barefoot, threadbare shorts, T-shirt, he was certainly not military. Nor was he a ranger, too scruffy. A poacher? Perhaps. There were plenty of animal tracks on the road, it was possible that he had been after four-legged prey. Twenty minutes went by and still no-one came. Leaving his pack, Jackson cautiously approached the fallen man.

Edward was not dead. Some terrible force had hit him unseen, knocking him backwards. His chest felt as though he'd been charged by a Cape buffalo. He could not move. After what seemed like an eternity, a face appeared above him. Jackson Mpande. Cold eyes stared down at him but Edward was too far gone for fear. The agony in his chest was so acute he was scarcely aware of anything else. He tried to speak but words would not form. Lung blood bubbled up and out of his mouth.

'Are you alone?'

Edward heard the words but they made no sense. He stared up with pain-filled eyes.

Cruelly, Jackson kicked Edward in the side. It was not a vicious blow but shock waves joined those of the bullet wound and Edward gasped at the added pain.

'Answer me, old man. Are you on your own?'

In that last instant before death lay with him, his mind cleared. He was unable to speak, drowning in his own blood, but finding strength, Edward knew he had to protect the young cub who would be hiding back along the track. He nodded. With his very last breath, Edward had the feeling he was flying.

Jackson stood looking at the dead man. He had told the truth. No-one that close to death would lie. Obviously a poacher, although his weapon was surprisingly good. Jackson knew that those who lived by their wits and the gun usually spent more on the tools of their trade than on themselves. This one had simply been in the wrong place at the wrong time. Dragging the body off the road and in to the bushes, Jackson made no attempt to conceal any other evidence. Night was coming and with it, the predators. Africa took care of its own. But he took the shotgun.

He retrieved his pack and set off again. Thanks to Edward's extraordinary act of loyalty, Jackson did not bother to backtrack and check the mine. Michael's footprints on the road just a hundred metres back remained undetected. Jackson Mpande had made his first mistake.

An hour had passed since Michael heard the shot. Muscles cramping, he moved, rising stiffly to his feet. It would be suicidal to follow the road. He crept forward through the bush and came level with the bend, now able to see along the next straight stretch of road. Empty. Still, Michael couldn't take any chances. Keeping out of sight, he pushed on as before, using every bit of available cover. His senses listened for the slightest sound, any movement in the shadows. Michael nearly fell over Edward's body.

He had known the man for less than a day, so he was unprepared for the tide of sadness that swept over him. 'Dear God, when will it end?'

There was nothing he could do for the old Zulu, but his spirit was a different matter. Using his knife, Michael cut a small branch of buffalo thorn acacia and laid it on top of the body. Even if it were never found, Edward's spirit would have somewhere to call home.

A few moments later, after establishing that the shotgun was missing, Michael found where Jackson had waited to ambush Edward. And then, incredibly, he saw footprints heading off along the road. The man was so cocksure he was still travelling in the open. So he must believe that Edward had been on his own.

'Think ahead of the bastard.' Michael's mind cleared. Jackson thought he was safe. But he'd proved to be cautious. Tracking behind him was dangerous. Michael still believed he knew where Jackson was heading. So he decided to get there first. If the tracks inside the reserve were still as he remembered, he could cut through and be waiting along the back loop road ahead of Jackson. And that was Michael's first mistake.

★

Ideally, Jackson would have liked to mine the two loop roads. However, there was a common stretch linking Okhuklo and Ngolotsha loops which lay closer to the western perimeter fence. Whichever loop the tour buses took, they'd still have to use that one section of road. He'd lost time over the poacher, and anyway, three mines close together could cause even more havoc. So Jackson changed his plan. Field flexibility it was called. Instead of exiting the park where he'd come in, he'd cut the fence further north and head across country to Ulundi. He could still make it to Kwa-Mashu the following day.

Michael stopped jogging and wiped sweat from his brow. He was back against the western perimeter but it had taken longer to get there than he'd thought. Mpande could well be on the first of the loop roads by now. He had, by his reckoning, another half-a-kilometre before reaching the common road that linked the two loops. The sun was nothing more than a crimson rim on the horizon. It would be dark in half an hour.

Jackson brushed sand carefully over the last of his mines. Done. Not before time. The dead poacher was playing on his mind. In his experience, the unexpected was often the cause of the unsuccessful. He couldn't wait to get out of the park and away. He'd heard a lion roaring a few minutes ago. This time of day was not a good one to be on foot. Not particularly superstitious, Jackson nonetheless had a bad feeling about this job.

He had committed the park roads to memory.

The western perimeter was a good kilometre from where he stood. He turned to leave, then froze at the sound of a sudden rustle not far off the road. His eyes picked up the bulky shape of a browsing black rhinoceros. Like most people who spend a great deal of time in the African bush, Jackson was not unduly worried about encountering dangerous game. Most animals were more frightened of man than the other way around. Besides, he had his AK-47. There was no wind. The animal probably couldn't smell him. Slowly, Jackson edged himself closer to a tree. The caution proved unnecessary as the cow lost interest in the bush she was feeding on and wandered further away. If she walked down the road . . . Well, that was a risk he could do little about. He was more concerned at the moment with getting out of the park.

Jackson's change of plans, Michael's determination to reach the outer loop before him, put the two men on a direct collision course.

TWENTY

Michael would have sworn he was fit but the last few months had taken their toll. The run through the bush to get ahead of Jackson and the fact that he'd had very little to eat in the past couple of days also sapped his strength. He had but one thought in his mind and that was to reach the back loop before Jackson. The animal tracks he was following would lead to a section common to both the circular drives. It was just ahead of him.

A trained man would have been more cautious. Jackson was trained. Michael was not. He passed within two metres of where Jackson crouched.

Jackson had been moving quickly along the road when he heard a twig snap, then another. Stepping quietly to one side and dropping into the darkness, he knew immediately that the sound had been made by no animal. There was a moment of stunned surprise when Jackson recognised Michael, then he was thinking clearly once more.

Michael stood still for a moment finding his bearings, then turned and made his way swiftly towards Jackson. The light was fading fast and he was concentrating on reaching the loop road. He didn't immediately notice the sudden presence of footprints. He'd gone eight or nine paces beyond where Jackson hid before realisation sank in. His senses screamed a warning. Diving forward, he rolled, pistol in hand, knowing it might already be too late.

Jackson watched Michael go past and realised that he only had a few seconds before his footprints were seen. Stepping onto the road, the Kalashnikov held waist high, he squeezed the trigger, holding low, braced for the burst of automatic fire. A single shot tore into the sand and Jackson swore viciously. The selector was still set for the ambush on that bloody old poacher. It gave Michael the few precious seconds he needed but, because he was still rolling, his shot missed too.

Everything seemed to be happening in slow motion. Michael saw Jackson flick the selector and take aim again, mocking evil in his eyes. He steadied his own aim. It was all taking so long. One agonising split second was taking forever. His finger tightened on the trigger.

The blast came. Not from Michael's Browning, he was still squeezing. Not from Jackson who, in that strangely dreamlike speed, was clutching his upper arm, turning, eyes wide, weapon spinning away in a lazy arc, as he started to run. Two more shots. From behind!

The bush came alive with shadowy shapes and shouted words.

'Got him.'

'Bastard's gapping it.'

'Van Schalkwyk, Pienaar, Macmillan, get after him.'

Michael was trying to make sense of it all. His world, his nightmare, suddenly in overdrive. Men. Shots. Voices. Jackson. Mines. 'Mines,' he roared suddenly, his brain miraculously crystallising. 'There are mines on the road.'

'What the fuck do you think we're here for, a picnic? We've got the mines. Right men, let's get that little Commie, I want to wrap this one up.'

A chorus of 'yes sirs' came from the darkness.

Michael picked himself up from the road, dusting off his shorts.

'You hit Englesman?'

'No. Thank . . .'

'You *are* Michael King I take it?'

'Devilliers?'

A heavily set man planted himself in front of Michael. 'Who the fuck you expecting? Nelson Mandela?' He was furious and making no attempt to hide it.

'No, I . . .'

'We had him. We had the bastard. Then you blunder on to the road like some demented knight on a mission of mercy. I told you, King. Don't fuck up.'

'Me! Me fuck up. What about you? Your lot only winged him.' Michael was suddenly as furious as Devilliers. 'You're not even supposed to be here. I had him in my sights. What are you doing here anyway?'

'Saving your arse.'

'Bullshit!'

'If I had any brains I'd have let him take you out.'

'If you had any brains you'd have let me know you were coming. What am I, a fucking mind-reader?'

'Shut up, King. Go and sit down before you fall down.'

'To hell with this,' Michael snapped.

'You fucking little boy scout. We *had* him, don't you understand? And now, thanks to you, we've lost him again.'

A shape materialised next to Devilliers. 'Sir.'

'What?' Devilliers bellowed.

The man cleared his throat. 'Ah, you might like to have this conversation later, sir.'

'Why?' Devilliers roared. 'What else have I got to do?' He lowered his voice and grated. 'This clown here nearly gets killed and we save his arse. You'd think he'd be grateful wouldn't you? But no. All he can do is tell me what to do with my orders.'

'Yes, sir.'

Michael thought he heard a grin in the man's voice.

'Now, thanks to Mr Bloody King, I've got three good men out there chasing around after that whacko terrorist. What kind of an idiot blunders into an ambush? We *had* him, Bob. We bloody *had* him.'

'Yes, sir.'

'Jesus!' Devilliers exploded in frustration. 'I don't fucking believe it.'

'What are you doing here? You said . . .'

'I know what I said. Bob, go and pick up that little shit's toys. At least we know he's not armed.' Devilliers squared up to Michael. 'Things change. Lucky for you, hey?'

Michael realised it was true. If Devilliers and his men hadn't come along who would have fired first, him or Jackson? Which of them would now be lying dead on the road? It was something he'd never know.

Bob returned carrying the Kalashnikov and Michael's Remington. Devilliers jerked his head angrily towards Michael and Bob handed him the shotgun.

'Let's go. I don't want to be out here all night.' He turned to Michael. 'By the way, I assume you don't know anything about the body back there?'

'That's . . .'

'Just as I thought, nothing.'

'Edward,' Michael finished in even tones.

'Not a damned thing.'

'Nothing,' Michael agreed.

'Deluxe.'

Devilliers thought for a moment. 'You said you were inside that fucker's head. Where's he gone?'

There was the sound of Devilliers scratching while Michael tried to work out what Jackson would do now. Finally, he said, 'The main camp's no good, too much security right now. He's got three men after him. He's wounded, we don't know how badly but probably needs medical attention. He's clever. As soon as he starts to think straight I reckon he'll hide, lose your men then either head for the western boundary or wait and hijack a tourist car when the reserve reopens to the public.'

In the gloom Michael saw Devilliers' head nodding in agreement. 'We can secure for a hijack so my money is on the fence. Let's go. Oh, and King, you so much as step on a twig and I'll break your fucking neck.'

'I'd like to see you try, you arrogant bastard.'

There was a long silence in the darkness. Then Devilliers said quite mildly, 'My parents were married.'

Jackson was getting desperate. On the road, when all hell exploded, his only thought had been to flee. He was good in the bush, sure-footed and keen-eyed, confident he could get away. He was barely aware of the throbbing in his upper right arm as he tore through the undergrowth. But the longer he ran the more it became clear that as good as he was, the men behind were just as competent. The shock of being hit had started to kick in, draining his strength. He had no idea how bad the wound was but he suspected more than a flesh injury. The ache was deep and getting stronger by the minute.

After ten minutes, he realised he'd have to out-think rather than out-run his pursuers. He had to reach the fence, it was the only way. The wire-cutters! They were in his pack back on the road. 'Double back,' he was thinking. 'They won't expect it.' He slowed, then stopped, listening hard. Yes, they were still there, following his footsteps by torch-light, a couple of hundred metres behind him. Moving swiftly but quietly, Jackson swung west then turned almost due north. There was nothing he could do about his trail but, with luck, he could still retrieve the wire-cutters and get to the fence ahead of them. He had the advantage of knowing where he was going. The men behind were slowed by the need to follow his footprints. At least they didn't have dogs.

The black rhinoceros was on heat, irritable, and in need of a mate. She had been heading for her favourite waterhole when the sound of shots rang out. She reacted instinctively, charging blindly into the bush, completely unnerved by the loud and unexpected noise. In panic, she was seeking the comfort of familiar territory, crashing through shrubs and low trees as though they weren't there. She covered a distance of nearly three kilometres before suddenly stopping to stand stock still in the dense undergrowth. Relying on hearing and smell, she would wait there for hours to make sure all was safe.

Michael, Sacha and Bob had fanned out and were carefully moving south-west. On Sacha's instruc-tions, they were not using torches. The single crack of a twig sounded so out of place. There, a shadow, coming towards them. It crossed a patch of open ground.

Jackson. He must have doubled back to lose the others. He was heading directly towards them. All three crouched, waiting. They could hear the laboured breathing. Suddenly he was there, moving fast, clutching his right arm.

With absolutely no warning the bush erupted and a black rhinoceros burst from cover, snorting with anger. She did not stop. Jackson might have been a bush, a buck or a man, she didn't care. It was there, in front of her, and her instincts said kill it. Head held high she thundered straight at him. Jackson turned and ran but Michael could see that he wasn't going to reach the tree. At the last moment, the rhinoceros lowered her head and thrust upwards, scything sixty centimetres of unpowdered, so-called aphrodisiac between Jackson's legs and tossing him upwards. The horn had penetrated flesh and bone. Jackson remained impaled. Irritated beyond belief, the cow lowered her head and shook it, trying to dislodge him. The wound ripped open. Jackson screamed. With one last violent shake, she was free of him. Snorting with renewed fright at heaven knows what, the rhinoceros blundered away. She'd had a thoroughly disagreeable night.

Michael was first to reach Jackson's writhing body. He shone his torch down. The horn had caught Jackson just beneath his testicles, penetrating upwards into his anus. Trying to shake him loose, the horn had ripped a massive hole in Jackson's lower body, finally tearing free with Jackson's penis and testicles. His entire lower torso was one gaping mess of entrails and blood.

'Erk!' Sacha's exclamation was made with no inflection, almost conversational. 'I'd say your man is done for.'

Michael's stomach heaved. Jackson stared up at him, his eyes pleading. 'Help me,' he whispered.

'Deluxe,' Sacha said. 'A fitting end for the bastard wouldn't you say?'

Michael thought of Jeremy, Jennifer, and Tessa. He thought of Edward lying beside the track and of Dyson in hospital. He thought of others unknown who might also have died at the hands of this man.

'Help me,' Jackson begged. 'Kill me.'

Kill him! It was all Michael had thought of doing. Now, as he stared down at his enemy, it was the one thing he didn't want to do. 'Die in your own time, Jackson Mpande,' he said harshly.

'Please,' Jackson pleaded. 'Kill me.'

'You heard the man,' Sacha said cheerfully. 'No can do. Drop dead.'

Jackson Mpande did drop dead. But it took him fifty-two minutes.

TWENTY-ONE

Michael was glad the moaning had stopped. He'd never heard a man in so much pain. The sound of it got inside him. The satisfaction he'd expected to feel was missing. *Jennifer and Jeremy. Can you hear this? Does it give you any satisfaction? Or are you weeping, as angels do, in the face of such suffering? Tessa. Can you hear him? Does it help you? Dear God! Let it be over soon.*

Jackson Mpande's death was as much of a relief to Michael as it must have been for Jackson. 'We can't just leave him,' Michael protested when it became obvious that Devilliers and his men were planning to go.

'What do you suggest?' Devilliers asked with heavy irony. 'Give him a decent burial?'

'Cover him with stones at least.'

'Forget it, man. There'll be nothing left by morning. Anyway, we've got a good fifteen kilometres to walk tonight.' He glared in Michael's direction. 'You're coming with us.'

'Where to?'

'Camp. In the wilderness area.'

Michael was surprised. 'How'd you manage that? It's off limits to most people.'

'Friends in high places,' Devilliers said shortly.

Something was worrying Sacha Devilliers. 'Our sources informed us that Mpande had four mines. We've only found three.'

'Not a problem. It's up a tree. Near that other body I know nothing about.'

'Disarmed?'

'Sorry, didn't know how.'

Devilliers sighed. 'We'll fetch it in the morning. I don't suppose the bloody thing is going anywhere.' He lit a cigarette. 'Good result back there. Untidy but good.'

'Are you going to explain what you're doing here? For that matter, how the hell did you get here so quickly?'

'Chopper. It's at Mpila Camp.'

'Okay, that's how. Now, why?'

Devilliers appeared to think about it. 'Why not?' he said finally. He inhaled smoke noisily. 'Remember I told you I'd been approached about Mpande?'

'Yes.'

'Well, the thing we've been working on for months blew apart, big time. The shit hit the fan and I lost two men.'

'What was it?'

'You don't need to know, King. Drugs. That good enough?'

'Yes.'

'I don't mind taking chances, know what I

mean? It's my job. But when the scum start threatening my family, that's different. Makes it personal. I got angry and that made me careless.' He grunted with self-disgust. 'It cost me two men and the entire operation. We had to pull out and fast. Just when I'm thinking what a fucking waste of time, I get a call from my other . . . the one I told you about. He's panicking big time. Says he doesn't want a fucking novice after Mpande. I'd have told him to shove it but for the fact that I didn't seem to have much else to do. Besides, we all need to get into the bush once in a while.'

'Lucky for me.'

'Nice to hear you say it, King.'

Michael grinned ruefully in the darkness.

'So we've set up camp on the river. Nice spot. No neighbours. Do a bit of training for a few days.'

'And the drugs thing? Exactly who do you work for?'

'Ah!' Devilliers tried to dismiss it. 'Look, I've told you I'm legit. I'm freelance – army, cops, Bureau of State Security, other organisations. In other words, King, I'm a paid but private soldier. I try to remain impartial, know what I mean. I was working for BOSS this time, most of my jobs come from them. So set your mind at rest about who I answer to. As for the job? It happens. I should be used to it by now. There's enough there for the bureau to take it on. They won't get the big boys but at least we hurt the network. It'll be a while before anything else can be set up.' He turned belligerent suddenly. 'Do you have any fucking idea what it's like? To get that close and then lose it?'

'I can imagine.' Michael had a fleeting thought that, try as hard as he might, Sacha Devilliers' idea of 'impartial' was well wide of the *Oxford English Dictionary*'s.

'Yeah.' Devilliers lit another cigarette. 'Lucky Strike, good name, hey? Tell me something, King. Just what did you intend to do with Mpande once you caught him?'

'Kill him.'

'Ja!' Devilliers sounded amused.

'I hated him enough to do it. I wanted him to die hard, the old Zulu way.'

'Stake up the arse? So, courtesy of *uBejane* you got your wish.'

'Something like that.'

'Know what I think, King? I think it's just as well that old rhino came along. You don't have the stomach for that kind of thing.'

'I believed I did.'

'And now?'

'He's dead. It's over.'

'Lucky you,' Devilliers said softly, leaving Michael with the impression he was talking about something else altogether.

Shortly after that Sacha Devilliers dropped behind Michael, leaving him free to think his own thoughts as they walked in the moonlight. A jumble of mainly unpleasant memories crowded his head but he let them come and, by the time they reached the camp, Michael felt that he could, at last, hope to find the peace that for so long had eluded him.

Sacha showed Michael to a tent. He was asleep within two minutes.

Waking with the dawn, Michael felt more relaxed than he could remember, with a hunger on him that could no longer be denied. The smell of frying onions was in the air and his stomach rumbled in anticipation. Leaving the tent he made his way towards the fire where various people sat around warming their hands on steaming mugs of coffee. Sacha sat at a table. 'Morning, sleep well?'

'Morning, like a log.'

A figure crouched at the fire stood up and turned around. Michael stared. In the early morning light, Annie Devilliers looked about fifteen, her blonde hair braided into a single plait down her back. She wore khaki shorts and a white T-shirt. 'Good morning.' The smile was brief as she went to the table and sat down beside her husband.

'Pull up a chair.' Sacha waved his hand vaguely. 'Coffee's on. Food won't be long.'

Michael poured coffee, helped himself to sugar and joined them. Up close, he could see lines of strain around Annie's mouth and eyes.

'After breakfast we'll go and pick up that other mine. I want it out of there and rendered safe. Think you can find it again?' He didn't wait for Michael to reply. 'After that you're free to go.' He glanced sideways at Annie. 'Your patient got his wish last night. One SWAPO gentleman, dead as a dodo.'

'He's not my patient.' Annie's voice carried just a hint of exasperation.

'He was your patient.'

She rose suddenly, snatching up her coffee. 'Have it your own way. Excuse me.' She made her way to a big tent nearby and disappeared inside.

'Wrong time of the month.' Sacha grinned at Michael, shaking his head. 'Women eh? Who can work them out?'

'Is she here for her own protection?'

'Ja, man. I told you last night. My family were being threatened.'

Michael made no response but it did cross his mind that Sacha might have shown a bit more sympathy towards his wife who, presumably, had been whisked away from her practice to spend God knows how long hidden away in the bush.

Bob slapped a tin plate in front of him. Four sausages, bacon, three eggs swimming in grease, baked beans and a heap of burned onions. It was the best-looking meal he'd seen in a long time. Sacha left the table saying only that he'd be back in half-an-hour and that Michael should be ready to come with him. The other men had also departed and were nowhere to be seen.

Michael was pouring a second cup of coffee when he heard footsteps behind him and, turning, saw Annie approaching. In her eyes there was something akin to disgust. 'I didn't think you'd do it,' she said without preamble. 'I really thought you'd come to your senses.'

'That's easy for you to say,' he said, stung by her criticism.

She sat down heavily. 'Was it worth it? Do you feel better now?'

'Yes. Does that surprise you?'

She brushed a hand tiredly across her forehead. 'An eye for an eye,' she said softly. 'It's a bit bloody basic wouldn't you say?'

She was very upset and Michael realised it wasn't just over Jackson Mpande. 'Basic or not there are things you still don't know about,' he told her quietly. 'Jackson turned up in London, murdered Tessa and then tried to kill my oldest friend, his own brother.'

'Oh, Michael.' Her eyes filled with tears. 'I'm so sorry. Forgive me. I can be a bit of a bitch sometimes.'

'I'm not sorry he's dead,' Michael said flatly.

'No,' she whispered. 'I daresay you aren't.'

'But I didn't do it, Annie. A rhino got him. I would have though. I would have killed the bastard. And I don't know how I feel about that.'

She reached over and put a hand on his arm. 'One day, Michael, you're going to be very glad that you didn't.' She seemed unaware that her fingers were brushing back and forth. 'I know what it does to people.'

'Sacha?'

She nodded and took a deep shuddering breath.

'It must be very difficult for you, Annie.'

'Yes,' she agreed. 'And it makes me so very angry. He has no right to allow his work to impact on mine.' She broke off, snatching her hand away from his arm. 'Forgive me, I shouldn't be telling you these things.'

Michael smiled at her slightly. 'Of all people, you should know how important it is to unburden yourself.'

She gave a tiny grin back. 'Touché, Mr King.'

'Want some good news?'

'Yes please.'

'You were right about Andrew. He could hear all the time. He's talking nineteen-to-the-dozen.'

Real pleasure shone in her eyes. 'I'm glad.' She hesitated, then asked, 'What are you going to do now?'

'Get my life back together I suppose.'

'Is Andrew a part of that?'

He nodded slowly. 'It won't be easy, but yes.'

'You won't regret it.'

'And what about you?'

The question startled her. 'My life is under control.'

Michael cocked his head to one side. 'That's not saying much.'

Annie looked away. 'It's better than some have,' she said softly. 'I knew what I was getting into.'

Michael went to say more but stopped himself. It was none of his business.

They were talking of other things when Sacha and his men returned. 'You ready to roll, King?'

Michael and Annie rose.

'You're not coming,' Sacha said curtly to his wife.

'Why not?' She looked set to argue.

'Because I say so, Annie. That's why.'

Behind him Sacha's men exchanged uneasy looks.

Annie stepped up to her husband. 'If I want to come, you can't stop me.'

'Bob,' Sacha called.

'Sir?' The man stepped forward reluctantly.

Sacha spoke to him but his eyes never left Annie's face. 'Stay in camp and make sure my wife stays here too.'

Furious, Annie spun around and walked stiff with anger back to her tent.

'Come on,' Devilliers snapped. 'We haven't got all day.' Without waiting he turned and strode out of the camp.

Michael opened his mouth to protest about the high-handed manner in which he had treated Annie but Bob shook his head and muttered, 'Better not, Mr King. He's a good man but he hasn't a clue how to treat women. The job always comes first. Leave it.'

Michael wanted to say goodbye to Annie but, with Sacha now out of sight and the others moving off after him, he snatched up the shotgun and set off after them.

The big male baboon led his troop along the dusty road. It was a large group, nearly fifty in all, strung out along the road for several hundred metres. Newborn babies clung to their mothers' bellies, older offspring grabbed a ride wherever they could. Individuals would stop to examine rocks, turning them over to check for ants and grubs. One cheeky male near the back leapt at a female in front of him. What took place amounted to rape but she didn't seem to mind, standing still until he had finished then resuming her seemingly aimless walk.

The dominant male at the front scampered off the road and into a tree, those immediately behind scattering into the bush. What had caught his eye was a curious round thing which he picked up, looking underneath in the hope of discovering something edible. Finding nothing, he lost interest in the flat object and tossed it out of the tree. It landed on its rim and rolled before encountering a scrubby bush and falling, right side up, just under its trailing branches.

The troop of baboon headed off across country towards their usual watering place.

'Here,' Michael said, recognising the fork in the road. 'This is where he laid it.'

'And now?'

'Up that tree,' Michael pointed. 'Hang on, I'll get it.'

'No, you stay put.' Devilliers turned to Macmillan. 'Shin up and pass the bloody thing down.'

The man unslung his weapon, laid it down beside the road and stepped into the bush. He climbed easily.

Sacha moved to the foot of the tree, ready to retrieve the mine.

'Nothing here,' Macmillan called down.

Sacha stepped back to see better. 'Are you sure?'

'Not a damned thing.'

He looked across at Michael. 'Are you certain this is the tree?'

'Absolutely.'

Sacha shrugged. He took one more step back and froze. They all heard his muttered, 'Shit!'

Macmillan jumped down and dropped to his knees beside Sacha. 'It's the mine.' He called out to the others. 'The boss is standing on the bloody mine.'

Everyone stared at Sacha. He had not moved. 'These things need a bit more than my weight,' he said calmly. 'What I want you all to do is get the fuck out of here.'

No-one moved.

Sacha smiled grimly. 'Do as you are ordered. Now.'

The men backed off up the road slowly. Michael went to follow.

'Hey, King.'

He stopped.

Devilliers was pale and sweating. 'I hadn't planned to say this so it could come out all wrong. And I haven't the time to fuck around because this thing could blow at any time. So listen and don't interrupt. Annie likes you. She liked you right from the beginning. A man like me, hell, there's no place for a woman in my life. Marrying Annie was a mistake. So here's what I'm saying. If I walk away from this thing I'm going to walk away from Annie too. She'll need a friend. That's all I'm saying, King.'

Michael saw fear in the man's eyes.

'Well?' Devilliers demanded. 'Can I count on you?'

'Why don't you come over here and we'll talk about it?'

'I don't need this, King. Can I count on you or not?'

Michael nodded slowly.

'Deluxe. Now, get the fuck away from here.'

Michael walked away and stood with the others.

They heard Sacha bellow, 'Here goes fellas.' Michael saw him dive over the low bush. Nothing. Devilliers was rolling and scrambling to his feet, running desperately towards them. Nothing. Fear was being replaced by relief. He stopped halfway up the road where they waited, hands on hips, grinning, when the mine exploded. The force of the explosion blew him off his feet, flat on his back, landing in the middle of the road. Even before the last of the flying debris hit the ground, they were all, Michael included, running back towards him.

Devilliers had a thin trickle of blood coming from his nose. Otherwise he appeared uninjured. 'Boss,' one of the men shouted.

Sacha Devilliers lay perfectly still. As they hovered anxiously wondering whether to move him or not, a deep, rasping chuckle began. He was coughing and laughing at the same time. It grew into a bull-roaring belly laugh that had the others staring incredulously. When he could speak he said, 'You'd think those fucking Russians could get something right wouldn't you?'

The conference was over, the delegates enthused and still talking about their rhino sightings. Sacha arranged for one of his men to fly Michael to Ulundi in the helicopter so he could collect his vehicle and camping equipment.

Michael retrieved his belongings from Edward's unlocked house. Then he headed north, alone, into the valleys of the Black Umfolozi River. He spent six days on his own, not seeing another soul. There, he spoke to Jennifer, Jeremy and Tessa. He remembered his childhood on UBejane. He thought back on conversations shared with Dyson and Wilson about their growing concern for South Africa and in particular, the Zulu nation. He recalled Tessa's turbulent youth and realised how glad he was that she'd found peace in her last few years. He cried for Jennifer. He ached to think that Jeremy had not even reached four short years before his life had been so brutally taken from him. And he missed Andrew.

He also found himself wondering if Sacha Devilliers really had walked away from Annie.

After six days of solitude, Michael King knew exactly what he was going to do next. Some of it wouldn't be easy.

First, he was going to visit Wilson and Nandi in

Kwa-Mashu. There were sorry words ahead but there was no way around them.

Then he was going back to England to collect his son. He was impatient to see him again and anxious to let Claire know that all was well with her oldest child.

And after that there was the rest of his life to see to. Those six days of soul-searching revealed to Michael exactly what he wanted to do.

He'd had three options. He could, as he and Jennifer discussed, consider a political career. There was a woman in Johannesburg, Helen Suzman, the sole remaining member of the Progressive Party in office after the previous year's elections, who might find a use for him. She was the thorn in the Nationalists' side, the one voice in parliament that dared to question them. Not that it made any difference to their increasingly repressive policies, it didn't. But what Suzman was doing by raising questions officially was getting them, and the answers, published in *Hansard*. And that publication was available anywhere in the world, for anyone to read.

His second option was to rejoin Umfolozi's black rhinoceros project. New funding had come from somewhere and it had been made clear to Michael in a letter that reached him in Johannesburg that he would be favourably considered as a member of the team.

When UBejane was sold, Michael's share had been placed in a fixed deposit account that paid high interest and rolled over every two years. The next two-year period was due to expire in six months. His third option was to use the money to buy his own cane farm.

The catalyst for the choice he made was Andrew. A life in politics was a busy one. Michael would have to be both mother and father to his son. And he couldn't do that if he was constantly travelling or working long hours. He ruled it out.

The wildlife project would allow time with Andrew and, depending on who else was in the program, the chance of company his own age. But ultimately Andrew would need schooling. And Michael couldn't bear the thought of his son in boarding school. He ruled it out as well.

He supposed he'd always known where he'd end up. It was the right choice for him and he was happy with it.

It took him a little longer to find Wilson than he'd expected.

When Michael tried to visit Kwa-Mashu to find him the authorities decided that his reason for doing so, to bring family news to a man who once worked for him, wasn't good enough. A permit to enter the all-black area was denied. Undeterred, Michael approached various Africans working in Durban until he found one who had heard of Wilson and agreed to get a message to him. After two not unpleasant days of staying at the Royal Hotel on Durban's beach front, he received a message from Wilson. They met eventually, about a kilometre from the sprawling township, the elderly Zulu looking furtively around before getting quickly into the canvas-covered back of Michael's Land Rover.

He drove inland for fifteen minutes, along dirt roads, through fields of lush sugar cane. There was a sliding window behind the cab but they did not speak. Finally, Michael found what he was looking for, a place where they could not be seen. They both emerged from the vehicle and embraced. 'We should be safe from prying eyes here,' he said to Wilson.

'We are never safe,' Wilson replied. 'Not any more.'

'What is it they fear? Why treat a meeting like this with suspicion? It's crazy.'

'So it is.' Wilson agreed. 'But we forget our manners, you and I. I see you, my son. What is so important that you would risk this meeting?'

'I see you, old father. Many bad things have happened. It is my duty to speak with you now.'

'Even as I fear your words my ears are open.'

Michael left nothing out.

Wilson heard him in silence. Whatever his feelings, they did not show. 'It is as the *sangoma* predicted so many years ago,' he said once Michael had stopped speaking. 'A great evil will touch the lives of two families. And so it has come to this.' Finally Wilson allowed tears to flow. They slid unchecked down his cheeks. But though sorrow racked him, so too did shame at the deeds of Jackson. 'It is possible to run from a great evil if it would try to catch you. But if that evil is inside, there is nowhere to run. Justice had to be done.

But I am thinking that justice is like a fire. It burns long after the flames have died down. My son, Jackson, broke many of our laws. This is unforgivable. His punishment is just. While I have no quarrel with this I have to tell you, *nkosi*, that I am glad your hands are not stained with his blood. If that were so you would never wash it off. Not in my memory or your own.'

'That's true, *Babu*, though I would not have hesitated.'

The tears had stopped. 'He was my son. He grew into a man I could not respect. We cannot always guarantee a good crop when we plant the seed. That is all I have to say.'

Michael could not help but admire Wilson's fatalistic acceptance of what must have been devastating news. 'It is over now.'

'No. It is only just beginning.' Wilson sighed. 'The *sangoma* tried to tell me. There is much to do and my blood does not run as hot as once it did. She said I must use my time well and be satisfied. I have tried to do this but now, as I near the end of my life, I find myself wondering if I have made any difference at all.'

'The way forward will be slow, I agree.'

'And the way behind is closed.'

Michael felt in his pocket and handed Wilson a packet of Amorpha Aromatic tobacco, for he knew the old man loved his pipe. 'There are two hard things in this life.'

'Tell me.' Wilson fingered the packet lovingly before producing a well-worn pipe.

'The first is knowing yourself and what you want to do with your given time in this world.'

'I agree.'

'You always knew.'

'The *sangoma* showed me my path. Without her guidance I would have been less sure.' Wilson rubbed tobacco in his palm, filled the bowl and lit up. 'And what is the other?'

'The other?' Michael smiled wryly. 'The other is even harder than the first.'

'Yes,' Wilson agreed, anticipating what Michael was about to say.

'How is it done?' Michael asked.

Wilson let smoke trickle around the stem of his pipe. 'It is done,' he said slowly, appreciating the fact that Michael was giving him the final word, 'by keeping in your heart that which, in your head, is sometimes impossible to follow. It is done by believing in the purity of your dreams. And it is done by allowing no other to poison your intent.'

Michael remained silent.

'You have come to a decision, my son.'

'Yes.'

'Good.' Wilson did not ask what it was. That Michael had come to him was good enough. 'Where will you live?'

'Where I belong. Zululand.'

'Ah! Truly a good decision. You are a son of this land.'

'Yes,' Michael agreed. 'And it is time my son became one too.'

'Your son is already of this land, *nkosi*. A river can never break free of its source.'

It was dangerous for them to be together for too long. Michael drove Wilson back to Kwa-Mashu and dropped him on the road where he'd picked him up.

'*Hamba kahle*, my son.'

'*Shlala kahle, Babu*.'

As he drove away Michael was thinking that while it was all very well for them to wish each other to go well and stay well, circumstances escalating within South Africa might mean that neither of them would ever know if the other had. He did not expect to see Wilson again.

Michael spent nearly a month back in England so that Andrew could get to know him again. The child treated him like a stranger for a few days, but within a week Andrew's affections transferred from Claire to Michael.

Dyson, who was still experiencing headaches and dizziness from his injuries, spent a week with them in Hertford. There was much to be said between him and Michael.

'I'm glad you went to see my father.'

'I had to. He had to hear it from me.'

They were in the garden, down near the duck pond, enjoying the Indian summer sunshine.

'Did he ever learn that I was still alive?' Dyson was referring to Jackson.

'No.'

'Are you sorry that you didn't kill him?'

'Yes and no. I hated him so much that killing him would have been a pleasure. Now it's over I'm glad I didn't.' Michael shrugged. 'It's complicated and it's hard to discuss this with you.'

'It is complicated,' Dyson agreed. 'But do not worry about speaking of it to me. I would have killed him myself if I could. However, while I wanted him dead I'm pleased that you didn't kill him.'

'Remember when we were kids?' Michael asked suddenly. 'How easy it all was back then.'

Dyson grinned. 'We couldn't wait to grow up.'

'Yeah! And look what happened when we did.'

Dyson was silent for a moment. Then, 'I was in love with Tessa.'

'She told me.'

'She knew?'

'Apparently.'

'Thank God!' Dyson rubbed a hand over his eyes. 'It was eating me up, the thought that she'd died without ever knowing.'

'I think she loved you too,' Michael said softly. 'She just couldn't come to terms with it.'

Unshed tears glistened in Dyson's eyes. 'How would you have felt if we'd got together?'

'Married? A bit worried about cultural differences.'

'That's all?'

Michael thought about it. 'No,' he said honestly.

Dyson nodded. 'Thank you.'

'You'd have been equally concerned about the racial thing.'

'I was.'

Michael sighed.

'You're right, *Nkawu*. Being an adult is hard work.'

When the time came to leave England, Michael had mixed emotions. He couldn't wait to get back to Africa but he was leaving so much of himself behind.

'If it doesn't work out for you back home, would you consider coming here to live?' Claire asked.

'I hear what you're saying, Mother, but no. This place is too tame.'

She'd smiled ruefully. 'I used to worry that you were growing up wild. In a way, I guess you were.' She hugged him. 'It hasn't done you any harm. I'm very proud of you.'

He left England promising to come back once a year.

In the departure lounge at Heathrow he was surprised to be confronted by Inspector John Dyer. 'Going somewhere?' Michael inquired.

'Nope. Heard you were in town. Came to see you.'

'What can I do for you?'

'I'm a patient man, King. I have to be, my job demands it. But I also have a tidy mind and I need to know. What happened?'

'Are you asking me to confess to murder?'

'No.'

'What if I said I'd killed him?'

'Your business, none of mine. Africa is off my patch.'

'Jackson Mpande is dead. A rhino got him.' Michael smiled slightly. 'Funny how things work out.'

'Know what I think, King? I think it's time you gave your guardian angel a rest.'

Michael had just put Andrew to bed when the doorbell rang. He wasn't expecting anybody, least of all Annie Devilliers. She held out two bottles of red wine. 'Sacha gave me your address.'

'I won't ask how he knew it.'

'What's that smell?'

'Dinner. You hungry?' He stepped aside and she came into the house.

'Starving. When did you get back?'

'Two weeks ago.'

'So why didn't you call me?'

'No reason really.'

'Bullshit!'

'Okay, I wasn't sure I should.'

'I rather thought that. Well, I'm here, how do you feel about it? Open one of these will you?'

He took the bottles from her. 'If you must know, bloody glad you're here.'

She followed him to a sideboard. 'You wouldn't lie about a thing like that, would you?'

'I never lie to ladies.'

'Lady! I like that.'

Michael opened one of the bottles of wine. 'I take it you're out of hiding.'

'Yes. Got an ashtray?'

'Will a saucer do? You'll find one in the kitchen.' He poured two glasses of wine and handed her one. 'Cheers.'

'Cheers.'

Annie sipped her wine, put the glass down and lit a cigarette. 'I'm going to stop next week.' She went into the kitchen and returned with a saucer.

Michael pulled a face. 'Crap! You're hooked, lady. Face it.'

'I mean it.' She burst into tears.

'Annie! God, sorry. Look, what's wrong, why are you so upset?'

'I'm not upset.' She was scrubbing frantically at her eyes.

He gently turned her to face him. 'So why are you crying?'

She pulled back, snatched the offered handkerchief, and stubbed out her barely smoked cigarette. She started prowling the room like a caged lioness. 'I don't know. How should I know?'

'You're the psychiatrist,' he reminded her quietly.

She dabbed at her wet cheeks impatiently. 'I'm crying,' she said slowly, 'because I don't feel like crying.'

Michael tried not to smile but failed.

She saw his grin and tried to hide her own, hiccupped, then gave a wobbly laugh. 'You must admit, it makes sense in a screwy kind of way.'

'This is about Sacha.'

'He told me to get lost.' Her voice was indignant. 'Not in so many words. In fact, for Sacha, he was quite eloquent.'

'Annie, you don't have to tell me.'

'I know that.' She frowned at him. Mimicking her own advice to others, she added, 'I don't have to do anything I don't want to do.'

'So don't tell me.'

'But I want to tell you.'

'Annie, are you okay?'

She stared at him. 'No,' she said finally. 'No, I'm not okay. My pride's hurt.'

'And that's what all this is about?'

She nodded. 'I didn't love him, don't suppose I ever did. He was a challenge to my psychiatrist mind, the only human being I ever met who is absolutely cold inside.'

Michael remembered Sacha's fear when he was standing on the landmine. His words, a man like me shouldn't be married. A cold man would not have a thought like that. Sacha Devilliers had known he was making his wife unhappy and loved her enough to let her go. Michael said nothing.

'Are you shocked?'

'No.'

'I am.'

'That's why you're crying.'

She sipped her wine. 'I'm going away for a bit.'

'Probably a good idea.'

'What are you going to do?'

'Get my own farm.'

'In Zululand?'

'It's my home.'

'Mine too. I miss it.' She wrinkled her nose. 'Something's burning.'

He rescued the roast lamb but the peas were beyond help. Annie made gravy and they took their meal on trays into the lounge.

She did not stay long. As she was leaving, she said, 'Mind if I look you up when I get back?'

'When's that likely to be?'

'I don't know. A year. Maybe two.'

Michael nodded. 'Be sure you do.'

EPILOGUE: 1999

The sky glowed a fiery red. From the house, Michael could hear the roar as flames raced through the cane block. He'd have been down there helping but his daughter had made it blatantly clear that she was more than capable of doing the job without her father underfoot. Michael had taken the snub philosophically, proud that Tessa was as good a farmer as any and content to let her take control. Besides, he reasoned, at sixty-one he deserved to take life easy.

Sometimes when he looked back, as he found himself doing more often of late, he wondered just where the last thirty years had gone.

Thirty years! The young man had grown old. Aches and pains mysteriously came and went. It took longer to get to sleep these days and he seemed to be waking up earlier with each passing year. His blonde hair had turned white, as had his matching moustache. Physically fit, he had some years back traded in his sports model figure for a slightly more rounded armchair version.

Thirty years ago, returning to South Africa with his two-year-old son, Michael had no idea what life had yet to dish out. All he knew was he wanted to spend the rest of it in Zululand. He sold the townhouse in Johannesburg and found a farm near Amatikulu, some fifty kilometres south of where he grew up. By UBejane's standards, it was small, just under 500 acres. While he waited for the paperwork to go through he spent time with Jennifer's father.

Shattered by the death of his wife, daughter and grandson in the space of a year, Harold Bailey had thrown himself into his farm work, trying out all the newest innovations as they appeared. As a result, he was able to bring Michael up to date.

The sugar industry was becoming less labour intensive. With the introduction of mechanical techniques many of the functions that had been undertaken by hand were now performed by machines. Using the new technology, farmers were able to make the same profit on less land. The era of the large, privately owned estates was coming to an end. Michael was glad of his father-in-law's advice. He'd been away from cane farming for five-and-a-half years. By the time he took over his own property he was eager to put into practice new techniques which he'd seen working well.

He and Andrew moved into their new home midway through 1970. It was a sprawling, Mediterranean-style brick house with tiled floors, large windows and arched doorways. The furniture from the Johannesburg townhouse seemed to float forlornly in the large rooms and Michael had the feeling that they were only camping in the new house. He told himself he'd buy more furniture, make the place more homely, but he never did. It was a house, not a home. Without Jennifer, it could never be a home.

Michael had agreed to keep on all the previous owner's staff, which included a shy young Zulu girl called Mirrit. She was supposed to clean and attend to the laundry but she was only fourteen and her skills were basic. But a kind of chemistry occurred as soon as she met Andrew. For Andrew, it was love at first sight. He adored her and Mirrit, in turn, worshipped Andrew. She had endless patience, playing with him, reading to him in halting English, strapping him to her back and going for walks. They became inseparable, which left Michael free to concentrate on the farm.

Like his father-in-law, Michael found solace in hard work. As a result, his farm flourished. He made friends with several neighbours and slowly developed a social life. The second anniversary of Jennifer and Jeremy's deaths was spent with the only other person on earth who felt them as keenly as Michael. It was a sad night for both men.

In a way, this anniversary was more difficult than the first. A year ago Michael and Andrew were staying with Harold Bailey, and their losses were still a raw wound. The first anniversary of the deaths of Jennifer and Jeremy, though more poignant than other days, was not so different from the rest of the year. Grieving, as both men were, neither had to face a surge of sorrow since they lived with it constantly. Now, after two years, neither of them particularly wanted to bring it all back, and yet they knew they had no choice.

The process was made even more difficult by the fact that Andrew, now three-and-a-half, understood every word of their conversation and asked a lot of questions – some of them almost too painful to answer.

'Grandfather, was my mummy your little girl just like I'm daddy's little boy?'

Or, devastating child-like logic.

'You're going to die first, aren't you, Grandfather? When you see Mummy and Jeremy will you say hello from me?'

Harold and Michael's eyes met over Andrew's head. If only they could be as pragmatic.

After dinner, with Andrew asleep on the sofa, Jennifer's father suggested they take their brandies outside. Seated in comfortable old leather armchairs, Harold, who was never one to mince words, got straight to the point.

'I dare say you'll marry again.'

Michael had always enjoyed a good relationship with his father-in-law. He realised there was no point in trying to save the old man's feelings. 'Not yet.'

'No. It's too soon, I can see that. But someone will come along one day. You'll marry and have more children.'

'Possibly. I'm in no hurry, Harold. If it happens, it happens.'

'Don't take this the wrong way, son. It's just that Andrew is the only blood link I have left with my daughter. I've changed my will. When I die,

Andrew will inherit this place. If he's under twenty-one, you will act as executor. I hope you don't mind. It was always going to go to you and Jen but now . . . Well, things change.'

'I think it's a terrific idea. Andrew's too young to remember Jen. This is a bond, a connection to her. Of course I don't mind, Harold.'

It was a relief for Michael when the day and evening ended and another year would pass before he had to face it again.

True to her word, Annie Devilliers returned to South Africa after eighteen months of wandering the globe. She arrived at the farm on a Sunday morning, driving a battered old jeep. 'Sacha gave me your address.'

Michael was no longer surprised that the man kept tabs on him. He pointed to the vehicle. 'Where did you get that old thing?'

'Durban. Isn't she beautiful?'

He went down the steps to greet her. 'How are you?' He was very pleased to see her.

She stood on the lawn, watching him walk towards her, hands on hips. She wore jeans, a man's white shirt with the tails tied around her midriff and the sleeves rolled up, and was barefoot. A cap was jammed onto her head and her hair was tucked up under it but long strands had escaped and he could see it was just as wildly curly as ever. Deeply tanned, the startling violet of her eyes radiated warmth. 'You look good.'

'So do you.' He stopped a short distance away. 'Are you back to stay?'

She nodded. 'Might set up a private practice in Empangeni.'

Michael raised his eyebrows. 'Think you'll get much business?'

'Enough.' She turned and looked over the farm. 'This yours?'

'Didn't Sacha tell you?'

She grinned. 'Well, actually yes.'

'How is he?'

'Busy. He sends regards.'

'And you? How are you *really*?'

'Fine.' She removed the cap, shook her head and curls went everywhere. 'Better than fine. How about you?'

'I'm okay.' He felt ill at ease and couldn't figure out why. 'Look, this is crazy. What are we doing standing out here in the sun? Come inside. Like a drink?'

She stayed put. 'Can we speak frankly?'

'Of course.'

'I mean *very* frankly. Straight up and out with it.'

'Try me.'

'Is there anyone in your life?'

'No.'

'Would you like there to be?'

'Maybe.'

'You are making this difficult.'

'Straight up and out with it. That's what you said isn't it?'

'Okay.' She squared her shoulders. 'How about me?'

He looked at her. She did not flinch, simply stared back. 'The idea has merit.' He grinned, suddenly feeling easier. 'You don't beat about the bush do you? Ever heard of girlish modesty?'

She snorted. 'Haven't time. I'm thirty-six.'

'You're completely different from Jennifer. It might not work.'

'I'm not asking you to marry me. Just that we try it. If it's not going to work we'll know soon enough.'

That made sense. Michael held out his hand and she took it. 'On one condition,' he said, leading her towards the house.

'What's that?'

'That you keep your bloody psychiatry to yourself.'

She ducked her head but he could see she was smiling. 'I'll try.'

Inside, he turned her to face him. 'I've been thinking about you quite a bit lately,' he admitted.

'Where's Andrew?'

'At a birthday party.'

'Good.' Those eyes told him she wanted him.

Their lovemaking had been a tentative journey where both were fearful of painful memories crowding them. The realisation that this was not going to happen dawned on them slowly. The more each gave, the more they received until finally there was no room for ghosts, there was only the two of them.

Afterwards, lying curled together, there was nothing in Michael's heart and mind other than

Annie. It felt so good to have her next to him, skin to skin. The sensation of sharing and trusting, giving and taking, had been missing from his life for too long. Later, he would search for guilt and find it wasn't there. The love he'd had for Jennifer would always remain, it had been too good and strong to ever fade away, but, as Michael would soon discover, the heart is a big place with an endless capacity for more.

Annie must have been feeling something of the same contentment. They lay together for a long time, not speaking, at peace with themselves and each other. Finally, she stirred and said, 'Mmmmm. Yum!'

He kissed her shoulder. 'Isn't the cigarette smoked now supposed to be the best?'

'I gave up.' She rolled towards him and put her arms around him.

'Well done.' He wanted her again. 'When?'

She was kissing his ear, sending shivers through him. 'Ages ago.'

Much later he asked her the same question. 'When?'

She looked a tad shifty. 'This morning.'

They had been married six months later.

Eighteen months after that, Annie gave birth to their daughter. When Michael suggested they call her Tessa, she agreed without hesitation.

She was, as he had pointed out to her, very different from Jennifer. She could be abrasive, impatient and she loathed domestic chores with a vengeance. But she had a great sense of fun, a quick mind, and an artistic flair that soon turned the barn-like house into a stylishly cosy home. She quickly made friends with Andrew. She loved Michael with unwavering sincerity and loyalty. She cried in sad movies. After Sacha, Michael's willingness to show affection never failed to surprise and delight her and she learned to reciprocate and took great pleasure in doing so.

And she'd lied about giving up smoking. It took another eleven years before she managed it.

Michael's thoughts returned to the present. The block Tessa had fired was smouldering but under control. She'd be firing the next one pretty soon.

From the age of ten, it became obvious that Tessa could be as obstinate as her namesake. Dolls and pretty dresses were not for her. Games of cowboys and Indians were more to her liking. She preferred the company of boys to girls. So when, at the age of ten, she announced she wanted to be a cane farmer like her dad, no-one doubted her. Michael thought it was pretty neat. Annie's attitude was, 'As long as she's happy.' She was very proud of the fact that Tessa had the confidence to be different for, as she said once, 'It takes courage for a child to be out of step with others.'

Michael, who had come to respect Annie's innate understanding of human nature, was inclined to agree. But he'd been thinking of another child called Tessa.

Tessa had finished school and then enrolled herself in an agricultural college. And now she was virtually running the farm. She was engaged to the one and only boy she had ever looked at. She had been six when she solemnly informed her parents that she would marry Nick Kelsall, 'But not for a few years yet.' Nick had been unaware of her plan but then, he was only eight at the time.

Nick's parents were friends of Annie and Michael and their farms bordered with each other. Michael had no doubt that one day the two properties would be joined.

Andrew, despite the inheritance from his grandfather, showed no interest in the land. A graphic artist, he lived and worked in Johannesburg and was married to a city girl. When it became apparent that there was little chance he'd take up farming, Harold Bailey was philosophical. 'It's yours to do what you will, my boy. When I'm gone it won't matter what happens to this place.'

But Andrew could see how much the old man loved his farm. 'You're going to be around for a long time yet, Grandfather. Don't worry, I won't sell it. I'll put in a manager. Dad can keep an eye on it. Who knows, I might end up a farmer yet.'

So far there were no signs that he would. After the old man passed away, Andrew had hired the best manager in the business, despite dire warnings from others about how you couldn't trust an Indian. Balram.

The second block caught and roared into life. Michael went back to his musings.

Sally now had three grown-up children: Dominique, who was very gifted in her chosen fields of textile design; Pascale, who went into journalism; and then a son, Charles, a brilliant young scholar who burnt out at university and turned to drugs. He was now on the long road to recovery but the mind-bending acid he'd abused his body with had done terrible things to his ability to concentrate and the only employment he could find was in a special workshop that made simple wooden toys. Sally weathered the heartbreak with the same kind of quiet dignity Claire had displayed when she needed it.

Sally had enjoyed moderate success in the cutthroat world of fashion design and her own label was respected in France and England.

Gregor followed his heart's desire and went into acting. He was now an established stage actor in Britain, regularly travelling to America for work as well. He married a model and they had one child, a son called Sean. When a cerebral haemorrhage took his wife's life at the age of twenty-seven, Gregor was heartbroken. So far, he had shown no interest in remarrying.

A few month's after the tragedy, in an effort to take his mind off his grief, Claire looked after Sean while Sally and Gregor travelled together to South Africa. They found the country of their birth so changed that when they left, both said they would never be back.

Throughout the 1970s, with apartheid still being practised despite an increasing wave of rebellion, violence was finally met with open defiance and retaliatory violence. Inkatha was revived by Chief Mangosuthu Buthelezi in the middle of that decade and attracted membership from almost every Zulu in Natal. Then, on 16 June, 1976, as students were protesting in the African township of Soweto, on the outskirts of Johannesburg, about being forced to learn Afrikaans at school, they were cut down by a hail of police bullets. Soweto erupted. Within a year, around 700 African children and youths had been killed. This set off a wave of protest which rapidly spread throughout the country. Boys and girls were actively encouraged to disrupt the system. They did, and they continued to die. Protest marches soon extended to other areas of rebellion. Work boycotts were called in an attempt to destroy the economy. Migrant Zulus living in hostels in Soweto paid no attention to the call for strikes and were attacked as they returned from work. This event set in motion the beginning of open warfare between Zulus and every other African race in South Africa.

At the start of the 1980s, a rift developed between the African National Congress and Chief Buthelezi which was to have far-reaching ramifications within an already wartorn South Africa. By the mid-eighties, international sanctions were beginning to hit hard. Inkatha was losing credibility yet again. Because of Buthelezi's quarrel with the ANC, a newly formed surrogate for the ANC, the United Democratic Front, was vying with Inkatha for followers and regular street clashes between the two were now occurring in the townships. The unthinkable was happening. Zulu was fighting Zulu. And no-one was spared.

In Kwa-Mashu, Wilson Mpande answered a knock on his door one evening and was dragged outside. He must have known what to expect but that didn't stop him sticking to his own principles. When he refused the crowd's demands that he switch sides from Inkatha to the UDF, a petrol-soaked tyre was rammed over Wilson's head and set alight. The 'necklace' killing was just another death in a land where literally thousands were dying each year.

Michael, who had heard of the necklace murder in Kwa-Mashu but had no idea it had been Wilson, only became aware of all the facts when a distraught Nandi was brought to him by her youngest son. The unenviable task of telling Dyson fell to him. And while the gruesome news devastated his old friend there was some comfort in the fact that Nandi and Dyson, who had not spoken to each other for twenty-five years, were able to spend nearly an hour on the telephone together.

The violence continued to escalate throughout South Africa. The economy was in ruins, the country in chaos. Then, six months after taking office, President Frederik de Klerk announced the unbanning of the ANC and promised the release of Nelson Mandela. Nine days later, the world watched as the tall political prisoner, who had not been seen for twenty-seven years, walked free.

Many people, Michael included, believed that the worst was over. Unfortunately, it was not. The

Zulus were divided. The more traditional followed Buthelezi's Inkatha, while the educated leaned towards the ANC and its policy of one voice for all blacks. Within the ANC, a radical arm was forming to continue feuding with Inkatha. And a 'third force' of police and army officers was being deliberately encouraged to exacerbate the violence. This 'third force', it was said, had been formed by the outgoing Nationalist Party.

Claire Dawson, now eighty and confined to a walking frame, increasingly begged Michael to sell up and get out. Michael and Annie discussed it a couple of times but their answer always came back to one thing. Africa was their home. But when Claire asked Michael in a recent letter, 'What chance do the Zulus have? They cannot unite. They have lost sight of their cause. I fear it is the end of them.' Michael tended to agree. So did the eighth king of the Zulus, King Goodwill Zwelithini, who asked, 'If Britain is at war, her people unite under their queen against the enemy. How could we face the problem here, when we are enemies among ourselves?'

In the first all-race elections conducted in 1994, Inkatha won an overall majority in KwaZulu Natal, though voter fraud north of the Tugela River was suspected by the ANC. It also won ten per cent of the vote for the national assembly. The political violence should have stopped. Instead, as well as continuing, it gained a sinister alter-ego.

Drug-related crime. The terrible carnage continued, visiting on whites and blacks alike. In KwaZulu Natal it was as bad, if not worse, than anywhere else in the country. The incidence of robbery skyrocketed with money and weapons being the prime objective and rape an added bonus. These crimes were largely committed by the twelve to twenty-five age group half out of their minds on drugs. No-one was exempted.

Michael, who hated the idea, was forced to install burglar bars, bulletproof glass and a rape gate in his house. Annie closed her practice in Empangeni. Driving home at night on her own was too dangerous. Older Zulus who remembered a different time when the young respected the elderly could only shake their heads at what was happening.

Farmers in isolated areas were particularly vulnerable and private security patrols were formed all over the country. Everybody had two-way radios within easy reach and cell phones were never far away. Nor were their weapons. Still, reports of murder kept coming in from rural areas.

After Wilson's necklace killing, Michael tried to convince Nandi to come and live on his farm. 'Please, Nandi. You will be safe here.'

'No, Master Michael. Nowhere is safe. I am returning to my home.'

She went back into the mountains where she had grown up and where she had first met Wilson. There, on the death of her mother-in-law, she was installed into the matriarch's large hut where she resided with all Wilson's ancestors. Over the years the village had changed like everything else had changed but, because of its remoteness, life still bore some resemblance to the old ways. Her two youngest children, though now adults, married with families of their own, joined her. Like most decent people, they were sick of the violence and fearful for their children lest they too get caught in it.

'When will it stop?' Dyson asked Michael in despair.

He had returned in 1990, two weeks after the unbanning of the ANC. No-one knew he was coming. Michael came in from the fields one day and there was his old friend sitting on the veranda waiting for him.

'Dyson!' Michael yelled.

Dyson sprang up, grinning like a fool. Though they'd seen each other whenever Michael and Annie took the children to England, it was different here. It was right here.

They behaved like kids again, cuffing each other, trying to wrestle each other to the ground. Both men were short of breath when they stopped.

'We grow old,' Dyson said. He was fifty-two and had lived in exile for thirty years.

'Are you back to stay?'

'Yes. I'll never leave again.'

'Want a job?'

Dyson shook his head. 'I'm going back to my

father's village. I'm going to live the old way. I want nothing to do with the new. I'm going to take a wife, have children and tend my cattle. I'm going to smell the fresh air, dance to the rhythm of Africa, feel the sun burn my back and speak nothing but Zulu. You, *Nkawu*, will be very welcome to visit me.'

'You'll get sick of it.'

'I'll never get sick of it.'

And he hadn't, though he did have to leave one more time. The first thing Dyson had done when he returned, after greeting his mother, was to visit the *sangoma*. She told him what he already knew. 'You have come home.' But she added, 'There are those who will hear your words. The time is coming when great wrongs will be put right.'

In 1996 the new South African regime instigated the biggest purging campaign ever undertaken in the history of the world. Called the Truth and Reconciliation Commission and presided over by, among others, the 1985 Nobel peace prize-winner, Bishop Desmond Mpilo Tutu, the aim of the commission was to learn, not to judge. Stories concealed over the decades were enough to reduce Bishop Tutu to tears on more than one occasion. Anybody who had suffered as a result of apartheid, or who had caused that suffering, whether they be freedom fighters, South African Security Police, ANC, Inkatha, United Democratic Front, Eugene Terre Blanche's Afrikaner Resistance Movement,

Nationalist Party members, ex-Bureau of State Security employees, Umkhonto we Sizwe, it didn't matter who, was called to appear before the commission. Both Dyson Mpande and Sacha Devilliers testified.

Michael, following the process through the media, found it hard to understand how so many people, on so many opposing sides, could get it so wrong. No-one was blameless. Not one faction could afford to point a finger at another. The innocent victims, ordinary African men, women and children who had borne the brunt of one form of cruelty or another, told stories of untold horror, hardships and heartache. South Africa should have died of shame. But it seemed to Michael that while some displayed evidence of a conscience, most were too busy trying to justify their actions.

Dyson gave evidence on two counts. His treatment in prison, and his involvement with Umkhonto we Sizwe. A victim on one hand, a perpetrator of suffering on the other. A typical example of the complex face of South Africa that had evolved over the past fifty years.

Sacha spoke unemotionally of his work and the reasons he believed in it. Yes, he agreed that the system had been less than perfect, less than fair. That was not his concern. He had been involved in preventing those who would undermine his country from doing so. Simple as that.

Annie, watching her ex-husband on television said sadly, 'He's a dinosaur really. A relic of the past. Look at him. Ramrod straight, stiff upper lip, no apology, no feelings at all really. If he suspects he's wrong he'd rather die than admit it. There's no place in this world for such people any more. I feel sorry for him.'

Just another facet in the complicated face of South Africa.

It had to get better. South Africa had to turn the corner. But when the pendulum swings so far out in one direction, it has to swing just as far out in the other. Eventually it would stop swinging. Only then would peace be found. Or so Michael fervently hoped.

Michael had kept up to date with the black rhinoceros project at Umfolozi, visiting the reserve several times a year. With a greater understanding of the animal's needs through research, better security against poachers, a habitat that agreed with the beast, the black rhinoceros was thriving. Not only in Umfolozi but all over Africa the animal was breeding and had been removed from the *Red Data Book*.

Annie came out on to the verandah where Michael sat ruminating. 'Checking Tessa?' she teased.

'No. Just wool-gathering.' He smiled at her. The long blonde curls had been cropped as soon as she noticed the first grey hair. She needed glasses to read and, when not in use, they hung on her chest, suspended by a chain. The violet of her eyes had faded a little but their beautiful colour could still give much younger women a run for their money.

She was a little rounder, a little slower but she still swore like a trooper and had no time for pretensions. 'You're beautiful,' he told her fondly.

'You need glasses you silly old bugger,' she laughed. But her eyes had gone soft and she placed a hand on his shoulder and squeezed. 'Like a drink?'

'Love one.'

After she had gone back inside, Michael shook himself out of his recollections. But not before he had one last ironic thought. All his life, and over and above any family affections, three things had remained a constant for Michael. His respect for the Zulus and the belief that they deserved their own independent territory. His love of South Africa and the desire to see all that was wrong with the system come right. And his concern over the near extinction of the black rhinoceros.

It came to him then that the only winner, so far as he could see, was the black rhinoceros.

Beverley Harper
Storms Over Africa

Richard Dunn has made Africa his home. But his Africa is in crisis.

Ancient rivalries have ignited modern political ambitions. Desperate poachers stalk the dwindling populations of the game parks.

For those of the old Africa, the old ways, nothing is certain.

But for Richard – a man used to getting his own way – the stakes are even higher. Into his world has come the compelling and beautiful Steve Hayes. A woman he swears he will never give up. A woman struggling to guard her own dreadful secret.

Richard has no choice. He must face the consequences of the past and fight for the future. To lose now is to lose everything . . .

Beverley Harper
Edge of the Rain

*The blood scent was fresh. Hunger ached in her
belly . . . the lioness slid forward as close as she
dared. The little boy seconds away from death was
two, maybe three years old. He was lost in the
vast, heat-soaked sand that was the Kalahari
desert.*

Toddler Alex Theron is miraculously rescued by a
passing clan of Kalahari Bushmen. Over the
ensuing years the desert draws him back, for it
hides a beautiful secret . . . diamonds.

But nothing comes easily from within this turbulent
continent and before Alex can even hope to realise
his dreams he will lose his mind to love and fight a
bitter enemy who will stop at nothing to destroy
him . . .

From the author of *Storms Over Africa* comes a
novel of courage and an unforgettable journey into
the beating heart of Africa.

Beverley Harper
Echo of an Angry God

*At the signal from the king, torches were lit,
throwing their flickering light onto the inky water of
the cove . . . Ng'ona saw the flames. At three
metres below the surface, he flicked his tail and
glided in a circle . . . The warrior stood alone . . .
With no hesitation, he leapt high in the air and
plunged into the jet black embrace of unimaginable
horror.*

For centuries, Likoma Island in Lake Malawi has
been a place of mystery, exotic ritual and human
sacrifice. It is also where geologist John Devereaux
disappears in 1983, while carrying out a secretive
survey of the lake in search of oil.

Fifteen years later his daughter, Lana Devereaux,
travels to Malawi, 'the warm heart of Africa', to
discover the truth. But Lana soon finds herself
caught up in a web of deceit, passion and black
magic that stretches back over two hundred years
and has ramifications that reach well beyond the
shores of Lake Malawi.

Following *Storms Over Africa* and the bestselling
Edge of the Rain, Beverley Harper's third novel is
a thrilling adventure that once again captures the
spirit of Africa.